UNIVERSITY THUGS

THE NOVEL

FREE CHEF

Above all, maintain ...

1 PETER 4:8

PART I

RISE

1

All week flyers were distributed. Saturday was THE JUMPOFF. The first party of the year. Doods came by the bus stop with their thick stack of glossy cards holding out their dap. It's going down Saturday my nigga you coming?

Heads nodded as the flyer was inspected for the cover charge (13 dollars) and flipped to the back where the girl was. Yo she go here? Nah just a picture they found on the internet.

Saturday came so Titus and Vonny went. It was at the frat house across the all-night tennis courts. There was a mulch hill out back where a friend could boost you high enough to reach the windows. When they got there, a pair of legs were already hanging over the sill. They said wassup and got yanked up too.

It was deep inside. All kinds of people. Supposedly the whiteboys checked student IDs at the door but couldn't all these people go to UVA. Had to be townies or just knew somebody that go here or maybe drove around and saw it was popping and decided to slide on through.

Titus didn't dance. He stuck close to the wall, the bottle of Masson tucked under the cape of his shirt. Vonny jumping on any freek he could. When he came back to the wall sweaty and panting and grinning, they took shots to the dome and leaned there on the wall being tuff, being bent, their vision blurred and fractured and the multicolored lights and bass fuzzing everything up, clowning who that nigga looklike over there hahahaha until the next pair of cheeks seized Vonny, a hot force pulling him from his chest, and his shoulders lifted off the wall which was running with sweat and tomorrow would be stained with denim and right now the water bottles all over the floor. People were sneaking in all kinds of liquors in water bottles because there was some stupid rule at UVA that black parties had to be dry. People slipping and stumbling on the discarded water bottles that had been stepped flat and AYE WATCH WHERE THE FUCK YOU GOING and glares exchanged. Everything taken personally. Everything consequential. Clumps of shit talking forming from time to time. Necks stretched. Bullnostrils. Hearts racing. The Masson bottle safe under Titus's shirt. Hard to breathe in here. The smoke. Fireflies in every dark corner sending up clouds and weren't enough windows and niggas were sneaking in those anyway minding the sill so their clothes wouldn't get dirty and brushing themselves off and diddybopping ...

Witnessing all this, the whiteboys was heated. Coming down periodically from the sofa barricaded 2nd floor where they all sat in their guilt and disgust. This was their house after all. They needed the money but was it worth it? Finally when one of their representatives came down and found one of the party organizers after much difficulty searching, This is NOT what we agreed to.

So when the lights cut on and they kicked everybody out, nobody went home. They sorta hung around after the fact. Out there in the driveway. Titus and Vonny still swigging the Masson. Everybody else from the party out there too. And the cops. Everybody standing and waiting and bullshitting and it was still warm out tonight because it was August. The first Saturday of the school year. Not even midnight yet. Trying to ignore the cops coming through the crowd nonchalantly waving their sticks. Let's move. C'mon let's go. Where officer? I don't care as long as it's not this driveway ...

Beyond the driveway it was slim pickins. No clubs nearby. The townie spots were trash. DC was 2 hours away. Richmond an hour. Though it was early, it was too late to drive anywhere far being as bent as they were. High as they were. Man Charlottesville was weak. Straight ass. Their best bet was to drink in somebody crib but the ABC store closed a while ago and nobody thought to stock up. They shoulda. The black parties always shut down early. Maybe the Corner? Fuck a nigga gonna do down there Vonny. You stay wanting to go down there ...

Bored leaning there by the stairs, they walked over a few feet to see what was going on. If there were girls there, if someone was wearing something they'd never seen before. If the people there a few feet away were somehow different than the ones they'd seen before. Something. Anything.

They saw Q and them eventually. They gave Q and them dap, tapped shoulders and bullshitted. Wassgood, wassgood. They adopted wide stances and mirrored one another punching palms lackadaisically. Watchall niggas finna do. Orrin tom bout goin down to the Corner. The Corner? Fuck a nigga gon do down there? Shit that's what I said. Paid my 13 dollars for this jonk. Aint no way I'mma drop anotha 13, 10 dollars to stand in no bar. Then we gotta pay for a pitcher. Yeah that's right. Yawls niggas got liquors at the crib? Naw. Drank all the brown before we got here.

The whole time they talked, they stood back and quietly examined one another's clothing. If shoes were clean. How shoelaces were tied and whether those were clean too. How the trim of the shoes matched the jersey lettering matched the bill of their caps. Whether they left the hologram sticker on the cap. How their waves or braids were holding up after being cooped up on a sweaty dance floor. How clothes fit generally. How hard it was to find the particular article of clothing. If you can pick that up at any ol mall. How much things cost. Things of that nature. They made these calculations without staring too obviously. It was the first party of the year, and time would tell if they could keep this up, if they could rotate their outfits the right way. Anybody got some trees? Vonny, man, you stay high! Look, look at his eyes. Naw, naw, I aint even smoke yet. Vonny patted himself down, Aint nuffin on me but blacks. I had just run out of some shit I brought back from home. Drew say he got a lil sum at the crib. Some lob? Huh? Lobsta? I don't know what they call it. Them blacks you got freeked? ... The bullshit lulled and nobody had a clue what was popping but they were done talking. More dap was exchanged. Every single person touched palms and tapped shoulders. Aye come holla at us if you hear sumpin.

The driveway slowly thinning. Cops came through and escorted groups down to the main street. People came back, resumed their interrupted conversations because man Charlottesville was weak ... straight ass ... slim pickings out there except for here ... so ... so whatchall niggas finna do? yall niggas hear back from them? thought yall said ... and the pattern repeated, less people coming back up the driveway each time, the effort too great as the clock ticked from Saturday to Sunday.

Vonny and Titus finally called it quits on the night, and were halfway down the driveway when they heard a voice offaways yapping at them. Going there he go right there. There LOOK. That long hair chinky lookin nigga. A big old dood, some football player, probably a first year or a transfer since they didn't know him, started walking alongside them. Vonny, with his phone still pressed to the side of his face, his soft hairless cheek, and he was purring sweetly into the phone when he felt that big ol hand on his shoulder and looked up. Wassgood big man? The football player said you needa stop blowin up shorty phone. Who shorty? You know who bitch nigga.

The big boy mushed Vonny in the face and Vonny's hat fell off and all of his half-Korean hair was hanging out crimped up looking. Titus tried to step between but hands pulled him back. There was cool talk in his ear. C'mon nigga, it's a one on one. You know the drill. Let these grown men talk.

Vonny was squared up with the big boy, his face level with big boy's chest. A lil yapping occurred and before the big boy was ready, Vonny dove for his knees like a champ. The crowd rushed forward jumping up and down, squealing, squeaking, shouting in tongues, people pushing eachother out the way to get a good look at Vonny kneeling on that big football player's chest and stealing on him clean with both hands.

Big boy's friends jumped in. When they jumped in, that's when Titus did.

Titus set his eyes on a little gumball head sitting atop a pair of silverback gorilla shoulders. He cocked back and swung. Kicked at ribs and stomped on fingers and shouting until someone from behind horsecollared him. On his back, rolling around on the ground getting his shoulders chewed

up by the gravel, he covered his face and the kicks came.
Somebody tried to pull him up to his feet. He ducked out of
his shirt and the cop swung his stick at Titus's bare shoulder. His whole arm went numb and he fell to his knees. GET
ON THE GROUND!!!! STAY THERE! My friend gettin
jumped! SHUTTUP! YOU STAY THERE! He lay on his
stomach and watched the cop sort through the pile. The cop
grabbed an arm and an elbow flew back and caught the cop
in the jaw. Another person came up and pushed the cop
down and ran off. As soon as Titus got to his feet, someone
stole him in the side of the neck—Aye, man, thefuck? The
townie stood back with a balled fist, strutted and preened.
Titus lunged at him but the townie took off in the opposite
direction, looking back with a big ol smile on his face, losing
himself easy in all the people fighting in the driveway.

The whole driveway fighting. Students, townies, doods,
chicks, whoever, in any combination imaginable. Here and
there the limb of a cop was visible. And in all those people
scrapping, there were no one on ones to be seen. Just people
trying to jump each other. Kicking at whoever or whatever
was on the ground. Running past and pushing random
niggas in the back and stopping only if someone fell then
proceeding to get in a few licks for whatever reason. Didn't
no one want to leave that driveway without getting a piece of
theirs. It was free so why not? Who knew when the next
sweepstakes would come?

The sirens blared from the road. Paddy wagons
crunching up the driveway.

Over by the grass, Vonny sat on his haunches trying to
put on his shoes. Titus picked Vonny up. FUCK THE
SHOES MAN! Stick man these my brovas!

They started toward the street where cars were honking
and high-beaming, the shadows of running people disap-

pearing into light. Vonny pulled up lame. A rock. Fuck! Titus helped him hop along on one foot, Vonny hopping and trying to slip on that second shoe. Cops broke out the spray behind them, the shouts taking a different pitch in the driveway.

They made it across the street past the all-night tennis courts. Taking cover in some bushes, they quickly inspected themselves, found no bones broken, only fucked up clothes, scratches, lots of shit they'll feel tomorrow.

When the last of the paddy wagons pulled away, Vonny came to his feet, brushing off the leaves. He'd been talking to Q on his cell. Q wanted to meet down at the corner. Orrin tom bout he seen one of them football niggas over there. The same one who pushed Drew from behind ... Titus looked up at his boy pacing, his voice going a mile a minute. Titus asked him point blank you tryna get me locked up for good?

Vonny stopped. He stood there panting, confused, the collar of his jersey stretched down to his navel, one of the sleeves ripped off. After a few moments, he sorta laughed, Guess you right. We gotta get our ass to the crib.

He helped Titus to his feet, where it was even plainer to see that Titus had no shirt on, and had recently engaged in something unlawful and very much in violation of the terms of his probation.

2

Going back to last year there had been a fuss about Peter Boyd, a columnist for the student newspaper, the Cavalier Daily, and the things he had been writing in response to one of the university's proposed diversity initiatives. The proposed initiative was this: before enrolling in classes, incoming first-years were required to take an internet-based diversity course. Failure to complete the training would result in a registration block.

In several Cav Daily columns, Peter Boyd decried the initiative, invoking several lofty values, plain, strong-sounding, easily-recognizable ones that he would return to across his columns, and he proclaimed that the university intended to indoctrinate its students without their consent. Words like TYRANNY were used to make this case.

There were several angry rebuttal columns printed in the Cav Daily, several angry letters to the editor, and an organized, well-photographed protest at the basement offices of the Cav Daily, all of which only emboldened Peter Boyd, who returned from summer break with an idea to start his own organization.

The organization's name was the Freedom of Thought Coalition. Its inaugural meeting was to start at 7pm tonight.

Seeing the flyers on grounds, student body president Alice Upshaw, a supporter of the diversity requirement, told a small group of friends to meet at 6, at the back of the Pav where the booths were, where it was more secluded. And keep it on the DL please, I don't want it to look like we're planning something.

* * *

A few minutes before 7pm, Alice and her contingent arrived.

Among them was Brooke Martin (pronounced Mar-TEEN), who people frequently mistook as a cousin of some remove to Alice, though Alice's family was from the British West Indies and Brooke was of half-Puerto Rican descent. It was their tall angular builds combined with the carmel, slightly yellow complexion that drew comparisons, and their hair, which had cycled through the trends at roughly the same intervals, cornrows one month, a bouffant another. Of course it didn't help they were often seen together first year; the association stuck.

When told of this resemblance, Brooke's face would light up, You really think so? but privately she hated it, only a few epithets capable of making her as upset, and immediately she reevaluated the intelligence of the person making the comparison.

Not only did she believe it was obvious she was more attractive than Alice, but after taking a class with Alice, and after living with her for 5 weeks in Spain the summer after first year, Brooke felt she knew the truth about the current student body president, that Alice Upshaw wasn't very bright actually, and had gotten by purely on her public speaking voice, which was deep, and of such a quality that strangers often swore they'd heard it somewhere before, from a commercial or a Civil Rights documentary on public television. That people were this gullible both saddened and angered Brooke. Despite these true feelings, she continued on the outward show of loyal friend and fellow sister in the movement for minority rights at UVA. When Alice called, she answered the phone immediately.

As they entered the small auditorium, which was about a third full but very much alive with bright chatter, the Freedom of Thought guys running the event, milling about by the lectern, watched the group of minority students now filing up the aisle. When they tried to resume their conversation, they felt one another's tight, awkward grins, and stood there growing more uneasy until Peter Boyd took the initiative and walked over, his hand extended toward Alice Upshaw. Madame President I'm happy you're here.

She raised her limp hand and had it shaken, and went back to her customary unmovingness, the rest of her group following her lead. Peter Boyd said he looked forward to the opportunity to begin a dialogue with her community this evening. Alice looked up at him, her eyes big and vacant, the dry erase marker tucked under her thigh, and said nothing.

Peter Boyd took the podium and asked if everyone could hear him. Good. This is wonderful. I'm glad to see so many people here. I don't want to go on too long. He cleared his throat. I had a few points prepared, which I might stray from. He swallowed and looked up.

Over the past 72 hours that comprise the existence of this organization, the Freedom of Thought Coalition has amassed over 1,000 signatures affirming, among other things, opposition to the proposed Online Diversity

Training Requirement. But I want to start by clarifying a few things about our organization, the FTC.

His hands still on the lectern, he raised up straight and scanned the room then went down to his script again. One, we are not opposed to diversity. Two, we are not opposed to efforts to increase sensitivity and dialogue about matters such as race and ethnicity. The Freedom of Thought Coalition began as a response to a lack of diversity in one—he raised his index finger—one key area—intellectual diversity.

Someone in Alice's group gasped mockingly and the rest of the group swallowed their giggling and Peter Boyd continued with no sign of noticing. He expounded on the primary role of the university as a marketplace of ideas, and how, just as Adam Smith's invisible hand guides us towards better ideas through open competition ... people in the room began turning to look at the snickering, whispering group of minority students near the aisle ... as a result, students end up being shortchanged when they are thereby deprived of a robust debate involving a wide, diverse range of opinions. It should concern us all when the administration endorses one narrow set of political beliefs at the expense of others. In fact we should sound the alarm bells when this endorsement resembles indoctrination.

Alice's hand shot up. Peter continued speaking. Alice waved it, then stood up waving her hand so he couldn't ignore her. Yes Alice I plan to take questions shortly. I very much look forward to hearing from you, from everyone actually. There's just one more thing I want to get to.

Alice was already down the aisle with the dry erase marker walking directly to the whiteboard behind the podium. He turned to look at her scribbling a web address directly beneath the web address already present on the board, the one for the Freedom of Thought Coalition's brand new website. People in the lecture hall were rising partway in their seats squinting at the address, and taking a moment to put together that it was for the website of a prominent Ku Klux Klansman that had famously run for president some years ago. People sat down again, checking with their neighbors that Alice's web address said what it said, and that it was reference to a famous racist, and by implication Alice Upshaw and her group were calling everyone in attendance racists too. This realization was met with incredulous sniffs and loud groans that could be heard across the room, and shrugging and headshaking, and Alice stood there, her expression unblinkingly smug and serene, and the rest of her group came down to join her.

Brooke was the last one coming down the aisle, the only one who remembered to grab Alice's purse and bookbag. She heard Peter Boyd say something into the microphone. It must've been incredibly witty given how the room surged with laughter.

Slipping out the door she looked back at the white whis-tled faces, curious what had been said, the people in there still laughing, their bodies doubled over. She adjusted her grip on Alice's bag and she rushed to catch up with the rest of the group who was already down aways out of earshot, hooting and cheering and counting their victory the same.

* * *

That evening, after a celebratory dinner, the conversations recounting what Alice had done, the looks on people's faces, and everyone hyping each other up and getting the other angry again, and when Brooke had driven back to her apart-ment and flicked on the lights, the sight of her dirty room saddened her. She tidied up, and made some coffee and told herself she would get some work done tonight. This semester would be different. She'd get back above 3.0. She thought about how on top of things she was first year. She had a 3.7 that first semester. And if she hadn't slept in that one time in Spanish, she'd probably have at least a 3.5 in the spring. Then second year happened. Geez don't remind me.

Brooke was sipping from her mug, noticing she'd made the coffee too sweet. She swirled it around to even out the sugar, and she sipped again, turning the pages of her textbook, feeling her attention wane so she went to her computer and read the Cav Daily, refreshing the front page several times to see if they'd written up a story of tonight's demonstration at the Freedom of Thought meeting. It was past 1am. I really really don't want to study. She turned and looked at the textbook laying open on her bed. Pattering her feet on the floor, she whined. Why do you have to be so boring?

She entered a search on the Cav Daily website for ALICE UPSHAW, and felt a rush of excitement seeing so many results, then quickly became frustrated that they weren't in any order, and that the button to sort by the date did not seem to work. She read some old stories on Alice from the time of her attack, last February, during the elections for student body president. There the familiar photo of her car with police tape going across the frame. The suspect Alice couldn't make out clearly, only that he was white and that he had a hoodie. And what he said, No one wants a nigger to be president. Then Alice's head was slammed into the steering wheel. Or did the head slam come first then dizzy, collapsed onto the ground, she heard the white boy say what he said?

Brooke looked through more articles, trying to remember, then her eye lingered on the pictures of the vigil, a girl she knew, Deidra, the subject of one big photo, Deidra's small button face lit up by the candle she was holding. Look at her cheeks. I never noticed how nice her skin was.

Eventually Brooke finished her coffee and her eyes were so painful and dry, she had to turn out the lights and lay down, her forearm shading her eyes. The hum of her fan soothed her, and she tuned into that sound drifting nearer to sleep despite her heart racing. She began thinking about Alice again, how set she was. She's got nothing to worry about from this point forward. Probably doesn't even know how lucky she *is*. Getting attacked like that. People get attacked every day. But her? Like that? At that moment huh? What a coincidence. If she did fake it, oh God she's so set. She wasn't even going to win that election. She even said to me the night before. I don't think it's going to be my year Brooke. That's how she said it. Don't you remember?

Brooke knew she was no longer talking solely to herself. It was her ex, Titus, who was listening. She imagined them together in a restaurant—no, not in public. Probably laying around in my room like this. She could picture the wry grin on his face as she paced and spit that venom about Alice Upshaw, a scene that had played out a few times in life but as of late only in her mind. If you want to know the truth Ty, I can't stand her. She didn't even know basic things in the ECON class we took together. You know she copied off me during the exam? Titus grinning in his wifebeater, Oh yeah? entertaining another retelling. You know I could take her down if I wanted. Alice was sitting right next to me like this, her hair down covering her face like this, you see? But I could see she was looking. Titus chuckling, How come you aint say nothing? Brooke shrugging there in bed, and moving her lips, I'm not going to put Honor charges on anyone. I'm going to mind my own business. I'm no tattle.

Titus then told her come over here and holding her, kissing her neck—God he always said that was his favorite part of my body. Only he would appreciate something like that. Imagining herself in his arms, she felt at ease and stopped thinking of other people and their secure trajectories of happiness and success. This easiness gave way. In came a rush of new anger and frustration, like a caffeine she was wide awake again—I can't believe his drunk ass. Came looking for a fight. I knew it. I shouldn't have even responded to his IM. I don't know about him sometimes. Mom would say that. Sweetie I don't know about this guy ... Maybe there's something to that comparison she makes. It sounds so terrible though. It's like she's calling him an animal. Not like. She *is* calling him an animal. A dog. What was that dog's name in her story? Poor thing ... oh he was standing there like a raving psycho. It looked like he wanted to hit me. I don't know. Maybe he has it in him. What a wimp.

Brooke kicked off her sheets and went back to her desk. She wiggled the mouse to wake up her computer, and let out a long, deep groan, and resumed refreshing the front page of the Cav Daily hoping to see something new.

3

After the rumble with the football players, Titus and Vonny laid low at the crib. They had a spot at Faulkner apartments, which was about as far from campus you could get while still being on it.

They wanted to let the situation breathe a lil but the gas was relentless. Their phones kept blowing up. The knocking was nonstop.

It seemed every dood they knew stumbled into their living room begging, absolutely begging to know what was really good. Palm punching, eyes bugged out. Was the beef really on with them football niggas?

Lots of people came through. Didn't nobody want to leave.

After hearing so many stories about all the forces out there against them—the football team, the police, this dean and that one—each came to the rational conclusion to keep his ass in here for now. Out there, it was too hot. Here, looking around at the other doods skipping class, was where he belonged. He felt like how the word MAN sounded in his head, and saw around him only that. MEN. REAL NIGGAS.

Not no PUSSIES or PUNKS. Not like the rest of them. Nothin but REAL ASS NIGGAS in here.

And they all got gassed up. Repeating stories. Embellishing. Allowing those embellishments to slide until everybody forgot what had actually occurred, how afraid and panicked they were. And allasudden every nigga in that smelly ass apartment was King Kong beating his chest, shouting how nobody was afraid of them football niggas! Just cos you big don't mean you know how to scrap ... yeah it was a straight textbook tackle, I done lifted him off his feet this high ... and so on ... Absolute gas.

But they never left the apartment alone. In twos or more, they ran to the store for dutches, other essentials. They were on high alert for slowmoving vehicles, people, basslines stalking them in the parking lot, the sound of too many loud deep voices in the next supermarket aisle, the swishy sound of officially-licensed windbreaker jumpsuits, untied Timbs scuffing up the floor. Even the absence of sound confirmed a threat lurking.

Truthfully no one knew how big the beef was, who was involved. Exactly what it entailed defied them. They knew a college football roster had over 100 players. Now there was talk that a basketball player took a cheap shot—add another 15. Then there were the townies. It was impossible to keep tabs on the townies. UVA wasn't located in Charlottesville as much as it was surrounded on all sides by it.

So they all crammed into that apartment surviving on nothing more than that noxious gas and Frito Lay.

Days passed. Grades suffered.

And one midafternoon someone woke up to piss and noticed, aye where Titus ass go?

4

As the blue bus made its way to central grounds, the sight of whitepeople jogging grew more common. A straggler here and there. A pair chatting along Route 29. Once the bus made the turn onto Ivy, whitepeople jogging everywhere. Titus found it strange. It was 90-plus outside. Humidity on top of that. Most limped along like they were bout to die. Why inflict that on yourselves.

Matter fact a lot seemed strange now that he was back. Couldn't tell what was new, what had always been there. The shape of people, faces, buildings. He came across a bulletin board with a sketch of the Charlottesville Serial Rapist. This the same dood from before? He still out there raping?

Proceeding with his head low, he avoided the bus stop by the Comm School where football players often posted up. What blared in his headphones seemed urgent, knowing, and he couldn't help that his step aligned with the beat. His bop grew heavier, his scowl thick, and he felt ready for whatever drama came his way. Coming indoors he tilted an earcup so he could hear around corners.

The lecture was endless. He waited in line to talk to the professor afterwards. He was in the middle of his speech about how he really needed to add this class—how he had to take a semester off for personal reasons, how he needed to go over 20 credits just to graduate on time so he could go to law school—when the professor promptly signed his course action form and handed it back. So if you're going to miss class for away games, please remember to get your TA an athletic memo okay?

Titus thanked him for his time.

He had another class, then discussion, then it was the class with Dean Daniels, which he'd been dreading all day.

* * *

Right on the dot Titus slid through the rear entrance, posted up in the very back by himself. Dean Daniels made no show of noticing him.

He tried his best to follow along. He wrote down whatever was written on the board, wrote when a lot of people were writing too, usually when there were lists involved, numbers and dates. Afterwards he looked down at his quarter page of notes and felt satisfied. During a stretch where nothing important seemed to be happening, he glanced around and cracked open his LSAT study guide. That so many of the questions looked like algebra disturbed him.

As soon as lecture concluded, Dean Daniels's eyes shot straight to the back of the room. He told the other students waiting to please step out. It will only take a second.

Titus let his head droop, smiling embarrassedly. No no I'm not going to yell at you Titus. I have too much respect for you. Coach Groh has spoken to his boys so I promised I would speak to mine. There will be no retaliation, understand? Let me take a look at you.

Titus came down the aisle, every inch of him scrutinized. Daniels spent a few more seconds looking him over, taking in every scab and bruise. He started packing up his briefcase, and grunted for Titus to come follow.

They made the short walk behind the amphitheater to the Office of African-American Affairs. His office was on the second floor.

The dean shut the door and got in that ass pronto. Pacing behind his desk, gesturing at him, every question a rhetorical one dripping with contempt. Every inch of wall in that room was covered by a frame—inspirational quotes, awards, pictures of the dean shaking hands with someone in front of the American flag—it all added to the attack but he just sat there, his raggedy looking ass sprawled in a chair while the dean asked over and over is this who you are? This? A scoundrel? Some thug? It's hard enough being taken seriously here and there you go skulking around— Daniels mimed a punch-drunk boxer, one eye shut. If this is who you are, why didn't you let us know sooner? You could've saved us a lot of trouble.

Titus had to take it. Dean Daniels was not a black dean, but THE black dean. Because of him UVA had the highest graduation rate in the country. It had been a big selling point for Titus's family.

Young man a lot of people don't want you here to begin with. We can't have black violent felons running around Mr. Jefferson's university, can we? That's not the kind of diversity people march for. What's worse is that you kept this hidden for years. Years. That's what upsets people the most. The Dean of Student Life is trying to put Honor charges on you. I spoke with her this morning. She said you lied when you applied here four years ago. Lied when you withdrew in the spring semester. Lied again on your readmission form. Being objective here, she's got a compelling case to revoke your enrollment.

Titus rose in his seat, Dr. Daniels I'm sorry but I got to stop you right there. You see the charges came down *after* I had already gotten into UVA ... and once again Titus began summarizing the timeline of his legal situation, which Daniels did not bother interrupting ... and my lawyer said that rule only applies to drug convictions because of federal financial aid guidelines, which doesn't apply to my case at all. So legally speaking I didn't have to disclose that information.

Daniels admitted that technically Titus was correct. But you want to know something? Don't play technicalities with the university. They'll play it right back. You'll never win.

Daniels fell back into his chair. He'd gotten most of it out his system. Frowningly, thinkingly, he massaged his face. He said that he would talk to Dean Staunton again. The best thing you have going for you is that you're a fourth year. You've made it this far so why not let you finish? I think I can convince her if I take more proactive approach with you.

The phone rang and the dean sighed, dispatching with the call quickly. He led Titus to the door.

They descended a narrow, steep staircase towards the lobby where, by the suddenly brightening faces, some from class, it was clear many were hoping to get a word with the dean despite not being on his official schedule. Daniels greeted the room with a booming voice and walking away sighed under his breath again.

When they came to the porch, Titus adjusted his pants. Aye Dr. Daniels I really appreciate you lookin out for me. I needed to hear all that up there. Daniels said not everything had been finalized yet. Either way it means a lot, you putting yourself out there on my behalf.

Titus turned to leave but had to tell the dean one last thing.

Whoever it is deciding, can you let them know something? I promised my parents I would graduate this year. That's why I'm taking so many credits. I gotta go over 20 this semester and next. That's the only way for the math to work. It's because I'm applying to law school. I want to go straight. I know myself. If I'm not moving forward, I tend to lose track sometimes. I need that momentum. Once I get it, I'm gone. I'm not trying to mess anything up Dr. Daniels. I promise to God I'm not. Can you let them know all that?

The dean studied the young man, actually seeing through the scabs and bruises for the first time, and sensed he was being genuine.

5

Brooke sometimes hung out with a girl she knew from the Virginia Dance Company, Susan Adelman, who was living on the Lawn now. They'd been meaning to catch up. Susan had spent the summer in Cape Town for a fellowship—Brooke moaning over the phone, uh I'm so jealous of you hahaha—and was dying to tell her all about it but whenever they saw each other on grounds, it was quick, and what little time they had to talk they complained of being tired and busy. Busy busy busy. They made sure to kiss each other on each cheek.

After trading a few emails, they found a night to catch up and Brooke agreed to come down to Susan's place on the Lawn. From the email Susan sounded very excited to tell her about the trip to South Africa. Susan wrote that she had something big to tell her, which was too much for Brooke to resist.

Parking was tricky and after circling again past the chapel she took her chances by the medical school. She made her way up a gravel alley, and it was always when she climbed the irregular stone steps to either colonnade did she feel truly transported to THE LAWN. The original UVA grounds that Thomas Jefferson himself had designed. Before she came to UVA she knew it was a big deal to live there. You had to apply and interview and they only took 50 or so each year. Only the best of the best. On a field trip in middle school she remembered peeking in the rooms and there would be someone reading in a rocking chair. They even looked real smart. Like a different kind of people altogether.

She'd been meaning to apply. But second year happened. She had consoled herself on the hope that they accounted heavily for service and leadership. But when she sat down to fill out the application, she felt so stupid writing her GPA on the line. Her extracurriculars too, they all seemed so random and scattered. She had never distinguished herself in any one thing. She was Treasurer of this club, Secretary of another. The only thing she was truly proud of was serving as one of the lead choreographers for Virginia Dance Company's Annual Spring Performance. Yet on paper it looked so shallow and insignificant. Girly even.

Susan's room was on the West Lawn so Brooke cut across the grass, feeling that she was in the presence of the Rotunda again, the soft blue moonlight falling on its pillars and dome. There seemed to be an event going on so the windows and porch were lit up in that orange incandescence which she loved and with the blue from the moon ... Brooke said to herself it wasn't fair. It was so beautiful.

Susan poured wine and proceeded to describe her thoughts following her time in Africa, the funk she had been in and how the realization did not come suddenly. When she could grasp her calling, she realized the signs had already been there. Susan kept setting down her glass to let her hands go free as she talked, whirling then cutting through the air, and clearing an imaginary table haphazardly and they both were laughing at her jumbling enthusiasm. Did any of that make sense hahahaha? Let's start again hahahaha.

It was getting warm in the cramped little room so they went out under the colonnade, Susan rocking in the chair as Brooke sat on the lip of the door frame, glancing over at the Rotunda as the event had let out, the people—older, a little stooped, cultured but not professors here.

Susan said that her vision was to teach kids how to cope with their emotions and resolve conflicts through ... Brooke finished the sentence for her, Dance? Dance is part of it. Really its more comprehensive. Brooke threw out the term Movement? and Susan snapped her fingers and pointed at her, Yes that's it. That's exactly it. Gosh I'm so illiterate right now. They need to revoke my Lawn residence. They laughed some more and right beside them a door shut and Susan's neighbor hurried past them in a bathrobe carrying a shower caddy. When he was out of earshot, Susan muttered something about him that Brooke couldn't make out, and resumed outlining her vision.

Susan pictured a devoted corps of recent college graduates deployed in the toughest inner city schools across America. It would start as a domestic movement and spread across the globe. It would have to. She stretched her arm out assuming an arabesque, the line long and lovely though Susan had been drinking, and Susan said that movement is universal. I really like that Sue. I don't know if you have a name for this organization yet but it would have to have movement in the name.

The neighbor came back after his shower. Brooke asked if she could use the bathroom. She was directed down to Room 37 where she would hang a right into the alley. It's a separate little building, you can't miss it. When Brooke came back Susan was inside typing on her computer and she gestured for them to go back outside where it wasn't so stuffy.

You know Sue everything sounds so exciting. I can just see it. Exactly how you described it with the desks pushed to the walls. You're a kid and you get so bored sitting in a desk all day, and at that age, you're allergic to reading. You gotta get up and move. Susan pointed at her again. That's it. Let's call it MOVE. Move? Yes MOVE. The MOVE Project. No not project. Initiative. The MOVE Initiative. Yes that's perfect. Susan stuck out her hand. So are you with me? Brooke was struck. Are you propositioning me? Susan got down on her knee and propositioned. Brooke laughingly gave her a big smooch on the cheek.

They drank some more. You don't think it's silly. No. I've read things before about kinesthetic learners in an Ed school class. Real interesting. Of course, we're dancers so we understand. You think you'd be interested? Interested in? But seriously Brooke. I'm practically begging you. Brooke giggling as Susan continued. I think about your ability to connect with these communities, and all the work you've done there, your experience, your energy, and I can't think of a better person to help me fulfill this vision. Oh Susan this sounds so great. It's really flattering. Is that a yes? Brooke's heart was racing. It sounds great Sue. I'm really excited. I know I'm asking a lot. You've probably got other plans after graduation. It's almost unfair for me to ask you to put those things on hold. Brooke pursed her lips, making a face to acknowledge that it was a good point, at least hypothetically. Susan's voice was distant. I know that starting a nonprofit is not glamorous work but at least we'll be in New York. New York? Yes, that'll be our base of operations. It's sort of a default option. I figure the corporate money is there. Brooke moaned, I LOVE the City, and they talked for a while about what they loved so much about it, their voices rising almost in competition with each other. And guess who else is there? Who? Susan went out to the grass and attempted a perfect passé en pointe before quickly losing her balance. Brooke tossed a hand over her head, letting her body sag as if she'd fainted. I've always wanted to see ABT live. Susan leapt around the grass. Setting down her glass, Brooke joined her, each grand jeté under the moonlight feeling better than the next. Seeing what moves they could still perform, pushing their limbs a little past what they could otherwise, with help from the wine and the romance of the setting.

6

Vonny had been cool most his life. He had certain God-given attributes that were not fully realized until puberty. Ones that would prove advantageous—his hair, his voice (this deep slowmoving Tidewater drawl). His personality was on point and more important, he didn't change it depending on who he was around. He had some natural musical talent. Could dance (and not too *too* good either). Was coordinated (ambidextrous, in fact) and faster than anybody he could pick up any game involving a ball or deck of cards or stick.

But like most cool doods, the secret came down to having an older brother. And Vonny was especially lucky. He had an older brother of the same height and build.

His older brother Shawn lived about an hour and a half away in Petersburg. Shawn made good money working for Amtrak, and had a nice lil spot down there by the river. Vonny would drive down every month or so and return with a bunch of clothes. Clothes nobody had seen before, except maybe in music videos. Then next month Vonny would drive down there, rotate the worn clothes with a brand new set, and so on.

Being seen around grounds, Vonny gave the distinct impression he was ballin. Dood always out there lookin official. Only athletes rocked such exclusives. But those doods were getting paid on the low. Vonny had no income whatsoever.

The weather turned, and it was time to stock up on coats, so Vonny made the trip down to Petersburg. And as soon as he laid out the old clothes for his brother, Shawn noticed something was off. A dull edge here. A pasty consistency to the leather there. Frayed stitching all throughout. Sup with those? You been breakdancin or sumpin? Them shits look retarded. Shawn's hands searching, Wait didn't I give you that Peppers jersey too? Where that go?

More and more questions came that Vonny couldn't answer. So he told his older brother the truth. He thought Shawn wouldn't be that upset after learning he'd won the fight, and that the other dood happened to be this big ol football player.

Fuck is you sittin there smilin for Vonny? You bout to be kicked out for bad grades. What, it's cool gettin kicked out for scrappin instead? Huh? You tryna kill dad, that's what you doon. I aint tryna kill nobody dog, don't try to put that on me. Besides, the guy mushed *me* first. I'm supposed to act like some punk?

Shawn told him to turn his ass around and go back to Charlottesville. I can't keep encouraging this shit. Encouraging what? How my supposed to leave when I just got here? I already paid for them trees. Lemme at least wait for your mans to come through. Paid??? Lil nigga don't talk to me bout money. You still owe me big time. You call me cryin how UVA put a registration block and what I do? And last time you came through here, what about that huh? You still owe me for that. Now you gotta pay for them runners you jacked up and that Peppers jersey. That jonk was an authentic, not no replica.

Vonny said he was short right now. Yeah yeah we all short. That's why grown ass people work. Mom and Dad work. I work. Even April working. Just cos the baby comin, don't mean the bills stop. Meanwhile you—Shawn was pushing him towards the door—you think *you* the baby. Everybody gotta pull their own weight on top of carryin you Vonny. You lucky I aint told Dad nuffin. If he knew HALF the shit I know.

Vonny hung his head in the doorway. Quit talkin crazy dog. You aint gon tell Dad. C'mon at least lemme hold a dub. You aint gon let me drive all the way up to Charlottesville empty-handed, is you? After I had just got here? You aint gon do me like that Shawn? Listen how bout I—

Shawn shut the door in his face.

* * *

An hour and a half later back in Charlottesville, Titus laughed at him. I told you he'd notice. That shoe whitener never works.

Chuckling a lil they began to reminisce on the rumble with the football players. It was a shame, they agreed, what happened to that Peppers jersey. How'd that sleeve come off? Sure that was an authentic? Hahaha ...

The brawl was only a few weeks old at this point, but felt even older given nothing had popped off since. They poked a lil more at the topic, nudged to see if there was any more life in it, but all the juice had been squeezed.

Titus said he was onto bigger and better things. He'd been doing pretty good lately. UVA had tried something funny with his enrollment but Dean Daniels had hooked it up somehow. Matter fact the old man had taken him under his wing.

Titus had that glow, the glow of having his shit together, which people who didn't have their shit together precisely noticed. It was the middle of the night and Titus still radiated it clearly.

He told Vonny come here and withdrew a small, white palm-sized object from his desk and handed it over. Vonny read aloud the name printed on it, THE SILENT TIMER. So special bout this again?

Titus sidled up to him.

See right here you type in how many questions you got and over here you put in the time allotted and when you press this big button right here—Which button?—that big ass red one you looking at. Press that and it'll make it so you spend an equal amount of time on each question.

Titus continued on about how the biggest error most people make on test day is the mismanagement of time, but with the SILENT TIMER, that wouldn't be a problem anymore. Not a lot of people knew about this device. It was his secret weapon.

Vonny stroked his chin approvingly. That's pretty official stick man. I do be getting hung up on questions.

80 dollars seemed like a lot to be charging though. Vonny studied the timer more closely. He turned it around to look at its back. Weighed it in his palm. It was as light as it looked. Won't really much to it, he thought. Just some circuits, screen, power supply. Learned how to do this in class already. That nigga who made this fucking filthy rich right now. Offa some stupid little idea.

Vonny's thumb fiddled with the little kickstand in the back that propped up the display. Yo they let you bring these in with you on test day? Yeah shit is certified my nigga I checked.

Titus said he could feel it working already. Compared to the practice test yesterday, he had already improved by one question. And that was from his first time using it. First time! And extrapolating from that, man ... Because when it comes to law school, all they look at is your GPA and LSAT score. They don't care bout nothin else. They don't even care about your major. Even you Vonny. You engineering but if you wanted ... Naw stick man hahaha you can go head with that hahahaha ...

Right then a yawn snuck up on Vonny. He stretched out his arms and chewed on it, going yup yup yup yup, and smacking his lips. Thinking. He got stuck in some thought as he stood there and almost forgot where he was, leaning against Titus's door frame. He was looking at the Silent Timer sitting on the desk, then at Titus admiring it, Titus kneading his hands together, then Vonny felt a sudden sinking in his chest. It confused him, the feeling, like there was a lotta stuff there all swirled in, but it only lasted a second.

Aye forreal stick man I gotta get on your level. I'mma quit messin around. I'mma stay my ass in like you. I can't keep drivin here and there. You know what we oughta do stick man? Maybe you and me, we can get on a schedule. Monday through Friday, like a 9 to 5. Treat this like a job. What you think?

Titus said that was a good idea. He already looked at it like a job. That was helping him get through taking so many credits this semester.

Vonny felt much better about himself, and slept soundly until the afternoon the next day. Not once did he think about being on academic probation, how his financial aid had been revoked, how he had applied for a credit card to cover the $4,000 he initially owed, and applied for another one because the first cash advance didn't cover the full amount, and the other credit offers, the money appearing from thin air, but the bills too, and the angry seeming language that had been popping up in the notices, and his brother spottin him ... but now Shawn trippin ... and ... and ...

7

It used to be Titus would wake up sometimes believing he was still in the Prince William County Adult Detention Center. Blinking up at the white ceiling, the white painted brick. Every minute of the day ahead accounted for and monitored. Then he would sit up and it was clear: I'm not there no more.

Less and less that happened. Less and less he could remember what it had been like in jail. The fine details. It used to be he could recall so many names. The men in his pod, the pastor, the different COs and their personalities, different wings of the detention center and so on.

Now he could only remember one guy well. This dood who was a former student of his mother, Ray Franklin. Met him one day outside chapel. Ray approached. Knew who he was and everything. Ray claimed his mother was his favorite teacher coming up. Oh word? He smiled, feeling his face twitch. Of all places he could meet one of his mother's former students. Dapped him up that day but the more he thought on it, the more it embarrassed him. It reached a point where he skipped the next chapel, so afraid he'd come across his mother's student again and who knew what would happen. Would he put hands on Ray? Blame Ray for making him feel the way he did. Tell him fuck out my face. She don't remember you ...

But he began to see the sign from God. He realized there was little separating him from the other men in his pod. Who was he but another sinner who had strayed from the path?

On the day of his release, he announced to his parents his plan to graduate from UVA this year and to attend law school directly. Becoming a lawyer was what he had been called on to do. He owed it to the men in there, men hardly different from himself. He didn't mention Ray by name but that's who he was thinking of.

His folks asked if he was sure. He said he was. Look how much we been around the system. It makes all the sense in the world. But Titus graduating this year? Yeah I have to. I always gotta feel like I'm moving forward. If I'm not moving forward ... Son nobody's putting anything on you. Maybe take a semester to get back in the groove? Ha yall make it seem like I been away forever. It was only 90 days. Let's get real, I did more reading in there than I ever did at UVA.

He needed to go over 20 credits in the fall and spring semesters to graduate on time. It was an easy thing to commit to in the summer, but once the schoolyear started, it was a different matter. Then that rumble with the football team ... And Dean Daniels had to check him.

Him and Daniels talked now on the regular. The old dean was right about one thing. Keep the door closed. It did wonders. Suddenly there was more time than he knew what to do with.

He pushed through the semester, grinded and grinded, and after a few weeks, he realized school was like anything else. A job. There was no special emotion attached to the tasks. Just work. A series of small transactions.

So he woke up early, continued waking up early, and would review his lists of to-do items on his post-it note, the tiny writing covering front and back, and dive straight into work. Just like a 9 to 5. No secret to it.

Every now and then he ran across some football players. His head told them there no threat, that the beef was over, but he would feel something stir in his body. His senses sharpening, his muscles becoming especially supple. But no drama ever transpired since that first party of the year. Most of the time of grounds he saw one of the older players who he'd known since first or second year, not one of these youngbucks who had started this beef. Besides, it was deep into the football season and these niggas had better things to worry about. Titus had even heard that they were good this year. They say that every year but who knows. Maybe they decent.

Finishing his work early, he'd crack a brew in his room and lose hours clicking through law school sites. Flipping through the brochures in his small collection. The pictures of people sitting in circles talking. Listening close. Being inspired. The buildings were bright and immaculate. All everyone had straight teeth. He liked to study the student profiles. He picked out the black people in the Diversity section and studied what they were about, what they had to say. Whatever they put down on their list of accomplishments. Whatever, it was all phony. But he liked it. He went to bed at night knowing he had them all clocked. He laughed thinking of their lil corny pictures. What it would be like to see them in person. Their reactions when he would roll up there with a bop in his step. These niggas aint even ready hahaha.

He could see himself in those places. Around those people. His ass sitting somewhere reading. Maybe in one of them pretty libraries with the light coming through the windows in thick rays you can see. Hardest part was getting in. It would be easier after. He'd be set up pretty good going forward. Big time man. He could see it. Depending on how he looked at it, it was actually about to happen.

He imagined returning to his mother's old church. It always killed him to think how she came to abandon her whole social life because of him. They used to go to parties. Have parties. There used to be people over all the time. Their house as big as it was. Big kitchen too. Since his father retired, since he himself started getting into trouble ... But he could picture it now. Going back to that old church, his mother on his arm, and going around rubbing it in those ladies faces that he was big time now. Loretta's son had made a name for himself. Just look at him in that sharp suit. A man now.

At the beginning of the semester, Titus had made an appointment with someone at Career Services. Their office was inside the football stadium down a hall past the trophy cases. The career advisor showed him a spreadsheet with the acceptance rates of UVA people who applied to law school. The numbers went back the past couple years, and were broken down by GPA and LSAT. He named some schools and her finger slid down the column with his GPA.

Did you take the LSAT back in June? I haven't even taken it yet. She picked a low number and slid her finger down the column until it intersected with his GPA, then did the same with a high number. So I could bomb it and I still got a decent chance? I don't want to mislead you Titus. This is a range of possibilities.

She explained that the people in the bottom quartile often had something compelling about them that couldn't be quantified. They could be athletes, ones that competed in the Olympics. Or could have written a New York Times bestseller. Owned a successful business. They had a great story. Do you have a great story Titus? Was there a peculiar challenge you've overcome that would impress an admissions committee? Yes most definitely. Are you involved in anything on grounds? Do you hold any leadership positions? He shook his head and she asked the same question about involvement in a different way, and he said no again, and she waited for him to come up with something and he was getting a lil embarrassed. Doesn't being an African-American ... ? Sorry to get point blank. That's a legitimate question Titus. While many schools don't use a strict quota system anymore, all schools actively seek out diversity. I wish we maintained records on that. I think the Office of African-American Affairs has those broken down. You should check with them. But you're right, being from an underrepresented group never hurts.

At the end of the consultation she gave him a thick stack of forms—pamphlets about workshops coming up, flyers for a series of meetings and tutorials for law school applicants. The most important form was this neon green one, the checklist for applicants applying this year. Altogether it was a lotta stuff. He felt good, like he had a whole team at his back. He shook her hand.

Throughout the semester he kept up with the items on the checklist. He went to a few of the events in September and stayed to the end of them even though the information was common sense. He enjoyed sitting in the back with his leg thrown over a chair and looking at all the other people applying, how anxious they looked while he himself was back here chillin.

In October there was a resume workshop which was held in the Career Services offices. He was expecting to see the career advisor he'd met with, but a different set of advisors ran the meeting. They made everyone partner up. The girl who was his partner played like she was real nervous having someone critique her work. When he took his first look at her resume, he felt his skull jump back. Gotdamn. What you use to lay this out? My older brother helped me. If you like, I can email you a copy. Just replace the information.

For the rest of the allotted time he squinted at her resume, trying to find fault with her action verbs, but it was so legit he had nothing to say. Where you get paper like this? She said she had some extra in her bag if he wanted some. No doubt.

That same day he went down to Madison House and signed up for a Little Sibling. He felt better about himself. There wasn't much of an application process. You just put your information down. No background check.

In a week he heard back and they assigned him Rasean Butler on Prospect Ave. He took the city trolley down and hooked up with another bus and walked through the neighborhood. Niggas were sitting on porches out there in the cold, fists thrust in their pockets. They stood up and looked at him, white breath coming out their hoodies.

Rasean lived at the only two story house on the block. There was an empty clothesline out back and a gravel driveway. The grandmother took one look at him from behind the screen door, Sheila not home. No I'm here for Rasean. I go to UVA. I'm with the Big Sibling-Little Sibling Program. Program? I don't know if he's signed up for that.

The mother, Sheila, came down and straightened it all out. He met the little dood in the kitchen. Shook his hand. Started asking him questions. I'm sorry he's very shy. That's all right. Can you take his brother too? Nah I'm sorry. The people from my program told me I couldn't do that. Putting on his coat, she said if she had known, she would've just gotten a sitter. I'm sorry ma'am but the program put specific restrictions on that.

He took Rasean to Clemons Library. Rasean didn't say much on the bus ride there. Titus kept asking him questions about school. If he liked this and that. What his favorite subject was. Lil dood wasn't much of a talker. Yo you watch cartoons? The kid finally looked at him. Oh yeah? Which one lil man? Took a few minutes but Titus was able to get out of him that his favorite cartoon was Dragonball Z. So when they got to Clemons, he sat Rasean at a computer next to him and told him to look up all the Dragonball Z stuff he wanted.

The lil dood knew how to get around on the computer so he left him alone. Titus was working on a paper. He was looking at a book in his lap and copying the blocks of text over and massaging those blocks into something intelligible, adding his own words here and there and it was all coming together. Rasean kept clicking around on that computer. Yo you finding your Dragonball Z lil man? Where is the printer? Over there.

Everyone in the computer lab seemed to be happy there was a little kid around. When Rasean waited in line for the printer, people stuck their hands out giving him high fives and asking him questions. It was cool. It didn't seem like much work to have a little nigga hanging around sometimes. Cheering shit up.

A female's voice drifted in from the side. Family visiting? It was Brooke. He was taking the sight of her in, that long neck of hers, returning her smile. Nah it's for Madison House. I gotta say Ty it's a good look. Oh yeah? He's so cute. He all right. I just wanted to say hi but I'll leave you with your Little Sibling. He still couldn't believe how beautiful she looked. Aye where you going? 2nd floor. Come by. Nah I won't be here but too much longer. Gotta take lil dood back. I can take you. Nah you don't gotta do that girl. Please it's been getting cold out. You don't want him to catch something waiting for the bus. Then what will the Madison House people say?

* * *

Somehow after dropping off Rasean and complaining to each other how much work they had left to do tonight, they grabbed a quick bite on the Corner and ended up back in her crib assuring the other that studying together like this would help them both stay up, and they were going to take it seriously and not think anything deep was going on here.

The studying yielded at some point. He remembered showing her the Silent Timer and explaining the buttons and how the device was transforming his life. That's great Ty. You always think of things like this.

Warm and tired, he put his head down to rest his eyes for a minute and woke up mumbling in the asscrack of his

LSAT study guide, disoriented, only to see her typing at her computer, and he passed out again.

He woke again to a darkened room. Still in her bed, her smells. She was touching him. He cooed, the throb of his pelvis full. He adjusted himself so he could accommodate her reach through the tangle of sheets. He was full boil. Her hand withdrew. He heard her footsteps leading away. The door snipped locked. The books were removed from the bed.

She lowered herself onto him. The gentle shrink-wrap sound in the still of the night. The beginnings of opera noises. The rusty yawn of the twin-extra long bed frame. She accepted him fully, bent down to him, her heavy breathing tickling his ears while he sopped her up with closed eyes. Sopped up neck, clavicle, chin, shoulder, chin, chin, clavicle. His lips eloquent, unbothered by patches of fuzz and staleness. Their bodies warm against each other. He traced her sides, her love muscles girding her narrow hips. He was smiling feeling a smile somewhere in the dark reciprocated. He strained to see that neck of hers above him. It was now wilting. Hair hanging out the sides of her head.

Her. Her first quaking brought her breath cool and quiet across his chest. Her toes released the sheets. She was laying across his chest whispering baby don't cum yet, okay? I think I have another one. She reared back, her rib cage full. Face to the ceiling, quickly her body became possessed. She collapsed onto him—Owww fuck Brooke witcho pointy ass elbows. Sorry I said I'm sorry. She rolled over and kissed him. He lowered his voice, I'm sayin tho ...

It was a minor drama and they sighed there in their sweat. She threw an arm over him. Baby I don't want to fight no more, promise? Then she rolled over and mumbled into the pillow that's it for me. You can now, if you want to. But not too loud please.

He climbed above, arranged her somehow in the darkness, the sleep still confusing his movements. He felt it catch after some probing, smelled the fresh paste and put in the work. When he came close, he stopped, gotdamning her in his mind that it was so good, wanting to say I love you right then and there, to forgive her for everything. She never came to visit him in jail. Not once in his entire 90 day bid. Never returned his letters. He'd been thrown away by her. But—didn't matter. In a short while every little petty bone in his body, every bit of ammunition he'd been cultivating and storing in his head, it was no more.

Their bodies curled together, she was stroking his forearm with the back of her fingertips. Have you spent more time thinking about us? He said he had. I'm glad. I've been thinking about us too. What you used to tell me about labels Ty, I get it now. You used to say that when you put something in a box like that, you can't just let it be and grow into whatever it's meant to and you end up stifling it. Pretty soon life is passing you by and you're not taking a second to enjoy any of it. And the original thing you wanted, it's not there either. You remember saying that? He was laughing gotdamn, you memorized all that? She laughed too. I missed you Ty. He squeezed her body against his, taking what she had said just now, the whole night thus far, as some apology. So he apologized too. Don't. I don't want to look backwards anymore Ty.

The next morning he woke, sitting up suddenly into a bright white room—the walls, the ceiling, nothing where it was supposed to be—then Brooke was there typing at her desk, a cup of coffee beside her. He lay down again remembering. Closed his eyes, enjoying the faint smell of ass that remained as it mingled with coffee, a familiar smell that he recognized but was brandnew to him again. A grown man's morning. He rolled into his side looking at her some more. Brooke wearing his white tee sitting cross-legged so that the cape of the fabric covered her body entirely except for her neck. That beautiful long neck. He lay and watched her quietly as she typed, admiring her, that neck, the grace of its line sticking out the white teepee of his shirt.

8

Midway through class Vonny got a message from Q on his 2 way: 9-1-1.

Vonny looked around the lecture hall. Everyone hunched over their notebooks. The professor wet his thumb and rubbed out a variable on the transparency. People turned to a fresh page, almost in unison. Vonny surmised that what was happening in class was important, and he debated in his head whether he should call Q right now or wait.

Vonny got up and went outside. Q confirmed that their weed connect George was one of the 33 arrested in the drug bust last night. The bust was a big one. The local police, University police, even the feds, they'd all been watching for months, which made Vonny a lil nervous. Not that he'd done any dirt. But still, the being watched part, and for so long.

Q came to the crib with the city paper. Vonny read the names of the 33 they arrested. George's name among them. He read the proud pronouncements from the task force chief, the boastful way the details were described of a clever scheme to catch some of the dealers. They created this fake fraternity and distributed fancy invitations to meet at the Rotunda at midnight. Being told you were invited to this exclusive, super secret society was too much for anybody to resist. So when these doods showed up to the Rotunda at midnight, the police loaded their asses in a van headed straight to jail.

It was too depressing to bear, so him and Q sparked up, and now there was more air around the problem and Vonny's mind began to work.

He knew this would be a prolonged drought, and was apportioning the days ahead according to the demands of his habit. He calculated how far his current sack, the one on the table over there next to Q's knee, would last, the minimum level of highness he needed before the next blunt needed to be rolled, then assuming another sack would materialize somewhere, then another, and he consulted with himself who exactly he knew and their dependability. These were steady, discrete measurements. He'd need to ease up a bit, that much was obvious but it wouldn't be too crazy. Something would turn up.

Just then the front door swung open. The rustle of plastic bags was followed by the sound of small luggage wheels being forced with a grunt over the threshold. A box fell onto the landing and was scooted along scratchily by a foot, and the dood making all this commotion came into view, clothes in hangers slung over his shoulder, partially obscured by puffy garbage bags and the fur lined hood of his coat. For a moment they thought it could've been, maybe just maybe, George, the man himself, or any number of their weed connects freshly sprung out of Albemarle-Regional, with a tale to tell, some scoop.

Instead it was the handsome, high cheekboned face of their long lost roommate Kev. There hadn't been a Kev sighting in weeks. They sat up grinning. Look like some-body in the dog house. Kev said it smelled like a dog house in here, Guess I'm in the right place, and smiled his big beautiful white ass smile. It was the most spotless thing in the room. Would either of you scrubs grab my computer out there? If you scratch it, I'll take away the tip.

Giggling they told him fuck you and got up to help, making sure to handle his things a little rough but not too too. Yo Kev you gotta let me hold them Barkleys. You? and looking him up and down, You gotta apply for a permit first ... They stuck a brew in his palm (luckily Kev didn't smoke) and got him to say a lil about him and ol girl, how it had been a long time coming, but Kev kept withdrawing the bottle every time they reached to clink it. It's okay Kev you can cry around us hahaha. We miss her too hahaha. Two years was a long time my nigga ... Brew after brew, they couldn't get him to break. The dood really was incapable of being upset. In all the time they'd known him, he'd never been anything other than what he was at this moment—happy, talking smack but not in a meanspirited way.

Just like Titus but even more so, Kev had the unmistake-able gleam of someone who had his shit together. It was as if Kev knew it was all a game and assumed you knew it too. Why wouldn't you? It wasn't that hard. Plus you weren't dumb, were you? Course not. And Kev was beating his chest now, swaying after the brews, quoting the Good Doctor that he was free freeeee at last Good God Almighty hahaha ...

This freedom talk should've made everybody hype, especially Vonny, who used to cruise up and down first year dorms with him. They played off each other well, both being pretty boys with the Asian persuasion, Vonny the half-Korean and Kev, a full Asian himself despite the rumors, a darkskin Filipino. It was a nice lil niche they had back in the good ol days.

Instead the mention of freedom made Vonny think about George in a jail cell again, the weedlessness and all the other bad stuff to come that couldn't even be imagined yet. Vonny sat back with a dry smile listening to his old partner talk about past conquests, and him prospecting the future, listing out who had been owed what, starting with the ones that were long overdue and going in that order instead of order of difficulty. It was strange to hear Kev talk about females in such sporting terms, but the film he played in their minds was a good one with lots of funny parts.

Vonny got up to take a piss and on the way back felt a sudden sinking in his chest. For a moment he was confused, but he recognized the feeling as the same one from the other night. Titus told him about this secret timer and it made him freeze there for a second.

Vonny sat, continued to act like nothing had happened, and nobody seemed to notice. BET was on, some urban shitcom.

His eye wandered from the screen, skipping around the empty cups and small piles of trash in the room, the tangle of cords under the TV. He tried to imagine where a tracking device could be hidden. Then he tried to imagine what the person on the other end saw and thunk. He could picture someone horrified that a college nigga like him spent so little time studying and so much of it chasing the things he did.

9

Once again Titus took the city trolley and fetched his Lil Sibing Rasean. He took the boy to the library and placed him in front of a computer while he got some work done, glancing over periodically at the boy playing a game and making a big show of being upset when GAME OVER happened to flash across the screen at a moment Titus happened to be looking. Brooke would arrive from a meeting, beaming My boys! My boys! and they dropped off Rasean and returned to Faulkner.

She rested her head on the wheel. He reached across and rubbed her back. That feels nice. If I could stay like this a little longer and not have to go out again. He shushed her, rubbed her back some more.

The next night they decided they both deserved a break so they went to the Downtown Mall and caught a movie. Afterwards they strolled along the cobblestones in their coats holding hands, noticing the other couples holding hands, and noticing their own reflections in the shiny surfaces and liking what they saw. Brooke was talking about how nice it was to watch a film like that when the theater is packed and everybody gets the jokes. It enhances the whole experience don't you think? He teased her about laughing at that one part of the movie where the joke was so obvious. Nigga you was he only one laughing all loud as hell hahaha —she elbowed him. He stuck out his leg to trip her, catching her before she fell. She hit him in the arm, and he deflected her blows, continuing to tease her. How many times I told you bout them pointy ass things? She looked around huffing, self-conscious that people might be looking, and took his hand again and they continued walking along.

They passed under wrought iron lamps, which had Thanksgiving decorations hanging from them. They couldn't believe the holidays were almost here. The next thoughts that registered were of time running out, which made them each sad, the sudden shortness of breath slowing their walk, then they squeezed each other's hand, knowing what it was the other was thinking. They walked untalkingly until a different urge came and they hurried to the parking garage across the street.

After making love they lay petting each other quietly, Brooke jerking up every now and then to look at the clock on her nightstand. She laid her head on his chest. I really don't want to go. Then don't. They'll understand. He thought of making a joke about how the people at whichever club it was never got none, and would be glad she was off getting hers, but thinking of the word he'd use—either fucking or getting a nut, neither of them fit the mood so never mind it felt so good just laying here.

She got up to fish through her purse for her cell phone and she stopped to deliberate again before calling. When Titus stroked her back with his knuckle, she dialed. She spoke quietly into the phone, scratching up her voice not too much but enough, and she lay back into Titus's arms sighing, the sound towards the end becoming a bit rough. What's wrong girl? I know I'm supposed to be relieved now but—she stopped herself. Titus held her for a long time without saying anything, assuming it was nothing. He had that weekend feeling inside him. Like it was allgood and he had something to look forward to but didn't know exactly what it was, only that it was going to happen soon. He stroked her side with his knuckle, slowly but not too slow, careful not to be ticklish. It was allgood. He ignored the fact she was wide awake, her blinking loud against his body, and he kept drifting nearer to sleep going uh huh, uh huh … Are you awake? Yeah. She apologized and he said it was okay and they went back and forth apologizing until Brooke said what she had wanted to say, that she felt anxious for some reason. If you really have to go, go then. You making me anxious. I'm not talking about the meeting. What then? I don't know. This is going to sound dumb to you but I feel there's always something I'm forgetting. It's like I'm so behind. He chuckled. Welcome to the club. The joke he realized didn't land how he intended. Squeezing her body he clarified. He said that he was behind on credits too, you see me busting my ass trying to catch up. I know you are Ty. I'm not just talking school. It's everything. It's like everyone else is so far ahead. They're set. They have something to bank on. What do I have? Nah that aint true. You know people fronting like they got it all figured out. She brought up Alice Upshaw. Her again? You stay comparing yourself to other people. Man that's your problem right there. I know that Ty. I know it. I know it and I can comprehend it in my mind. But I go about my day feeling like I'm this big fraud. She covered her face, When you call me fake, pulling away from him, I don't want to make you angry Ty. It's okay, I aint mad. When you call me fake, it hurts because it's true. All of these clubs, these events, none of it is adding up to anything. It's just so that I look busy. What about the dance organization you bout to do with the whitegurl? I don't think it's going to work out with Susan. What? I thought yall was making moves? We had a discussion last week. I'm not sure you could call it an argument but it wasn't good. Yall beefing now? Over what? Ty it's so stupid. You know how we've been applying to these grants. Well Susan found one. When she showed it to me, it said it was for African-American women. I'm thinking oh shit, she thinks I'm ... so I look at her and tell her well Sue technically I'm not black. She doesn't believe me. So I tell her again and she goes what do you mean you're not? I say Sue I am *not* African-American. You've seen my mom, she's white obviously. My dad is from Puerto Rico. But your last name's Martin. No Sue. It's supposed to be pronounced Mar-TEEN. And she goes oh. Just oh, like that. No sorry Brooke for assuming. No sorry for pronouncing your name wrong the whole time. None of that. Just oh, and this look on her face. She's obviously embarrassed but I can also tell she's disappointed. What, that yall couldn't do that grant? Was it for a lot of money? No it's worse than that. She said she was sorta counting on me to be black. Those were her words. Some stupid reason about building relationships in the African-American community. She wants to start in DC, then go to Detroit. She was envisioning me as some sort of liaison, and now that's in jeopardy, at least according to her. She didn't say jeopardy but it's obvious that's what she's implying. What? Yall can still go to the hood and build relationships. We cool with the Puerto Ricans. At the end of the day people just wanna know if you can help them. Yeah Ty I know, that's what I told her—Titus chuckling, do she know *I'm* ...? Yes of course she knows my boyfriend's black. I've talked about you plenty of times. She's even seen you on grounds, oh I saw Titus today at the bus stop, blah blah blah. She's so full of it. I mean she apologized eventually. She said she overreacted but I don't know. I've been thinking about what she called me, a *liaison*. That's a funny thing to call someone. And I've been thinking about it some more. She's just using me Ty. This whole time. You believe she looks at me like a collaborator? I'm no equal to her. I'm some mascot.

Titus laughed, Hell you been? We all fuckin mascots here. They don't give a fuck what we think haha and squeezed her body and realized she was sobbing. My bad girl. No it's fine. He began kissing her breathily along her neck. After a while it suffocated her sounds and she leaned into his kisses, holding his one arm wrapped around her waist as she sobbed and sniffed, the both of them rocking in her narrow bed. He was whispering in her ear fuck the whitegurl, fuck all them. You aint them, and they aint you. These people here, I never been around a faker group of people my entire life. You watch and let them keep talking, and they bound to say something to let their true colors come out. That's why you gotta keep your circle tight. You don't gotta be friends with everybody. Not saying you gotta be mean. I just say whatsgood and keep it moving. She asked who he considered in his circle. Truthfully here it's just you and Vonny. What about Kevin? Oh Kev? Kev my peoples, Q too. But you asking about the inner inner, he added a few more inners and she laughed, tickled by him. You and Vonny, yall the only ones who know all about me. Dean Daniels? Now you just playing girl.

The next morning they had breakfast at O Hill and came back to Faulkner, the rest of the day still ahead of them. They put in some laundry and went one building over to the computer lab. It was empty because it was a Saturday and the studying was good. But their breaks got longer and longer, and pretty soon Titus, still smiling, threatened to take himself and his Silent Timer back to his crib, Okay okay I'll stop but you have to promise too, and they got another decent stretch of studying in. Brooke didn't want to use the restroom down there so she walked back to her place and he got his best stretch of studying in her absence.

When she came back, she explained that it took so long because she was on the phone and that she had forgotten she had a study group to go to. When? They're just about to get started. He said he was good staying here. Their parting kiss surprised the both of them and they looked at each other, puzzled yet pleased, and they kissed again, him reaching around for one of her cheeks, at which point she pulled away. No one's here. He picked her up and they went into one of the rooms and closed the door. Did you lock it? Nah it don't lock. Under the fluorescence they made all the faces at each other and sounds and it was allgood. The both of them spent, they dribbled liquids onto the chair and floor, laughing, just laughing. Surrounded by the screensavers, the absurdity, how wonderful it was and dumb and so funny. Not just the buttnakedness. Them two together. After how it had ended, the drama that ensued. Finally pulling up her draws and her sweats, Did you ever see us together again? Yes of course. On the way out she mooned him. Him laughing, Go head on hahaha …

10

After weeks and weeks of HIAF 2001: EARLY AFRICAN HISTORY, it got to the point where Dean Daniels didn't need to say a word and at the end of class would leave the briefcase on the table for Titus, and Titus would come scoop it up and follow along, handing it over to the dean on the porch of the Office of African-American Affairs, the journey there hardly predictable, sometimes straight there, more often not. The days becoming colder but no deterrent to distance. As soon as class ended the line formed. The dean nodded, sliding his arms into his coat as he was groped at with complaints and asskissing and luck being pressed. As he approached the exit, the people still went on yapping as he pushed open the door without so much as a glance back at that briefcase, at Titus. And Titus, true to the expectation, retrieved the briefcase from the desk and added himself to the rear of Daniels's entourage. Dr. Daniels I don't think it's a coincidence that the 3 of us had the 3 lowest scores on the midterm. We're the only ones in there. Daniels hands clasped behind his back walking along, Yes there seems to be an irregularity ... The Griot Society is having a showcase this Saturday. Please will you come? Ha don't ask me. Ask Mrs. Daniels.

Every so often, when it would be just Titus and Daniels for some portion of the walk back to the OAAA, Daniels would ask how things were going and Titus would say good and they'd bullshit and carry on, Daniels putting more into the conversation. Daniels really liked talking about his son Josh. That got him going more than anything else. Even the race stuff. The fact that his son played basketball and was getting recruited by a buncha places. Daniels was name dropping names that Titus didn't know. Coaches or something. Calling him directly. They adored his son too. Tell Josh we'd love to have him visit. Titus kept nodding along, oh yeah? The dean was so proud. I have no doubt that he'll be successful. You know how I know? He's got the right mental makeup. Daniels paused, tapping Titus on the chest. He's got a healthy ego hahaha. Gets it from me HAHA-HAHA. You have no idea how important that is. But in order for him to take the next step, he absolutely must learn to subsume himself to the team. Much easier said than done of course. They don't call it sacrifice for nothing. The trick, as I see it, is finding a program that cares about cultivating the man first, then the ballplayer second …

He went on about his own college basketball days. Walked Titus up to his office and showed him a black and white photo. Some college up there in Vermont. He went on and on. Friday nights it was New York City. Drinking and dancing. A little bit of fighting too. It was a different time then. You didn't have to worry about some guy pulling out a gun … During the week he would play dumb while the tutors did the work for him. Laughing he recalled this all. Somehow I still flunked a few courses. It almost embarrasses me to say I got away with it. But in my life I've written a better second half than first. I hope there's something that can be taken from that. Listen, you want to hear a secret? Well almost. Not many people know I served in Vietnam. I don't like talking about it. It still makes me emotional thinking how naive I was. I still think about my friends. How naive we all were. Scared too. Now I've never been incarcerated but I have been locked up. That boat ride is 30 days each way. Now that's confinement. Seen some crazy things on that boat.

One time the dean asked him if he had a life philosophy. I'm sure you're wondering what mine is. Titus nodded. Show me yours and I'll show you mine kind of thing? The dean laughing boisterously and Titus working up one side of a face to a grin. Then the dean's laughter died down. He had stopped in his tracks. He was staring at Titus. Service. And he continued looking at Titus and Titus was nodding slowly. You know what I mean when I say that? Yeah devoting your life to others—Not just others. Ideas too. I have the great privilege of serving the black community of Charlottesville. Every night I ask myself what have I done today that has left the community in a better place than it was before the day started? And I think those out. I even count them. The Dean nodded his head counting in demonstration.

11

A few weeks had passed since the drug bust. The situation in the Charlottesville weed game did not improve. A lotta doods were going home on weekends talking big shit, only to return with crumbs, excuses. Vonny knew they were lying ass niggas. So it's like that huh? Alone a few times he drove down to Petersburg to see his brother's boy (Look don't tell Shawn ...). Drove a few other places chasing whatever whispers there were from other doods.

He went out with newly-single Kev a few times. If he couldn't have trees, maybe some cheeks would take his mind off. That didn't go nowhere. Kev kept saying this place and that place was poppin, and Vonny would drive him there, and they'd roll up to some out of town spot where they didn't know nobody and didn't nobody speak English and by the look of them they could've might been terrorists.

All this driving and Vonny was running low on loot. He was already in the hole from the financial aid stuff and the credit cards but that was neither here nor there. The hole was that much deeper.

He went over to student health. He had heard there was a cold study that paid pretty good. When he got there they told him he had to have a cold to participate. I thought yaw said *without* colds. The lady up front showed him the flyer, he guessed maybe to make him feel even that more dumb, and he left telling himself that it was a ripoff anyhow. It only paid 300 bucks or a Palm Pilot.

So he called around seeing what was good. Rob said they were hiring at the phonathon. Rob worked there and was on the flyers and the official website wearing this corny teal polo. Vonny always cracked on him for that and Rob always said they made him wear it for the photo shoot. It aint even my shirt. Yeah right nigga lookin like a M & M hahaha. And they got down to business. Is it hard? Not really. They give you a script. Just don't be sounding like no nigga on the phone and you be straight.

Vonny slid right in there. In about a week he felt he was getting a hang of it. The office was upstairs from the Blockbuster on Ivy. There were about a dozen other callers working. 2 per desk except for Vonny who had a station all to himself in the back. There were bells pinging and murmuring and smiling with voices. Just smile and dial, they told him. Smile and dial. He had to tune that out and focus on the ringing in his receiver ... ringing ringing ... When the answering machine picked up he scratched another X into his weekly log. Hello my name is Vonny Childress he said to the machine. I'm callin on behalf of UVA Giving. I was trying to reach— forgetting midway through his sentence, he glanced at the printout again, covering his face as a yawn stretched up his chest and through his arms—Trisha, Trisha Danwood. Smacking his lips. Yeah Ms. Trisha I'm sorry I missed you tonight but if you uh ... He set the phone on the receiver. Shit. He had read the wrong name. The number was for Charlie Mettenburger. Frowning, he ran his tongue along his teeth. Nigga prolly aint givin up no loot anyway.

He massaged his face feeling surrounded again by the sounds of little bells being pinged and the smiling and dialing. I might just gon quit this shit. He looked at the weekly log. It was X's all the way down this week. He hadn't realized. Looked kinda cool allum marks for some reason. Like a cool little design. Ha.

For the next few calls he started placing each X a little offset from the previous one. X after X, he was making a little wave down the column. Going one way until he reached a crest and slowly moving back the other direction. When he reached the end of the column he got bored with that little game and put his feet up on his desk, blinking at the ceiling and looking directly into the glowing fuzz of fluorescent lights. He knew he was ass at this. Prolly the worst one there. But he had to think there was at least some trick to getting people to give you money. Some way he could freek it. Staring at the ceiling his ears sifted through the sounds of human voices, the pleasant tones, and he began to pick up on some words and phrases. People was using the word LOVE a lot. LOVE this. LOVE that. Shoot I guess that's it.

For the next hour or so he was moving down that list of numbers determined he'd get someone tonight. Didn't have to donate. Just to holla at someone at least. Kick some game to or whatever. Just smile and dial. Smile and dial. Ringing ... ringing ...

Someone picked up. Took him a second to realize and he looked around before remembering where he was. Hello my name is Vonny Childress and I'm a fourth year Student in the E School. May I speak with Vincent—he squinted at the printout—I'm sorry but I don't know how to pronounce this.

It's Arbogast. Well uh can I speak to him? Speaking. Mr. Arbogast would you love to hear about some exciting things happening around the university? Silence. Hello? Hello? Yo you there? There was a quiet snickering on the other line. You sir are a piece of work, you know that? Never satisfied. Take take take. Is that what the Dream is? Taking? If you believe that, then, well, be prepared to be devoured. It will devour you whole, I guarantee. I guarantee.

Vonny clicked off the line letting his smile die out into his chest. Then he looked at the window, tired, the black of the night beyond, but all he could see was reflections of the office space inside, the people smiling and dialing.

12

Titus and Brooke had reached a point where they could talk openly about a future together. He evaded her questions at first but she called him on his bullshit. This was their last year at UVA, and if it weren't that serious, they wouldn't be spending this much time together. We'd be getting our hopes up for no reason. How you know I aint running around behind your back? Now that's some, Brooke covering her face laughing and was about to jab him in the belly, I don't even know what to call that hahaha, and glancing around sensing they were too loud.

They were at the Harris Teeter down the way. She'd done a string of cooking for him and now he owed her. He was lingering over the flat cuts of meat on display, unsure about the names on the labels, picturing each pressed into a Foreman Grill, whether there'd be problems.

About moving up to New York next year, she asked if he could see himself there or not. I gotta decide now? All I need is a Yes or No. Why? I aint going nowhere right now. Well I have to know. That aint a reason. Well I *need* to know.

He tossed something into the cart and they moved along, him pushing the cart nice and easy, her leading the way with the checklist.

So we make some plan now but will you be there? She asked what kind of question that was. We talk all nice now when things are good but what happens when the time come? Ty you won't let go of that will you? How many times do I have to say I'm sorry? She put down the shopping list to show how earnest she was being. They pecked each other on the lips.

Well the plan is to apply to a buncha places on the East Coast and see if I get in somewhere. The highest ranked school, that's where I'll go. It aint more complicated than that really. She said that he would get in somewhere good. Really? Someone with my situation?

She told him about Fatima's brother who went to jail and how he eventually went to law school. Shit what he get knocked for unpaid tickets? It was serious Ty. He spent a year in jail. A year in jail huh. Musta been drugs or weapons. You ask her. I'm not gonna ask her that's personal. Shit Fatima told you and you don't even like her. No we're okay around each other now. Since when? I told you about that class we had together. When was this?

They continued walking along the aisle. He asked what law school he get into? It was either law school or business school but I know for a fact it was Cornell. Titus chuckled, warming to the idea. If it had been some bullshit school he would've dismissed it. But aye, we talking Ivy League here.

Brooke was looking at the spices, shaking each little jar, apparently judging them by sound. He chuckled aloud. Fatima brother huh? Went from behind bars to passing the bar? Cornell Law School? I'm pretty sure they Top 10. Brooke corrected herself. She was sure it was the business school. In any case you know the Ivy League is starving for minority representation, especially black students. Yeah I hear what you sayin. I get a nice boost. But really they got me in there competing with other black people. They got me in there with your Huxtables, people from Africa, the Islands. Shit we all the same to them. Well there you said it Ty, they're all the same. You'd definitely stand out then.

They strolled about the supermarket, looking for anything else they could use around the apartment. They began pawing at the idea ... what if Titus were to make his personal statement about that? I've thought about it before. Yeah I'd definitely stand out. She said that wasn't a bad thing. It's an incredible story. Me sticking a nigga up by the side of the road? No the journey—seeing the sly smile play across his face, she began laughing and he teased her for being gullible. So you've really thought about it? Of course. It aint like me to put myself out there like that though. You know me. My parents, they always be talking about, let's turn the page. It aint good to be stuck on the past so much. So what you talking bout now is embracing it, his voice trailed off. She asked what he was thinking. You really believe these people would be comfortable around a black man with a record? Not no minor shit neither. She said that she was comfortable around him. I never think about it until you bring it up. Well that's you. She said that they'd know anyway wouldn't they? Don't you have to disclose that some-where on the application? That's a good point. If they know anyways ... and his voice trailed off.

He said he didn't need to talk on it further and as more things were tossed into the cart, he continued thinking on it, probing along for cracks, and the idea of basing his personal statement off his armed robbery conviction didn't sound so stupid no more. Pretty soon he was afraid of stumbling upon a reason not to do it, so he quit thinking on it and resumed pushing the cart down the aisle, Brooke ahead of him looking at the shelves, her neck tall through her puffy coat and she was so beautiful especially when she wasn't trying.

* * *

A student in the front row tapped the back of her wrist. Disbelieving Daniels turned and looked at the clock high on the wall behind him. Yes of course. Thank you for reminding me Lisa. This matter absolutely must be addressed. I'm sure you all have heard what's going on with the Alphas. A few skips of weak laughter across the lecture hall as bookbags were preliminarily zipped.

Daniels crossed his arms and stood there thinkingly for a few moments.

If you know me or my record of advocacy, you know where I stand. It's disgraceful. Nothing more to say about it. There can only be 1 of 2 explanations. Either these young men didn't seek advice from the national office or they've been grossly misinformed by their elders, the latter of which I highly doubt. But you know what I keep coming back to? And I told these young men this last night. Martin Luther King Jr. was an Alpha. That's what I keep coming back to. Dr. King. He'd be rolling in his grave right now. That's what I told those young men. Rolling in his grave. The Dean tugging at his pants and putting his hands in his pockets and pacing a little. I truly would love to believe incidents like these are isolated. But this problem is a major one. You see when black students attend a white university, they find themselves overcome with whiteness. Subsumed and consumed by whiteness. You can't blame the parents. They could come from a strong home but the moment they get here, they cave. I don't know what it is. So easily they forget the values and traditions of the black community. They choose to abandon a collective history of which they are a part, whether they like it or not. Let me repeat that. YOU ARE A PART OF OUR COLLECTIVE HISTORY. Never forget that. But so many students forget. For what reason? Why turn your back on a GREAT people? You'd have to ask the Alphas. Ask them, is the white man's ice truly colder than our own? Say it Amir. A young man up front looked around before mumbling it. You ask them the next time you see any of them on grounds. See what they say. They'll probably tell you no it's not about that. What they told me last night, Daniels hunching over and working up a stage whisper, Dr. Daniels it's about bringing the community together. Improving race relations. Moving forward. Daniels stood up straight now and resumed his normal tone. That's how they explained it to me. That's why they left the Black Fraternal Council. I told them you're the biggest black fraternity on grounds and you abandon us? You all are sell outs. I've seen my fair share of tomming across the years. This takes the top prize. The dean shaking his head and muttering. Race relations. Here's the difference between the leaders of my generation and this one. I'm not here to improve race relations. Do you even know what that means? I'm not going to waste my time getting white people to fall in love with me. I could care less and I promise you your life will be much easier if you drop that illusion right now. I'm not falling for that crap. I am and will continue to be an advocate for black people and black people only. 40 acres and a mule and these house niggers over here are happy. Not me. We're taking what's ours and—AND collecting interest. You tell those Alphas I said that.

Daniels excused the class. People got up slowly, care-fully, and walked past him minding their distance as the dean glowered over his open briefcase arranging his papers. Titus rolled up to the front, going back and forth in his mind if he should ask him now or wait. Aye fuckit. He went up and asked the dean point blank. The dean smiled. Titus grinned back, unsure if that was a yes or not. Briefcase in tow, Titus accompanied the dean as the dean walked hands clasped behind his back.

They went along McCormick until they were back behind the Lawn where the gardens were. Looking at the bare trees above them, Daniels asked if Titus remembered how pretty they were at the beginning of the semester. With the flowers, you remember? Titus nodded his head saying he remembered, then the dean led them up through an alley to the Lawn itself where Daniels stood gazing across the grass, over the patches dusted with orange and red leaves, at the rooms along the far end, the students going up and down under the breezeway humpback in their sweaters, and Daniels was murmuring the names of the black students residing in those Lawn rooms, asking if Titus knew them. Yeah I had a class with her before and the convo proceeding like that.

They continued walking along under the colonnade.

You know Titus it would truly help if I knew your reasons. Yeah of course, Titus shrugging his bookbag higher onto his shoulder and tightening his grip on the briefcase. He ran through his explanation. How his personal involve-ment in the legal system inspired him to be a lawyer so he could help young black men much like himself and funny enough he didn't realize this until recently and I kept coming back to it, I mean, it was right there in my face ... so on and so forth, trying his best to convey the conviction and continuity he had rehearsed in his head but the dean kept stopping to wave and say hello to people, every single black person they came across, and Titus was feeling kinda dumb just following this nigga around holding his briefcase and having to pause and go not knowing if the dean was really listening in the first place. So you wanna be a defense attorney? Yeah I see myself doing that. I have many lawyer friends Titus. All kinds of attorneys. It's a necessary service they perform but not at all soulful work, I'm sure you already know that. The firm'll own you till you're 35. Titus chuckled obligingly. Why not teach instead? Or work with young people in some capacity? Titus said he was open to it. His mother was a teacher—Yes, I recall that. What grade level? Fifth. She taught third for a while. They continued walking along. Teachers, they help shape the moral character of entire communities. It used to be that teachers were held in as high regard as pastors. The church and the school, those were the 2 bedrocks of the community. For a long time it was that way. Still is, I hope.

They descended a stairway and came across the parking lot where the OAAA stood in an island of grass, the screen door out front ajar. Titus handed over the briefcase, squinting, thinking and finally telling the dean I appreciate everything you telling me and I'll think about it. Titus I'm not here to dissuade you. We're just talking, are we not? Titus looking at the ground dawdling his feet, so sorry to get point blank with you about the letter. The applications are due in January and I wanted to give you enough time. If you don't got the time, I understand. It's pretty late to be asking. But can I be honest with you Dr. Daniels? Titus glanced around at the parking lot, the porch of the OAAA, came closer and lowered his voice. My time away, I plan to talk about that in my personal statement. It has a lot to do with my decision. A lot. Not many people know my situation and I think it would be right if one of my recommenders could speak to that too. And the only people who know are you and Dean Staunton.

Daniels set his briefcase on the porch and lowered both hands to his knees. Shaking his head and grinning down there. Standing back up and licking his grinning lips, trying to speak but his own laughter stopping him. You know I used to see you around all the time Titus and you're a lot more clever than I ever gave you credit for. You'd make a tremendous lawyer, I have no doubt. So can I count on you Dr. Daniels? I admire how you're going about this son. I say this all the time in class about people's refusal to come to grips with the past. We'd all be so much for the better if we can do that, Daniels chuckling, and I see you're taking that to heart. I'm very proud of you young man. A very bold way to go about it. I mean that in the best of ways. It's an incredible story. Behind bars at one point to taking the bar. Quite a rhyme to it.

Daniels couldn't stop smiling. When he finally shook Titus's hand, the dean said he'd been wondering when he'd ask. We've spent all this time getting to know each other.

13

Vonny decided it was time to man up with the studying. So he called around for the notes. His bread and butter for this stuff wasn't coming through, even a few of his backups, so he was starting to get nervous. He called the OAAA. They asked who his peer advisor was. Don't got one. I'm a fourth year. When is the midterm? Next Wednesday not this. They said someone would call him back. Before they got off the line, he made sure to mention he was on academic probation.

They got back the same day. Hooked him up with this chick named Sisi. She said she was up in there yeah. He explained his situation. I'm saying so is you gonna hook a nigga up? She said she wouldn't just hand over the notes. That would be an Honor violation. But I sympathize. She said she would be studying tomorrow at Clemons. Would be there the whole day. She said she had a system. She liked to frontload most her studying about a week before and taper off as the date neared and the day before was just review then her favorite ritual go out to see a movie. Oh word? What movie we seeing? She laughed. He liked hearing that. Sounded kinda cute over the phone. Some cheeks. It was a big class and he almost never barely went. Maybe she was a little freek. Maybe the whole class was fulla freeks and he didn't even know he barely went.

He was chuckling to himself indulging in this fantasy as he was going around the den hunting for a stray bag he recalled from a few days back, lifting cushions and clearing away chords, and looking through old drive thru bags and finally settling on gathering all the roaches he could find and picking through them with a paperclip excavating anything that wasn't yet burnt.

Felt ashy as hell the next day at Clemons. Hadn't been there all semester. Sisi said she could tell. You looked so lost. Yeah well ... They got to tutoring. She stopped every so often and looked at him horrified and would complain, ooookaaay, now we got to go back to the beginning. Eventually, there wasn't a beginning to go back to and she began talking to herself under her breath making these slick remarks. You think I can't hear you? Well Vonny that's the point. If you gonna say some slick stuff, just say it. She threw up her hands. I don't get it and I've been racking my brain right now. What exactly have you been doing all semester? Don't talk to me like I'm dumb. I'm not dumb. I'm not saying you're dumb. It's like you don't care. I care. How you know I don't. If you cared, you wouldn't be on academic probation and I wouldn't be wasting time reviewing stuff I already know. It's like how is this possible? How are *you* possible? You're a fourth year. How'd you get this far? He didn't know what to say. He started smiling, brushing off his pants. Well you know they say it's good review to teach other people, to explain things out loud. That's when you know you really know it.

Huffing, I can't believe this dood, she went over to the water fountain. Automatically he appraised her backside.

Yup. I knew she won't tom bout nuffin back there. How you gon be African and not have no booty. He scooted closer to her notes. His eyes grew. Couldn't believe it. Her notes were on another level. They were handwritten but looked typed. But in pencil. Couldn't believe it. He flipped through. Man. She had a system of colored tabs and lightning bolts and shaded box inserts and underlines. He started laughing good gotalmighty. She took two sets of notes. One for lecture then, from what he could tell, she went back and organized those notes and synthesized them with the stuff in the book. She put an arm across her notebook. I am NOT going to be facing Honor Charges. Yo keep that shit down. I TOLD you yesterday I wasn't going to hand over my notes. Aye how is that cheating? The professor said we could bring that index card anyway. She started zipping up her bookbag. I'm wasting my time. Fine leave then. You like the worst peer tutor ever. I come here for help and you wanna make me feel bad the entire time. Talking all that slick stuff over there like you better than somebody. It's all memorization anyway. Hold up, is that what you think? Memorization? They have machines for that. I'm not going to graduate from here and be someone else's cog. You maybe but not me.

When he got home from the library, he retained nothing. He couldn't make sense of the little he'd taken from her. He suspected she was holding back anyway. She probably had some beautiful index card written in five different colors that could fold up into a helicopter and fly away. What this bitch call me? A cog? Man forget it.

When he had a chance to cool off, he honestly considered her question: just how in the world had he made it this far? The first time he was placed on academic probation, this was back in second year, he talked to a counselor. After he told the counselor about his problems concentrating, she diagnosed him with 9/11 syndrome. Many people are experiencing these symptoms she said. This has been a traumatic event for all of us. And just like that he got out of it. Too bad that don't work no more.

Without any weed in his system, his body was disgruntled. He hit up the dining hall, asking all the workers there if Andre was working, this townie he'd bought a crummy ass dub from one time. Nobody said they knew him. Somebody snickered. I bet I know why you asking. Vonny raising his arms at his sides, So why is you messin around then? Is you gonna hook a nigga up or what?

14

The Silent Timer was FLASHING—FLASHING—FLASH-ING. Titus was out of time.

He hurried through one more question, the FLASHING—FLASHING—FLASHING loud in the corner of his eye, trying to concentrate on the passage before the guilt of exceeding the time limit overcame him and he dropped the pencil flexing the cramp out of his hand.

Sitting at his desk he rubbed his head dreading. What the fuck man. Before his irritability could get worked up too much, he flipped to the back of the LSAT study guide and checked his responses against the answer key. He flipped back to his section and tabulated the total correct of that last section and added all the sections together and ... his heart sank. How am I getting worse? You practice more you supposed to get better. He sat in his chair staring at the tabulation with his raw score at the bottom. Then the key that translated that to the adjusted scale. And the big number at the end ... It made no sense. Absolutely no sense.

This was the second time this week he bombed. The last time was supposed to be a fluke. But again? So soon? God so soon ...

He had 2 weeks to the day, to the exact day until the real thing. He'd taken 5 full-length practice tests—actual authentic tests, not some bullshitass made-up ones from the company—actual real live tests!!! 5 of them!!! 4 tests with the timer. Gone through the entire workbook and all the recommended drills and activities. He did everything that was prescribed. It wasn't even noisy in the crib this morning. Vonny still sleep. All the conditions sterile. Got good sleep last night. Didn't drink not too much. I'm usually pretty good at multiple-choice.

He checked the answers again. Tabulated the total. The same. He consulted some materials he got from Career Services. Maybe he misremembered the target score. Staring at the page, Nope. Not even close. Not even in the league.

He didn't want to tell himself he was worried. He consulted his body, the sensations there, the numbness in his ears. He didn't want to think on it any more.

He stepped into his boots and walked across to Brooke's. How'd you do Ty? He worked up a smile not saying anything, allowing her to infer the best. She smiled. Oh I knew it. You've always done well at multiple choice. Shruggingly he laughed, I aint say nothing haha.

They had breakfast at O Hill. He still wasn't saying much. She rubbed his arm, kissed the side of his chewing face. You're up so early. I bet you're tired. Sure am. So how long was it? He sat chewing and staring at her. She clarified her question. The test. How long will—Shit can't you count? Titus what was that for? I'm sayin Brooke. I left your crib at 7am and I got back at—She was looking around at the other people in the dining hall, Ty not right now please. I regret asking. If I knew you'd—she stood up hastily. Damn you leaving? I'm refilling my drink. Oh.

He continued eating as he watched her walk away. Pissily watching her and pissily eating. Muttering inside his head that he had just told her that he was tired. You knew that the muhfucker is like over 5 hours long. 5 hours of your brain on full throttle, just GO GO GO GO!!! And you still got the nerve to ask me some fucking question you already know the answer to. You know some people really like smalltalk but I don't even fucking understand it.

On the drive back to the crib, he reached over and put his hand on her thigh. An apology. Her hand on the wheel, easy and purringly she leaned across and touched her head on his shoulder. Titus giggling, C'mon now, don't tell me you can see the road like that. She drove leaning sideways, and he kept his hand on her thigh and the two-lane road wound past the Catholic church, and there were trees, and houses with yards.

Climbing a hill, the car began to veer slightly across the yellow line and she jerked the wheel back. He said okay okay okay I told you shit and removed his hand and she sat up clearing her throat. It was quiet at the stoplight. She asked if he'd given any more thought to next year. Not more than I usually do. I'm just focused on that test right now. Have you narrowed down your list? I got a speech impediment or something girl? I told you. I'm just focused on that test. I can't think that far. Damnit it'll take you 2 seconds to tell me what schools you're applying to. Aye can you just focus on driving? This was what happened last time you wrecked your Nissan.

It was quiet in the car again. He was massaging his eyes, shutting them hard, and when he opened them he saw the time on the car's dash. 4:15 PM. The hell? Already? The sun gonna go down soon. He was allowing his voice to be exasperated. She did not respond. She dropped him off back at the crib and said she wouldn't be free until later. She had some meetings. On a Saturday? I told you Ty I had that study group. Then I promised I'd meet Susan because we're so far behind. Remember? This morning I told you I'd be working on the phone script and you—Yeah yeah I remember. Dancing for Peace. No it's called the M.O.V.E. Initiative now. As long as she aint making you dance for no popcorn chicken. She got you doing enough shuckin and jivin.

She let him out at the bottom of the hill at Faulkner. Standing outside the car, he leaned his body into the driver's side window and hunted for a kiss. She turned away. Hell you mad about girl? Do we have to do this now Ty I'm already late. Oh all right. Good luck with them meetins then.

He watched her pull off.

Vonny came home from work and they threw dice in the hallway. Clickety clack. Snapping fingers. Quarters bouncing. Titus was down a few dollars. His mind half there. Half somewhere else. Wheels turning. He had a few theories on his subpar performance this morning. Now he felt the problem had nothing to do with last time. Two flukes in a row was entirely possible. But maybe it *was* the same issue. Maybe I need to put more time into it. Need to find the time from somewhere tho. Where? It's gotta come from some place. Don't go to class next week. Tell Brooke we need to ease up a lil. I don't know.

Vonny cleaned him out of a few bucks and was gloating about it. Aw nigga I let you win. You got allem credit card bills ...

There was nothing else to do so they hit the brews. The brews hit them back. They watched ComicView and got a workout laughing. Titus still thinking meanwhile. The whole time thinking, strategizing, plotting. He concluded that it was the Thanksgiving Break that had thrown him off his game. His scores were steadily going up until then. I'm still getting back into the swing of things. These last two I had to get out my system. Now I should be straight. Better now than test day right?

Vonny got dressed to go out. You coming? Nah gotta wait for Brooke to come home. You know Kevin ass comin. Kev? Aww man ... If you not coming out with us, at least talk to this Henny for me. Vonny poured shots. Aye nigga I said only one and you pouring it to the second line! Vonny kept pouring. The Henny kept going down smooth. They were bent and very giddy and when Kev came home ... Kev, after several to the dome, smiling that big beautiful smile, even slightly more homo looking, threw an arm over Titus's shoulder ... I used to be a good boy like you, real obedient. Nigga you stay callin black people *boy* hahaha. I'm beginnin to think you racist. Me racist? How can I? I'm half black myself didn't you know? Oh yeah? Yeah from the waist up I'm Filipino—Slugging Kevin in the arm, Go head man hahaha you a clown!

Titus decided that going out was in fact good for him. He needed that break. After that full-length test this morning. Right what the doctor ordered. He called Brooke's phone hoping for her voicemail. Getting her voicemail. Aye I'm going to that black party over there by the bridge whatsitsname. You know what frat I'm talkin bout. With Vonny, Kev too. Just call his cell when you get out. Aye look. Just come through there if you want. I know you don't really come to these shits. But let me know.

Who knew if she ever called. It was so loud. And with Vonny and Kev up on them freeks. And Titus hugging the wall bent as hell. Titus even venturing a step or two beyond it rocking a barely perceptible 2 step. Then retreating to the wall again, still embarrassed despite being bent and the reggae set being hard to refuse for everybody else.

The room was so crowded no one was looking at him. Only feeling what flesh was directly attached to their pelvis or thigh. Seeing if it was moving the right way, if it was big enough, hard or soft or firm in the right ways and drunk and high and willing enough and had a history of being discreet and friends who would conveniently look the other way or if the owner of that dick or ass or coochie or what have you—whatever floats your boat—wasn't just doing this outta pity or annoyance or maybe you was harmless to her/him, only a friend, and what's dancing between 2 friends? Cos shit it's only dancing it don't mean we married or nothing because that's how shit always start, people catching feelings over people just dancing ... sure it look like fucking ... feel like fucking ... and there was so much going on for other people to worry about cos people was worried about their own damn selves and how this night would end.

Still Titus retreated from his 2 step, coming to terms once again that he wasn't no dancing nigga, and proceeded to gulp at the Henny and wince and eyeball niggas he thought might could be a prollem. A nigga was yapping over there too loud. I know him? Then this nigga over there bumping into people too much.

The only ones he worried about really was them townies. Wasn't even stressed bout these football niggas no more. That shit done blown over. But townie niggas man. Not too many of them tonight, not that he could see. But this corny nigga Leon dancing over there. Always see this nigga around with some custom Jordans on. Scowling, slowbreathing, Titus watched Leon dancing nearby and he began to wonder what if I were to step to him one day and tell him straightup, yo you gotta come up outta them sneakers bruh.

What would he actually do? That would be something wouldn't it? You know how easy it would be? What if I were to do that right now? He laughed to himself, looking around at the sagging drunk faces. That's the prollem. Aint no UVA doods scare me. Not even no athletes forreal. Cos even them niggas gotta answer to a coach. That's why you gotta keep your eye on them townies man. Aye I can't blame em. How would you feel if boujee niggas kept coming through your town every year? Buncha soft ass niggas. You know these college niggas won't do nothin. So what is it to steal a Huxtable in the face real quick? What was it? What would they do?

The party ended without incident. Ended when it was supposed to end. All the squad cars cruising slow on the street to greet them upon exit. It was skinny stinging rain so everybody took their asses home.

Brooke said she got his message. Don't call me when you're that drunk. She had her arm across her door. Oh I see. I try to be considerate and you go talkin out the side of your neck like that. It's disgusting Ty really. You know how you get when you're drunk. You know what Brooke? I'm real sick and tired of you tryna lecture somebody when you poppin pills like some fiend. She snorted. Get the hell out of my face Titus. Or what? Call the police? I dare you. You aint gone violate me. You too pussy. He sat on the landing in protest. Oh just look at you Titus. Like a baby. Grow up. YOU grow up. Love callin people names. I swear you was bout to call me a bitch again. In the courtyard below, people staggered drunk and boisterously across the wet grass with jackets held up over their heads, shouting up toward the stairwell where Titus and Brooke were. Titus shouting in return that he was just chillin. Yall have a good night now HAHAHAHA. Stay dry niggas HAHAHAHA ...

When his laughter died he was panting and groaning from the effort it took to sit upright. He wavered unsteadily and hooked his arm through some bars on the railing so he wouldn't tumble down the stairs. So are you just gonna sit there all night? As long as it takes. He continued talking, saying some vile vile things and she had already gone back into her apartment when he looked up to see if he'd cut her with anything. I always knew you was phony. I put you on the list. You know I coulda put someone else's name down. Maybe they would've actually came to visit. You know Vonny came. Me and him aint boyfriend girlfriend, so don't even use that excuse. His head spinning and wobbly, he focused on the sound of the rain, the coldness of it, the freshness. Anything to keep him from vomiting all over himself in this stairwell. A web of spit dangled from his lip. He tightened his arm around the rail and slumped forward hearing the sounds.

* * *

The next morning Titus tried to act as if nothing had happened. He thought how bad could it be? She picked up when I called.

Entering her room he knew something was off given how clean everything was. She told him to sit. We need to talk. He hunkered down in a scowl and she talked to him, her body straight and tall, her whole demeanor bright as if she were giving some sort of presentation, her hands moving broadly and deliberately, and her expressions matching. Hold up. Is this an ultimatum? Look at it how you want but I need an answer. When? Now? She looked at him calm, but a little forced. By this point he had determined that this was an ambush, a dirty dirty ambush, and he wasn't going to leave until she got knocked off her high horse, sitting there acting so calm.

He told her that he knew this was why she wanted to see him, and she corrected him calmly, No *you* called me. Don't try this bullshit like you better than somebody Brooke. You tryna ultimatum me. That's not even a word. Nah I see what you tryna do. You think you the one callin the shots here. Titus I told you. I've got my life to plan, and while I know you've got your own plans too and it's been good to see you putting your mind to things, I think I'm entitled to an answer. I'm not forcing you to *do* anything. I just need to know. Shit you always want to put the press on a nigga huh? I don't get it. Everything is allgood Brooke and you gotta do this. You always gotta put labels on stuff and timetables. And I know exactly why too. It's Alice. Brooke finally smiled and continued looking at him unblinkingly as he talked, like he was a fucking idiot, as he paced through his logic.

You see that's your problem right there Brooke. You keep comparing yourself to other people. It all makes sense. I was thinking on this the other day. You tryna be like Alice and you want me to be like that cornball she go with. Titus you are crazy. You see that look you gave me just now? You know I'm right. I got you clocked. I know you better than you know yourself.

You know what, leave. Get the fuck out of my life. We're done. He was mumbling to himself, grinning. You heard me boy? I said leave. We're done. He got up and under his breath, Fuck outta here you broke ass Alice Upshaw. She shrieked GET OUT and lunged for something on her desk to throw at him but ended up knocking over her keyboard and an empty travel mug, and she was crying violently and he finally left hearing her wailing, and that made him even more disgusted and hateful, at her, himself and the whole situation and he felt so gross and sad at what he'd said, but he was so locked down a path in his mind that it would be more trouble to apologize.

They didn't talk to each other for a day. Then it was 2 days without contact. When the one week point came, he finally acknowledged that it was over. Something about 7 whole days seemed significant but maybe it was a wrap long before that. Who had time to think about that, how fast or slow things collapsed, what he had built up to this point, the life that could've been. He had things to worry about.

15

The LSAT testing location was all the way out in Lynchburg. Titus signed up for a carpool through Career Services. It was last minute but they were able to find him a ride. The evening before the exam a little Mazda rolled up and he hopped in the back with his bag. He made a lil chitchat with the whitedood driving and the whitegurl in the passenger seat who he swore he had a discussion section with before. She spoke to him as if it were their first time meeting. Once they got onto 29 he pretended to sleep the rest of the way. When they dropped him off at the Best Western they asked if he wanted to grab some dinner after he had a chance to freshen up. Nah I'm good. I hope you're not staying in to study. Haha nah it's a lil too late for that. You've got my number in case you change your mind. If not, we'll see you bright and early tomorrow.

Titus tried to think of relaxing things he could do and the first thing that came to mind was taking a bath. There wasn't a tub at the apartment, and the last bath he recalled taking was as a kid. After the bath he went to the vending machine for a soda. He unwrapped the cheese sandwiches he'd packed and emptied a bag of Bugles onto a napkin and that was dinner. He set the heater, prayed and tried to sleep. Nah couldn't. The motel had free HBO so he put that on. Some shitty movie he didn't feel like watching. Now what to do. He leaned on the railing outside looking out at the parking lot. The glint of the lights on windshields. It was getting too cold so he went inside. Walked around in his room. Actually walked. He knew it was dumb walking like this in this smallass room but he walked, kept his legs and arms moving and swinging and he was in his boxers barefoot humming just humming a random melody. Door to nightstand and back. Around the bed past the dresser and mirror. Lap all the way back to the door. Stopping at the mirror. Flexing in front of it. Flipping on the light so he could see all the definition in his abdomen. He was perfectly content in terms of temperature yet he checked the heater once more. Walked from front to back and swung his arms. The more he walked the walking began to feel to him like pacing. The word PACING in his mind began to worry him. Nah I aint nervous nah. Just a lil hype for this shit. Excited. He yawned though he was wide awake.

In his bag by the nightstand was his LSAT book. The better part of him knew he shouldn't have brought it. No good reason to. He'd put in the weeks and months of work. The absolutely last thing you want to do—THE LAST—is tire out your brain the night before. That shit'll take the whole day. I should be sleeping now anyhow.

He looked at the time and for some reason he wanted to call Brooke. She would be up and home by now—nah nah what am I thinking? It's Friday. I aint bout to drop no money on no long distance. Guess that's why niggas be on cell phones these days. He rolled over again and looked at the phone in the dark. He was about to take this huge giant leap in his life and it only seemed right to hear her voice. Something big and life-changing was going to happen tomorrow. He should talk to her. It was like he was leaving to go somewhere far. Like getting shot up into space as dumb as that sounded. He had to tell somebody he loved them and thank you for everything. He was about to be great shortly. Some big shot. And tomorrow was going to be the genesis of that and I told yall man. God got a plan for me. And the urge to talk to Brooke grew stronger. She knew. Despite all the bullshit and all the riffraff and nonsense and static and drama, she knew that about him. I always believed you would be somebody great Ty. Brooke looking at him softly, her head tilted and that neck showing and collarbone, and the sight of that in his mind about broke a nigga heart right there. The way she look at me sometimes man. She could be genuine when it's just me and her. Just me and her and she aint so pressed bout how she coming off to other people. I always believe you'd be somebody great ... he was hearing that in his head again and was happy and comfortable with the heat in this room and was laying in bed again with the sheets pulled to his chin.

He got onto thinking about this one time they were at the Ruby Tuesday's and they were flicking water at each other with their straws all giggling. Such a suckafalove. He would never do nothing corny like that now. No way. Flicking water, can you believe this guy? Tickling and shit? Damn near had a food fight with her in the middle of Ruby Tuesday hahaha. Everything funny and Stop—No you stop hahaha. He was trying to remember, if it was, yeah it was spring, way way back. First year. Right before they brought charges on me. He remembered just feeling so good and so connected to this girl like I know this sounds corny girl but you sure it aint even been a month yet? It feels like so much longer than that. She had such a clever way of looking at it. It's not like in high school Ty. In college you can spend every waking, sleeping, eating moment with that other person. Time is more dense here. Again he thought on how he kissed her in that restaurant, again feeling warm and weightless.

He was in a good serene place, not forcing sleep but it could happen at any moment, precariously drifting on the edge of consciousness when he heard some people walking past his window outside. He got out of bed and peeled back the heavy curtain. 2 doods out in the parking lot smoking with their hoodies on and pajamas. Shivering and rubbing their arms and spitting and smiling at each other. College looking doods. Maybe bout that age. My age. The thought now came to Titus that prolly a buncha of people in this Best Western is LSAT takers. Driving in to take the test tomorrow. Maybe the whole building. Just about. Cos what kinda people would visit Lynchburg in the beginning of December? The thought of the entire Best Western full of LSAT takers. People worrying, stressing, struggling to sleep the same as him ... it was too much to think about right now. The hopes of all these people. All of us going for that prize. Man that's a lot of paths. He was tingling, a little fearful of where his mind was going. All these other people, the paths they took to be here, all those paths converging with his. How much better prepared they were. All these people prolly had the money to pay for the prep course. I shoulda paid for that prep course. My folks got the money why am I fronting? Shoulda just asked. Maybe I been wasting my whole time with this shit man doing the booklet wrong. I didn't even read that first chapter, HOW TO USE THIS BOOK. You know I just realized that the other day that there was actually a first chapter. Fuck I was

jus goin through doing questions at random. Even ran out
of practice tests after a while. Hadda tell Vonny, Vonny go
erase these answers for me so I can take this again and I
don't even want to see the answers I had marked before, so
he did and I took that shit again and could still see the
marks and that might've threw me off worse, those old
marks some wrong and some right and then I had to worry
about if I was wrong and right before and damn, the things
I heard about the people who took the prep course. They
got a different book. 2 books matter fact. 2 thick ass books
that you can't even buy in the store. Shivering and jittery,
Titus went to his bag by the nightstand and pulled out his
book and read that first chapter HOW TO USE THIS
BOOK quick and greedily and immediately regretted not
reading it because it told him that once he took the diag-
nostic he was supposed to progress through the book in a
certain manner if his score fit in a certain level, and if his
score fell into a different bracket, he was to progress in the
book in another fashion and fuck man how come I just
didn't take the 5 minutes to read this fuckin shit man?
Fucking bitch. I knew it. I knew it. You keep doing this
dumb shit yo. It's like you do this trifling shit on purpose
man. You make me sick. Absolutely sick. I wanna throw up
you make me so disgusted. He grabbed the booklet by its
thick spine and flung it at the wall and was standing there
huffing and with his head so congested and throbbing
looking at the divot in the wall. Throwing his hands up,
fuckingbitch now I gotta pay for that too. Standing there
panting. That was so stupid. Why'd I have to do that huh?
Rubbing his head he paced—yeah PACED—as a nausea
began in his belly and he needed to be away from it so he
threw open the door and the shock of cold air on his bare
skin—it snapped him out of it. He returned to the room,

not too crazy hype no more. He sat on the edge of the bed wondering why he threw that book at the wall, and what it was that came over him.

In the morning the Mazda came right on the dot. Titus had his stuff ready. His three pencils, sharpened this morning with a manual sharpener. An extra eraser. His timer. Some backup batteries. They didn't need to come back to the motel. When they got to the campus, they told one another good luck before splitting up into their respective lines according to their last names. He removed his skully. Presented his stub and his ID, what was in his pockets. They tried to give him a hard time about his timer but he showed the manufacturer's note printed on the back of the device— THIS TIMER IS SOLELY DESIGNED FOR MANAGING TEST TIME. IT IS INCAPABLE OF MAKING NOISE. IT IS NOT A CALCULATOR, CAMERA, COMMUNICATION, DATA RECORDING OR COMPUTING DEVICE—and they waved him on through to another line, a smaller one. Some dood behind him asked if that timer thing worked. Haha well we'll see won't we.

They made a quiet chain gang shuffle down some hallways. They stopped at a classroom door. One by one names were called. He sat in his predetermined seat watching the remaining others file into their seats. One girl came in with this big wooden board under her arm. He'd seen her out in the foyer with it, and was curious. It looked like she was carrying some art project. Maybe she was here for something else. Now, a few rows over, she laid her board over the desk and tightened it down with some velcro straps. People were looking at the proctor, expecting some sort of intervention. The girl spread her test materials across the wide wood surface, which had been lacquered up thick so it was smooth and shiny. She had enough room to lay open her test booklet without it overlapping her scratch paper, and she had a miniature white rubber toy there, it looked like a sheep, musta been a good luck charm. Titus fondled his timer. Slid the battery tray open for a peek. Looked at that girl's setup some more.

The door was shut. It was then he began yawning. He couldn't help it. Yawn after yawn coming up through him as the proctor read the instructions. He knew he was nervous. A couple rows over the girl with the big desk contraption had her head bowed, eyes closed, rocking rhythmically in her seat. You know what that's a good idea. Titus closed his eyes and thanked the Lord. He prayed thanks to his parents next. He pictured coming home to them at some point in the future. How glad and proud they would be to see him after he'd been away so long. The brightness of their faces. Things different. Then another shaky stuttery yawn came up through his body and he was brought back to the present where everyone was packed and lined up and there weren't any windows in the room.

PART II
RECLINE

16

Back home in Portsmouth, Virginia, a good 2-and-a-half hours southeast of Charlottesville, Vonny sat in his room looking at the date on the letter. He couldn't make sense of how recent it was. His last exam was only a few days ago. The registrar hadn't even released official semester grades yet. Winter break had barely started. A few moments later it made sense. Yeah, that's right. They come for the money first. Just like last time.

Just like last time, when he was notified that he'd been put on probation and he owed $4,000, he went out with his boys later that night. A bar on High Street down by the water. A lowkey weeknight. A few pitchers in the booth. Just like last time.

But tonight. Tonight the bartender handed his card back. You got a different one chief? Vonny said run it again and the bartender said he had tried it several times already. Listen I'm not tryna blow up nobody spot here but you got a different one?

Vonny reached into his pocket and put his elbows on the bar, fanning out the credit cards from his wallet. He had a system to remember which ones still had money on them. The ones on the front was supposed to be good to go. He musta slid a card in wrong and gotten everything mixed up. The bartender bug eyed, You don't expect me to go through those one by one do you? Vonny said hold up and continued flipping through the cards. Listen maybe your friends can pick this one up. Vonny grinning said hold up and the bartender said that as long as he got the $45.76. If not I'm keeping your driver's license.

Vonny's boys said yeah we spot you. But they told Vonny to slide over here right quick let us holla at you. They huddled up at the far end of the bar near the exit. Vonny dog we gotta make moves. On three okay? Naw man bartender got my ID. On three, ya hear me? I need my ID. I gotta take my dad somewhere tomorrow. One. Two …

Something happened and Vonny was outside himself, watching what was about to occur, how that wouldn't fix nothing at all, and that there was only one way this all would end. He became weak. His hand found a loose chair and he sat down. His boys stood over him, What is you doin??? I'm telling you yo I can't. Why not? I'm too bent. No you not. Get up. C'mon bartender not looking. The door just over there nigga c'mon. The bartender leaned over the bar, Sup fellas?

Tooth sucking his boys made a show to look into their wallets. Vonny looked in his too, shuffling through the cards again. There was a card with a picture of an eagle flying over a lake that he did not recall seeing earlier.

The card with an eagle flying over the lake was also denied.

The next day his father, the Reverend Dr. Earl Childress, drove him to the bar to settle up. When they got back to the crib, that's when he came clean to his pops. Told him straight up. The reverend did not understand right away. Told him to try harder next semester. That he shouldn't fool around so close to the finish line. Dad I aint gon be in school next semester. I'm on suspension for a year.

He watched the realization slowly become born across his father's face. The reverend squinted, crossed his arms. He wanted to know when these troubles started. Vonny paused a moment thinking should I tell him *everything* everything, then surrendered to the cold, watery feeling in his stomach and just started talking.

Last year when they revoked his grant, they put a registration block on his account. In order to enroll in his fall classes, he signed up for a few credit cards and took out some cash advances, and one thing led to another ... at the first mention of credit cards, Reverend Childress shut his eyes and turned his head away. The reverend sat like that listening as Vonny continued speaking about his plan to pay everything back. About getting a job at the phonathon. About going to Student Health and looking into some cold studies. Supposedly they had one study coming up during spring break. It was supposed to pay a couple hundred bucks if you were willing to stay in a hotel room all week.

His head still turned away and with a calm voice, Reverend Childress said that none of this made sense. Something had to have proceeded it. Son look at me. Tell me the truth. These troubles with your schoolwork, how far back do they go?

Vonny ran his hands through his hair, scratching, wincing. Honestly dad right from the jump. As soon as I got to UVA, it was clear. Everybody there was on point. They was so far ahead of me and—What about all those math awards in high school? No, it don't matter. That's high school. UVA, it's a completely different echelon of competition. You telling me you not as smart as them? Naw they not smarter. It's like this Dad, Vonny punching his palm, I'm learning this stuff for the first time while they reviewing. You see? Yes. From the beginning, huh, I could see that. But you're a fourth year. You couldn't catch up in all that time?

The discussion ended with his father saying he would help with the credit cards, not everything, but only enough to get them off his back for now. Vonny would have to work to pay the rest. And tell me what's the name of that black dean they got there at UVA? That man would know what to do. Maybe they don't know you're graduating.

All in all, it didn't go as bad as Vonny had imagined, though he himself didn't feel more relieved. All of it pushed out of him, he still felt like a scumbag. His mother wasn't taking it too good. She ignored his hello, walking past him in the hallway without raising her eyes.

His father reached out to Dean Daniels. A plan was laid out for Vonny. The math of the retake already calculated by Daniels's office. If Vonny would have scored at least a B+ on the final exam, his semester grade point average would have been back above the threshold. Will you need a tutor? Vonny was trying to remember exactly which class Daniels was talking about, which one with Professor Jackovides, when he felt his father watching him sternly and just rolled with it, saying naw Dean Daniels I think I got it.

* * *

Vonny, when he was home from school, still played the keyboard for his father's church, the Living Word Worship

Center of Portsmouth. The worship center had been converted from an old house some time ago. There were about two dozen folks attending service today. They sat in folding chairs in the main room, which had once been a master bedroom, part of a hallway and part of a kitchen. Vonny sat on his stool off to the side. He was looking at a spot on the floor as his father delivered the sermon. From time to time, Reverend Childress gripped the sides of the pulpit bending down to glance at his notes. The pulpit was small and had wheels and kept rolling forward a lil every time the reverend bent down to it.

When it was time for the final remarks, the reverend wiped his mouth with a napkin and came out from behind the pulpit folding his hands across his belly. Vonny sat up and scooted his stool towards the keyboard. He touched some keys, coloring the room with some right hand, guiding his father with music, helping the reverend as he began his slow way up the aisle patting his head with the napkin.

I know sometimes amen that we have some things amen that we feel we can't get there. And while we are struggling amen trying to get there, sometimes it's a situation we don't even understand (Yes). Sometimes there's a house we're trying to get rid of and we don't know how to go about it (Amen). Sometimes it's family in tremendous trouble (Oh yes amen). Sometimes we're going through it. Hallelujah. But we have to stop just for a moment and speak to the situation (Yes!). Speak to the trouble in our life. And speak to the one who is the author and finisher of our faith (Faith yes amen), and allow Him to do (YES! praise the Lord) what he's been commissioned to do. And that's Jesus Christ. He's able to make a way out of no way (No way yes). All we gotta do is trust in him. And pray I'm going through. I pray that we'll all go through together. No matter what it is hallelujah all you have to do is call somebody and let us hallelujah amen walk with you. We're not the answer. But we know who has the answer. Now let's go to God and pray. Heavenly Father ...

The reverend doctor led them in prayer, then the room turned to song as he lowered himself onto the front row of chairs, his legs stretched out and he was holding his napkin, eyes closed, singing along with the congregation. Vonny played the chords, looking over the people hymning and his mother standing in the back, arms raised, shifting her weight from one foot to the other, arms raising higher and higher, face lifting higher, and he thought to himself man momma got a big head. He was used to it but sometimes it caught him off guard. This Korean lady in the middle of all these black people. But she had the Ghost in her. Everybody had it right about now.

Vonny allowed his fingers to move with the spirit. He was going along good but he got a lil fancy with it—one of his father's eyebrows jumped—so he backed off and cruised around in circles, the melody descending slowly in spirals until it landed somewhere nice.

They broke bread and fellowshipped in an adjoining room. Vonny brought over the radio and put on the gospel station. His father was being told to sit. No reverend we'll make you a plate. Dr. Childress was brought a white unbuttered piece of bread, cold vegetables and some peach slices. Well hallelujah amen.

Vonny told a group of ladies it was good to be back and that he wished Christmas break were longer. How's school? You makin good grades? He kinda looked at the ladies sideways and grinned, Could be better. Hahaha, aint that the truth! You know Vonny your father's doing much better. It's good to have you around to help your mother out. They all turned and looked at the reverend walking up and down the room, swinging his arms, bending down to talk to people. They watched the deliberate sway and pitch of his walk. You can really see it's all coming back to him now. Just the other day I was telling your mother you can't even tell which side was the bad one.

17

Vonny's makeup exam wasn't until after the New Year. The day after New Year, his father gave him some money for food and gas. Enough to last through the weekend and onto Tuesday, the day of the exam, after which he would come back home. On his way out of town Vonny hit up his mans for some lob. Couldn't smoke it yet. Gotta conserve.

Once he reached Charlottesville he sat with his books in the den. The apartment was so cold. He sat for a little while bunched up in a blanket looking through his books and he had to lay down after a while he was so bored and cold. He sat listening for any activity outside. There was nothing. No one was back from break yet. He watched TV. Nothing good on but he left it on anyway because it was so quiet. Might fall asleep it's quiet as hell in here. He took his shoes off and read laying on his side. His eyes grew tired. It wasn't dark out yet. He closed his eyes. Just resting them for a lil while. Not used to all this reading. He told himself over and over not to sleep because there was all this studying he needed to do with the test on Friday. He lay with his eyes closed convincing himself naw I aint tired. It's not even dark yet.

Then he remembered he hadn't eaten since this morning. What was that? Like 4, 5 hours ago?

He called Gumby's. 40 minutes was a long time to wait. He paced the den with the blanket draped over him checking the time on his phone. Hongry as hell tho. Can't lie.

He took the PS2 out of his luggage and hooked it up to the TV. He could squeeze a game in right quick. Pizza will be here next thing you know. Prolly forget about it. He got a game in on the computer and just as he predicted he had forgotten about the pizza and was surprised and happy when he heard the knock on the door.

He ate too fast. Caught the itis immediately. He was burping, smiling, weak. Licking the roof of his mouth. He loosened his belt. His stomach hurt a little but at the same time he felt good all over.

It was finally dark and Vonny thought on what a nice long day he's had so far. Long ass drive. Hit the books. Talking to himself about all that he had accomplished today, he began breaking up a dutch and reaching into the baggie from back home. Aye I still got till Tuesday. Plenty of time.

He burned the dutch to the halfway mark playing Madden. He slept. God knows how long or little because when he returned to consciousness it was still dark out. Cold as hell. He covered his head with the blanket. Slept. Poked his head out of the blanket a few times telling himself he wouldn't get up until there was light out and it would be warmer in here.

When it was time finally to get up again he lay there swaddled in his mink blanket staring at the ceiling hoping for the room to warm up. He was afraid of what might happen if he sat up and out of his blanket into the cold air of the empty apartment, how painful and unpleasant that would be first thing in the morning. He waited around for a while until he finally had to take a dump. Shivering there on the toilet missing his blanket. Hustling back to the couch shivering and blubbering his lips going Jesus dog.

The sun finally angled just right through the blinds so the rays landed where he lay and he was warmed up enough to sit up and gather up some of his old homework problem sets. He spent a few hours looking at those. Learning. Things clicking into place. He put in some good time. He felt real good. Honest. He took a break. Finished the rest of his pizza. Considered for a long while to finish the rest of that dutch from last night. The dutch just laying there in the ashtray. He was staring at it. He checked the time on the phone. It's only 2. Got plenty of time. Holding the dutch to his lips and with his thumb on the wheel of the lighter, Naw it's too early for trees. Wouldn't get nothing done after this. He put the dutch and lighter down. Picked up the remote and watched TV for a while. Nothing good on. It was a Saturday in the middle of the day of course nothing good on.

With his blanket draped over him he went to his bedroom and turned on the computer. He had some flicks saved in a secret folder called Yup. It was buried deep in the hierarchy of his computer file system. He didn't have to consciously remember how to get there. The muscle memory told him where to click and scroll and he was finally there at Yup. He busted off one right quick. A tremendous feeling from the bones in his toes all the way up through him. That's wassup right there. Yup. After recovering he got another one in and lay in bed with his body absolutely spent and devastated and he wished, Oh God wished maybe there was some cheeks out here. Gotta be someone back from Break. He signed on Instant Messenger looking to see who was signed on too. Nobody really. A few niggas but they stay signed on even though they not even there. He turned the volume high so he could hear alerts from the den where he sat with his old homework problem sets spread out on the coffee table in front of him, the pages laying across all the junk on the table. The open pizza box, the ashtrays, the blunt guts, the blank and burnt CDs, all of it ashtrays at some point or another, hard flat surfaces to break dutches on.

Sitting in the empty den of the apartment, looking at the various stapled packets of his problem sets, Vonny tried to remember the one he was working on last. They all looked the same. Vaguely familiar but not. Something about them. Looking at all the pages laid out like that he said to himself bruh that's a lotta stuff. A whole lotta stuff to go through. Looking longer, he realized these shits aint even from the right class. None of these niggas Jackovides. You serious?

He went through the pages shaking his head and realizing the worst. He tried to laugh at himself but naw there was nothing funny about this shit. They bout to kick a nigga out and here I am can't even study the right notes. Looking at the wrong ones the whole day. Hell wrong with me? He slipped off his shoes and rolled onto the couch swaddling himself in his mink blanket. When you turn into such a dummy? A nigga was sharp as hell back in high school forreal. The hell happen forreal? Was a nigga really smarter back then?

He felt drained out and spent and absolutely useless and cold. Useless. Absolutely useless. A waste.

It was the perfect time for that dutch. Might as well. Day already blown. He sparked it and a cool stillness came over him. It's a wrap man. Wrap status all the way. Still can't even believe this shit. He drove to Taco Bell. Ran into this dood, a student. The dood had got shot a few years back and dropped out because of it. Now he was back. Vonny was talking to him a while but was so annoyed and angry at himself, he was barely paying attention.

Dood wanted to talk and hang out some more, but Vonny said he had to go back to the crib to study. What? School don't start for another week hahaha. What's good with that hahaha?

Vonny ordered some more food to take home. Sparked another dutch. He thought on how smart he was back in high school. Used to get 100s on everything. Used to be the first nigga to turn them tests in. Take me like 5 minutes. Walking up there and turn back and see all these niggas scrugglin. This was the gifted class too. Didn't even had to study. Straight 100s tho. 100 every time. Shit was mad easy. Never had to barely study. Either I was a genius or they had us doing some baby math.

He kicked off his shoes and got on some Madden. Take my mind off. Played a couple games on All-Pro. Beat the computer. Turned it up to All-Madden to see if he could beat the computer then. Got skunked in the first quarter. Computer cheating bruh. Pick 6s. Breaking tackles like the Incredible Hulk or something. Computer on some bullshit bruh. He tried with a different squad. A better one. Picked a scummy one for the computer. A little more fair that way. Computer still beat him. He put the sticks down. MAN! Computer really on bullshit bruh!!! I don't see why they even got an All-Madden if they make it that hard. Grief.

Eating the rest of his Taco Bell his mind searched and found what he believed to be vulnerabilities in the computer's scheme. He had an idea of how to beat it. What glitches and tendencies to exploit. It's a computer after all. Just code. Can't even think for itself. He got on the sticks. Rematched with the same squads. Didn't win but look, progress. Some of his theories seemed to work. Re-did the squads, tried the same theories. He got up on the computer late. Lost on an avoidable set of fourth quarter mistakes that he fully recognized, which is why he didn't feel too bad about it. He was tingly. Had a positive mindset. Had it really figured out. Yeah. Got the joint clocked now. Yeah. Know exactly what I did wrong too. Rematched again. Got skunked in the first quarter. Hit reset. Naw, naw let me re-do the squads. I know what I gotta do but let me do the squads different, it's all good.

He spent the entire night on Madden. Battling with the computer. Measuring himself against the best of what it had to offer. All-Madden. Somewhere around 2 or 3 in the morning he checked the time on his phone. How am I so wide awake bruh. The fact that he felt so awake despite the hour, despite all the food he'd eaten, the itis, the trees he'd smoked, the cold, all of it. Despite all that, he was awake. Alive. Could go longer. It was a Madden marathon for the ages.

6 in the morning now and Vonny had beaten the computer twice on All-Madden. The first time he beat it he grew a lil emotional. Like so genuinely happy for the first time in the longest. Doing something that he didn't think he could do. Something he never imagined he could do nor heard of

anyone doing. Just how many niggas out there can say they beat the computer on All-Madden huh. He knew that getting gassed on that accomplishment was sorta dumb in the grand scheme but what the hell. It's something at least. At least I know I did it.

He finally put down the sticks and went to the blinds to see the light in the morning. Kinda look nice out there. Small banks of snow rimmed the lot but the pavement was dry. It was cold out and wisps of vapor lifted off the hood of his car. The air out there look real fresh. He put a jacket and shoes on and went out to the landing and leaned there on the rail breathing the air and feeling the stillness and emptiness, his body tired and worn in a good way, his character strengthened he felt. I can do it. I'm a quit messing around. I'mma actually do it. He saw a door open across the courtyard and a Chinese student carrying a laundry basket. Vonny lifted his chin. The other dude kept his head down and disappeared to the basement floor of an adjoining building with the basket. Damn bruh. We almost cousins yo.

After a quick nap, food, he sat in the den again, resolute in his mind that he was going to knock this studying out. He had the right notes out. The right problem sets. He had printed out the old practice exams that the tutors sent him (shit I shoulda been looking at these the whole time). He had everything. TV off. Quiet. I'm a knock this out. Boom. Be ready. Quit messing around. He put his fingers on his temples chanting I'm focused man, I'm focused maaan, I'm FO-CUSED ... MAAAN over and over. You know what, I'M GOING THROUGH. I'M GOING THROUGH. I'VE GOT MY EYE ON THE FINISH LIIIINE. I'M GOING THROUGH.

Chanting, closing his eyes and rubbing his temples, he was trying to decide what material to go through first. What would be the most efficient use of his time. Of course the old practice exams first, I know that. But which one? So what do I do after that? Rubbing his temples. Thinking. Planning. Visualizing the progression of work.

All that was tiring. He had a headache. All this thinking about work. He kicked off his shoes and rolled onto the couch trying to still chant and plan. But at least more comfortable like this. Tomorrow Tuesday tho. Shit. Already? He tried to think of it in terms of hours. That would make it better. If he could think in terms of hours then he would know that he had about 20 or so. Which sound like a lot. Which IS a lot. Yeah. 20-sum is a lot more than less than 1. He wondered the time exactly. His phone was charging in his bedroom.

Then it struck him that he should call one of these tutors Daniels mentioned. He found the email with their numbers. Time is it now? Like after 9? He grew embarrassed. Like the night before the test and I'm only calling now. I must look trifling as hell. He fidgeted, growing even more embarrassed. Hopeless. It's too late to call.

Past 10 o'clock now. He went to the Yup folder on his computer. Came quick. He was still shaking afterwards. This test on his mind the whole time. His breathing shallow. Might as well get another one in. Then another one. Not even bothering to use a sock or napkin. Growing numb but shaking still. Cum all everywhere. The smell of it. Whattam I doing? he asked in his mind still clicking and scrolling through the Yup folder, searching for the right flick, one that would hit the spot. The right one. Needed it. He was growing numb and he needed something special. Whattam I doing? Hell wrong with me? He called one of them tutors eventually. It was past midnight. Where you at? I'm not even in Charlottesville. What? Dean Daniels said yawl was down here. No, I'm in Bethesda right now. It's late Vonny. Naw don't worry about it, I just had a quick question. If it's quick I can answer it. Naw naw I think I got it. I'm sorry Vonny I didn't mean to shoo you off. Listen I'm getting up now—Naw it's all good don't even worry. She was still talking to him and he hung up, his arm numb, releasing the phone and letting it tumble to the floor. He sat there in his chair for a while, his mink blanket draped over him, the cum drying to sharp naps.

Nothing more he could really do. But a part of him hoped still. Like he could be saved by something. Like he could be captured suddenly. Taken over. His body possessed. By someone, something that would snap his body out of it. It know exactly what to do. Do all the work. And he'd be carried along by it. He waited and waited.

* * *

Vonny blinked his eyes awake. Under his cheek, the page of the homework problem set had become pulp. Running his tongue around his mouth, he felt the enamel stripped off his front teeth and a potent shitstain taste in the back of his tongue. In the kitchen, he took a birdbath with the yellow dishsoap and a handful of napkins from Taco Bell, and patted his balls dry, careful so none of the napkin would come off. He went back to his room, stepped into his shoes, and left for central grounds.

It was an empty, creaky 70 seat lecture hall. The TA sat on a platform up front. Behind him was a clean chalkboard with fresh sponge strokes.

The questions, just variations of the ones he'd already seen before, weren't hard as much as they were slippery, and he hadn't the swivel in his mind to catch the right answers.

The TA put his book down and wrote the ending time on the board.

Vonny filled in the rest at random, going what the hell, a couple deep breaths rising inside him, and handed in the test, relieved to be finished not only with the exam, but a whole lot of other things. Where you going? If you wait a moment, I can grade this for you right now. Vonny told him naw. Just email it to me.

His father called. So you aced it? I think I did pretty good. Your mother and I, we prayed over you. You passed son. I know you. You've spent your whole life excelling. Remember back at Norcom you won that math award? Vonny said he was coming back that night but he laid around the rest of the day. Smoking. Eating. Madden. Lots of Madden.

A storm came overnight and the next day looking out the window at his car submerged in the snow, he called his father. The snow was sticking in Portsmouth too. It was best he wait this out. The reverend wired more money into Vonny's account. Another few days worth. Just in case.

18

One of those afternoons watching the mailtruck from the stairs at his parents' home in Manassas, Titus hurried down the steps, reached into the mailbox and found the envelope with his LSAT score. He had done poorly, lower than even the bottom range of his expectations, but looking at that number a lil voice inside him said of course, and he put the sheet under his arm with the rest of the mail and carried on with his day.

He didn't want to think about it. Because the more he thought about it, the dumber he felt, and more and more it seemed everyone had been lying to him. Coming out of jail bright eyed, bushy tailed. Thinking how he was shootin straight to the top. How come nobody told him the truth? Maybe they thought it was cute. From behind bars to passing the bar. This little jailbird got a dream ... Even Brooke. None of them really believed. Not those people at Career Services, Daniels, none of them.

So he repeated to himself it is what it is and that God had him and he had to trust in that. He clung tight to another bit of scripture, GOD WILL NOT PLACE A BURDEN ON A MAN'S SHOULDER IF HE KNOWS HE CANNOT HANDLE IT, all the while struggling to shake the thought that he'd come face to face with what was inevitable.

He fondled the details of the test day again, how clumsy he was with the Silent Timer, and he was there in that test room hearing the proctor announce 5 MINUTES LEFT and he looked down and saw he was only on question 17. The same cold panic came over him now and he buried his head in his pillow, squeezing his eyes shut, squeezing his face, trying to collapse inside of himself. Why didn't I just cancel the scores when I had the chance? If I woulda canceled them, it would be as if I never took it. Clean. Like it never happened. I would just have to apply next year, that's all. He stopped squirming. I could just wait a year. Why the rush? More time to get my application together. Could take one of them prep courses too. A calmness came over him. Why rush and do a half ass job? Wait a lil and get that shit tight?

There was knocking on his bedroom door. His pop. Your Grandma Boothe on the downstairs phone. She would like to speak with you. Then came more knocking. Slow, sarcastic knocking. You gon pretend to be sleep again? I know you're up. I can hear you blinking.

Dutifully Titus went downstairs and spoke to Grandma Boothe over the phone, and dutifully had his dinner which was waiting for him. His folks asked what been wrong. Nothin, just bored. Bored, how? You been going out every night.

The next day mom had to be back at school to teach and he was home all day with pop. Pop retired from the Manassas Police Department a few years back and still spent a lot of time following crime on the local news. His father was polishing a church shoe in the den, when a report about an unsolved murder came on the TV. Well of course they won't talk. You think it's easy being a snitch? And he went back to polishing before remembering there was another warm body in the house. He glanced over at Titus's sulking figure on the couch.

So you just gon lounge around all break? Titus said yup, that's why they call it a break. Then you complain to your mother and I you're bored. You know she'll be worrying over you all day at work. So what's it gonna be? The news anchors shuffled their papers on the desk. After the forecast, Pop said let's go outside and shovel the driveway before your mom gets home.

By let's Pop meant *you*. Titus didn't mind the fresh air. By the time the driveway had been scraped clear, Titus's hands and feet were so cold and numb they no longer felt attached. He was moving his heavy limbs around and think-ing. If I wait until next year, hell am I gon do? Lock myself up and kill myself studying again. I aint fallin for that Silent Timer shit that's for sure. He hung up the shovel and made up his mind he'd stop worrying about it the rest of the day. It happened. Whatever he'd decide moving forward, he know he didn't want it to be like this no more. Like a fucken fiend. Killing himself. Can't take another year like this. 24 credits. I don't even know how I survived. They knocked me on Oceanography ... rest of them wasn't too bad. Next semester'll be easier.

He apologized to his father for acting funny earlier. His father's gaze remained hard. Whatever's eating you, you've taken care of it? Titus said it was nothing. You know I aint dumb son. Nobody said you was. Son listen to me. Are you listening to me? I don't want you to be in a situation where you're in a situation, understand? You gotta be smart. I hear you pop. It aint nothing. Is it street stuff? Titus shook his head. Somebody pregnant? Titus smiled, Go head pop, and though pop wasn't smiling he was giving off that vibe, and went back to polishing his church shoes.

19

Knockknockknockknock—Vonny pressed pause.

At first he thought it was Housing coming by to tell him to leave.

Knockknock.

Hold up I'm comin.

He set the controller down and drew the mink blanket over his shoulders. Sat there. Maybe they'd go away on their own.

Knockknockknock—TOLE YA I'M COMIN. Walking up to the door slow and heavy with embarrassment, preparing in his mind some excuse or explanation or maybe he'd just play dumb or something. Through the peephole he saw a nigga out there. Graunchy looking. Hat. Dark coat with bright patches. Somebody he might've known.

The dood came in laughing appreciatively, kicking the snow off his boots giving Vonny dap then looking Vonny up and down, I wake you up? Vonny shook his head and the guy bust out laughing, hahaha, don't YOU look comfortable. Hahahaha. With your jammies on and everything hahaha.

Vonny remembered where he knew this dood from. He'd run into him at Taco Bell. This was before the makeup exam, which seemed so long ago. Wasn't. Now he remembered the dood's name too—Joe Reed.

Joe pulled up a chair in the den and talked a mile a minute removing his coat. It's bad out there. Snow don't know how to stop in Virginia. Yah get it much worse down here believe it or not. I couldn't even get the whip up that hill back there hahahaha. Look, look, dood extending his hand to make sure Vonny was listening, I left the whip down there by the side of the road and WALKED up. You heard that? WALKED. Almost fell out on my ass a few times hahahaha. Joe put his coat back on and sat back down. Looked around. That this year Madden? Yeah. You don't want to see me on them sticks son I'm nice with mine, then looking over his shoulders, Anybody else here? Just me. Joe began rubbing his arms and looking around. There someone we can call about this heat??? Cold in here as it is out there. Hahaha. Vonny explained that unless you notified Student Housing that you were going to be here over the break, they cut off the heat. Joe said if that was the case, he didn't see why they couldn't cut it back on. You got Housing number? I think there's a sheet over there by the fridge.

Joe went to the kitchen to look for that sheet with the numbers. He got someone on the line and used Vonny's name. Vonny sat there reviewing what he knew about Joe Reed, which wasn't much. He knew Joe was older. Remembered seeing him around a few years back. Had heard about Joe getting shot outside the Outback Lodge. For some reason that wasn't some big scandal and he wasn't sure what happened to Joe after that. He might've could been dead. Vonny had lost track. Vonny could hear Joe peeking in the fridge, the freezer, walking around the kitchen, opening cabinets and shit, sucking his teeth for being put on hold, his general phlegmy way of speaking, and a few other niggarish mannerisms. Vonny could even tell when Joe was rearing back and rolling his eyes.

With his phone pressed to his ear, Joe poked his head back into the den and asked Vonny whatchu still doon here anyway? Don't you got nowhere to go for winter break? No family or nothing? Hadda do a re-take cuh. Yeah that's right. You told me at the ... at the? Taco Bell. Joe put his hand up, carried on his conversation with Student Housing, then resumed speaking with Vonny. Yo you won't believe this shit but I BEEN here. I aint going back up to New York no time soon. I was staying with my nigga over there by Dale City. Then his lady was trippin, I don't know, so I had to be up outta there—hello, you there? Yeah. Request? I didn't. Me being here was unexpected. I see. I had to re-take an exam. It was last second. Can you? How soon? Faulkner. He asked Vonny what the unit number was and the information was relayed to the person on the line. Joe hung up and said they would send someone down to flip the switch.

He came back into the den, sighing in relief, and started patting himself, feeling around in his pockets. Then he reached into his coat for a bag of weed and box of dutches. He took a CD case from the coffee table, blew it off and got to work quick. Vonny didn't even have to ask him to do that. Joe licking the leaves, So you pass that test tho? Not looking like it. Damn, son. We got another goner. Yeah they fittin to kick me out. I was on probation but now they bout to put me on suspension for a year—For real? I was just kidding. You serious? You talked to Dean Daniels? He can get you outta that. Shit he the one that got me the re-take. What year are you? Hearing Vonny say he was a fourth year, Joe's eyes became real big. You gon really need this then.

They blazed and got on Madden. Vonny could tell right away that the dood wasn't no good. Joe ran with the Falcons and would roll Vick 30, 40 yards backwards, breaking the pocket to the left and he'd throw these 60 yard bombs across his body going to the right that didn't come close to nobody. And Joe would yell and bite his finger while the ball was in the air and when it landed way off the screen out of bounds he stood up and yelled and he'd run the same play over and over and shout I ALMOST HAD YOU RIGHT THERE! and OOOOOHH YOU GOT LUCKY THERE. Vonny was up 3 touchdowns in the first quarter, going easy on him actually, not saying a word, the haze in the room making him thankful and civil and blessed and full of essence.

Trust me when I say this, Joe setting down the controller, that nigga Daniels will get you across the finish line eventually. Call that nigga again. That's the only reason he here. You seen all them articles about him? The ones he keep mentioning in them emails? UVA got the highest black graduation rate in the country. Niggas quitting college in record numbers but not here. That nigga Daniels got the touch I'm telling you. He got in my ear too. I wouldn't even be here if it weren't for that game he was spittin. Pointed at a map of the school and said, This here belong to you. Joe laughing. It sounds corny but I'm tellin you, you had to be there.

Yawningly Joe stretched and looked around. You smoke all those Black-N-Milds by yourself? Not all back-to-back. Good. Them shits'll tear your chest open you not careful. You freek em? Yeah. That might help a little. You gotta take care your lungs. My doctor tell me I shouldn't even smoke no squares. Supposedly I'm allergic. Joe started patting himself again. He pulled out some cash from the snap pockets on the outside of his coat, some more cash on the inside pocket of his coat. He started patting the pockets in his jeans. He had some painter style jeans with skinny pockets down at the knees where he found some bills wadded up, some folded tight, coins. A nigga trying to order some food over here. I was bout to say Gumby's but it look like you been had plenty of that. How bout Domino's? You got some loot?

Vonny went to his room and came back with a 10 dollar bill. It was his last big bill. The rest were ones and coins. Joe bust out laughing again. What is you wearing? Fuckin long johns? Holding his chest, laughing, asphyxiated. He wearing … he a lumberjack … hahaha. And a blanket? You go everywhere with that blanket, huh? You know you remind me of that nigga in Charlie Browns. What's that nigga name? The one with the blanket going around sucking his thumb? Hahahahaha. Fuck Charlie homeboy ahahaha. Yeah that's me. Vonny sat down and watched the graunchy nigga count the money.

Dominos wouldn't pick up. Gumby's neither. It had begun snowing again, fat old clumps. Joe said he had something in his car. He said if he didn't come back in five minutes to check for him haha. He might just fall and break his neck out there haha. In ten minutes Joe came back shivering and stomping the dandruff of snow from his shoulders. He had a plastic bag with his cell phone charger, a bunch of black frostbitten bananas and a tub of peanut butter. In order to keep the peanut butter warm he said he had to keep it between his legs while he was driving. He guaranteed that didn't affect the taste. Also in that bag was the DVD box set of the Chappelle Show. He said he had bought it at Best Buy the other day before the snow storm. They popped it in the PS2. 2 discs into the season, the heat came on and Joe took off his boots and laid on the couch going I told you this nigga crazy.

The snow growing like a flat top fro on the mailbox outside, they got through the whole season that night and the next day they watched it again, Joe watching the same episodes back-to-back-to-back, rewinding the jokes though they had stopped being funny to Vonny, Joe pounding his knee and stomping on the floor and looking over at Vonny who with some effort drew a corner of his face to a smirk. See I told you that nigga CRAZY son. Snickering. Running the bit back again. Another dutch. It was all forgivable with the weather not letting up. Joe kept going back out to the car and coming back with more bags.

* * *

Days passed. Looking now at the trashbags of Joe's clothes shoved into the corner of the den, Vonny guessed the nigga was staying here now.

Once the snow let up a little, Joe's townie girlfriend came through. The ploughs made a pass over the road and she took the bus. Showing up at the apartment, hair straight down, she wore navy blue bubble goose and walked bowlegged like a tomboy to the den in calf-length fur-lined Timbs. She didn't talk much. She enjoyed sitting around listening to niggas talk. She sat cross-legged, her elbow on her knee looking more the lady. With long fingers, she balanced the dutch, babysat the thing for a long minute then she glanced down at the glowing cherry, drew the twig up to her face and blew without coughing. While old girl was in the bathroom, Joe asked if Vonny wanted to make some loot. Shit that's why we're all here right?

Vonny rented out his room for the night. Joe brought his own sheets.

While they were in there, Vonny took it upon himself to snoop through Joe's stuff. Under the cloak of TV sound, he poked open some of the trash bags expecting to see a tuft of weed. Joe would always reach in his coat pocket for a sandwich bag and when that one was smoked through, he reached in his pocket for another. Never saw him go to the main supply tho. Vonny imagined a trashbag swollen with the stuff somewhere.

Mostly it was clothes he found. Pinwheel hats, a couple sizes too large for Vonny. A pair of jeans still with the markdown tag from Marshall's, some faded RL Chaps shirts in springtime pastels, a pair of white basketball shorts that had been bleached because the black swoosh was brown. Countless white tees, wifebeaters. The nigga wore the same white tee with the pale yellow stain on the collar. Vonny found some prescription medicine bottles and looked away feeling guilty, then he got over that feeling and looked in a bag of official-looking papers, which seemed like the perfect hiding spot. He excavated layer after layer of papers until he reached the bottom of the bag. He put the papers back it the correct order and beneath the shriveled grab-handles, he saw a letter on the top of the stack from the Office of Financial Aid, December dated, NY addressed. Lots of zeroes. The letter said it was happy to restore the remaining part of his Holland Scholarship to cover the rest of the academic year.

The next morning Joe and his girl were still in there. Vonny called home and gave it to his pop straight. The phone line was quiet. You there dad? I wanna know did you try your best. Vonny said he did and there was another silence and his father said well I guess you gotta find work now. It'll be good for you. So when will your mother and I expect you? Vonny said he would try to get down tomorrow. He had to figure out a way to pack up all his stuff.

When Joe and his girl were done with the room, Vonny ducked under his desk to unplug the cords to his computer. He heard Joe come into the room again. When you leaving? Maybe today. I don't have as much as I thought.

Joe lingered around as Vonny rounded up his things. With everything unplugged, the sounds were that much louder and depressing. The rustle of trashbags as things were shoved in, opening of the closet doors, heavy things being dropped. People were getting back from winter break too. Cars coming and going. People in the stairwell shouting directions, I'M OVER HERE, and keys jingling.

Joe asked if he'd turned in his keys yet. Not yet. I was going to drop them off in the RC's box on the way out. Just put tape in the doorway if you wanna stay. Vonny running his hands through his hair thinkingly. Or I can give you the keys if you want. Thing is tho, I don't want them charging me. Joe said he had an idea. He explained it. Vonny agreed. The room was vacant now. He didn't see why Housing wouldn't let someone new slide right in as long as they could pay. Joe got on the phone with Housing right away.

20

Titus decided to move forward with the law school application process. Another year studying for the LSAT, sitting at home all day with his pop, nah, no way. He set himself a deadline of finishing all the applications before heading back to UVA for the spring semester.

He and his mother spent a lot of time on the personal statement. Coming home from the schoolday, his mother would need a few minutes with her green pen. He'd read aloud her corrections. A few days of this and the statement was pretty much done. He looked at the marked page in his hand, certain phrases leaping from the type, LEAVING A MUTUAL FRIEND'S GATHERING ... I JERKED THE STEERING WHEEL ... PASSENGER SEAT TOO ... TOOK ALL THAT AWAY ... EMOTIONS GOT THE BEST OF ME ... and allasudden he felt hopeless again. He couldn't recognize any of this. None of it was him. The idea of putting his past out there, Ma I don't got a good feeling. She told him it was natural to get cold feet. This was a big step for him. He sat wincing at the details on the page, the paragraph describing his act. He asked his mother if it was too much. I want you to be honest Ma. I *am* being honest. She went back to hunting for typos with her green pen. I don't think it focuses too much on the past. Here, look. Here you talk about what this experience has taught you, what you're going to do about it. She finished making her edits and presented her copy to him. He read the statement aloud, backing up occasionally over the rough phrases and smoothing those out, then they focused on the paragraph with the statistics, which transitioned from the personal stuff to the matter at hand, a career in law. She made him read the end, even though it had no corrections, and by that point she was tired.

She reminded him before going off to bed that if the admissions officer wasn't broken to pieces by the end of this, then you haven't done yourself justice. There was no shame going for tears. He hugged her, smelling her deeply. I love you Ma. You know you my heart. It's that I want it so bad. Titus you already make us proud. If you're going out tonight, tell them to turn down—Pop already told me.

He didn't go out with his boys that night. He was up late on the downstairs computer. He sewed up a questionnaire on one of the online applications and had been fooling around on a few others, his mind fried, but there was something deeper there bothering him. A layer. He came across the conduct section.

HAVE YOU EVER, EITHER AS AN ADULT OR A JUVENILE, BEEN CITED, ARRESTED, TAKEN INTO CUSTODY, CHARGED WITH, INDICTED, CONVICTED OR TRIED FOR, OR PLEADED GUILTY TO, THE COMMISSION OF ANY FELONY OR MISDEMEANOR OR THE VIOLATION OF ANY LAW, EXCEPT FOR

MINOR TRAFFIC VIOLATIONS, OR BEEN THE
SUBJECT OF JUVENILE DELINQUENCY OR
YOUTHFUL OFFENDER PROCEEDING, OR IS ANY
SUCH ACTION PENDING OR EXPECTED TO BE
BROUGHT AGAINST YOU?

He closed his eyes and rubbed his face. He was already
answering this in the personal statement. Did he have to
write out another separate statement? Did he really? Could
he just put SEE PERSONAL STATEMENT?

Just fucking around, he clicked the NO box. Immediately the big ol box beneath the question disappeared, the
one where he had to put his explanation. The page seemed
a lot cleaner. The way things were supposed to be. He
clicked the YES box and the explanation box came back.
The cursor inside blinking back at him. He felt a little
funny.

The next day he came back and clicked and unclicked
that box. He looked through other applications and marked
NO wherever he could. He said he wasn't actually gonna do
this. He was just messing around. He stared at the screen,
the order and cleanliness of space now that he didn't need
to explain what had happened that night when he was 17.
When he was 17. Not even the same person anymore.
Depends how you define it. Right? Yeah wouldn't it?
It would.

He realized he was breathing hard, the whine in his ears
loud and all enveloping. He sat there with it. Breathing his
in outs. Riding the wave, feeling whatever it was coursing
through him. He got off the website and crawled into bed.

* * *

The next day Titus waited around for his parents to leave the house, then dialed the number to the application credentialing service. Listening to it ring, he told himself he was calling out of curiosity. Just to see, nothing more.

When he got a hold of someone, he asked his question and they told him he didn't have to do a thing. On their website, he could simply select what letters of recommendation would be forwarded to which school. In the case of Recommender Fred Daniels, all he had to remember was to NOT click Daniels's name. That's it? Yes. Is there anything else I can help you with? Will my recommender be notified? The woman on the phone said no right away, then there was a pause. If he were to call the schools themselves and follow up, that's another thing. I'm not sure how each school handles—But you all won't say nothing? That's correct. Titus thanked her for her time.

He was fighting the urge to get gassed up. Nah I haven't made a decision yet, grinning inwardly, knowing which way he was leaning. All day he allowed himself to consider it longer, and allowed himself the pleasure of being surprised at how things could come together so easily if he actually went through with it, how uncomplicated everything would be. The more he thought on it, the more plausible it became, and he admitted to himself that he was actually considering it.

Every now and then logistical matters intruded. What about the schools that wanted Daniels to mail them directly? Do I even got enough time to switch everything up? But he came off those thoughts, and stroked and stroked the possibility. He sniffed, suddenly angry. Shit it aint on me to disclose. YOU wanna know then YOU go look it up. I aint gonna help you, fuck you think. Before I even get my foot in the door. I aint fallin for that. What you think would've happened if I had told UVA? Would I even be here right now if they knew beforehand I was stickin niggas up? Huh? What you think? I'm sayin. Use common sense. That shit might work on them other people. Why the hell make things more complicated? I'm sayin. Why make things harder on yourself by bringing that up, like what's that gotta do with the man I am today? You don't walk around and that's the first thing you say. After you tell them that, then what? It won't matter. Nothing else would. All they see is a nigga with a record. Fuck outta here.

Maybe another day passed before Titus decided to go through with it. It didn't take him long to make the changes. The ease and simplicity of the entire process shocked him. He went through the credentialing website unchecking the boxes. Pages, blocks of type disappeared like that, sucked away somewhere. The new personal statement he was able to knock out while his mother was at work. After he removed the references to his prior conviction, he realized he could slide in some general stuff that pretty much applied to himself and the whole thing came out almost as long and still made sense. It was just a statement. They don't put too much weight on that. His pop drove him to the post office the next day where he mailed out the few forms that couldn't be accepted electronically.

His mother was a little heated that she didn't get one last pass at the materials. Pop shrugged. I assumed he had checked with you first. There you go assuming Jeremiah. Why you upset at me? Nobody tells me anything around here. I'm just a taxi service. Nobody's upset. Just disappointed. Loretta how else this boy gon learn but to do some things on his own? She set down her fork and explained some of the mistakes she'd been finding. She was listing out mistakes she'd never mentioned before. Listening to them, Titus grew annoyed at all the little petty things she'd noticed, but he knew she was right ... Mixing the blue ink with the black. Repeating the same words over and over. You know these people are looking for any reason. You remember that dean, she was snapping her fingers at Titus across the dinner table asking him the name of that dean and he told her. That's right, Staunton. Ma put her elbows on the table, her mouth hanging open as she chewed, eyes rolling in disgust, the disgust taking a moment to pass through her before she was able to speak again. Remember what she said about us. We drove 2 and a half hours. You remember how hot that drive was? You remember. Two hours just to hear this woman call us liars to our faces. And this dean was smiling too. You remember that? Yes I remember. THAT'S the people we're dealing with. Pop sat thinking and chewing. Chewing he was looking at his son. Next time boy you check with your mother. Won't be a next time pop. Shoot, that's what you think.

There wasn't much left of break. What was left he filled as much as he could with sleep. He lingered in bed a little longer and lost track of time lying there in his room. Now and then he thought about what he had done but he always stopped himself before the thought formed an edge to it. In those moments he would say to himself I did what I had to do. I just have to get my foot in the door. They'll understand. Someone. And that familiar feeling that something was wrong, that it was all going to end terribly and in the worst way possible, left for the time being, and he would feel better somewhat. He managed to convince himself that the chill coming over him was relief. Drinking a Corona with his boys the night before he went back to UVA, the thoughts slowly turning ... turning. Thinking whew that was close. Coulda fucked up big time. Woulda been a wrap for me.

21

Vonny hung around UVA a lil longer. He had himself set up on the couch. Everything he needed. A pillow and mink blanket, enough slack in the phone charger. He was good.

He would hang out and smoke and listen to music and play Madden. Samo. Sleep would come up and take him while he was out there in the den with the last of the scragglers looking to settle a score on the sticks, and he would wake up a few hours later, the dream very vivid, an adventure of some kind, he was jumping and could jump over buildings, jump up outta a dangerous situation with some bad guys who were out to get him, and the dream was almost pulling him back, then he would feel his foot knocking into a controller, and the urge to piss became critical. He more or less had to feel his way to the bathroom, going on nothing more than instinct and muscle memory through the heavy residue to find it, and afterwards instead of hanging a right to where his bedroom had been (Joe and his girlfriend had been awoken once or twice, Joe laughing), would continue straight through the hall to the den where he got a good few more hours of sleep in.

Besides that right turn after the bathroom, life was pretty much the same. He'd done the rough calculations. He was about the same level of contentedness as before, as what he would be otherwise if he had to go to class. The same amount of work got done, he suspected, Madden, food eating and so on. The only other annoyance was his lack of cheeks lately but that always comes and goes. Like the wind blows haha. He could use a new pair of shoes. An edge up perhaps. Niggas came back from break rocking a few new color combinations. He noticed. If he had gone back after the test, he would've had the chance to get his gear right but ... yeah I been slacking. His mind ran through the things he'd seen people wearing, nodding occasionally, I gotta get up on those ... like all things the lack of cheeks probably came down to money.

So he gave slanging an honest shot. Went up with Joe somewhere in the country. North. They sat in the McDonald's parking lot, waited, the heater in the Maxima broken and Vonny wished he brought a blanket. They were parked at one end by the dumpster and they watched the farmer-looking people get out of their trucks and go in the McDonald's.

Finally the tan Honda pulled up on the passenger side. Joe told Vonny to crank down the window. The other window, tinted. It rolled down slow and the nigga in there was shaking his head and sucking his teeth. Joe asked whatsgood my nigga? The other dood seemed too embarrassed to talk and it was like he wanted to get this over with. Joe handed Vonny a convenience store bag taped up secure with the money. Vonny aimed and threw it into the other car and the guy caught it with one hand. As he counted, the dood pulled a black garbage bag from the passenger side footwell and tossed that big pillowy thing at them without looking. It bounced off the door before Vonny could grab it and fell to the wet salty ground. Joe cursed. We right over here. How the fuck you miss a wide open window? I aint picking that up. Your mans should've caught it. What? Why you acting funny style, my nigga? Tell your mans to pick it up.

When the tan Honda left, Vonny opened the door and picked the bag off the ground, shook the wet off it. Joe started pulling out of the parking spot. Yo you don't even want to check it? Son do it feel like weed in there? Feel like plants. Joe told him good then to toss it in the back seat. He explained his connect was a good dood. Funny-style sometimes but a good dood trust me.

And that was the extent of Vonny's foray into slanging. He sorta knew it would be the case beforehand, but now he knew for sure it wasn't for him. He couldn't see himself working that much, being on call at all hours, couldn't see himself collecting from people, being mean to them if they came up short, implying to people. Maybe his older brother Shawn could. But no, not Vonny. He didn't even have a pistol like Joe. Joe laughing. Whatchu need a ratchet for Vonny? You won't have no weight on you.

Vonny had to tell him them shoes simply didn't fit. Joe was cool with it. This aint no career for me neither.

The phonathon wouldn't take Vonny back. Only currently enrolled students were allowed to work there. So he called around some more and his boy William said there was some openings at Best Buy. But not up front in customer service with me. In the back. You good with that? Yeah I'm good. Long as it aint outside. Can't stand nature.

William put in a word and Vonny got hired right quick. The first week or so he sat in the break room watching training videos. It all seemed common sense. The manager came in at the end and said Got it? then took him and the other new doods into the warehouse and had them practice on the pallet trucks. Steering them shits this way and that.

Working nights was all right with him. There was no way of telling the difference. Everything in piles, rows, bare bulbs in the ceilings way up there. Everything in every direction looked the same.

22

Titus cleared his throat, spread his legs and stared vacantly at the wall before him. The cup grew warm in his palm. He pinched off the stream and reached for the other cup on the lip of the sink. The tech standing armscrossed by the door with a clipboard asked him how his break was. It was straight. Ate a bunch. You? The tech rubbing his belly proudly, I had the same problem hahaha. I'm still recovering. Still? Titus handed him the cups and waited for the bus back to grounds in the bright windy cold outside.

He took the city line to the green then hooked up to the blue and stayed on that for a while looking at people outside shrugging their faces deeper into their coats, then he got off when the bus looped back behind Cabell. He walked up to the OAAA and handed over a packet of forms to the workstudy. He was explaining to her what the forms were and how they were organized when Daniels walked in. Titus just the man I wanted to see.

Daniels removed his hat and gloves and shook the young man's hand vigorously. I promise that your letter will be finished this weekend. I've been thinking about it constantly. It will be very sincere, I know it. I want to make sure I get it right. Titus said thanks once again and that he brought the forms. The dean nodding, Yes I can see that, and Titus saying that he already filled out what he could and provided the stamps and envelopes and put them together with paperclips and everything should be clearly labeled—Good good—and Titus reached into his bookbag and handed him a red square envelope. Well this doesn't look like law school materials. It's to say thank you Dr. Daniels—No I refuse. This is completely unnecessary. My mother said you gotta take it. There's a invitation in there too. My graduation party. It's in May. I'm sure you busy but she said she'll need an answer soon if you don't mind ... Titus continued mumbling his appreciation and Daniels stood beaming and the two of them shook hands once again and Daniels announced to the receptionist and the few people waiting down there that they were looking at the next Thurgood Marshall hahaha. Titus was heading out the door when he remembered. He caught up to the dean who was halfway up the stairs. I been meaning to ask about our meetings this semester. You had said that we didn't have to meet since I had that class with you but this semester I'm not taking you so ... ? Yes that. Well Titus my door's always open. Titus studied the dean's expression for a moment, then understood. Oh thank you Dr. Daniels. Goodness, was your time with me that oppressive? Nah I didn't mean—Yes yes haha I was only kidding. You've come a long way Titus. I'm awful proud of you. After all you've been through. I knew it wasn't going to be easy. But your work's not done here. No sir it isn't. I want you to focus on finishing up strong. Thank you Dr. Daniels.

As soon as he got back to the crib, Titus made sure to check the credentialing website again, that under RECOM-

MENDER FRED DANIELS there were no checkboxes, which meant the forms he gave to the dean today would be seen by exactly no one. The letter the dean was writing, thinking about it, Titus felt like an asshole.

Felt like an asshole the rest of the day. Being fake like that, he couldn't recall the last time he'd been that fake. It shocked him thinking of how easily he slipped into that, even his little Hollywood laugh when the dean called him the next Thurgood Marshall. Hours later Titus was still blinking in disbelief. Maybe I would make a good lawyer after all. Somehow the joke wasn't funny. He continued drinking. Then became conscious of the fact Joe was looking at him grinning. You be knockin these back huh? What you say? Joe made the gesture with his hand. Titus looked down at the bottle in his palm. Nah this only, what, my third?

Together in the den they squinted at the bootleg DVD, the fuzzy action and talking, and could tell that it was probably a good movie, and tried their best to follow it. Joe got up, chuckling that he had stopped making sense of why they wanted the ninja lady dead, and came back to the den holding a brown bottle saying you wanna try one of these? Titus said he saw them in the fridge earlier. I thought only whiteboys drink that. It's different. I kinda fuck with it truthfully. Joe brought him one, cracking the top off with the end of a lighter. Titus watched the vapor disappear from the mouth of the bottle, and after hesitating a moment, took a sip. It's different aint it? Them whiteboys swear by these! After Titus finished swallowing, he admitted he could see why they did, though he himself would never buy this at the store. As the bootleg movie played, they drank, Titus occasionally holding the bottle out and looking at the label and chuckling to himself, and a few more bottles went down

that way. Joe said that a white boy did in fact bring these
beers over and Titus took the opportunity to finally ask
what he knew full well to be the case, whether Joe was
slanging out the apartment. Kev had been asking him to,
saying he himself wasn't the confrontational type. Shit so
I am?

Without taking his eyes off the screen and barely raising
his voice Joe said he had a few people he dealt with. Not no
major weight or nuttin. Only reason I ask is that my PO
might come through. Watching Joe shift around in his seat,
Titus emphasized MIGHT again, and spent a few more
minutes trying to downplay the possibility. This led to Titus
explaining his legal situation, a very lengthy, more or less
chronological account that stretched back to middle school
when he started running with the goons and knuckleheads.
He went on to talk about high school, smoking boat,
running up on weed spots with ski masks, forreal I was so
reckless then. With some pride, he described how a hit had
been placed on him when he was only 16 years old. At a
party he had fired his pistol in the air after someone had
pulled a knife on his boy. No one was hurt, God forbid, but I
was so stupid back then. So wild. Lucky I had an OG inter-
vene on my behalf or else I'da been dead. When Titus
finally arrived at the part of the story where he had finally
been caught by the law, the details of sticking up Jermell
Knight and Dawnisha Randle on the side of the road next to
Battlefield Park, this after Jermell had cut him off in traffic
half a mile prior, these details glossed over as the point of
his youthful wildness had already been established, and the
brews by this point made forming syllables strenuous. Plus,
he'd been going on this long without Joe interrupting.

Joe began talking about coming up in the New York
foster system, sticking mostly to dates, ages, facts of that

sort, then how his mom died of cancer when he was 9, his brother being shot dead too when he was 11. He had one other older brother still alive though, and a sister, 17, still part of the system. Both of them still in Brooklyn. Joe went on about his sister, how the service only cover but so much, and how he don't even think she seeing as much of the check as she should be, which is why he started sending her money. Joe wouldn't go into much detail, but he kept repeating that he'd been through a lot coming up in the system. Titus asked what about getting shot. My older brother? Nah you. Joe peeled up his shirt. Titus got up close, kneeling on the floor to look at the dimple in Joe's chest and the 2 dimples in his large but taut belly. Exit wounds? Taking a sip of brew, Joe shook his head and put his shirt back down, chuckling. The skinny nigga who did this, he thought I was somebody else. I think I know who too. There was somebody in the club with the same Iceberg sweater on, the one with the cartoons, member those? Titus said he remembered those sweaters. He used to have one of them. He even had one of them Warn a Brother shirts, member those? Joe said he remembered those too.

By the time Vonny came home from Best Buy, Titus and Joe were ready to head off to bed but seeing Vonny in his corny Best Buy polo led to a few jokes and they felt another wind, and after a quick run to the store, partook in another round of brews.

Vonny was demonstrating how months earlier he had cinched the football player's knees together before driving him to the ground. Vonny's mildly Korean eyes were big and crazy lookin. Forreal I ain't tryna throw down no more but if they still think we punks after what we did? and he looked over at Titus who mumbled he wasn't scared of no football players. But there comes a time when—Titus rubbed his eyes and forgot the point he was making. His mind had drifted and he was thinking of his encounter with Daniels from earlier, how fake he'd been, how easily it came. Maybe it meant nothing at all.

Joe was off to the side laughing, shaking his head, calling them crazy for going at them big boys. Before going to bed, he said his final piece. Don't get me wrong, Joe grabbing his belt buckle and jimmying it up and down, if it's getting critical, knawmean? I'm not gonna let no man lay hands on me. But look, aye look, there just TOO MANY of them niggas and yah know not all of them niggas get playin time nor do they care about getting kicked off the team. It seem like a lose-lose to me. But aye, what do I know? This yah beef and I ain't tryna call nobody no punks.

After Joe went to bed, Vonny was still hype from his reenactment and was walking around the den in his Best Buy polo aimlessly swinging his arms and letting his feet knock into things on the floor. An empty french fry container was kicked into Titus's foot.

Slumped in his seat, Titus was processing the sight of Joe grabbing his belt buckle, and was thinking whether that was an empty gesture or some true indication.

He asked Vonny and Vonny said yeah he had seen Joe's pistol. He keep it in his sock drawer. He say he got papers on it too.

* * *

Titus overslept. He boarded the blue bus off the hour, and in that empty bus was assailed by the shock of each bump and pothole, and considered staying on until the blue looped all the way back to Faulkner.

He stepped out into central grounds and since his discman was out of juice, he could hear the people inside the buildings,a voice of a professor striding confidently through a point, and past another building chairs scraping and a professor raising her voice over them to deliver instructions, and down by Cabell Hall bongos and chanting and he could see in the first floor window the people going around slowly in a circle, stepping wide and stalkingly, and the teacher standing by with a stoic expression, an African looking lady with dreads. For some reason Titus knew that they were all barefoot in that room, and he remembered there was green colored tile in there from a lecture Brooke had brought him to one time. Or was it one of her dance performances? The tiles in there were green he knew.

He hung around the outside of the doors of the lecture hall debating with himself if it was worth it to come so late. He pinned his hopes that someone would come out the door and he'd slide in casually, but something inside him said it was just too quiet and the minute he walked in everyone would be looking up at him coming through with his bookbag and sweats and I got these Timbs on, and they prolly went over the main concepts already. He was annoyed at himself for being such a bitch, then another part of him said fuckit it's only the second week. Probably won't be on the midterm, and he was off to pick up some batteries at the bookstore.

Then to Memorial Gym. He hit the bench, and in the back there was a separate room with a heavy bag. The smell in there reminded him of jail. In that back room alone he did his pushups and situps and shadowboxed in his socks, admiring his shoulders in the mirror, the veins and striations, as his fists recoiled, and he put on the thin worn mitts from the checkout counter and walloped the heavy bag. Circling the bag and cursing at it, playing along, potshotting, and felt what he was doing was corny so he got more organized and the punches came cleaner and there was a snap to them that left indentations. Some thinking happened. What's even the point of another semester? Then a little later, how bad does a person need to do for them to rescind an offer? I can't be failing of course but ...

A familiar voice called out from behind, Quit scaring the white people.

Standing there cheesing was Kev. He had on this home-made sleeveless tee cut raggedly from the collar down to the waist. His nipples and ribs were showing, which made Titus smile. Shit if they gotta prollem, let em come down here, and he re-seated his knuckles in the mitts and squared up to the bag.

Kev rolled up to the other side of the heavy bag, braced himself against it, and told Titus to drive his hips more. All that grunting and all you giving me are these pitty pat punches. Hips huh? Where'd you learn that? Bruce Lee. You mean your uncle? Ahhh somebody got jokes finally ... The chain above shook and clinked then both were out of breath on the floor. Now it's your turn faggot. Me? I just got done lifting. Look, this is how high I can raise my arm. Can't even feel it.

They put their coats on and grabbed lunch at the Pav. Kev was already at it, flirting with the old ladies in their hairnets, flashing his white smile beneath the fur lined hood of his coat. It lifted Titus out of his congestion. Talk came easy. They caught up on gossip about the music world, beefs, unexpected collaborations, all with far reaching implications. Next Kev revealed he had been recruited to the Fashion Show—yooo hahaha they gon make you wear a thong!!!—and was explaining the science behind his new diet and how it was going to achieve the impossible: the simultaneous building of new muscle and burning of fat.

Titus noticed the croutons piled to the side of Kevin's salad. You don't look fat to me. Just eat whatever you want and exercise more. Kevin said that all the doods in the Fashion Show were following this diet, and the results were proven. Filipino people, he claimed, weren't naturally cut, not like the brothas. There was no way he was going down that catwalk next to some of these African doods, each and every one of them with 8 packs, while he himself could only rock a 2.5 on a good day. Slapping the table, Titus almost spit out his drink, GO HEAD ON! and they both roared with laughter, drawing a few meek glances that quickly turned away.

Kev had other big plans. He was applying to this organization that put you in the hood to teach for a few years. It was an impulsive decision. He already had something lined up with a consulting firm after graduation, but someone was handing out flyers outside class one day, and he went to the website, watched all these videos and now he was all about closing this thing called THE ACHIEVEMENT GAP.

The way I look at it, and I'm sure you agree—Kev's tone altering, acquiring the whispery seriousness of the famous actor narrating the videos—there's a fundamental problem we keep ignoring. Your mother's a teacher so you know exactly what I'm talking about. *This*—and both of his eyebrows arched on the word then the next important one—is *the* Civil Rights issue of our generation. And it's inexcusable that, depending on your zip code and who your parents are, a child can be completely shut out from opportunity in this country. We have to reach them before it's too late.

Titus said he agreed with everything but that last thing, he couldn't necessarily cosign that. It's never too late. I mean I hear what you sayin but that's not what a Christian goes by, feel me? As long as you believe Jesus is the Son of God, there is always a path to redemption.

Seeing the blank, almost startled look on Kev's face, Titus apologized for bringing God into it, so he made an example of Kevin's dieting, that after a lifetime of bread and soda, a person like him could suddenly call it quits. A grin returned to Kevin's face. See Kev? You know I'm right. If it's not possible for people to change, then what's the point? Why try to eat better, or study more, or quit smoking or, or whatever. You might as well kill yourself.

Kev confessed that he missed rice the most. His diet would likely end the minute he stepped off the Fashion Show stage. And that's the point I'm trying to make here. After a certain age, we are who we are. That's reality. Of course there are deviations. Phases. But after a certain point, sad to say, it's a wrap. The real you, when the pressure's on, it always comes out. Think about it another way. Ever notice that most of life's problems come from this notion that we have to change someone? How does that ever work out?

Titus sensed there was something wrong and deeply dangerous about what Kevin was saying, but it sounded so comforting, maybe even right in certain cases, that he tucked away the idea where he knew it could be found later, and moved onto a new subject.

Before lunch ended, Titus confirmed the suspicions about Joe. No major weight but yeah, it was true. He was slanging. Kev shrugged it off like it was no big deal, then the corner of his face smirked conspiratorially. It's not like I'll be around much.

Kev had a new girl, and when he said who, Titus fell to giggling, so much so that he had to close his eyes at the absurdity of his roommate's good fortune. Nigga wasn't you the one callin *me* obedient?

M.O.V.E. Against Violence received very little interest from potential corporate sponsors. The school districts were at least friendly over the phone, but were much too busy with standardized testing to schedule any sit-downs. The last few times Brooke and Susan talked, Susan had nothing to report. Brooke believed she had caught a whiff of attitude again, and simply stopped asking. Stopped calling. It seemed better that way.

Halfway through her final year at UVA and Brooke felt she was back to the beginning, the very beginning. She began to wonder openly to herself what would happen if she graduated and there simply was nothing *there* afterwards. There had always been a next thing and thing after that but what if this was it? What if she had already peaked in life at the tender age of, Jesus, 21? Getting into UVA would be her greatest accomplishment after it was all said and done. Maybe she had been living these past few years on the downslope, unaware that the lustre had already worn off just that bit.

She constantly imagined the nightmare scenario of graduation. It would be May on the Lawn, after all the pageantry, and the hats flung into the air and everyone else was going somewhere and when they would ask her so where next? and she couldn't avoid it any longer. Would she shrug, play it cute somehow? Was she the type of person to make light of that, of being a failure? Would the other party then turn away, embarrassed on her behalf, maybe hiding a smirk—Brooke's stomach turned. She hugged herself, her crying body. I've got to be able to hold it together. Maybe I won't go to graduation? Mom would understand. Dad? I could just fly out to see him. He only wants to spend time with me ...

Brooke continued fondling that nightmare, somehow transfixed, and concluded that it'd be less trouble to lie. She'd go to graduation and simply tell people she had something lined up back home. Something corporate, don't ask haha.

Regardless she felt she would burst if she held it in any longer.

Her mother was more surprised than upset. Sweetie it sounded like New York was a sure thing. The last time we talked, you said you received the grant for minority women. Mom. We only applied. We don't hear back for a while. For a while? You have a business plan. You had tee shirts made, my God! This, this, I thought you said this other girl, this Fulbright Scholar, she doesn't know what she's doing? I thought she did Mom. I don't know anymore ...

January nearing its end, she carried a heavy feeling that she'd missed out on a string of fabulous opportunities, things suited exactly to her that were gobbled up by less qualified, less deserving people, and they were sitting back —she could just picture their heads tossed back laughing, their molars.

She grew bitter and scrounged around her emails and the bulletin boards and the career center for a good week, determined that there was still something out there left for her. A few times she believed she'd found something but would learn that the deadline had passed or that she was ineligible because she was a fourth year. It seemed that all the best stuff went to juniors. What was I doing last year when all these things were available to me? She thought of pointless club meetings and post meeting gossip sessions and a class that had occupied so much of her time and worrying ... She beat herself up about not keeping up and made an oath to herself to be more vigilant about every grant opportunity, program, paid internship that had to do with ... well, she didn't know exactly, which was the thing.

She knew she qualified into a number of advantageous categories: female, Hispanic, multi-racial, and so on. And if she were so inclined, she could make a case for herself as black somewhere down the line. Look at my father. Where do you think I got this curly hair from?

Yet there didn't seem to be a direction to any of her searching. She could be anyone doing anything. And as much as it hurt to admit this, it didn't even have to be in New York. Just a city somewhere with a pulse. She could see herself in DC. Lots of UVA people were going up there, right? What was she able to tolerate? Anywhere but Chesapeake. No way she was going back home. Not after four years of college. How would that look?

Brooke got in touch with her friends in the Latino Student Union. She got back into Sustained Dialogue, attended a meeting for the Minority Women Coalition. Everyone was happy to see her again.

She ran into some friends who were involved in the Black Student Alliance. They were headed to dinner and

Brooke joined them. Someone asked if Titus was taking her to Winter Ball this year, and before Brooke could respond, the person was scolded for not being up to date. That's okay, we were together for a little while last semester but you know. Gave it one last shot? You could say that. They said she should go anyway.

The people around the table who were going without a date were identified to her, and they all perked up. Yeah come with us. We have a room. Where is it? The Omni. Alice and Sharif will be there. You remember ... and other names were listed out to her, people she knew. Normal people. Brooke said she needed to find something to wear. It would be short notice. She didn't bring anything from back home. They teased her for being dramatic just now. Girl don't even front. You can grab something off the rack at Ross and still look good.

Later that week Brooke was at the Fashion Square Mall trying on dresses. She crossed her arms at the wrists, peeled off her sweater. Assessing herself in the dressing room mirror, she turned at an angle, stepping back and turning her body another way, manipulating the light and shadow against her skin until she wasn't so bothered by what she saw. She tried on 4 dresses, none evoking strong feelings from her but the people she was with really liked the copper one so she went with that. It was asymmetrical but not in a modern way. Girl you have beautiful arms. Doesn't she? Don't ask me to raise them. Hahahaha ...

Fighting to get her seatbelt fastened over her coat, her cellphone rang. Susan's number. It'd been weeks. Weeks she had been forsaking her time being a pretty little ethnic mascot who would lend some street cred to this clueless whitegurl's urban ambitions.

Brooke answered anyway. Susan wanted to know if Brooke was sitting down. Well I'm sitting in my car hahaha. It's sooo cold out hahaha. After a dramatic pause, Susan announced that Johnson & Johnson wanted to meet next week. Brooke screamed OH MY GOD and said that she was coming over right now to celebrate. Oh honey I'm not in Charlottesville. You're with Ryan? I was having such an awful week girl, I had to see him. Susan apologized, saying she felt she'd been a brat last time they talked—Oh no you weren't—Yes I was. Then Johnson & Johnson just called and you were the first person I thought of. I still remember that night on the Lawn, telling you about this vision. You're as much a part of this as I am. Brooke laughed warmly. I was so sore for days. I hadn't done a grand jeté in months haha-haha. Me too hahaha. I won't start up again hahaha.

Susan said she would call back because her boyfriend didn't like it when she was on the phone so long. She and Susan said love you to each other before getting off.

24

Winter Ball was the Saturday after the Super Bowl. A few of Titus's boys drove down from Manassas. It was the afternoon when they arrived. Vonny didn't get off work till 9. Meanwhile they chilled at the apartment. Passing around that 151. They passed around the bottle watching TV. Bare arms and wifebeaters and doo rags. Giddy inside but not making too big a deal on the outside but their minds wowing about all the college freeks at the Winter Ball tonight. A picture being formed in each of their minds.

A shot of 151 down the chute. Someone checked the time. Another asked the time. Heads nodded. Turn down the volume on the TV because someone wanted to hear a song on the laptop. The iron was plugged into the wall. The bottle kept going around. The more they hit the Bacardi the skronger they felt. Like diesel in their veins.

The TV turned back up. Aint nobody wanna hear that shit yo. You aint feelin that? Nah. That nigga get on my nerves ... Another shot down the chute. Bare arms and wifebeaters. Someone kneeling over the towel on the floor pushing the iron up and down a pair of heavyweight denim turned inside out. Another shot down the chute. Eyes watery. Grins widening. They couldn't sit still. They looked at the TV. Had to stand up. Bopping their heads. Swinging their arms. Muttering lyrics and hooks and swinging their arms punching palms and yo what time your boy say he was getting off? Took a shot. Felt so on point. Like you couldn't believe.

They dressed. Say college nigga you still know how to throw em? Ha as if I forgot. Titus and P both peeled off their Coogies draping their garments carefully on the backs of chairs pinching right at the shoulder seams and laying them gently so as not to incur any wrinkles. They went to the hallway and raised their dukes. Palms open. Feinting. Bobbing. Twitching their shoulders. Laughing when the other flinched at a feint. Giddy. Sliding around the floor on their socks almost stumbling and laughing. And it was midlaugh when P got caught—Titus flicking his hand out not meaning to make contact, well maybe just a tap if anything, a graze across the nigga cheek—but the 151 (3 or 4 shots by this point, Titus lost count) had already distorted his motor skills to such an extent that the harmless flick of his hand landed as a loud palmslap flush against P's cheek —WHAP—and the niggas back in the den immediately ooooooooed and shouted YALL NIGGAS REALLY GETTIN AT IT HUH? Giggling but incensed, P flailed back at Titus, really really trying to lick him good but only landing on forearms and they both had big huge grins on their faces and were giggling and their feet sliding and P grabbed Titus's arm to hold down his guard—Aye watchu doon nigga?—and with a big grin on his face P shot through with his right arm really tryna pop that muthafucka in the lip. Nigga I swear you get softer and softer being up here. But Titus wiggled and blocked whatever P was throwing (the open hand eventually curling into a light balled fist that caught Titus flush on the side) and Titus reached out with his leg to trip P and P said aye aye don't dump me nigga and the way he said it sounding like a bitch made Titus let go and that's when P dove at him and they wrestled on the ground bumping against the walls ... Panting, undershirts dirty, they stopped and went back to the den. They cracked Heines and looked at the TV debating on who got the best of who, both their faces sweaty and eyes bloodshot while everyone else watched for the hundredth millionth time the same shit on the TV ... Someone asked the time and was told the time by somebody else. Yo how come your boy work so gotdamn late? I know. Who the fuck work till 9 on a Saturday? What he do, work at the 7-11 or something? Someone gripped the bottle of 151, took a shot and passed it. They wiped their mouths and looked at the TV, all of them sitting there in their Coogies, smelling of baby powder and Coolwater cologne and liquor, adjusting the knots in the backs of their doo rags and waited like that for Vonny to get off work so they could get to the Winter Ball. They came all this way from Manassas shit. Won't be nuttin left allem other niggas there already. First come first serve. Titus sitting with his elbows propped on his knees surrounded by his niggas from back home feeling good man. Not talking. Nothing more to say. Listening and staring at and eventually through the TV his eyes becoming unfocused and his head numbing around the fact that ol girl Brooke would be there.

* * *

When Vonny came home he got dressed quick in his 3/4 length blue gators and his blue Coogi with the hood attachment and a pair of black dusty Girbauds and they rolled up to the Omni.

Vonny called somebody and they were let in a side door and they took the elevator up and stumbled loudly onto the main floor where an old guard sitting on a stool perked up and raised his voice towards them as they walked away ignoring. Excuse me. EXCUSE ME. Can I help yaw find something? They followed the sound of music until they got to the ballroom and saw the couples on the parquet floor 2 stepping. Females in tubegowns balancing tall plastic sculptures of weave on top of their heads and the fellas had on cream tuxedos with long tails in the back and it was enough to make a nigga feel overgrown and underdressed. They kept looking. All couples. It was kinda weak. They walked around the perimeter of the parquet, agitated and looking all at everyone. Hassan said fuckit pass me the Bacardi and they all took swigs and felt less self conscious. Skrong again. Titus's boys wandered onto the parquet bobbing their heads and rubbing their palms together trying to see what they could pick off. Then the DJ put on some quiet storm and the couples clutched each other tighter under the shower of strings and crooning echoes and them niggas leaked off the floor getting the hint. What's good with the freeks playboy? Vonny said you looking at em. Larry said let's see what's good upstairs.

They took the elevator up and found themselves walking up and down the hallways looking at the rooms with the open doors and people was drinking in there and listening to music and laughing loud and having themselves a good ol time. They kept walking up and down the hallways looking in every room avoiding the rooms with niggas inside until they came upon a room with nuttin but shorties in there.

They hollered at them for a lil bit. Sitting on the edge of the bed conversations. Letting them sip a lil of that Henny and everyone was having a good time laughing. One darkskin shorty waved for everyone to quiet down. She had to have everybody say their names. I don't got a prollem sharing my liquor with nobody. Only thing I ask is that you tell me your name. Niggas gave names. Suppressed guilty smiles. An arm over shorty waist and calculations were being made ... so there 7 niggas and 3 shorties ... and then niggas continued laughing and being pleasant and kind and these bitches was a little dumb too and all them niggas was giving each other high fives in they head, exchanging glances and quick smirks and hoping nobody would fuck this up. One of the shorties got up and her wrist was grabbed. Where you going? I told my man I would only be a few minutes ... and with the battle of attrition being waged there was 2 shorties left in that room and 5 niggas and them shorties was at least 7 drinks in and a nigga started rubbing on a thigh and she smiled. Purring. That feel good shorty? She smiled meltingly, the tip of her tongue lingering between her teeth. Then rubbing her breast. Giggling, but your friend is looking. P didn't even know that nigga over there. He started sucking on her neck and pushing her down onto the covers and straddling her waist. Pinning her down like that and undoing his belt. Someone cut the lights. Another someone closed the door.

* * *

Titus and Vonny hung back at the edge of the parquet floor and passed the 151 between them. Brooke had arrived. She was here with a big group, and Titus was trying to parse who was paired with who, but there didn't seem much rhyme or reason the way girls was dancing on girls, and on boys, different boys, a few he knew for a fact was gay, a few he suspected was brothers on the DL, except this one pretty boy he'd never seen before. A real smiley nigga. 360 waves rippling in the strobe lights. Long points on the sides. This pretty nigga kept dancing in Brooke's orbit. His back to her. Then right beside her. Stepping on the same part of the beat. It only seemed inevitable. Three songs in, a reggae joint, was when it happened.

Titus frowning suddenly, Nigga I feel like you over there analyzing me. Vonny laughing. Stick is you just gonna stare at her the whole time? Titus ignored him and continued staring. He grew impatient that the bottle wasn't being passed fast enough. When it was passed faster, he was annoyed. Nigga I already put my hand up! When I put my hand up, that means I'm good. He stared at Brooke some more, then covered his face laughing. Comical man. Uh huh. Titus said he had to take a piss. Yo that's a good idea.

They looked for the toilet in the typical places you would imagine a bathroom being. But away from the ballroom and out in the bright tiled reflections of the hotel, they realized how bent they were.

Titus carried on about Brooke. You know the thing about Brooke is she real manipulative. Yo go head with that stick hahaha. I'm serious. You see the way she glanced back over her shoulder. See? C'mon stick it won't that deep. You gotta let go of that. Gotdamn Vonny I aint sayin it's deep I'm just sayin it's aggravating. Yo but I'm just laughing at her inside man. Shit is comical to me. Like yeah I see what you tryna do Brooke. Go ahead and try. Pure comedy.

Someone told them the mens bathroom was past the waterfall and they looked there and somehow got lost and had walked into a laundry room and had to retrace their steps, bracing themselves against the wall to walk straight and followed the sound of bass until they were at the entrance to the ballroom where the ice sculpture was. They looked at it. They were dizzy and really had to piss bad. Beginning to feel their teeth chatter it was stinging so much.

It was Vonny's idea to go back past the waterfall over there where there was some plants and it was dark. You go first stick man and I'll watch out for you. Titus unzipped. We good? Yeah you good. Then Titus kept lookout while Vonny went in a different plant. Vonny's teeth were chattering and the tips of his fingers tingled and he moaned. Haha. Couldn't help myself stick. Ha. Feel so good cuh.

Zipping himself up he emerged from behind the plant. 2 security guards were talking to Titus. Vonny was about to go back behind the plant but one of the guards said Hey you. The guard tapped his wrist. Let's see it. See what? Wristband. Vonny glanced at his wrist. Then the other one. Began patting himself. I had mine on just a second ago. What about you? Titus shrugged. Gentlemen this is a private event. I'm going to have to see wristbands. Or else what?

Another guard approaching with a hand up. Sir I think it's time to go. How do you know I don't have a wristband? C'mon sir it's time to go. I've been watching you the whole night. The guard placed his hand on Titus's shoulder. Titus pushed it away. The guard put his hand on the shoulder again and Titus slapped it off quicker and removing his Coogi and undershirt and squaring up to the guard chest to chest, Do that shit just one more time, Vonny holding him back going stick man ease up. More guards walked up going Whoa whoa what's going on? He doesn't have a wristband. Sir this is a private event. We're going to have to see a wristband if not we'll have to ask you to leave. I'm just minding my own business and this dood want to put his hands on me. We have to ask you to leave. Fine.

Titus picked up his clothes on the floor and started towards the elevators. Where you going? My ride is upstairs. You can't go up there. You need a wristband to go up there. Why don't you call em? Titus didn't answer right away and the guards approached again—Yeah I thought so—with their hands on him steering him away from the elevators and Titus jerked around, I gotta get my friends they're up there. No I think you should stay here. Get your hands off me. They pressed him against the wall and told him to calm down. Now how am I gonna get home huh? He sat down on the ground as the guards stood around him, talking to each other, some looking away. They were all waiting, then a few cops walked up in their heavy boots and belts jangling and scratchy radios. Double taking at the fact he was shirtless. Let me guess he's had something to drink tonight. I haven't asked but I wouldn't be surprised. The cop bent over to talk to him. Can you tell me your name? Titus looked at him and said nothing. Sir I'm going to need you to cooperate here. I didn't do nothing. I was minding my business. Then that guy, yeah you, grabbed me. Titus looked up at the ceiling, blinking hard, trying to gather himself. Look officer. My father police. Retired. I know the drill. I know no rentacop can put they hands on you. That dood over there just a hallway monitor. Sir the Omni security has informed me that you don't have a wristband and if that's the case, I'm going to have to take you down to the station for trespassing. WHAT?!? Titus covered his face, distraught. But I didn't do anything officer. Why you taking his word over mine??? He clamored to stand up but the cop pushed him back down and continued to talk slow at him. Sir how many drinks have you had tonight? Titus looked past the cop who was talking at him and saw all the security guards standing around. All the cops. All those people just for some stupid shit like this. All over a fucking wristband. It infuriated and offended him deeply how big a deal they were making over this stupid shit. C'mon. Over a wristband? How many people do it take just to ask me to leave? The more he thought the angrier he got so he rolled halfway to his side and stood up, panting and bracing himself against the wall and the floor was spinning. He lurched towards the glass doors. Whoa where are you going? Move I'm going home. He stuck out his arms swimming past whatever bodies were in his way. He felt himself being lifted off his feet and pinned to the wall. Sir I need you to sit back down. Move outta my way. You said I was trespassing so I'm just gonna leave then if I don't belong here. He jerked his arm against another restraining set of hands and they shoved him against the wall again, several more hands holding him down, their boots squeaking against the tile and their hot breaths loud in his face. Titus began kicking his legs out and thrashing and yelling LET ME GO and there were a buncha people in the foyer watching and yelling hey it's just one of him and a dozen a yall. With the crowd of onlookers edging closer a few cops let go of Titus and had to shout for people to move back and when one cop pulled the stick out of his belt the other did too and the crowd started pissing and moaning this is police brutality and someone else laughingly in the back cupped his hands and shouted FUCK THE PO-LICE and someone finally looked at who was being shoved against the wall back there and said hey aint that Titus? People jostling to get a closer look, pressing in on the cops, squeezing against one another in their formal wear, butler tails and 3 piece suits and long gowns and most of the girls had taken off their heels because it was that time of the night already. Yeah IT IS him. Get Brooke hurry. People clapping their hands trying to get the attention of the cops.

Officer. Hey officer. He's a student here. Then a buncha people started yelling that, yelling it angrily HE GO HERE! HE GO TO UVA!!!! and the cops shrugged and said it made no difference. Eric Hatley managed to get to the front of the crowd and with an arm out trying to assure the police officer that he wasn't going to make any problems, he told the officer look my name is Eric Hatley. My organization is co-sponsoring this event. What seems to be the problem? The officer didn't hear him so Eric turned to one of the security standing near and asked. Trespassing. Trespassing? Yup. He doesn't have a wristband. Laughing demonstratively, Is that all? Eric began reaching into his back pocket for his wallet to pay saying if that's the discrepancy here and as he moved toward the cop with his hand in his pocket he was jabbed with the stick right between the cords in his neck. He bent over gasping dryly because of the pain and the crowd was shouting WHY'D YOU HIT HIM FOR???!!!!?? and shoving forward and Titus heard all that and with his head spinning and the hard floor under his feet sloshing back and forth wildly he thrashed his body even harder against the restraining arms shouting his lungs bare and he didn't even know, couldn't hear what he was yelling, only felt deeply that he was a live current of energy, so alive and increasing with energy and getting skronger and all these people around him shouting were feeding him pure strength and it came down to his mind and if he knew in his mind he could do it he could throw all these faggots off him who was holding him down. Just toss him with his godly strength feeling the power in every fabric of muscle and bone and he screamed YAH NIGGAS BETTER GET OFF ME!!!!! and he was beginning to stand against the weight of several full grown men and was slowly dragging the pile and finally one of the cops said to himself fuckit this is a clown show and

popped the tag off his can of spray and stuck it in Titus's
face and triggered the stream. Titus jerked his head away
and collapsed to the floor. The burning shot straight
through him and his eyes shut and his throat narrowed and
he couldn't breathe or scream but could only squeeze his
eyes and teeth together and the shouting inside himself was
so intense it roiled his organs and his bladder and his
sphincter gave. Suddenly everyone in the room could taste
the hot pepper in the air and the crowd scrambled covering
their faces and some coughing and screaming through their
coughs with tears streaking down their faces and a few
titters of laughter, and Eric was still bent over gasping trying
not to swallow and there were several sets of hands rubbing
and consoling him and in the scramble he was clipped and
fell over and helpless he was choking on the pepper in the
air and was pulled to his feet crying and Vonny the whole
time was too slow and too bent to react to any of this and
was still shouting Yo stick man be easy! far past the point of
no return but the pepper in the air snapped Vonny out of it
and moved his legs and he was bounding down some stairs
skipping 2 and 3 steps with the echoes of wild slapping feet
and shouting in that stairwell giving him more urgency. And
meanwhile Titus's boys were still upstairs roaming the hallways peeking room to room after shorty had passed out.

25

At some point after the spraying, Titus could open his eyes again and see the other men in holding, all of them sleeping curled up on the metal benches and on the floor. There was a dull cloudy ache in his head. The clean cotton shirt he was wearing, it wasn't his. His wrists were tender. He was incredibly thirsty. Upset at himself, upset for being here, he dug down for some Psalms, did some promising to God. The next morning he was released on bond.

On the drive home Vonny told him that Brooke wanted to see him right away.

He called his PO first. His PO thanked him. You don't want me learning this from somebody else. She asked him if he was leaving anything out. Was he on something? Nah just liquors. Did he resist arrest? Course not. She said the disorderly probably wouldn't stick, just the trespassing. She didn't see a need to call a proceeding. I went to college too I know how it goes. But please Titus don't put me in a position where I have to violate you. You're my college boy.

Before hanging up she asked one more time if he was leaving anything out, if there would be anything on the police report that would surprise her. He said no.

He had gotten in an hour or two of sleep before the phone rang. It was Brooke asking if she could come over.

She came over and they sat in the den with Vonny comparing stories of what went down last night. Titus said all he remembered, which wasn't much. He said he didn't even remember seeing her there. Brooke said she didn't believe him. Aye I already told you the last thing I remember is standing by the dance floor with Vonny and looking out at them people dancing. But not me right? Nah. Like I said, me just standing out there with Vonny and next thing I know I got these niggas kneelin on me. Like a dozen doods and I don't even know if I knew they was police at that point. I thought I may have been getting jumped. I just know I can't barely breathe and my face on fire.

Brooke shared what she remembered from the night before, omitting the part about being there with her date Debon and Titus staring at them the whole time, but she kept Vonny in the corner of her eye and Vonny nodded along looking at the floor, his hairless babysoft cheeks, and his eyes, hooded, quiet, was he high? she couldn't tell, maybe that's the Korean side. Her account next focused on the confrontation with the police, which she didn't see herself completely but she had talked to some people and was still talking to some people about.

Titus nodded tiredly. She stopped a few times and asked if he remembered this part of her story and he said no. Again she stopped and asked and he said no and she looked at him wide eyed, really you don't remember???

Titus was getting annoyed but was too tired to raise his voice. He just shook his head and chuckled, It was that 151 man I know it. Vonny chuckled and covered his face still chuckling. She said she had talked to some people and there was going to be a vigil for Eric Hatley at the Rotunda tonight at 7. Vigil? He's scheduled to be out of the hospital any time now. Just in time for it. He's supposed to speak. Eric Hatley? What happened to him? Titus was sitting up now and Vonny said yeeaah, stretching, grinning, and said what had happened to Eric. I was standin right there when it happened too. Titus was frowning, his head cocked to the side as he heard how Eric tried to show a cop his student ID to prove he went here and maybe the cop would at least listen and not arrest nobody—Hold up you say Eric reached for his wallet? Yeah. Show me. Vonny shrugged and demonstrated without getting up from the loveseat, his leg still thrown over one of the arms.

Though it hurt his ribs, Titus laughed incredulously. You tellin me this dood???? talkin to a uniformed police officer???? actually stops??? reaches with his HAND back here??? LIKE THIS??!!?? Vonny covered his mouth chuckling, now realizing, yeah I know right haha. Brooke asked what's so funny about Eric being attacked and hospitalized? Titus asked that he'd been attacked and hospitalized for what? For losin his gotdamn mind that's what. Shit nigga. I'm telling you Vonny. Some of these niggas aint never spent a day in the hood. They need to go visit some time. Get them instincts sharp.

Watching those 2 laugh Brooke readied in her mind ... yes, if she brought that up he would definitely feel it ... no that wouldn't be mean no, it would just be stating the obvious ... but she said nothing and brought up the vigil again. It's not just for Eric. It's for anyone in the community who has been the victim of police brutality. Titus shook his head. Brooke asked him to just listen. Aye I know yall mean well but I talked to my PO and I'm just happy she aint violating me. I aint tryna push my luck in no organized protest. It's not a protest, it's a vigil.

She did some explaining and he sat back listening. She said it would be a good idea if he shared his story. It would encourage others to come forward. He rolled his eyes and she kept pushing through and got to the part about Eric working on a letter to the editor for the Cav Daily. Please tell that nigga don't put my name on it. Well it'll be hard not to Ty. Nah you know what Brooke, I aint tryna win no award for having my ass beat by no cops. It's like every time I fuck up there's gotta be a whole sit down and discussion and post-game analysis and I'm like shit let's just keep it movin. No one's putting you on the spot Ty. You don't have to speak tonight. You just have to show up and show your support and after that we'll grab something to eat. You know I don't like going to these protests. How many times do I have to tell you it's not a protest? Shit you know them boys will be out there either way. Titus smirked and looked over at Vonny. More than 3 of us in one place and they put the BOLO out on the radio. Vonny laughed and said yup. She looked at them, BOLO? Yeah be on the look out.

They bout died laughing. She was real heated watching them and she brought up Titus's personal statement for law school, how he was okay sharing his story there ... and she left it at that. Titus stopped laughing. Whatchu tryna say? Oh nothing. It just looks convenient from my perspective. Oh you always do that Brooke. That's like your line right? Convenient???

Vonny looked down at his phone and got up mumbling that he had forgotten to make a call. The front door shut behind him.

That convenient shit you always use that on me. Like I'm some big hypocrite here. Ty I'm just wondering why there's an inconsistency. Inconsistent? You callin me fake to my face. In my own fuckin crib? Ty I don't understand. Why are you so reluctant? It seems you have a problem with us but we're the ones out there fighting for you. I don't got no problem man. Well it sounds like you do. You and Vonny, sitting here laughing about it the whole time. Like everything is so amusing. Meanwhile there are people who look exactly like you getting—Oh stop it Brooke, just stop it—No, you think you can slide around laughing this off like there are no consequences. What? Me? Me, I can laugh. I earned the right. I almost get violated and here your boujee ass go talking bout consequences. You aint even black neither. You Spanish. And only half too, don't even get me started. Your ass can't even speak—BROOKE SCREAMED and Titus watched her with outward indifference but he immediately regretted what he had said, and sat shaking his head in the ensuing silence, the offending words repeating in his mind. He apologized.

I don't care what you think of my background. I'm not one of these mixed kids who can't figure out their identity. I know who I am. I'm not ashamed. Unlike you. When your friends are around, you're different. I'm not saying anything new here Ty.

Hanging his head he said he didn't want to fight no more and just wanted to know, and I don't want you to take this the wrong way, but what do you think will actually come out this demonstration? Look at me. Look who you talking to here Brooke. She looked at him straight on, her legs hugged to her chest in the chair, and she felt his earnestness.

He began talking about his father, his voice lower, mumbling so she couldn't hear some parts but she did not interrupt his speaking, which felt to her like a confession, though they'd talked about his father many times before. Man they made a whole big fuss about my pop being the first black cop in Manassas and you know what they did to him? Didn't matter he won in court. They just figured out another way to keep him in his place. Now you talkin bout a *vigil*. So you think holding some candles gonna make a difference? Eric lil letter, that'll accomplish somethin? Yall really makin moves huh.

She said she understood where he was coming from but if his conclusion was to do nothing, to let something like this slide, well I can't go along with that. We have to do something Ty. It would be wrong of us to sit by while bad cops prowl the streets. These are bad cops that did this to you and Eric, not good ones like your dad. Now think, are you honestly saying we should be passive and let them get away with this? What'll they do next? Take someone's life? Hold up I'm not saying we should be passive—Then what do we do Titus? He thought about it, recognizing the insinuation, however subtle, that he'd been called a bitch, but he no longer wanted to fight. I guess nothin wrong with showing support. I still think there's something more, I don't know. I can't see the ignorance stoppin.

He walked her back to her place. They stood outside her door, his hands pulled inside his tee shirt, arms tight at his side, and he was hopping around and shivering. She said he didn't have to come all the way up the stairs. Nah it aint hurt too bad, nothing broke. It'll be easier going down. Isn't it scary Ty? You never used to black out like that. I was watching you shouting and yelling and your eyes, they were open, and come to find out you're not even conscious during all of that. He fought the urge to correct her, to say I wasn't sleepwalking, just bent as hell. Yeah girl. I know it's bad. She hugged him and kissed him on the cheek. He liked the way she looked just now, her Winter Ball hair still intact. She smelled good too. He didn't want to say bye yet. You hongry? She said she was going to grab something after the vigil, remember? He said call me before you go. I might feel better. No you just rest. Your face, I can tell there's still some swelling.

* * *

There was sleet that night so the vigil was rescheduled for the next night and by that point Titus had changed his mind. He rode with Brooke down to central grounds.

The night was clear and deep black against the stars. The gathering of people came halfway up the steps and everyone had gloves on and shuffled side to side singing with their candles. The song died down and the group of people near the top of the stairs conversed and decided the next song, bellowing out the first line and the rest of the gathering caught up in a few measures, wavering and singing like before. When one candle went out another candle was tipped toward it and the flame came alive again and the feeling of thanks and kinship pervaded, the sense of something grander, nobler and truer being summoned and witnessed and beheld. There wasn't a heaviness or an anger as everyone stood there singing. Titus had outlined to Brooke beforehand that he was gonna stand off to the side and wasn't gonna give no speeches so don't even try it cos I will walk out. He stood off to the side now holding his candle in one hand, unsinging, unsmiling, unwaving his body back and forth but he could feel something softening inside him. Brooke was with some of the main people at the top of the stairs arranging the audio equipment and he was looking at her pointing and delegating and he felt deep inside him there wasn't nothing wrong being here. It was nice coming together like this. There were two university police standing off to the side with their armscrossed talking

to each other. Same ones he seen around. But he wasn't
bothered. He couldn't help but think of church for some
reason. His mother and her Sunday hats. They used to go to
the First Methodist but his mother said they talk too much
there so they started going to the nondenominational
church behind the Manassas Mall. It took some getting used
to. The TVs. The loudspeakers. But he supposed all
churches was getting that way now. At the top of the steps
some dood walked up to the microphone stand and started
playing the trumpet. Titus recognized the song. Dood was
good. When he was finished everyone got back to singing.
Then during the singing people's heads started turning.
Titus squinted down the Lawn where everyone seemed to
be looking and he could make out a dood coming up slowly
on crutches up the right colonnade. Some doods were at his
sides helping him. People kept singing and turning around
and looking over there and it took Titus a second to put
together the fact that it was Eric. The man of the hour. One
person handed their candle off to a neighbor and jogged
down the colonnades to help. Then another person jogged
down there too. Pretty soon you couldn't see Eric, just the
contingent of bodies marching past the columns, the candle
flames flicking back and forth across their bodies. As the
contingent approached the singing died down and Eric
emerged. He was hopping along carefully on his crutches,
solemn faced and his whole body panting. He had to take a
break. There were some cheers and Eric broke into a smile
and resumed hopping along. Some people tried to talk him
out of going up the Rotunda steps but he waved them off.
He handed his crutches to somebody and made like he was
gonna hop on one foot the whole way up the steps. Like that
people flew under his arms and helped him up and
arranged him at a spot all the way at the top of the steps

between the big columns where Brooke was standing off next to the loudspeaker. Eric was handed a lit candle and he began speaking to the crowd. The first thing he said was something to the effect of look around you, look at all the strength around you. Something to the effect. Though we all hurt together, we hope together whatever whatever. Tonight is the night for healing.

Titus couldn't exactly hear the words because Eric needed to lean closer into the microphone so he walked around the side of the crowd up the steps and was close enough to see Eric reading from a folded up set of stapled pages, looked about 4 or 5, which made Titus wonder how long it took this dood to write all that and if someone helped him. It's been going on for too long and sadly many in our community are unaware of this reality ... Titus was mainly listening to see if Eric would mention him by name. He had told Brooke over and over that he did not want Eric blowing up his spot. By no means necessary. Brooke I'm telling you don't make me hafta go over there and straighten a nigga up. Oh stop it. You'll do no such thing ... Someone was standing there turning the pages for Eric because his other hand was holding the candle. When they got to the part where he was going over the events of Winter Ball, Titus held his breath expecting his name to be called and Eric just said he was intervening on the behalf of another student and left it at that. Relieved, Titus tuned out a lil and was just watching the dood read, not even listening. Looking real close tryna figure exactly what injuries this nigga had from getting poked in the neck with the night stick. Didn't see no marks on his face. Studying the soft elastic sleeve around one knee, studying. Was that it? The nigga sprained his shit crying on the floor like a lil bitch? Ha. You don't see me cryin. Them boys sprayed me point blank, threw me up against the wall. One nigga kept kneein me in the nuts. My ass actually went to jail too. I'm the one who actually was taken into custody. It was such a good point Titus looked around at the people standing next to him as if they'd heard it. They were looking up at Eric, completely immersed, and in their eyes, the flame flicking back and forth, Titus saw, and he was growing angry for seeing them, he saw tears. Tears! What? For Eric? Shit I had cuffs on my wrists. I still got burn marks from that. I'm the one who spent the night sleeping on a metal bench not him. Shit I get locked up and this nigga up here talkin like he Nelson Mandela. He looked around grinning a lil, mad and crazy feelin.

Titus continued listening and he was conscious of the fact he was getting agitated. He didn't know why. He was watching this dood read from his speech and he couldn't shake from his mind the idea that this dood was being a phony. Titus began listening to the words, preying on the next line. By virtue of my skin color ... I stand in closer proximity towards police violence ... Please. He was soon disgusted by this dood and was not ashamed by it. He reveled in the fact. With your faggoty ass scarf talkin how you walk in fear of police violence. By the virtue of my skin color ... O stop it. Just stop it nigga. No one mistaking your faggoty pea coat wearin ass for some hood nigga. I see them tight gay ass turtlenecks you wore to Daniels class man, quit tryna fool these people. Walking down the street no one mistaking you from ME. Pssshh. People aint that gullible now. Nobody scared of your corny ass don't even front. Only reason they poked you cos you dumb enough to reach. Pssssh. Whatchu expect? Why the fuck you reach for yo wallet you dummy? That's the first thing my pop taught me. You talking to the law, don't you ever EVER EVER for any gotdamn reason reach back there. You should know that nigga. Now look at you. Cryin. You fake niggas stay profiting off our backs man. Titus felt his face collapsing into his chest, into inescapable gravity, and even the taste in his mouth, literally the flavor in there, began to change and tasted wretched and foul, and he was shaking and buzzing all over, each molecule vibrating so loudly the sound in his ears closed up. Brooke was still standing up there behind the loudspeaker with her head down. She wiped away a tear from her cheek and Titus said that's it. He had to walk away.

He felt his legs moving hurriedly down the steps and down the colonnade and he ducked down a side alley until he reached the main street. He was bracing himself for a confrontation. When Brooke would come up yelling behind him and she'd tell her that this was a mistake. Why? Don't ask. And playing the scene a different way in his mind, angrier and there would be shouting—QUIT TRYNA CHANGE ME! YOU KNOW I AINT WANNA COME TO THIS SHIT SO WHY KEEP FORCING ME! I AINT LIKE YO FUCKIN FRIENDS AIGHT!!!—and she'd run away crying and him thinking good I told you. So he kept his legs moving faster and faster and he heard no one coming up behind him. A half hour later his hands and ears and nose were numb and painful, his boots soaked completely so that the suede he knew was ruined by the salt. At least he was home now and safe. He was feeling so thankful and happy that there was still some brew left over from Winter Ball. He called Vonny and told him to pick up another 12 pack when he got off work. They sat in the den hitting the brews and letting the brews hit them and Titus told him all about Eric and his lil boo boo in his leg and he finally said aloud his line about Nelson Mandela and Vonny bout died laughing.

26

The television flickered in his room as Eunice drifted to sleep in his arms. Joe Reed looked at the screen, not fully absorbing what was happening in the movie, what was being said. He was concentrating on not waking her up. He couldn't cough or shift his weight or nothing funny. Everything in him said to make sure she stayed like this. At peace. Sleeping in his arms. Not a care in the world right now. His arms fell asleep. He kept thinking over and over how nice this was. To be here at this very moment in time. Like this. He won't supposed to be here. His mind was casting back, nothing in particular coming but a general sense of turmoil long behind him and warmth all enveloping. Loved ones looking down on him. He luxuriated in those sensations, a tinge of pain creeping in eventually, which he knew would come and he cast it aside, and concentrated on the face of his mother and his brother serene and lovingly looking down on him but it was too much, seeing the two of them, and he came out of it, watching the movie on the TV again and looking down at shorty sleeping in his arms.

He began to cough. Squeezing himself to stifle the sounds. Eunice turned her head and swallowed, What time is it? Iown know. How long I been sleeping? A lil while. Eunice blinking up at him. She put one hand up to his cheek. What happened Joe? Nuttin, no that's nuttin. Are you crying Joe? Nah. She sat up onto his chest and looked at the TV with him. They watched and watched, warm in the room, laughed at the stupid jokes, his mother and brother's presence receding.

* * *

Vonny was due in Petersburg for another clothing rotation. The jackets and jerseys slung over his shoulder, he was bout ready to dip when Titus came out his room scratching his ribs asking if he could come too. Vonny said he wouldn't be back till late. Yeah I know.

In the car each leaned to his own window, the seat reclined way back, and drew his hand occasionally to his chin like there was something deep to reflect on. From time to time they glanced when a car slid up on them on the freeway, holding the glare if it was other niggas, nonchalantly looking away if it wasn't. Untalking and content most of the drive to Petersburg, they spoke to each other in the dead air between tracks. Their most prolonged conversations were about what to play next. Vonny always forgot to label his burnt disks but could remember by the placement of the disk in the stack, and if that didn't work, by the scuff marks.

Right around Hadensville Vonny did wonder about the terms of Titus's probation. Didn't they say he couldn't leave the county? It was so obvious a question Vonny didn't ask it aloud, so he went on assuming what was convenient, that Titus had worked something out with his PO. Truthfully a part of him was scared to ask. He kept to the speed limit.

Shawn was in a good mood with Titus around. Happy someone new could hear him bust on his lil brother. Hahaha Shawn you crazy nigga ... Vonny told me your girl expecting. Yeah, you should see her. She about to go on maternity leave. She could barely get up the stairs here. They hit the brews and it got late.

On the way back to Charlottesville, Titus mentioned a Golden Gloves Tournament up in DC. You working Friday?

A few days later they were up in DC watching the 132 pounders go at it, and feeling at ease they were out of Charlottesville again. They struck a conversation with the fight fans sitting next to them, rooted for the same hometown heroes, genuinely felt happy that their fighter had won. Afterwards there was an after party and they found themselves at a 2-story club for the grown and sexy. The one that Michael Jordan supposedly owned. They 2 stepped feeling the electricity of the place, of the possibility of ball players coming through, who knows, maybe His Airness himself. Then drawn into an orbit they danced on some cheeks and had the cheeks dance on them. There were stallions, so many about, the kind and variety impossible back at school, almost enough to go around. What was they thinking spending so much time down there in Charlottesville? All this had been going on in the wider world.

When they ran out of money, the stallions had no time for them but still they could fall back on the possibility of Mike coming through, or somebody else on the team, so they lingered, people from the fights earlier triggering blips of recognition but not enough to be friendly here.

When the club let out some females were fighting in the parking lot. It somehow stayed contained to them and on the drive home Titus and Vonny were laughing about how quickly those two got tired. At the end they were just grunting and holding each other hair and when they got separated you see shorty face all covered in snot and drool? whereas at the tournament earlier them skinny doods were bouncing around letting them fly the whole time. Could've gone a few more rounds. And wouldn't it be cool if we had the kinda bread to buy a bottle and let the hoes come to us? How much a bottle run? You seen that whip when we was pulling out? Had them Sprewells spinnin and the car chillin there on the corner?

They were so hype on the drive back the alcohol seemed to have burned through their system. They had to pull over to piss. The next morning there was no hangover. Just the taste in their mouths and in their heads of someplace else. Anyplace else. The sun couldn't go down fast enough.

Joe and Eunice were doing a lot of the same thing. Smoking in his room watching movies. Occasionally a customer came and went. He told stories growing up. New York. The different families. Things he seen. Occasionally it would get deep. She listened.

He was repeating the same stories after a while. If not the same story, the same kind. He could tell she wasn't paying attention. The way she seemed impatient with whatever they were doing. Eunice pulling away from his arms. Do we got to watch this again?

They didn't go out to eat much. They ate from wrappers. He would call her and he'd come scoop her from her mother's apartment. He called, she answered.

More and more she was having problems calling him back. She would be out somewhere. Not checking her phone a whole day. Then a day and a half. She said she was out. Declined to name with who. Joe analyzed this acting out of hers, this foolishness. It all came back to him. Something he was doing. He sorted through his memories, the small burps of conversation in the movie, other things he'd done and said in her presence, then concluded it was something he *wasn't* doing. Eunice wanted more.

He was able to get a hold of her and they made plans. He pulled up to her mother's spot. There were flowers waiting in the passenger seat. Tiny plastic dandelions sprouted from a ceramic unicorn base. It was a nice lil something he spotted while waiting in line at CVS. Eunice frowned picking up the trinket. Joe you don't gotta do all this. Nah nah gahead it's for you.

They went out to eat and he had to stop a few places before they were back at his spot, smoking and watching movies, when he dropped it on her—I never thought I could love somebody. Annoyed she had nothing to say he asked why she act sometimes like they don't go together. Oh Joe why you want to get all deep right now? Girl I tried to call you like 5 times the other—I told you I was out. Out? I got my own life too.

She said she had to use the bathroom. Was gone for a while. When she came back she was all matter-of-fact when she asked for a ride home. I gotta take care of something. I can't sleep here tonight.

He was studying her, the way her voice was, the way she was sitting so still on the edge of the bed. Who'd you call out there when you was in the bathroom? She looked at him. Don't look at me like you own know what I'm talkin bout.

She stood up gathering her stuff and muttering Joe you crazy. There was another circle of arguing and playing dumb, which led to more accusations and sulking. After a long silence her voice was kind, small, childlike. She told him she had an early doctor's appointment tomorrow, that's why. You sick? What is it? Is you late or something?

She didn't say anything right away, so he continued to ask if it was that. So you late then? How? You take a pregnancy test? She looked confused by the question, by him. His voice exploded happily, as if he had solved the problem. It was that easy, an over-the-counter pregnancy test. No need to trip hahaha. They should just go to the store right now for one. They not expensive hahaha.

He was standing up now and running his hand across his desk for his keys, You can't be jumping to no conclusions girl. Mighta been something you ate. You know the weather been crazy lately. I don't know Joe. Just take me home okay. Yo you could save yourself some money and time if we just go to the store, you know that right? He held her, asked her a few times if what he said made any sense, his voice deliberate and kind, if not enthusiastic. She kept shaking her head slowly, looking away tryna hide her face from him. As they got up to go, he noticed something. You don't want your flowers? My bad. She came out holding the unicorn base and he dropped her off at her mother's crib.

When he got home he felt the strong urge to smoke. No one was home and he smoked a Newport with the bedroom door open, expecting Vonny and Titus to come bounding in bent and laughing. He listened to cars coming and going in the lot. He looked at the TV for a while and after the movie was over he searched around his room for dutches.

He burned one out in the den looking at his hand between pulls, the way the light from the lamp fell on the bumps and grooves. The haze helped his mind get unstuck and he was more comfortable entertaining the thought that he, shit, he might could possibly be ... oh hell nah. Let's not get ahead of ourselves now. Regardless he sat thinking on it, trying on that bit of reality. Wearing fatherhood like an outfit he walked through a mall with it on, holding little shorty hand, then in a bodega getting candy, and waiting for the bus, and on the bus shorty sitting on his lap. He could see himself whispering in a little boy's ear, pointing, teaching. Something about it felt right.

* * *

Richmond rose before them. Exit signs. Elevated on-ramps. Motels. Fast food. Vonny and Titus weren't sure where the club was. They were lost on some side street and with his elbow resting on the sill, Titus's thoughts drifted back to Brooke again. It would hit him at strange moments. The fiending, fantasizing. The utter romance that would cloak him in warm velour. Outta nowhere. Right now, he imagined, Brooke was in her room studying. Trying to at least. He could see her neck in the soft light of the study lamp. Her eyelids listing, the book boring. She rolled over in bed and hugged her pillow thinking of him—Vonny mumbled in the driver's seat. Hell this Franklin Street at? You remember passing it stick? Vonny turned the car around and they began trailing a long slow moving caravan, the cars chock full of rowdy niggas, plumes of breath and smoke, arms chickenwinged out windows.

The club was called the Icebox. 21 and over. Dress code: no Timbs, no hats, no athletic apparel. Out front there were four bouncers in 3-piece suits. A bouncer gripped Titus around the belt, pulled him a wedgie. Titus stuck his arms out and turned on command and said his slick little line. Niggas usually pay me for what you doin. Haha. When his money was collected, he was stamped and tagged.

The club was thick with sweat and churning bodies, the smell of the wet street outside mixed with leather coats and ass. It was a long narrow slaveship with a row of booths along the wall with white tables keeping with the theme of ice. There was the bar in the back, which was white too with black lights overhead and liquor bottles on glass shelves. There was a dip in the middle of the room where a few people were dancing and most stood around like the undead watching the same small group of females. Vonny had one hand on the bar, Gimme a Long Island. Titus ordered a Heine.

They found a corner at the end of the bar beside a no-access staircase where they could drink and not get bumped into. They watched people, waited. It was too loud to do any talking. Titus wasn't in the mood anyway. His mind was elsewhere, at Brooke's bedside. He kept plumbing through the vivid details of what he was seeing back in the car, finding the vision harder and harder to see, and the more he tried, the more he felt like he was playing a stupid joke on himself for believing that shit. It's been a wrap. Who am I kidding. After he finished his beer, he looked into his wallet and considered another round.

One of the bartenders was female. He noticed that when niggas paid, they tried to touch her hand on the exchange. She ignored them, their smiling. When she turned for a bottle on the shelf, doods got on their tippy toes, put both hands on the bar boosting themselves up for a better look. With an arm around their homeboy, See you got the sistas, then you got the bitches. Look how they dress and you tell me.

Titus watched the bartender move down the line taking drink orders, her black shirt and slacks snug against her body. He waited for the peek of her yellow midriff when she reached up for a bottle on the shelf. Under the black light, he could see the smears on her sleeve and the little pieces of lint when she came up close and collected his money. Her belly was clawed faintly with stretchmarks. She didn't smile not once. He was thinking I like a woman like that. Not too nice to niggas. Not too gassed up on her looks. Know how to handle herself. A single mother prolly. Never been with one but they prolly more mature. Know what they want. Aint into playin no games. A solid round the way chick. She laid his change on the counter. He said thank you and left a dollar tip.

They drank and waited, went over to the other side of the club by the booths when they saw a vacant table. The booth was quickly taken and they went back to their original spot by the staircase, sidled up beside the niggas who replaced them, and there was nothing to do but to drink and wait. They waited. And waited and waited, bopping chins to the music, hazarding a gentle 2 step, conscious there were no females in their orbit. The back of Titus's shoulders found the wall again and he was thinking. Man look at me. I used to have my head on straight. Hell am I doing here on a weeknight. He looked over at Vonny swinging his arm sipping on his cocktail, nodding his head. Titus forced some good thoughts onto himself. Massaged and massaged and felt there was good news waiting for him in the coming weeks. He'd already gotten into George Washington. They said YES right away. Not the highest ranked though. But one of them Top 10 schools. The Ivies, yeah. Getting into one of those bigtime joints, he could vision it and at some point in the future being suited up at some cocktail party and looking back on this moment, at this nowhere spot in Richmond and thinking how far this was.

Worst case scenarios drifted in too. What if this it? What if I been fooling myself the whole time? and picturing disappointment on his mother's face, his father consoling her. He'd done the right thing. As long as he got his foot in the door, it would be okay. He threw back some ice, rolled the cubes around in his mouth. He went back to looking for the small group of females from earlier, stretching out his neck, even getting Vonny to start looking too, and that was when something popped off on the dance floor. There was yelling all around.

Watching the crowd clump toward the shouting, Titus grew excited and felt the thighs and seat of his slacks pulling taut. With a wave of his hand, he untucked his shirt and got on his tippy toes for a better look. A pair of niggas stood chest-to-chest comparing adam's apples, barking. You wanna get retarded cause I can get retarded. Do something, nigga. Oh I can get retarded. Then do something. I aint bout that talking. Someone else from the crowd came in— Sup boy—and swung on one of the doods from the side. The dood ducked, the crowd surged forward and in an instant the whole club was swelling, reeling, cheering— Titus's drink got knocked down—then the crowd laughing and somebody watching nearby took exception with being bumped into and he let his hands loose then the other dood's boys swooped in and there were pockets of fighting everywhere and the 2 original doods were swinging at each other blind, their shirts pulled up over their heads, chains swinging and getting tangled, tables with drinks knocked over, and someone swung on Titus and the blow glanced across his shoulder and he turned and saw a man in a black turtleneck rearing back for another one and Titus turned on the ball of his foot and swung and through the yelling in the room he heard the distinct crack of the man's jaw and saw his eyes roll back into his skull and his hand hummed, FUCK, and he shoved another person nearby who looked like he was about to do something. Another person fell over and more drinks were spilled. He grabbed Vonny but someone yelled THEY POKING NIGGAS IN HERE!!!! and he lost hold of Vonny's shoulder with everybody stampeding towards the narrow mouth of light that was the exit. The slaveship rocked and he felt himself slammed into a wall of bodies at the entrance and he kept looking over his shoulder for who had the knife, then remembering Vonny but people kept ramming into his back and shoving toward the exit as the shouting piled on top of him, WHO GOTTA BURNER? IS THEY SHOOTIN???? THEY SHOOTIN OR NOT??? I CAN'T SEE!!!! He pushed and pushed against them and was inevitably pushed toward the exit, his feet coming off the ground and he was more or less carried by the stampede until he was out into the cold air. He sprinted toward Vonny's Corolla parked in the lot across the street. He waited in his damp clothes, both disgusted by it all but happy, his body fully awake and electric and shaking and his gray breath tumbling and turning and rising in the cold air—he couldn't believe some nigga tried to steal him gotdamn—and Vonny finally came up in his loud blue slick-bottom gators panting, his Coogi sweater wet. Damn, stick. Niggas tried to swing on me! I doan even know nunna these niggas! Hahahahaa! HAHAHAHAH!!!!!

Catching their breaths, they watched a bouncer drag someone out onto the sidewalk by a shirt collar. Dood swung first and the other bouncers got him to the ground and made a circle and began stomping, their shoes shiny in the streetlight. The wind blew their ties back in their faces. The dood down there eventually stopped getting up. People in the parking lot began wandering their way toward the front of the club again. Whispers from the bystanders slowly approaching. He gone, dog, he gone. Naw, he aint. He just sleep. Where his people at? Shit, if that was wunna my boys it would be real serious right now, feel me? The bouncers stood and talked loud amongst each other, embarrassed, guilty, stuttering, agreeing, wanting everyone nearby to hear the justification. They were practicing the story for the police. You say he the one with the tool, right? I saw him reaching like this—I saw that too. You did the right thing. What was you supposed to do with a man reaching like that? It was me or him. People from the crowd started shouting. Sayin he won't even the one with the burna. That nigga done left out the back! But the bouncers ignored them and told everyone to back up.

When the police came, Vonny and Titus drove to the Down Under Lounge on South Street and they thought they recognized half the crowd there from the first club.

Even though he had deduced Eunice had misled him about the pregnancy, Joe didn't let their thing die right away. For a few days he kept calling, kept driving past her mother's apartment, kept telling himself there was some reason she led him on like that. The story that took root in his head involved her being in some kind of danger. She lied in order to protect him.

Then another story, the godhonest truth, emerged. One of his customers confirmed that she'd been riding around with some dood in a jeep. Joe laughing after a stint of blubbery curses. Know what I deserved it. She'd been going around some other dood's back when we first got together.

Satisfied with karma Joe got back to the things he'd been neglecting. He was set to graduate this summer and he'd been putting off thinking about getting a job.

The whole time he had simply assumed an opportunity would be there waiting for him once he got back to New York. All laid out and ready for him once whatever paperwork got processed, like a lot of things in his life. It was mostly a matter of calling to follow up.

A few weeks ago he'd gotten some business cards and pamphlets at the Minority Career Fair. Matter fact one of those companies called him. He'd been meaning to call back. He looked through his desk drawer for other loose, important papers, and fell into the process of catching up.

He got caught up in his classes and calling whoever needed to be called and by the end of the week he'd completed applications to several engineering firms with offices located in the Tri-State area. Even a few in Northern Virginia, defense contractors. That one firm that had reached out to him had already filled the position but encouraged him to check the website for more openings.

Turned out there were several entry level positions if he was willing to move, which he hadn't considered before. His home, his universe was New York. It's not that he had hard feelings for Virginia. Matter fact it had grown on him. The only part he didn't like were his allergies but everything else was cool. Reminded him a lot of Staten Island. But living here long term? Over New York. New York was New York. It didn't need to be explained beyond that.

But maybe it was good to stay open minded about things. Over the phone his brother Zeke said he'd been thinking about leaving. Really? New York? All of it? Not just Brooklyn? Yeah for a while I been thinking. There's gotta be more out there. I been on this same block since, since—

laughing drily—forever and I aint never even been down to V-A to see you. Not once. You realize that? Ever since Lou went away I been thinking. So many things, places I never seen. Joe asked what about Crystal. You know she'll be fine. The other day you know what she told me? She told me this boy at school ... She did that? Laughter. She cold. I told you ...

With his brother's blessing Joe applied to a few more positions. He gravitated first to city names he recognized, ones with sports teams. Texas had an allure onto itself. Anything in Texas was clicked. He clicked on a few more spots, satiated, and looked at the Diversity sections of the company websites imagining friendly people were awaiting him.

* * *

Titus slept in, having slept through his mother's call, and swallowing a few times to make sure he didn't sound too hung over, he called back. She said some mail came from Yale. Is it a thick or thin envelope? It's a few pages in there. No more than 3. He told her to open it.

Hearing her read the first few lines of the letter about missing documentation, he barged in with his What??? What's this all about??? and having beaten his mother to the punch, he tried to drown out her concern by continuing to say he was so confused, even angry with Yale for losing his paperwork.

You know what? It was probably the post office ma. But I thought you said the application was online?

His mother returned to the notice and read again the name of the documentation that was missing, PART IV CONDUCT, and read HAVE YOUR POSTSECONDARY

STUDIES BEEN INTERRUPTED FOR ONE OR MORE
SEMESTERS FOR ANY REASON? On the page here they
photocopied the box. It's marked NO. I don't remember
marking NO. Well it shows here the box is marked NO. Is it
in my handwriting? It's not handwritten. It's typed out, like
on a computer.

Again he broke in with laughter saying he was
completely confused. Clutching his head, making the face
of disbelief, he said into the phone it was hard to keep track
with all the schools. There were so many. I told you Titus.
That's why I wanted to go over everything one last time. She
said he was lucky that they at least *sent* a notice. You know
the kind of people we're dealing with son. They only need
the smallest reason.

Afterwards he sat in a cool silent patch, no distinct
thoughts forming yet. Then it hit him, the full weight of
what he'd done. He'd lied about his criminal record and
been caught. This was the beginning. Not only was it clear
that he'd never become a lawyer, they wouldn't even allow
him into law school. He sat in disbelief how the dream had
vanished. That part of him. All that time he'd spent.

He held his chest, then began patting on it, punching it,
his heart was going so fast. It continued to race and he was
hapless to it so he lowered himself to the floor, looking at
the objects in his room unrecognizing and his chest, for all
its heaving, wasn't allowing him to breathe.

27

Dean Daniels asked about the letter of recommendation. I spent a long time on it. Titus shook his head. What does that mean? I disabled it. Disabled? Titus began detailing the process of going on the credentialing website, how the applicant could configure which letters went to which schools, if any, and the simple clicking and unclicking of boxes.

Daniels watched Titus explain, saw the young man sitting in his office moving his mouth, the sounds coming, none of it was making any sense. When the dean could finally piece together the full extent of what the young man had done, the cold-blooded self-sabotage of concealing his felony conviction on the law school application forms, the breath rushed out of him. He held his hand up for Titus to stop, please that's enough.

He studied the young man's face, the embarrassment there, and himself felt resentment that such a mess had been made. A secret life of stupidity and recklessness had been allowed to live on this long, and no one had done anything about it. And as always—*always*—he would be the one who had to clean it up. He wanted now to tell the boy to fix his face, stop looking hurt over there. You're no innocent party. But Daniels collected himself, looked down at his own long dry fingers and began talking.

Please answer for me, in as simple terms as possible, why? I'm real sorry Dr. Daniels. Your letter would give me away. I'm not referring solely to the letter. *All* of this. What you've done here. Only someone with mental issues would do this to himself. When Titus couldn't respond, Daniels continued. Coming to terms with your past? That was the point wasn't it? You couldn't learn last time, could you? Titus said he didn't know who else to come to. I apologize Dr. Daniels. It aint easy coming to you to say I messed up. Daniels sniffed.

It was quiet in the office for a while then the dean said he wanted to know, wanted to hear Titus say it—Did you lie? Yes I lied.

They sat there some more, surrounded by all the pictures on the wall, the certificates, inspirational quotes.

What I did, I think that maybe you'd be able to tell me if, Titus wincing, you know I think I might of automatically disqualified myself. Yes that is a distinct possibility but you know I'm not the one to ask. No, no I think I did Dr. Daniels. I think I really hurt myself this time. Titus made a clucking sound in his throat. Like laughter. Yeah I think I mighta did just that, then a broad smile broke across his face. Don't you think Dr. Daniels? I mighta just thrown it all away?

The dean said nothing. A thought was preoccupying him. That he himself was to blame. He'd let this happen somehow. Then all Daniels said was that nobody was sure at this point. Why not? What do you mean why not? They just gon find out anyhow. If not now, I'm going to sit for the bar and they'll do the background check then. Young man Daniels was repeating, his hand up, let's focus on one thing at a time. Didn't you say you came here looking for my help? You do still intend on going to law school, do you? Titus clucked again, Yeah. No it's not time to laugh things off. You are the most important participant in your rescue. Look at me. Do you still intend on going? Titus nodded. The dean asked what the nod meant. I still want to go. Want to go where? Law school. Wherever they'll take me.

The dean explained that he would make a few calls to some lawyers. He knew some other folks in admissions who might be able to offer some general words. We just need a picture of our options. Then we will decide. Or rather *you* will decide.

As he was helping Titus out the door, Daniels remembered an email that had come in recently from him. When's your appearance for court? Oh that. Monday. At 10 I think. I wrote it down in that email but I can check again for you. No I remember getting your message, I just wanted to double-check. Do I need to ask if you can keep a low pro until—I got midterms next week. Good then. I will let you know if I hear anything.

From his office window, he watched Titus cut across the parking lot with the hood pulled up over his head, and followed the young man's slow, broad-shouldered stalk carrying up the flight of stairs. Daniels fixated on the seat of the young man's jeans, sagged so low the boy could barely raise his leg to climb the step straightaways. Had to turn his knees out ... Daniels shook his head inside himself. I don't know how they can walk like that. Like a full diaper. He looked at his watch and fell back into his chair where the heavy dread returned. Already he could see this matter would occupy him for a few days, probably more, and would require an inordinate amount of effort and suffering. With his hands clasped in his lap, he slid down his seat and shut his eyes.

Monday came. Titus performed his testimony on Vonny one last time before rolling up to the General District Court-house in downtown Charlottesville, the only ones there wearing ties and tucking in their shirts, though their shirts still smelled like the wet streets and leather coats and asscheeks of some out of town club or another.

It was a misdemeanor morning in the chamber. Men sat there in security jackets or in paint splattered jeans along the pews, bored, their arms up over the back of the bench and looking around, not used to being so still and quiet on a weekday. Daniels arrived in a gray suit, long overcoat and scarf. A few men nodded to Daniels and the whole pew stood up quick to let him through, wiping off their pants. Daniels shook the hand of a man in an Allied Security jacket, told him God bless. Daniels sat next to Titus, unspooled his scarf. My my you two look nice.

The bailiff called up Titus Stevenson. Titus gave the judge the facts, the Yes Your Honors and No Your Honors, his voice clear, emboldened that the arresting officer didn't show. Then came witness time and Vonny said his piece. Punching his palm, Vonny laid it out there a bit more casual than they practiced but he hit all the points about Titus being unarmed and on his way out of the Omni when the cops jumped him and sprayed him. When it was Daniels's turn, he put his hand on Titus's shoulder. Your Honor this young man has been under intense one-on-one counseling with me since the beginning of the academic year and I can assure you this will be the last time he appears in your courtroom. You know my track record Your Honor—Yes I know you do fine work at Mr. Jefferson's university Dean Daniels—This young man has abundant help at the Office of African-American Affairs. He's not leaving your courtroom alone. We're a family at UVA. We've all got a keen eye on this young man's future. Nevertheless I cannot help but notice a disturbing pattern of overzealous police spotlighting at many of the events sponsored by the African-American community...The judge was looking at Daniels hard as the dean went on for a lil while on the race thing, then the judge finally raised his voice. Dean Daniels this young man was drunk, trespassing at a private event and if I'm reading the report correctly, was without a shirt in the middle of winter, is that correct? A few titters of laughter in the courtroom. Please Dean Daniels quit while you are ahead. The gavel was banged.

The disorderly was dismissed but they caught him on the trespassing and obstruction of justice. Titus paid the clerk 70 dollars thinking to himself man you could find bobo sneakers that cost more than that.

Daniels asked him why on God's Green Earth were you not wearing a shirt? I took it off. Took it off? Yeah I guess I was angry, I don't know.

In front of the courthouse, a round bank of old snow lined the street. Daniels fixed his scarf and turned up the collar on his coat. So have you heard from any law schools yet? George Washington accepted me back in—then Titus's eyes narrowed thinkingly and now understanding what the dean had meant, shook his head no, no other schools. They shook hands and it looked like Daniels was about to say something more but he just said alright then I'll see you soon and walked down the sidewalk to his car. Vonny squinted at the dean walking away and asked why the dean was acting funny just now. What you mean funny? It must have not been that deep an observation because Vonny was already onto the next subject asking Titus if he was hungry. Yeah starving.

28

Before Dean Daniels would share his advice, he felt it necessary to point out to Titus that he had spent an unusual amount of time on him and that he'd been questioning lately whether the gains they had made in the fall were illusory or if it was his own mistake not requiring Titus to continue on with HIAF 2002: MODERN AFRICAN HISTORY in the spring semester. I pegged you for the type that doesn't require constant supervision. But no shirt Titus? Really? I think you might need some psychological counseling young man I'm not kidding. That's the only answer I can come up with.

Titus looked on impassively, but not in a disrespectful manner and explained, well, it was one of them things I guess.

The dean was struck by that odd phrasing and began telling of a chance encounter with Barbara Staunton, the Dean of the Office of Student Life, at the beginning of the semester, this was before the incident at Winter Ball. Remember her? Titus's forehead moved. See? I knew that would get your attention. She certainly remembers you. You know what she said to me this woman? Only one thing. How *is* Titus Stevenson? The dean let that hang for a second, a sneer on his lips, and it looked like he was holding back some laughter, as pleased as he seemed to be revealing this information. He repeated Staunton's remark, the emphasis on *is*, growing more angry at it, and asked Titus what meaning he took from her words. I'm still on her radar. Not just you, not just hers.

Titus frowned thinkingly for a moment, then said he understood, I guess that makes sense.

Do you Titus? I've got a few theories myself. No, I shouldn't share them with you. Wild speculation. But a part of me suspects she's trying to build a UJC case against you. Judish???? What?What for?

Before Daniels could explain, Titus had stopped listening and begun chuckling to himself, comical man. Judish? Why? Everybody know Judish can't do nothing to you. They just make you write a letter if you get caught drinking in the dorms. What are they gonna do to me? Make me write a apology letter to the Omni? I'm already graduating.

Immediately regretting that he said anything, Daniels mumbled that Dean Staunton had done something like this before, not quite sure if that was even true or if he had confused something along the line.

In any case Titus they've got a pair of nooses ready. A pair. I don't know about you young man but I'm not going down easy. I'll do what I'll need to do. That's not an empty threat. Can you promise me Titus no more nonsense? Please? I know it was one of those things but we're only 2 whole months away from graduation and—Daniels lost his train of thought momentarily. I was about to tell you no more surprises but nothing surprises me anymore. We get scared and things happen, by their own accord it seems. There doesn't seem to be a meaning sometimes. You look and look, Daniels paused, lost again, lost somewhere in memory, and came out of it. Oh listen to me Titus. You're making an old man beg here. I'm beginning to lose respect for myself.

Titus promised he'd keep his head low. No more nonsense, no more nothing. I just want to graduate and gettonup outta here. The dean said me too.

They got to business. Daniels told Titus what he needed to do about the applications. An addendum. Nothing fancy. Be direct about what happened, apologize, move on. Titus said he figured it would be something like that. Daniels told him there were no guarantees that would undo anything but at least you're covered now. They can't come back down the line when you sit for the bar and say you misrepresented yourself. Titus asked what about George Washington? Yes what about? They already accepted me. When was this? Back in January. They were the first ones. Daniels said even them.

* * *

After the meeting with Titus, Daniels was agitated and he remained that way the rest of the day, though the explicit thought would come and go. He had a meeting at First Baptist this afternoon and he found himself drifting away in the middle of talking. He threw his hands up laughing, I can't seem to piece together a sentence tonight, and his colleagues laughed and said it was okay and the meeting ended a few minutes early.

His wife turned out her lamp and said she loved him. She rolled over and he continued reading the sports magazine. He thought of calling his son who was on the road again, another televised game up in DC, but the page kept turning and he found himself drawn in closer and closer to the article. It was about a former big time college football coach who'd been fired from a few places and was now finding some small measure of redemption coaching at an obscure liberal arts college. The college did not have a football program 10 years ago and was now fielding bids to play the big name schools, which would bring in a lot of money.

The article made Daniels feel good and he turned out the light, the feeling still there. Looking at the ceiling, he saw crying women and children. The child, must not have been older than 4. Josh was about that size I remember. The children crawling up the ditch and he found himself lunging toward him, or was it she? He couldn't remember. Just couldn't remember though he'd been here so many times. They're so young at that age. Pulling the child down by the arm and throwing it toward the earth and his buddy unloading a round and it was sprawled there. Then the mother lunging toward the child and his buddy again TAP TAP and the woman fell short.

* * *

Coming home from work, Vonny was exhausted. At the end of a long shift tonight, he had made up his mind to quit Best Buy.

Driving home he had tried to convince himself this was a long time coming. He just needed a reason. He wasn't used to all that standing and moving. The repetitiousness. It got extra cold in the back too. That was the worst part. On the loading dock there was a chair. Between shipments he would sit in that chair pulling the hood of his coat over his head and blowing into his hands to get the feeling back in them. When the boss wasn't looking he played on his 2 way.

Today the boss came up to him. I've walked past 3 times and there you are. Vonny stood up apologizing. But the boss wasn't finished. He asked if Vonny was tired. Vonny shook his head. Well you're making *me* tired. Sitting there like that you end up sucking all the energy out of the room. I bet you didn't even know that. The boss hesitated, standing there licking his lips as if another prepared remark was coming, then walked away shaking his head sniffing like Vonny was the dumbest pieceashit who ever lived .

Vonny never liked pulling out his college credentials on people. It didn't seem right to put people on different levels on that basis. Yet watching that manager walk off birch-ested and gully after that talking to, it was one of the few times in his life Vonny felt the urge to pull rank on some-body. Don't talk to me nigga like I'm some dummy. I bet you don't even know that I go to—then Vonny realized that even that wasn't true. He wasn't no student no more. Hadn't been.

This realization left a taste with him for the rest of his shift, and whenever the boss walked past, Vonny felt strange and ashamed, almost scared of him.

At the end of his shift Vonny went around and gave dap to everyone. Laughing with them. They all knew the time. They said they were about to quit too matter fact but ... then Vonny said of course, he didn't blame them, and they asked if he had another job lined up somewhere. Maybe there they could be coworkers again.

Waiting for his car to heat up, he thought on the bills he'd been meaning to pay, reconfiguring the math now that the Best Buy thing would be out of the equation, and a big ol number was looking back at him. He'd have to call his father for another spot. But last time—a cold, watery feeling returned to Vonny's stomach. Last time his father didn't say yes right away like he usually did. They were working on the house. With Shawn moving back in, and April, and with the baby coming. Maybe they could fix things up. Add a little more room. Things are tight Vonny. You really need it?

Vonny looked back at the bright Best Buy sign on the other end of the lot. He hadn't *officially* officially quit yet. Didn't tell the boss. Didn't sign nothing declaring it so. But shoot ... somebody there prolly already told him tho. When the car was warm, he backed out the spot and the farther he got from the store, the more he knew he didn't want to go back.

* * *

After the last class of the day, Titus took the bus home. Though he had left the meeting with Daniels a lil pissed about being called a psycho again, and was also angered by the thought of a broader administrative conspiracy against him, he was at least relieved that he knew what he had to do with law school.

He made the statement direct. He said that something had happened that he wasn't at all proud of and he wanted to make it right. He didn't want to make excuses.

WHEN I WAS 17 ON THE EVE OF MY GRADUATION, I GOT IN MY CAR AND LET MY EMOTIONS GET THE BEST OF ME. A FRIEND AND I WERE LEAVING A MUTUAL FRIEND'S GATHERING AND HEADING DOWN A DARK TWO-LANE COUNTRY ROAD WHEN ANOTHER CAR SWERVED DANGEROUSLY AHEAD OF ME, CUTTING ME OFF. I JERKED THE STEERING WHEEL AWAY IN AN ATTEMPT TO AVOID HIM AND

ALMOST LOST CONTROL OF MY CAR INTO A NEARBY DITCH. IN A MOMENT, MY LIFE FLASHED BEFORE MY EYES. I SAW MYSELF IN A CAP AND GOWN SURROUNDED BY LOVING PARENTS. I SAW ONE OF MY FUTURE CLIENTS EMBRACE HIS MOTHER AFTER THE JUDGE HAD RENDERED A NOT GUILTY VERDICT. IN ONE FLASH I SAW ALL OF THE PEOPLE WHO HAD IMPACTED MY LIFE AND THE PEOPLE OUT THERE WHO WOULD NEED MY HELP IN THE FUTURE. THIS CAR THAT SWERVED IN FRONT OF ME ALMOST TOOK ALL THAT AWAY, AND THE HOPES AND DREAMS OF MY FRIEND IN THE PASSENGER SEAT TOO, WHICH IS WHAT I FELT AT THE TIME. OF COURSE I KNOW NOW THAT MY EMOTIONS GOT THE BEST OF ME. I AM NOT PROUD OF WHAT HAPPENED NEXT. BUT MY FIRSTHAND EXPERIENCE IN THE LEGAL SYSTEM HAS ONLY STRENGTHENED MY PASSION FOR A CAREER IN LAW. I KNOW THAT THE SYSTEM IS NOT PERFECT AND THIS IS WHY I WANT TO HELP CHANGE IT FOR THE BETTER. MY EXPERIENCES HAVE ONLY MADE ME HUNGRIER TO HELP THOSE WHO ARE CASUALTIES OF THIS FLAWED SYSTEM. WHILE I HAVE BEEN FORTUNATE TO BE FROM A FAMILY THAT COULD AFFORD A PRIVATE ATTORNEY, I CANNOT REST KNOWING SO MANY OTHERS CANNOT ENJOY THAT PRIVILEGE. HERE ARE SOME STARTLING FACTS ...

He got up to use the bathroom and came back, the cursor on the screen blinking. He kept thinking if this was the way he and his mother had worded the original statement. At the time he had kept asking her if it was too much. She said no. But don't focus too much on the past. Focus more on what you're gonna do. And baby above all else you gotta make em cry. You gotta go for those tears. Have no shame.

He took another break and had a brew this time, enjoying the warmth and certainty he was feeling now, his mother's words floating like an essence in his room. He put another line in his addendum about feeling violated. When that car cut him off and his life flashed and all that...dun da dun da dun VIOLATED. Something about that term I don't know. He deleted it. For a minute he contemplated what people meant when they used that word. If it only applied to females. If it went beyond a sexual connotation. He figured that it could be used broadly but he had a hard time coming up with many examples. The more he thought about it, the more offended he was at himself for attempting to apply the term to his own situation. Then the joke sprung up in his mind, that he felt *violated* for using the term *violated*, and hanging his head laughing at himself, he didn't care if he even used the phrase correctly.

When Vonny came home from work, Titus rose from his desk happy and shouting, let's go out. I'm tryna get bent tonight.

* * *

It had been a minute since they'd gone to any of the local bars. O'Neills wasn't too deep cos it was a Wednesday and people were already leaving early for spring break but they saw some people there they knew. Said whatsgood and booshitted for a lil. Then them niggas went their way, said it was jumpin somewhere else they heard. Oh word? Maybe we'll getup whichu later.

Titus and Vonny sat at the bar drinking their Long Islands. Not talking much. Taking the straw and punching down some of the ice and looking at the mirror behind the bar. Vonny put his hand on Titus's shoulder, warmly looked at him, and said something. Titus leaning in, What? I said I got Law and Order right here dog haha. Titus chuckled, Vonny continued. So you gon stand up in fronna allem people in court and you got dood sittin over there with his life on the line, and what happens if you mess up? You forget your opening statement? Titus shaking his head laughing, I guess the faggot gon fry. They laughed. Aint your pop a preacher Vonny? You never ask him how he do it? I don't know if it's the same kinda pressure stick man. Oh sure it is. Your pop got whole souls on the line. Say I defend a nigga and say he gets convicted. What's a 12 year bid when the soul live forever. Vonny grinned at him, You real smart nigga man, and clapped him on the shoulder. You remind me of my pop. You aint never think of becoming a man of the cloth? I did for a while. Still might could be, you never know. Vonny started talking about his dad, all the reading and studying he did to prepare for his sermons, how sometimes out of the blue he'd look at him and his brother and he'll try a line from his sermon on them, walk in the room while him and his brother were playing Nintendo, and pop would perform like he was doing it forreal forreal, like it was Sunday and we say all right amen pop. That sound good and we go back to playing. Then he say I know it sounds good but did you think about the words boys? The words.

Titus and Vonny drank some more and got bored so they got up and messed around a lil bit at one of the pool tables. They called out their shots. The scratches were prolific. There was some whitegurls the table over and Vonny said yawl wanna do teams? The whitegurls looked at each other and said sure. Boys against girls or co-ed? Vonny had both hands on his pool stick and squintily looking at them tryna be cool said let's mix it up.

They shot 9 ball and bent over one another and called shots and laughed and had a good time. Vonny whispered in one of them whitegurls ear where she was going after this but she kept pretending she couldn't hear him. He asked again and she said home and it was at that point he asked her straightup aye why don't you let me beat? and a nervous smile on her face formed then she flicked her hair wiping the smile away and scurried to a stool beside her friend where she remained between shots.

Titus and his team ended up winning so Vonny's team was supposed to buy the next pitcher but the whitegurls said it was okay and they were done playing. They sorta drifted away after that and Titus and Vonny decided they didn't want to spend no more loot so they went home. On the ride back to the apartment Vonny said that he prolly was going back home tomorrow. HOME home. Oh yeah? How long? A minute. I think my Pop said he could get me a job down there by the shipyard. You quit the phonathon? Yeah stick a while back. Just quit Best Buy tonight. Fuck you gon do in a shipyard? A longshoreman? Naw stick. They got me on the ships. Supposed to be related to engineering. Vonny explained the nature of the work, and that there would be some training period, after which he could be designated a master welder. So basically construction? Yeah but for ships. They get paid as much as a engineer. I have to call my dad to see if it's still cool. Wait wait you quit Best Buy? What for?

They sprawled onto the couch and the loveseat in the den. Vonny kept talking. Punching his palm describing other plots and schemes. If the shipyard thing don't work out he'd try to freek it with real estate. Had a boy out there doin that. Didn't een sound hard or nuffin. You just gotta take some class and get certified. Needa credential for every-thing these days. I gotta quit messin around stick man look at me. I just been sittin here booshittin. Vonny went to the fridge for another brew. He was still wide awake. I see you stick and I see you got yo shit on point. You missed a whole semester and you still gon graduate on time. And me? Look at me stick hell I been doon yo?

Titus said he got nothin to be shamed of, we all grindin. Vonny took a long pull and winced, putting his hand on his stomach old man-like. I don't know how you do it stick man. I be sittin there sometimes thinkin how do he get up erryday and grind like that? Erry day. With me, I know what I need to do but for some reason I just can't make myself do it. That's my problem. It's like I know what I gotta do but it's like shoot I'd rather chill to be honest. I'd rather, he shrugged and took another pull. You gotta tell me stick man what's the secret. Titus said you already know the answer bruh it's God. Vonny said yeah you right and he took a sip sighingly and looked at his phone with his feet up on the couch for a good half hour. Yo stick. Lemme use your room for the night. Nigga how you know I don't need to use it? They both had a laugh at that one. But seriously. What her roommate look like? Vonny shook his head grinning, They not cool like that.

The night dallied onward and Titus kept going in and out of consciousness, his hand shielding his eyes from the overhead light then his arm falling away and he'd wake up again irritated by the light. At some point in the night, Titus came to again and Vonny was still awake laying on the couch looking at his phone. Titus asked if shorty hit him back yet. Vonny said naw and Titus asked you still need my room? and Vonny said naw again so Titus slumped toward his room and crashed facefirst onto the springs.

Titus slept in and the next morning was surprised to find Vonny, his bags of clothes that were pushed up against the wall, all that gone. He sat on the couch where Vonny had slept so many nights before. He let the fact soak in. The nigga actually did leave. And he sat there some more. He noticed that the PS2 was still here.

* * *

Late into the night, Daniels sat on the edge of the bed, wrung out, shuddering occasionally. We stopped shaving Janet. That's when I should've known. His wife draped her arm over him. Rubbed him and said it's been a while since the last one. I could tell something was bothering you all day. She got up and came back a few minutes later with a damp washcloth. We're out of mozzarella sticks Fred. He draped the washcloth over his head. It's all right dear. This is fine. They sat in the dark waiting for the tremors to pass. She laid him down ignoring his breathless talk of being a butcher, and even the old people too, and this women and her baby, Josh was about that size I still remember and she shushed him. Janet we didn't have to do any of that back there. It didn't have to happen. Any one of us could've stopped it. Oh you all were scared kids. Just scared kids over there. He asked his wife to roll him a joint. It would help me sleep. You didn't need one last time. Please Janet? I'm asking. Sure but can you go in the study? I've got to meet with the Telluride people tomorrow first thing and it gets in my hair. He was quiet for a while. I don't think I need it. You sure? Yes. Janet you're right about us. We were kids. But in my heart I know that's no excuse. To be naive? How does that make things right? His wife shushed him, kissed him and adjusted the towel on his head. Think of what you've become since then. All the good you've done. You've built something real Fred. A place people call home. God recognizes that. She slept on her side facing him.

PART III

REVEAL

29

For spring break Brooke went up to New York with Susan. It was a working trip. Their first day in the City their itinerary was clear. They wandered, playing things loose for half the day, and grew guilty that they had wasted the time so they set to imbibing as much culture as they could, visiting two museums, broken up by a skip through Central Park, and bought tickets for the closing night of the winter season of City Ballet (to their disappointment, ABT's season had long ended). At their hotel, they went over their big day tomorrow, pitching memorized statements back and forth at each other and begging the other to do it as if it were the real thing okay? and offering limp critiques of intonation and delivery.

The JP Morgan meeting was in the morning. They had no trouble finding the building on Park Avenue. Nonchalantly Brooke responded with the floor number to the gentleman by the buttons, her voice straining to go that low. Their hearts pounding in the waiting area, they smiled tightly at one another and went back to tossing the choreography of the presentation in their heads, rushing through the phrases impatiently, almost thrashingly. From time to time, they leaned over to the other and asked in a whisper if she should wait for ... and the other nodded hurriedly, uh huh yeah good, wanting to get back into her own head.

The basic plan was this. Susan would thank Donald Wasterman for his time and would launch directly into the revelation she had while visiting the schools in Cape Town. As she described turning this vision into reality, she would gesture to Brooke on the word REALITY, and Brooke would take things from there. There wasn't time for her whole story but she should emphasize her work in under-resourced communities around Charlottesville and the Hampton Roads area. There was a chance that Mr. Wasterman would barge in at several points in their presentation, probably early on in the VISION-TO-REALITY section. He might want to know the details of movement therapy but we should assure him that everything was backed by research and that we would go into it after I let you introduce yourself and say your piece. What if he's real insistent? If he's insistent, I can give him the broadest of overviews but we have to get to you, your firsthand experience in these kinds of communities so that everything flows right. Because you have to describe what it's like in these classrooms and from there we can bring in the Tennessee study because it applies directly to US schools. Brooke said it made sense.

Mr. Wasterman broke in early, looking up after thumbing through the xeroxed packet. How about the name? The name? He shrugged. M.O.V.E. Against Violence, it doesn't exactly roll off the tongue, does it?

Susan was crying afterwards. Brooke whispered, Can you hold on until we get to the lobby? and held Susan's twitching hand down, down. By the time they got to the lobby she said she didn't need to cry. I still feel like shit.

Back at the hotel Susan was sneering into her phone. She went through the blow-by-blow with her boyfriend, waving one of her shoes around mocking the things Mr. Wasterman had said, then she collapsed onto the edge of the bed in self-pitying laughter admitting the man was right about the curriculum needing work. Brooke would chime in from the side, plugging any holes in her account, and was getting riled up herself just thinking about the smug exec's questions and how she herself would've answered them. She had little doubt she would've done better. During the presentation she had caught something about Susan, this her first time actually joining a pitch with her, an annoying cadence in Susan's public speaking voice. There was something about it—the way it flipped up at the end of statements? Maybe it was the buzzwords. Yes! Jesus, the buzzwords. And the lists of three! Good god, enough with the verbs we get it. No wonder.

She glanced at Susan sitting cross legged in bed. Her mother on the phone now, the conversation was more subdued. She didn't sound like some little girl when we practiced last night, did she? No, I would've noticed. Brooke then thought about the times Susan had taught choreography for the Virginia Dance Company, if she had known this about her then. She then supposed, thinking of the many meetings Susan had taken on her own, maybe that's why. I should've been there from the start. Then she remembered their tiff from the fall over her not being black, the disappointment in Susan's voice, then the line about being a liaison—or excuse me, mascot. Only if I knew then what I know now ... Compromising your vision Sue???? Please.

You're the fancy Fulbright. Maybe you should've been playing that part ...

They had good seats for the ballet. In the beginning they studied feet very closely, inferring all that they could from that, and making sense of the hierarchies as they allowed hands, arms, the placidity of faces into their fields of vision. Though little creaks of sweat were showing in the makeup of one tall double-jointed girl, none of the dancers seemed to require strain, even breath. Brooke and Susan watched on, completely caught, each beginning to project themselves into the choreography, making the same turns and leaps, their toes pointing, every line long, and every now and then a flourish of movement occurred that was so impossibly difficult for them to imagine doing that each laughed to herself in her seat, and turning sidely exchanging a look at the other, Did you? Oh God ... At one point Brooke felt the sweat forming at her temples, so caught in the virtuosity of one of the principal dancers, a girl with an exceptionally thick neck (only apparent when viewed straight on) as she danced a solo in one of the later acts, and when the applause went up at the end, Brooke stood without apologies clapping fully, aiming her cheers toward her. Brooke made so much noise cheering she drew the eyes of several dancers who, hands pressed to their chests and mouthing thanks, genuinely seeming appreciative. Brooke wondered aloud if there was a place the dancers hung out after performances. But where? Susan asked. There's so much to do in the City. Hearing that, Brooke remembered where she was, that outside this theater was the City—Oh God!—a place that she had thought about constantly but only in terms of movies and television shows, perhaps an accent of an acquaintance at school. But now? Now it was out there. At once she could feel the oldness and newness of her life coming together at a defined edge, what had been and what was going to be, and the teetering, oh, it sent chills, and right here, RIGHT HERE, oh … All was forgiven with Susan. She embraced her friend, a drunk vaporous effervescence coming up through them, as the balletomanes stepped past and around them, muttering that the performance was rather flabby and the company had seen better days under prior direction, and the crowd carried along towards the exits, full of wool and the occasional guffaw, dry smirks and former dancers striding proudly with outturned feet into the windy outside past the fountain and to the line of cabs waiting streetside.

For the week of spring break Joe stayed in Charlottesville. The days were like the others, which wasn't half bad. He'd been nurturing his weed business back to where it was at the beginning of February. That first week of February, back around the Super Bowl might've been the pinnacle of his earning. He spent so much time on the phones. Up in people's ears. Was around more often. Him and Eunice were not that serious yet. Business would probably never be that good again, not with other people slowly creeping back into selling. But things were finally steady again. He sent some money his sister's way. Had enough to put aside. Even enough he didn't feel guilty spending on himself. A new pair of clean white uptowns. You could never go wrong. He kept them in the box wrapped in its original tissue paper. The weather wasn't there yet. Maybe in a few weeks.

* * *

Brooke's interview at the Tisch School of the Arts was towards the end of spring break week. It had been hanging over her, especially since she hadn't the time to visit beforehand to make sure she knew the right building, and had gone the whole morning with a vague sense that she was in the wrong place, the wrong train, the wrong platform, the time falling away each wrong step she was taking, and she nearly considered giving up and turning back to the hotel. What was this job to her? Who were these strangers? When she saw the violet NYU banners, she was directed from landmark to landmark until she reached the appropriate building.

The interview was going well. At the end she had the opportunity to ask the interviewer questions, and was told that her questions were great, which Brooke took as a sign of her own thoughtfulness, and was so high and smug off that she wasn't even listening to the responses. Her questions had been calculated to sound as if she had studied the job description carefully, and had done her own research into the Tisch school, and had enough presence of mind to note any inconsistencies, possible conflicts, places that could mark trouble for the lucky person who would get the administrative position, but the interviewer laughingly remarked that they hadn't run into any issues with that yet, and that it was a good idea to put a system in place for that contingency. Brooke said she would love to be the one to do that, and sitting tall with her chin tucked, smiled with all of her except her mouth, thrilled those were the final words of the interview. Leaving the office she spent some time admiring herself in that moment, not forcing things, not in her own head like she usually was.

The corniness and triteness of the line became apparent to her as she reached the elevator. Now her whole assessment of the interview was changing. Nagged by the feeling she had left something behind, she hesitated watching the elevator doors open and the bodies emerging. She stepped in and waited as the elevator went down each floor, people entering and leaving, and she took quick inventories of anyone who seemed to be a dancer or artist, or anyone that looked to be in graduate school or was generally older and looked like they read books. Stepping out into the floor she remembered that the interviewer frowned a little when she replied that she hadn't found a place to live yet, and that something dry and sarcastic was said subsequently, and that the interviewer knew that Brooke didn't understand the joke. I should've said something at least.

That night they met up with some other UVA people at an upscale hotel lounge. The floor-to-ceiling windows looked conqueringly out at the skyline. Everyone dressed up. These people were only faint acquaintances back at school but here in the City everyone gave hugs and kisses and was so interested in hearing about the other's adventures all week. They took turns with stories. Susan and Brooke's pitch, delivered with the buzz of a few cocktails and without a senior executive across from them, drew universal praise and a few pledges to join their cause. Everyone bobbed their heads drinkingly, more loosely as the night went on. The songs became harder to refuse. At first Brooke and Susan decline to break out any serious dance moves but people kept goading them, the M.O.V.E. Against Violence girls, and they did a few freeky things, on their own then on each other, and fell to laughing and didn't really dance much after that.

Everyone was standing near the bar when Brooke realized someone was holding her waist. She turned to look at the face of the whiteboy doing it, the whiteboy listening intently to a story being told. This guy, she remembered, didn't go to UVA but was a friend of a friend ... When he was introduced, where did he say he graduated from? She could only recall that it was ranked somewhere below UVA, but was still prestigious. The features of his face, alien up close but somehow not offensive, went on listening. She allowed herself to imagine. It wouldn't be bad, would it? Smiling to herself. There were too many people around though. We haven't even exchanged a word yet. He'll probably do something corny soon anyway. Tell me I'm exotic. Ha. She moved up and a few inches to her left to fill a void in the bodies near the bar. His arm fell casually off her hip. She took it as a good sign he did that.

Enough time passed and he said into her ear, let me pick this one up for you. She said she was ordering for her friend too. He looked down at her, and from behind the smug, almost demeaning smile of his, I'll take both of you then. She grew warm, embarrassed for him somewhat, but her gaze lingered a bit too long on that strange face of his.

It was done. Now only a matter of logistics remained, a dance around the nosiness of other people. With everyone continuing to drink, the margin for error grew so he put his arm around her waist again, but so that all the UVA people could see it. Nobody seemed to mind, and took them in as if they were together, an outright couple, what you all didn't know?

The party was thinning. They could've left a while ago but Brooke and the whiteboy remained by the bar. The whiteboy teasing her about something neither would remember, perhaps how exotic she looked after all. Susan, clearing a strand of bang that had stuck to her lip, shot one more glance back at Brooke and her new acquaintance, the light and glass surrounding them, and left.

The next day Brooke and Susan boarded the Chinatown bus back to Charlottesville. Susan had her headphones on, sleeping most of the way.

When people came back from spring break, things were slow for a while, everybody with stuff from back home, so Joe laid low looking for another small hustle to make ends meet. Somebody told him that the joint right now was online poker. He tried it. Wasn't feeling it straight off though he could see the potential. It just took too long. He kept his eye out for something else. Something dealing with the internet. The future had to be there somehow.

He began thinking of what separated him and other doods on the street, any number of people he knew out there on the block back home, and it had to do with computers. He could corner the market there somehow. But how? Spending more and more time on his computer, he came across an advertisement for a dating website called BlackPlanet. It was especially for black people, and these females put pictures of themselves on there. They seemed like real pictures. So he started a page and put up a picture of himself he had saved in a zip drive somewhere, which took a long ass time to find but he found it, and had to cut out his brother Zeke, but you could see a lil piece of Zeke's hand, and with his brandnew page he started messaging these women. After the third one, he realized why I aint just copy the message and send it again, which he did for the rest, all Virginia addresses.

He didn't think much of BlackPlanet after that initial flurry of messages. Played his poker. Went to class the next day. Said wassup to people. Titus needed a ride somewhere so he took him. Ran to the store for himself. Dutches, squares.

When he signed into the BlackPlanet site again—a message. His heart was stuck somewhere up in his lungs when he clicked to open it.

It was a real person with a phone number that ended up being real. They talked for a while. About where they were from and she thought it was cool that he was actually from New York—haha, I thought you was just wearin the hat like everybody else—and he drove out there the next night, almost an hour and a half away to some townhouse in the middle of dark country, and they burned a dutch and were kissing and she petted on him and it didn't get farther than that. She said she had a man.

Joe left on pleasant terms, promising not to call her home number anymore.

He drove home cheesing, thinking on this little pit stop in his life. As he got closer to Charlottesville, the woman farther away but fonder in his mind, he knew he discovered something in this BlackPlanet website. He snickered to himself, aw I can't believe niggas aint even on this yet. This internet shit.

* * *

Law schools were getting back to people. People were getting into good places too. Big name places. Even people Titus didn't think much of. This coulda been a sign. He didn't know. Don't want to get gassed up again. It was still too early. The schools said they'd received his addenda. Now the waiting.

Duke said NO. For some reason it came to him as a surprise. They were supposed to be a safe bet. Safe but still up there in the rankings. A place he could see himself going. It already had a slot carved out in his mind, a life there, the trajectory carrying onwards. He had developed a fondness. Now that was done. Him and Duke, they were strangers again. Ma said it was allgood. North Carolina was too far south.

One day he was coming back from class and saw the mailman. The mailman was having trouble closing the little door on one of the boxes. You good over there man? It turned out that the culprit was his box. The mailman handed him the mail directly. Among a scroll of junk, mostly graduation notices and delinquent notices from Vonny's credit card companies were envelopes from 3 schools. Thin envelopes.

He opened them all quickly in his room. Harvard, Cornell, Penn. After he had read each NO and checked again if he had misread the language, he felt mostly a relief. He at least knew now. It was alright. Yeah I already knew. He shrugged. Yeah can't blame em. I lied about my record. I shoulda known they would react this way.

He was cool with it. Went about the rest of the week. Tryna see the bright side. Tryna come to grips. God was telling him to wait.

But he kept on hearing through the grapevine about the other people getting in. Places that said NO to him saying YES to them. Some was plausible. But the flagrant ones. What? Amir? That nigga? I had class with him man, you sure? How'd he get into U Penn? You sure it wasn't Penn State?

Titus brushed aside the part of him saying nah just let it go, and giving into his urge to know and set about doing some due diligence on people, pinning down hard numbers and writing out his guesswork on paper. It wasn't past him to ask straightup whatchu get on the LSAT? What your cumulative GPA? And shit his numbers was in the vicinity. Was better than some. Even his LSAT, which he had thought was in the basement.

He held his head up high, and he was full of disdain inside, Oh I see. It must be all those bullshit extra curriculars yall be doing. Musta got them pretty resumes too. That good paper huh? I see. Yeah that, and besides the obvious with my situation but that's neither here nor there ... But I see. Ha.

And he held onto things that way for the time being, no longer ashamed that a lower tier school like George Washington was the only school fucking with him. Fucking with him regardless. He was happy that it had turned out that way. He was riding with G Dub. Me and you G Dub we gon fuck niggas up. And he saw himself a righteous man about to venture out. Surveying the landscape in his mind, the fake, wicked people out there, so many of them, even more than he thought, and he told himself repeatedly that he was lucky he could tell people apart so clearly now. He had them all clocked.

Texas Instruments was in town conducting interviews for its Summer Internship Program and as soon as Joe was notified of his appointment, he drove down 29 to Ross and got himself suited up. He liked what he found and tempted himself with thoughts that he wouldn't need to keep the tags and receipt. A grownman needs a killa suit after all. At least one. He paid a girl to braid his hair, one of Eunice's friends incidentally. Eunice was not mentioned.

His scalp was still swollen the morning of the interview, though walking through the Scott Stadium parking lot he felt clean and sharp and so on point, and catching his reflection in the trophy cases down the long hallway, he knew it was worth it, all this money he'd spent getting himself GQ'd up, and was about to pat his tender scalp again when a door was opened and a hand was extended in his direction, a big white smile behind it, You must be Joe.

The interviewer was a deep deep brown, of some ethnicity Joe could not determine, maybe Indian or Hawaiian or something, maybe mixed, and his interview style reminded him of a caseworker that had been assigned to him when he was in middle school, probably one of the better ones, who didn't seem like in much of a hurry, and spent as much time talking about himself as doing the interview. But talking about himself not in a way that was trying too hard to impress you. Just about a pretty place he'd visited in Texas where he lived.

A few questions were asked about computer languages. Then it was over before he knew it.

The interviewer was guiding him out the door, a hand in the small of Joe's back going on about how he would like Texas. It's not what you think. What you see in the movies, sure some of that's true. There are some beautiful green parts. Rolling hills. He said he worked with a few Northeasterners who were acclimating well.

There was another applicant in the waiting area. Another black dood but Joe didn't recognize him, also in a suit, but Joe could tell it was a lot more expensive, the certain shade of gray it was. Walking past, Joe caught a whiff of dood's cologne. It smelled real nice and Joe lifted a lapel of his suit jacket to his own nose, then his sleeve, and caught the dark heavy smell of smoke, then sniffed his fingers, thank goodness, at least they still smelled like lotion.

It seemed like a waste of a fine suit and fresh braids to go home already, so he cruised along grounds before making a run to the store for dutches and ... he felt good that people were being so nice to him. I might should wear a suit every day gotdamn ...

* * *

Over the phone Vonny said I don't know what to tell you stick. You must gotta need connections to get in. Titus said nah, squishing sounds coming out of his mouth, I aint even tripping tho. They letting niggas in they know they can control. I know that. You hearme Vonny? Titus was drinking, pacing, and the phone cord was dragging from carpet to tile and to the hallway outside his bedroom. I know somebody said something about me. More drinking occurred. Titus was laughing. I tried to tell em it was stupid. I told my Ma— Ma something don't feel right. It was a sign Vonny. Aye you listenin? What I say? Somethin aint right. Exactly. But look, Titus with both his hands up, the phone tucked in the crook of his neck, I aint even tripping tho ...

* * *

The season was turning. Any day now the clocks would spring forward but it was past the point of denying. It was the season of lovemaking with the windows open. Long thinking. The season of white sneakers. Joe could finally break them out. He unwrapped the tissue from his uptowns, smelled them deeply, ah victory. The days were growing longer. Nights warmer. Despite his allergies returning, it was allgood. Every time he went to class, he saw some girl he'd never seen before and his heart would be pumping again. Such a suckahfahlove.

He was on a good stretch, he realized. A real good one. Historic almost.

Then night would come. He was in places he'd never heard of. Weird names like Henrico, Culpeper, Mechanicsville, Gainesville, Haymarket. Sometimes the addresses were bogus and the BlackPlanet girl didn't pick up the phone and it would be midnight at some gas station and the bugs were huge and of some new species. Other times he got to an actual place with an actual woman. On one hand he could count the times he smashed. He was feeling pretty gully.

Regardless, he liked driving. He liked the kind of thinking that happened on these drives, the places his mind went, old places, new places, the 2 lane country road curving under him.

His sinuses clearing at night, he became amenable to deep thoughts about his origins. He thought about the arc of his life. It was still rising at this point, he concluded. Things were going to keep getting better and better ... But there was something ridiculous about being in the South. He wondered why here? Why Virginia? What a weird name, VIRGINIA. Growing up, the idea of being a college nigga had worked out differently in his mind. He always thought he'd talk and act different. Start wearin nice sweaters and all that. Instead he stayed the same ol Joe. Average Joe. Thinking on his life story, the whole shape of it, he recognized that there were lots of tough things in it, lots of things that told him to give up. Every moment was either proof of his willpower or more writing on the wall that he should've done died earlier, to assume his place as another statistic. Two and a half years ago the townie clapped him point blank and he remembered staring up at the green awning outside the club wondering if he had died already and that he would be trapped inside a dead body like that for the rest of eternity, staring up, being moved around, having dirt tossed on him, the whole world black. But maybe, just maybe, if the world would become light again he might see his brother and his mom and they both would be all right and happy, just happy.

Jake stopped him a few times on these country roads. The highway patrolman, tall and striking a silhouette like a park ranger, remarked on the smell of cess, patted Joe down, stuck him in the back of the patrol car. You wait here. Mussing through the BlackPlanet printouts littering the car, jake found the llama under the passenger seat. Sir, I got papers for that. Well I gotta call it in.

After an hour Joe was on his way, the country road delivering him home safely.

After a while, all this traveling made him feel he was living the life of a superhero, some nighttime vigilante. He wanted it to stay this way forever. That sun would go down and there would be gas in the whip. I don't need nothing more besides that.

30

Brooke had been promising herself she would take things much easier. With only a month of school left, and things with M.O.V.E. becoming settled. A week after returning from New York, the Colgate-Palmolive people got back to them. Despite the discouraging meeting that had focused on the shoddiness of their business plan, the company agreed to terms on funding and pledged to set aside a small space for them at their Park Avenue headquarters. That night she and Susan celebrated by buying Colgate toothpaste and Palmolive dish soap. The next day they began phoning and writing potential donors, emboldened that they had a Manhattan— not just anywhere in Manhattan girl, Park Ave!!! Park Ave!!! —address, and could flash the name of a major company as a partner.

More good news came. The Tisch school got back to Brooke with a YES. She told herself that she knew they were going to say YES, and began to think of how she nailed the end of that meeting. She was high for days, forgetting momentarily and suddenly remembering that ... it was such a good feeling that finally, yes, finally, OH GOD and Brooke felt whole about where and who she'd be come the fall, and could look so many people in the eye on campus. She scheduled all these lunch dates and other excuses to catch up with people, glowing so much that they'd be forced to ask, and she'd have so much to say.

But with things beyond being a foregone conclusion, it was impossible to focus. It's not like she wasn't a night owl anyway, as much as she tried to curb her habit of all-nighters. Yet after all these years it seemed that she could only get down to schoolwork long after midnight when the meetings and study groups had stopped and the post-meeting dinners and the lingering around exchanging loose ends of gossip and before she knew it, she was the last one left again.

Nicole, a friend from Dance Marathon, had cleared away the cups and was doing the dishes, there at the sink with her sleeves rolled up and Brooke still yammering on about her nonprofit with Susan Adelman and about her dayjob at Tisch and how excited she was to be in the City again and the food! and the museums! and the people! but my god, what kind of people can afford to live in Manhattan? I might have to live on the street hahahahaha and Nicole with her feet up on the couch stretching her arms overhead and swallowing a sudden yawn, Excuse me, giggling, with my mouth all open I must look trife, hahaha. No I should go. It's a weeknight and I still have work to do. No no I'm not kicking you out …

Driving home Brooke glanced at the time on the dash and laughed at herself it was so late. How am I gonna pull this one off. In her room she ground up a smurf and sniffed it. Powder hitting the back of her throat, she phlegmed up coughingly, swallowed and waited, searching for the symptoms. She was whispering to the chemical bonds forming in her bloodstream and propagating throughout and latching onto her neural pathways, whispering Let's go. The sound in her ears closed up. A high, barely perceptible pink hum took over. And about a foot from the tip of her nose, she could see everything with remarkable clarity and focus. Settling into her desk she looked at the computer and worked unthinkingly.

When she finished with the paper the humming in her head was drowning out everything, even her breathing. She was happy. It was still dark out. She pushed PRINT. Up on the screen popped an error message, which she studied with a deep seriousness and intent. She followed its instructions by turning off all of her programs and restarting the computer. For good measure she detached and reattached the cable between her printer and her computer. A different error message came up. Hmmm I guess that's progress right? She fiddled with a few more settings, clicking specific X's and then a more disturbing message appeared. NO PRINTER FOUND. I'm looking at it right here what do you mean you can't find it? She stared at that message. You know what I won't even mess with you anymore. You can wait.

Pulling the sheets around her in bed, she rolled onto her side away from the bright screen. I checked the cord I swear. It was plugged in at both ends, I know it was. I was printing out the flyers for Dance Marathon. This was last week. Haven't used it since. It was fine then. She lay listening to her heart beat expanding in the skin around her temples. You know what? It's probably Sheekah again. I knew it. I told her last time. If you need to use it, ask. That too compli-cated for you? It's not like you can't get your own printer. Such a mooch.

Brooke tried to sleep but the inventory in her mind continued. She always printed out her papers the night before. Her mother always said sweetie if it could be done today, do it today. It was probably something simple too. A setting that needed to be switched on or off. A simple click. She closed her eyes, felt the burning in the lids. She got up and went to the computer lab. Just get it over with. She punched in the code on the door and had her pick of the computer workstations. All were empty. She opened the file to print and immediately noticed a typo. Jesus why does it even matter she muttered to herself as she proofread once again. A man in coveralls walked into the room. She didn't hide being startled. And laughing gently she apologized. He said nothing and stood behind her. She asked can I help you? He said nothing. She continued to work pretending to ignore him, though the heavy smell of his sweat was settling all around her. Her fingers searching for the PRINT button. He unzipped his pants and started jerking himself off right behind her. Right behind her head. She could hear it. Sounds coming from the base of his throat. She couldn't move or talk. Too petrified, too afraid to comprehend how afraid she was, and it was hard to say how long that lasted, he was still going when the printer nearby began spooling and buzzing, and she jumped out of her chair and threw open the door and ran across the grass not even looking behind her.

* * *

Titus was yanked into consciousness. SOMEBODY BANGING ON THE DOOR OUT THERE SCREAMING. A female. He sat up and tilted his head. It's our door. He ran up to answer it and Brooke collapsed through the doorway eyes big and gulping air and he could barely understand what she was saying about keys. Panting and shivering I left em. I left em. Joe called from behind his bedroom door everything aight? Ty I left my keys there. He's going to get them. Who? There was this guy—she couldn't finish the sentence and began crying. He helped her to his room sitting her down on his bed. Joe knocking on the door, Everything aight in there? Yeah Joe we good man. Titus held her arms and was trying to look her in the face. Brooke, aye Brooke. Talk to me. What's going on. Her breathing shallow and fast and she swallowed air and gathered herself enough to say, pausing a long time before saying There was a man in the computer lab—and not able to finish and she began sobbing again so he let her and sat with her on the bed rubbing her back. He hurt you? Her face squinched up, It was so stupid. I should've waited until tomorrow. It didn't even have to be done tonight—Yo Brooke answer me. This nigga touch you? He knelt in front of her and looked at her sweatpants and her hoodie and nothing was torn and she gathered herself enough to tell him that the man stood behind her while she was sitting at the computer and he unzipped his pants and started playing with himself right there right behind—He stood up HOT, scowlingly stepping into a pair of sweats and boots. Fuckin gotdamn nigga how long ago was this? Just now. JUST NOW?!!!!??? He shut his eyes tight. Breathing. In. Out. You say a man right? Not a student? Yes. So what was he? Black? White? What was this nigga green purple tell me. Black. And he was older, she wiped the wetness from her face, I don't know. Like middle aged. He was dressed like he was a janitor. I thought he was in there to replace some paper towels I don't know. I guess I should've known.

Stomping across the hallway, Titus saw Joe's door cracked open and he pushed it all the way. Joe sitting on the

edge of his bed. Shorty aight over there? Titus told him they
had to go and aye bring your tool okay.

Titus and Joe ran across the courtyard and stalked the
empty rooms of the lab, Joe with his pistol raised poking
around the corner and into each room like how he saw cops
doing in the movies. All the computer monitors were asleep
except for one and that was where they found Brooke's UVA
lanyard with her apartment keys. They checked the bathroom. Nothing. The maintenance closet was locked. Titus
put his ear up to it and walked away muttering that the
nigga was gone. Long gone. Joe put his ear up to it too and
they both went outside and walked around the building,
then around all the buildings at Faulkner, each with a
picture in his mind of the Charlottesville Rapist. Titus
picturing an old time hustler in faded blue coveralls, a real
skinny scragglyass nigga with a slink in his walk. Joe's
mental image, largely inspired by the police sketches he'd
seen at the bus stop and tacked to bulletin boards all across
grounds, consisted of a babyfaced nigga, prolly mixed with
somethin, wearing a fat ol beanie, prolly got a lil gut too.

They combed the hill behind the complex, hearing
themselves crunch twigs and kick through bushes. They
rounded back to the main road facing the dry brush twisting
into thick dark thatches across the street, the hot hate in
their blood dissipating. Joe said you stay with your lady.
I'mma hop in the whip and drive around and see what I see.

Brooke stayed over. Titus pulled up a chair, put his feet
up on the edge of the frame and looked out the window
across the courtyard for any signs of movement. She turned
over. Can you get me some water?

When he went to the kitchen, he saw Joe still up
smoking a cigarette by himself in the den, a controller in his
lap, the blue of the TV washing over the room. Titus went

back out there once Brooke went to sleep. Joe reported that he hadn't seen nuttin out there son but a buncha trees and empty streets. Good lookin out though Joe. Joe dropped his cigarette in a soda can and picked up the sticks and started playing. So shorty all right? Straight, she asleep. She don't needa go to the hospital or nuttin? Nah. You sure son? Get checked out? I could drive. She straight man thank you. Titus watched Joe play a lil then said honestly Joe the guy aint even touch her. Joe pressed pause and held his chest, Really? Yeah she straight. Thank god son that's a relief. Sorry for soundin like a broken record earlier but I just can't stand hearin females like that. You never wanna hear nobody in pain, especially not no shorties. I don't even think I can sleep tonight hearing her cry like that. The door too. Hearing someone bang on it. Titus said that it fucked him up too hearing stuff like that. He asked Joe what was good with him and his lady. What lady? Joe went on to explain and got onto explaining BlackPlanet and was about to show him some profiles on some females on the computer when Titus said he should check on Brooke.

The next morning a detective came. They used Titus's room for the interview. She and the detective chitchatted for a bit. She was struck he didn't have a legal pad or anything to write with. The convo flowed easy and Brooke was thinking how young he looked for a detective, that we might be the same age. Then they got down to business. I know that some of these questions may be difficult to answer but I want you to try your best yes? She answered his questions, going back to the beginning when she was at Nicole's. Filling in the details there and step by step approaching the moment in the computer lab. She hoped she was being detailed enough, the detective watching her deeply as he sat in the chair across from her, nodding rhythmically as the story came out, stopping her with some small questions once or twice like who was there with her at Nicole's? and what time do you think it was when she got to the computer lab? and so on. He thanked her and as she was drinking her water, he watched her. I don't know if anyone's ever told you this Brooke but when you talk, you have trouble making eye contact. That observation hung there then the detective grinned, I'm sorry. I didn't mean anything by it. I should've kept that to myself.

He went into his bag on the floor and set a thick binder on his lap. He explained that he was one of the people working on the Charlottesville Serial Rapist case and that the binder represented all persons of interests related to the case. If she could take a look through it, that would be a big help. The binder was so thick that the cover didn't lay flat on his lap, but fanned out at the open end. I know it looks intimidating but if you need to take a break, stand up and stretch, let me know.

She spread the binder across Titus's desk saying a few calming words to herself and began flipping through the pages of mugshots. Each page a plastic sleeve with 9 mug shots each. She began to grow a little—and she was embarrassed to feel this way, the word forming in her mind —*scared*, as if the men in the pictures were there and could see her. She was imagining that she was vulnerable with each page exposed to her face, so she flipped through faster and faster, becoming a little more panicked until the detective behind her asked if she was all right and she stood up quickly. I need to refill my water. I can do it for you. No it's fine. I need to stretch my legs anyway.

Outside Titus asked her if she was okay. Yes I think we're almost done. Titus put his head down in his book again and she smiled at that image of him.

She returned to the room, a bit more composed and resumed looking through the binder again, putting out of her mind that silly idea that the men in the pictures were actually there, actually looking at her. She formed a mental image of the man she had seen last night and turned each page allowing the possibility of that familiar face to jump out at her. Pages flipping and flipping. She had to stand and stretch again. More pages flipped. Black faces them all. Chins tilted down. Tilted up. No rhyme or reason. Just every face black, male, 18 going on 40 ... At a certain point, a part of her felt that she had come up against something, a truth so blunt and obvious and imposing it was if she was being taunted by it, by someone, and she grew warm all over with shame. You defend them so much. You're so in love with these people, more than your own. They're animals. Can't you see? She responded angrily in her head that this whole thing was a farce, I mean you kidding me? It's like the police were so lazy they took every black man ever arrested and threw them in here ...

But soon all these thoughts and all thinking itself subsided and it was just work this flipping. Just get it done. Flip. No. Flip. No. Flip. A flicker of recognition. She flipped back. No not that one. No not that one. No. No. No. There. Titus. Was it? Yes. The face so swollen. Misshapen. He's not even standing up straight looking at the camera. Why's he looking down like that?

The detective coming up behind her, Are you seeing the man from last night? She pointed at Titus's picture. He should not be in here. I'm sorry Miss? This picture, him, this guy, he doesn't belong here—the detective looking at her squintingly—you all have made a mistake. We're in his room right now. He's not the guy you're looking for. It came to her suddenly, the pepper spray, that's why, and why he wasn't standing up straight. They were probably propping him up. Was he even conscious? Brooke felt her throat clench, a revulsion emerging, and her hand twitch, the need for it to cover her mouth, which she was able to resist.

The detective apologized. He said he wasn't the one who put the binder together. Look I don't care. That picture needs to go. Could you give me a reason for doing that? She looked down at the binder, unable to say why. The detective smiled and picked Titus's picture out of the sleeve and put it in his coat's breast pocket, apologizing once again. The flipping resumed and she reached the end saying that she didn't see the guy. The detective gave her his card and told her to stay in touch.

Titus asked her what was good with the laughing he heard earlier. Oh Ty he was nice. Real easy to talk to. Titus sniffing, Don't think a moment he your buddy now. Yeah I know. Titus told her to stay home today. You could stay here if you want. Oh Ty I'm okay. I need to change. Shower. He offered to walk her over to her building but she said no it was okay. She'd commandeered enough of his life. Nah girl I don't look at it that way. Then a kiss happened between them, the initiator of which wasn't entirely … she was surprised and pulled away. She told him she'd call him later and thank you. And she walked over to her apartment a few buildings down, a few flights up, her eyes never fully adjusting to the brightness and she was in her room again.

31

Vonny felt among men at the shipyards. He felt this way especially in the mornings. Driving up he would see the crowds of men already gathered out front the hangars and along the chainlink fences, the hard hats nodding at one another in sideways conversations. The big giant crane hung overhead, over everything, looking bigger than even the aircraft carrier with tiny men crawling in and out its holes. Looking at that big giant ship in the distance, Vonny knew, and throughout him felt, that he had never contributed to something this significant. Before he started working at Newport News Shipbuilding, his pop told him that he would be helping out the country. He was told that again on the first day of training. That he'd have the privilege working on the biggest, most advanced ships in the world. The country needed young shipfitters like him, especially now because of the war, and for that he should feel a deep sense of pride.

Up to this point he had never really thought of himself as a patriotic person. He had never really thought in terms of the country or of a world populated with countries, though he knew these were facts. It's that these facts hadn't a reason to occupy his mind before. Why would they when you had stuff going on? People to see, places to go today. School, work. He didn't think of other countries at all besides those with restaurants nearby. He would sometimes realize that his mother was from a different country, and that she had had a whole life in Korea prior to him, and that things were set up different there. Did she have patriotic feelings for Korea? She feel something whenever their anthem played during the Olympics? She still remember the words right? Every so often his father would mention his time as a young missionary in Africa, which evoked in Vonny generic images of potbellied kids and packed up dirt and women holding stuff on top their head and the shape of a continent on the globe, a big ol chicken nugget ...

Being a ship fitter paid good, real good. Yeah, that was one of the main things, if not *the*. Matter fact, paid about as much as being an engineer. Being a shipfitter you had to take classes too but the company pay for that. That was on top of paying you to work. And you're off by 3 every after-noon. That's wassup.

One of the olderdoods broke it down this way. Once you figure out college isn't for you, you know you have to work. This right here is work. This aint no air conditioned job. Sometimes you'll have to crawl up tight spaces. Other times you'll be in the shop all day with the torch. When it comes down to it, we solve problems. I know they lecture about that at college. Well we do it every day.

It was all good at the shipyard. Vonny could see himself here until they let him back into UVA. It would be a whole year, shoot, if not longer, the math being what it was. The first few weeks flew. But he sensed something off about his situation. It was so cozy, so perfect for him, there was bound to be something wrong. He went to welder certification training every day wondering, waiting to find out what it was exactly. He'd go back to these thoughts at lunch sitting in the shade with the rest of the young guys. Vonny would think to himself, So this is it? This how it's gon be?

The olderdoods were always talking news. News news. Not sports, though how they talked about it seemed familiar. Vonny started listening to the news on the radio on the way to work. Was surprised to find out there was a vote for the president soon. This realization made other things them olderdoods talking bout more clear. He was able to follow the plotlines better. Parse out motivations. See who was pulling for who. What was likely. What was only dreams. He was able to make private predictions about who would show up to work in what kinda mood. He didn't really have a strong opinion yet he knew why people had strong feelings about things. He realized about himself that he enjoyed seeing things from the different sides. It was neat to him how the different sides fit together and made sense. You just had to step back far enough. It amused him to hear people getting so heated. At some level he thought they were pretending to be that mad. How can yawl be so upset? It's not like the world was ending. Though he knew it was sometimes fun to play along. Talk a lil smack to each other. Nothing too deep. The camaraderie made him miss Madden, miss UVA. He regretted leaving the PS behind. Calculations formed. Maybe by the end of the month he would have enough saved for a system. Or he could drive up to Charlottesville to pick it up? Then he'd have to be back in time for work. Would he fall asleep on the road? Man what's that traffic like?

He found somebody at work who played Madden. One of the youngerdoods he was cool with, Antonio, though he lived out in Chesapeake. At least he had his own apartment. Vonny was nervous beforehand but once the ball was snapped, it was clear his reflexes were still there. He could see things develop. Without even thinking he was up 3 touchdowns. He didn't even talk no smack when Antonio said they should switch up squads.

Vonny had a good setup at the shipyards. He put that first paycheck towards one of his credit cards, the yellowish one with the deer looking up from the tall grass and the sun was setting behind it. This card had been one of the first and he was soon caught up on it.

The training hit a new part where he needed to be in a different building. The man behind a desk was taking down his information, a pudgy, strong-looking olderdood who seemed real annoyed, like Vonny wasn't talking fast enough. Vonny sat at one of the computers in the corner of the trailer, breezed through some clicking and typing and spent most of the time arms crossed staring through the screen when the videos were playing. The earmuff headphones didn't sit right on his head and made his ears hurt after a while. With those on and all his hair, he was hot and uncomfortable. As soon as he finished a unit quiz, he removed his headphones and stretched and tied his hair up again. He looked round at everyone else hunched at their computers, the expressions on their faces extreme—pain or boredom—one guy was scratching his arm, his teeth bared like a dog when it had a good itch behind its ear. The guy behind the desk who was annoyed at him earlier was typing at his computer with his pointer fingers. It made Vonny suffer watching those thick, stiff fingers hover over the keys, and the olderdood's face grimacing with effort.

* * *

Vonny came straight from work to the hospital. He took a nap there in the waiting room of the maternity wing, his clothes still damp because he had to work outside and at the end it rained. The baby was born sometime in the early evening. His brother Shawn came into the waiting area with Reverend Childress's arm around him, Shawn's face wet and swollen with tears. Vonny sat there with his brother, his arm around his shoulders, the other people in the waiting room occasionally looking at them with tilted heads smiling. He asked his brother what it feel like bruh? There's no going back, that's the first thing that popped in my head. Soon as I saw the doctor holding her up by the legs, Shawn shaking his head, living the moment again. It's a miracle Vonny. Life come out of life. What wasn't here before, now it is.

Vonny continued thinking about that phrase, Life out of life. He'd never heard it put that way before. It—it really made him think. The idea of things coming into existence. Out of other people. That's what had happened to himself. What happens to everybody. Miracles. He'd never seen his brother so moved. Life outta life.

Vonny kept coming back to that phrase while he was at work. He'd be looking at the hull of the aircraft carrier peeking out over the low slung buildings, going man and beginning to absorb the meaning, life outta life. Could come out of nowhere too. Man. That's wassup. He drifted off again in the computer training center. The same ornery fella behind the desk with the sign in sheet would be trying to type with his pointer fingers. The expressions passing over the man's face—agony, hopelessness, curiosity, amusement —flowing one into the other connected. Vonny was staring at this olderdood a while. He wondered if he had kids. If he had been touched by what Shawn had.

At the buffet a few days later his family gathered, some visiting from out of town. The tables were pushed together longways to accommodate them all. Joining hands, they listened to Reverend Childress say a blessing and they set out to the food stations with their plates, wafts of steam rising from the trays, and Vonny was reading the printed labels of the food on the clear glass sneezeguards when a little hand reached past. The parent helped with the tongs, What do you say? Excuse me.

He noticed kids in the booths playing. The strollers in the aisle. A pregnant lady going by leading her children as she balanced plates in both hands. Everybody having babies these days. Maybe it's always been this way.

He liked being around the baby. Close by. Not necessarily touching it. In fact, he hadn't held it yet. Even now when Shawn and April held the baby out to him he backed away, naw it's alright. Maybe later. He sat looking at it sleeping in the car seat. The baby had a name. Little Miss Janette Turner. He didn't think of it yet by a name. Or even as a she. It was still *Baby*, still something else, purer, still trying to figure out itself. He was fascinated at how the skin looked. Soft but there was like a dried film. The shut eyelids reminded him of the knuckles on a thumb. Man. And just sleeping too. Sleeping through all this. Like a lil piece of breathing meat. Sitting back in his seat needing to take a break from looking, Man so little. Everyone sat eating, and it wasn't very talkative but everyone was content. It was clear there was no other place anybody wanted to be.

Vonny got up for one last round of food. On his way back, that's when he heard the voice. It was clear, deep and pure and clear, almost whispery it was kinda relaxed-like. PLACE YOUR TRUST IN ME. The voice came from over his shoulder and he turned smiling, ready to acknowledge the stranger with the sweet voice. A couple was walking past with their trays muttering Spanish. One of the workers, Chinese, was sweeping things into a dustbin. He looked around some more not finding the tall, deep-chested man who fit the description, and became self-conscious he was spinning around for no reason. As he took another step, the voice came again, again from over his shoulder. I'LL BE THERE WITH YOU.

He felt a chill in his stomach and told himself not to panic, and went back to the table with his plate. Showing no outward signs, he sat absorbing, processing, chewing, afraid that if he moved too suddenly, the voice would come back again, this time angry and shouting. After a little while he began to relax and felt he wasn't crazy, then another part of him opened up and he began to consider the possibility that what had happened was somehow special. Whoever had spoken to him wasn't out to get him. In fact the opposite seemed more likely. And he finally asked the obvious, the presence smiling on him and approving as soon as the question formed in his mind. Is it You?

Sensing the response, he returned to his plate, smiling inwardly, a relief, a peace, this vast plain spreading open inside. Yet he was still conscious to make things go as normal as possible on the outside, trying to stay loose in his movements, keeping up with conversations going on around him, occasionally entering into them and laughing. He listened to what people said, looking at all the faces, and no one seemed to notice that something was different, that what had happened had happened and now they were looking at an altogether different person. Occasionally he glanced at the sleeping baby beside him who was the only one who seemed to know.

32

Titus took Brooke up on lunch, though he refused to accept it as a gesture of thanks for the other night. It had been a while since they'd caught up. The other day with the detective in his room, they really couldn't. Yeah. She could pick the spot, it don't matter where.

Brooke drove him down to the Corner. People were out, moving up and down the street in loose groups. At the crosswalk Brooke took a chance and reached for his hand. He took it naturally, squinted both ways at the traffic before stepping into the street. By the time they reached the other side, she decided that today, it would be all right today. She was glad she called him. It was the right thing to see him again. They passed along the street under the awnings looking at the tired sunburnt faces in the bars, and rounded into an alley. A staircase took them up to a bistro she liked going to with dance company friends. She liked the kind of people there and knew it would be busy and alive.

It was busy but they were seated quickly by the balcony. They looked over the railing at the grass and trees across the street. The brick building of the medical school. The sounds from the street below wafting up laughter and slowmoving cars and warm chatter.

I know you don't want to hear this Ty but I want to say thank you for the other night. It means a lot to me. Nah you don't gotta do that girl. You was banging on my door. Anybody woulda did that. He was rubbing his arm, his gaze averted. She thought he looked absolutely cute. Shy like the day she met him first year. Not a lot of people know that about him. She was smiling at that memory, at him now. You didn't have to sleep on the floor the whole night. That was very kind of you. Nah not the whole night. Me and Joe was out looking for a while. Then we was up talking, Titus scratching at his collarbone, still unwilling to meet her eyes. We was talking for a while, a smirk forming, so nah I didn't sleep too long on the floor. It's alright.

The food came and they ate. In the quiet work of eating, she couldn't avoid thinking about his mug shot in the detective's binder again, whether it was worth it to tell him, if anything could be accomplished besides him getting angry. Then she came to thinking of Winter Ball. Him thrashing around shirtless. He just wouldn't listen. We kept trying to calm him down. That sinking feeling of helplessness came over her then, and she was shuddering inside having that moment replayed. No that's not him. He was drunk. Brooke looked across the balcony and caught the glint coming off the cars passing below. She realized she was slouching, her chin touching her interlocked fingers. She sat up straight and picked up her fork. She hoped to god he wasn't doing anything right now to call back that image, and dared a look at him.

He was eating quietly, unaware that she'd been talking to herself. Yes. This is him. She asked how he liked the pasta salad. He took a big long-developing swallow. Good. She asked if he had a busy day today. He began to complain in general terms about work he was pushing off, then said he didn't want to get into it, and sat chewingly, his annoyance coming to an end with a shrug. We both gon be up outta here soon so I can't stress too bad. She said she couldn't believe it, one more month, can you? He said he been done with this place. It can't come fast enough.

She took this as an invitation to ask, so she did and he set off to reporting the law school results thus far. She felt an urge to apologize to him, to make excuses. But if you get into Yale, that would be wow, that would be big. Columbia too. Those are both, what, top 5? Yeah. We'll see. I'll prolly end up going to G Dub. Don't say that Ty. What you mean don't say that? What's wrong with G Dub? I didn't mean it like that. You sounded pessimistic there for a second Ty and I—I, she was hoping he would save her somehow but he continued looking at her confused, scowling, and she left immediately to the bathroom. She returned, the apologies streaming out of her. He laughed, told her she meant nothing by it, G Dub barely made the Top 30, and there some accreditation drama going on there that had to do with diversity, and stood to hug her, the apologies still spasticating her movements so with arms wrapped around her slender shoulders, he squeezed tighter and swayed with her a lil while and they both sat to eat again.

She told him about her plans in New York, couching things so as not to sound like she was bragging, but not underplaying things so much to draw attention to herself, which she'd been guilty of on other lunch dates lately. He said he was happy for her. You always wanted to be up there and now it's happening. Yes I'm excited. I can tell. She was going to ask how he could tell but he was looking out across the balcony already, which sent her worrying she'd gone on too long. The waiter brought boxes.

After lunch they ended up back at Faulkner, at her crib. They were catching each other up on music. She liked everything he played for her and eventually were laying in her bed holding each other looking at the ceiling babbling and not saying nothing too deep to each other. DC to New York wasn't so bad. Anything on the East Coast is driving distance. The Chinatown bus took 7 hours from here, and that's including the rest stop in Delaware. From DC I imagine it would be ... Nah it wouldn't be bad. Just gotta be smart with my PO.

He sat up out of bed and called for some pizza and laid back down with her. I don't know what happened Ty but I got tired all of a sudden. Aye you just chill. She closed her eyes breathing and letting everything sink. She could feel him wide awake beside her, the vibrations of his blinking eyes, his throat swallowing, his stomach. Her mind sinking, she felt her mouth moving. Asking him what he thought he was doing. What you think? Then his lips soft on her collarbone. She stretched toward him and the warmness. Her arms overhead and he peeled off her top. I'm tired Ty. She arched her back and he slid off her shorts and he kissed her navel. You hear me? I'm tired. He peeled off his clothes and entered her, the groaning in his throat deep and at the base and vibrating across his chest and shoulders. Isn't your pizza coming? He didn't take very long. His goosebumps and the air blowing cool from his lips. He gave her a napkin and lay beside her. Her eyes closed, her consciousness there in a thin tendril but there, still awake.

They lay for a while, half covered by sheets, the fan oscillating in the far corner. She asked what was that? Why you asking? I don't know why. He asked was it good? She said yes. After a few moments of quiet in bed, a sound spurted up from his throat, man I'm still hongry as hell. He lifted the lid on the pizza box asking her if she wanted a piece. She said sure and didn't bother to ask what kind it was. He stood chewing. She could hear all manner of tongue thrusting and bodily liquids. You don't want your slice? She said no, she had changed her mind. You can have it.

When he sat on the edge of the bed eating her slice, she pulled away and rolled over, her movements annoyed. He asked what was wrong. She said that her arm, it was getting pinched or falling asleep or something, she couldn't remember a second later what she said, she just wanted him to stop making so many sounds like that.

When he was done eating, he understood that signs were being sent but which ones? what for? but whatever. All he knew was he was unwelcome so he left with the pizza box, thanking her for driving him earlier, for the meal. She faintly protested that he should stay but did not walk him to even her bedroom door. She felt much better when the door was shut and the crack of light beneath it was clear, and finally relieved when she heard the front door close shut.

33

A few days after hearing God speak, Vonny heard he'd been laid off from the shipyards. They told him it wasn't personal, that something unforeseen had happened, delays in Congress awarding contracts to ships—So all you new guys are bearing the brunt of that—but Vonny didn't need an explanation. This too was part of God's plan. Though he hadn't heard the voice since the buffet, this was indeed the Lord speaking again, the Lord telling him he was needed elsewhere.

Vonny said his goodbyes, each of the olderdoods telling him he'd go far just keep working hard, then twisting earplugs back in, they returned to work.

It wasn't clear what the next move was. Present on his mind was the vastness of this world. A single planet, and all the variety of climates and wildlife it contained, flashed before him. He saw a solitary bird flying through the Grand Canyon. Now it was a long pole of a gondolier slipping into the water. Then he was laying on his back looking at the stars.

Yet his mind kept coming back to Charlottesville. He had a need to venture out, to be a man in this world as God had intended, but as big as the world was, he still needed to go somewhere where he knew people. After his brother had moved back home from Petersburg, there were no options left.

He asked the Lord, I don't need to go back till next spring but ... forreal? Charlottesville? That where you want me?

Waiting around a few days for a response, Vonny began making inferences on the Lord's behalf, then shortly after that, began making moves.

The UPS depot in Charlottesville was hiring. They got back to him right away and he drove up for the interview. When they notified him the next day that he landed the supervisor position, he packed all his stuff in his car and drove up. He was on the verge of signing a lease on an apartment when he called home and told his father for the first time he was moving out the house. They askin first and last month for the deposit—What???? Where are you? Charlottesville. Charlottesville? How? I drove. Drove? Son you know that's not what I'm asking ...

After fussing a bit, Reverend Childress agreed to put some money in checking. But let me be clear, you're on your own after this. No more help, not until you go back to being a student. A lil while later they talked on the phone again and his father had time to cool out. So you're a working man again. Good. Your own place. This will be a good experience for you.

Sterling Apartments was a new spot out there in the woods, so new that half of the complex was still under construction. No one had lived in his unit before. The cabinets, freshly painted, stuck a little. The Sterling people provided some furniture—a couch, coffee table, another table to eat on —but he had to go to Walmart for a lamp, other small things he soon realized were essential. The TV would have to wait.

Since God had spoken to him, he hadn't a single puff of weed. In terms of brew though, he had held out as long as he could but on one of his last nights in Portsmouth, he had split a pitcher with his brother and decided that drinking was all right with the Lord, as long as he didn't get too too drunk. The trees was something different tho. For some reason, setting foot in Charlottesville once more, the urge returned. He had to run to the gas station for some Black and Milds and had been smoking them back-to-back like a fiend, too impatient to freek them.

After class Titus came through and they split a pack of Killians. Hahaha fuck is good with the jacuzzi out there? Then Q and them came through, each rubbing Vonny's newly shaved head. Don't he look young now? I was bout to say the same thing hahahaha. It was bout time he did, shit. I was gonna sneak up on him when he was sleep, Vonny mushing back, you won't gon do nothin ... Someone began breaking up the dutch and Vonny feeling the tingle, looked away. When it was offered to him he said no, smiling lazily. UPS drug test. You aint driving no truck, hahaha, I don't see why they trippin. Yeah just go to GNC and get you some goldenseals. Fuck that, you could just go to Kroger and get cranberry juice. The dutch was taken outside and Vonny did not follow it. Bent as hell and restless with no TV, he went outside eventually and everybody shot hoop in their jeans and clean sneakers and ended up getting too tired after chasing all those loose balls that had careened into the grass and the volleyball pit.

At the end of the night, Q and them dipped, and only Titus was left. Vonny was going around picking up the bottles and dumping the ash tray into the trash.

Titus watched him from the couch, watching from one eye as he knocked back his brew and talked aimlessly about going to G Dub next year, this decision he was facing whether he should live in DC or live at home and take the metro in. He sat drinking some more, nurturing this skeptical feeling he had about Vonny, all this cleaning, the refusal to smoke ... this allasudden good behavior, it had to come from somewhere. He called over to Vonny who was by the sink doing dishes. Yo you miss it? What, my hair? It's gettin too hot for long hair stick haha. Gets too itchy, I had to switch it up. But forreal—Vonny drew his hand up to where his ponytail used to be—I keep reaching for it still. So we'll see. I can always grow it back.

Titus laughed to himself, somehow unconvinced by anything Vonny had said just now but none of that seemed to matter anymore. He was in a good mood. He walked over to Vonny and handed him the bottle he'd just polished off. In my opinion you look even gayer with the short hair, and tried to mush him in the side of the head but Vonny preemptively mushed him first. So it's like that now huh? And they both were giggling with their dukes up, and they stayed up for a few more hours talking, just talking, so happy and relieved just talking and having someone there who could understand.

34

Joe's sister had a birthday coming up and he was thinking of getting her one of those mp3 music players. Not the name-brand one, but another one that was good still. With a rough picture of the gift in his mind, he strolled the aisle at Best Buy until he found what he was looking for locked behind a glass case. He asked the store person some very detailed questions about the product and evaded the attempts to steer him to the expensiver namebrand one. Crossing his arms grinning. Why I wanna pay more for less hours of music playback? And look, it say here that this come with a cradle, a 6 foot internet cord ... The store person turned the key on the glass case, admitting Joe was right. The box felt very light in Joe's hands. He walked with it proudly to the registers.

Waiting in line, a song came on. The song. The one that reminded him of Paul.

His brother didn't like the song or nothing. Joe had associated the song with the time period. When he was 12 and living out there with the Andersons. A yellow house. Bunch of other kids living there. Some bigger who used to pick on him. But at least it was Brooklyn. The boomboxes in the bodegas would be playing the song all day. It wasn't even a sad song. Not a good song neither. The lyrics made no sense if you listened but was supposed to be about love. It was real popular and everyone liked it and you could even play it on the radio because there was no cursing.

It used to be Joe cried whenever something reminded him of his brother. He'd have to go somewhere and steal a minute or two. Then he'd be done with it. Wouldn't think about his brother again. Wouldn't carry those emotions along. Not until the next thing came that reminded him of Paul. God knew what the next thing would be. It would just creep up on him and he'd need to go somewhere. His whole body would well up tight. He would cry for a few breaths. Then a calmness prevailed, the vision dissipating of his brother's final breath, kneeling there on the floor looking down at Paul and with that breath the soul releasing, and Joe went about his day. Days, weeks would pass before it would hit him again. It would always be something little. But between little fits like that Joe would be decent.

Regardless, he was angry he had to watch his brother die. It could've happened at any time. Why didn't them niggas bust down the door the night before when I was staying with the Andersons? I had to be there and see that crap. He was ruined. Why'd he have to look? He could've stayed in the bathroom like he was told. He could've closed his eyes and held his brother and waited like that for the ambulance. Why'd I have to see that? Now every time I close my eyes ...

He had to take medicine for it. For other things too but the medicine made an immediate impact on that. Before he couldn't do anything to stop it. He'd be hapless to it. Over time and with the help of his medicine he just surrendered to those moments. His eyes closed, he could see it vividly, the moment the spirit left his brother. The subtle shift in his brother's weight in his arms, the releasing of tension, then slumped, eyes open but inside they were dim, and Joe was covered in piss. And waiting there and waiting there on the floor of the living room with pieces of the front door around him, waiting for the sound of the sirens. The medicine made it so there was distance. He could stand outside of those visions just far enough, just long enough, and feel ... yeah it still hurt. But not as much as before.

The cashier rang up the person in front of him. It was Joe's turn now, he could see it. He had to move one foot. Then the other. He placed the box with the mp3 music player on the counter. Will that be all? Yeah, Joe clearing his throat, that's everything. Joe laid his bills on the counter, counting them in separate cascading stacks, which the cashier watched admiringly.

In the time it took the cashier to gather the money and print the receipt, Joe was standing there wavering again, very far from where he was actually. The song was playing and he was standing there stuck. Then the cashier pushed the bag across the counter and Joe walked to his car and put the keys in. Then he just sat there blinking. Yeah he had seen it. The whole thing again. The release. All of Paul relaxing. Gone that instant. Something was wrong tho. None of it, it didn't feel right this time. It felt far away for some reason. Too far. There was no effect. Paul might as well been a stranger.

The next day he called his therapist. Is it an emergency? the receptionist asked. The word EMERGENCY flashed big in his mind and when he saw it like that, big and blinking, he grew a lil embarrassed and said nah it's not an emergency. Dr. Eugene wasn't able to meet until Friday so Joe had to make sure he was straight until then. He drank a lot of water and took his current medicine as prescribed. For a stretch of a few hours he made a conscious effort to smoke less. He walked up to the gym and shot hoop for the first time in forevers. He talked to his sister on the phone. She had gotten the money he sent a few days ago but not the gift yet. I can't wait. Thank you sooo much. You all right Joey? You sound a lil off. Like you preoccupied. Do I? Just busy. Exams. You'll see what I mean in a few years ...

Titus said come through Vonny's new spot off grounds. They got a jacuzzi there. Joe made an excuse. Found it easier to hide in his room the next time.

Dr. Eugene asked how he was holding up. Did he need his levels checked? Was he consistent with his medication? I been thinking bout my brother a lot lately. Paul? Yeah. He told the doctor what happened at Best Buy, standing in line and hearing that song, and then that strange old feeling of being stuck, and how Paul for some reason, he felt like some stranger. How are you feeling right now? Right now I'm fine. Maybe it's because you here and we talking about it. But I know as soon as I leave this office, it might go back to ... What kind of thoughts are you having? For the remainder of the session, Joe was coached by his doctor to articulate thoughts and feelings, and Joe did so, his arms crossed, naming things, specks of mental phenomena, as he had been doing for the greater part of his life. After a while he grew tired of describing and it seemed anyhow he was telling people what they wanted to hear. He gave into that, serving his responses to the waiting blank expression sitting across him, serving it up a certain way so the interview would be done quicker and he could get on with his day.

The doctor wrote him a new script. In the parking lot, Joe looked at the slip of paper for a long while. He was thinking of the milligrams that would come into his body and how they would play their games with him. It's the medicine doing this to me. I was all right the other week when I went off a few days. I was good. Everything was fine. I don't even need it. When I tried to get back on, that's what fucked me up.

He didn't have the courage to follow his impulse to tear up the prescription into tiny unrecognizable little pieces. He began to fold the slip then, annoyed at himself for being a pussy, crushed it into a ball and stuck it into the bottom of one of his busiest pockets where he bet on himself forgetting about it.

35

This year the year-end BBQ was at Faulkner. Titus left for class in the morning, stood and joined the clapping at the end of one lecture, and was on the bus back to his apartment before noon, his stomach empty but he was in a positive mood. Someone had told him that the organizers were going to get the grill going earlier this year. Last year people got to drinking on empty stomachs haha ... then once them boys came with the paddy wagon we just went back in the crib and drank there ...

Listening to the familiar scene, Titus thought on where he was when these events transpired, a picture of the bright slick day room of the jail flashing in his mind and he continued listening, out of sorts but in a good way, shocked that he'd done what he set out to do, get all the way caught up and graduate. The fact hadn't stopped seeming surreal.

Now he got off the bus and smelled the grill, and walked up the hill to where a Tahoe was pulled up onto the curb, the driver inside talking on a cell. It was DJ Tone Capone. He'd graduated a few years back. Titus knew him, gave him dap and Tone complained about having to wait for his mans to help with the equipment, so Titus ended up helping him lower his speakers from the back of the truck to the curb. Tone said that's all that he needed. He could roll the dolly out from here. They both looked at the crates and turntables and the heavy clump of cords remaining in the truck. Titus was about to help him with the rest but was stopped by the smell of meat being laid on the grill. Tone noticed it too and they both went to the courtyard and said wassup to the grill-master who refused their dap and told them he wasn't fallin for that. Yall niggas wait on the side. Why? You know why. Hahaha go head nigga hahaha. You know if we big boy you, you won't do nothin. And the grillmaster brandished his tongs and dukes were raised and they were all laughing and jabbing and parrying through the smoke, and Tone ran back to his truck because it was unlocked and all his stuff was out on the curb. Titus took the opportunity to slip back into his apartment with a napkin full of chips and a half cooked drumstick.

The fridge was out of brews so he had to wait until Joe woke up to ask about making another run to the store. Titus waited and waited, cursing how Joe had been sick for a minute now. How come his ass don't go back to the doctor? Then Vonny strolled into the den eating from a plate and bobbing his head to the bassline coming from the courtyard, and they grabbed another plate outside and said wassup to the loose crowd of people and got DJ Tone Capone to play some hard shit, which sounded so good over his speakers, like the beat was going inside and coming up through them simultaneously, and it was hard to peel away, but they drove over to Barracks before the party got too deep, and got enough brews and liquors to last a few days. Vonny used his credit card. Don't worry stick I get paid soon.

They took one shot each and saved the rest for later. Joe was up now. They could hear him in the shower clearing phlegm. Joe said he couldn't take a shot right now, maybe later, and went back into his room.

Dog he look terrible. I know. Yesterday I told him go get checked and he said nah it's my allergies. I said whatever it is, it sounds like it's getting worse. Vonny turned his head away, trying to stop giggling at something. Shorty musta broke his heart real bad hahaha. Man Vonny you dumb. Let's see what's good out there.

Titus and Vonny went out to the landing with their cans of Steel. They sat looking out at the courtyard, the people hugging and picture snapping, other people talking and being able to hold a conversation while each 2 stepped to the music and drank from Dixie cups and balanced full plates of food, and there were people in the stairwell across the way huddled around what looked to be a dice game. Scratching his chest beneath his wifebeater, Vonny stood to get a better look and sat down on the step again, and said he shouldn't go too hard tonight. He was getting tired already. What time you work tomorrow? The same time. Early.

They drank some more and recognized a drunk smiling face down in the courtyard and unable to stand, waited for the dood to come to them. The dood squeezed past people and was coming up the step rubbing his palms with the naughty head shaking look like awwwww shit like they were old dogs or something. They gave hard ass dap to the dood, pulled in for the shoulder—Awwww of course yall up in here with the Steel hahaha—and after the Hollywood laughing and exchanging of addresses and phone numbers (the dood had a little pocket spiral notepad) he melded back into the courtyard. Titus and Vonny tried to figure out dood's name. It was nowhere near the tips of their tongues, though they entertained themselves trying to remember, and got hungry and went back to the gazebo for more food, and got stopped by some people, and leaned in unsmilingly for some pictures and went back to the stoop to watch the Alphas do their thing twirling the canes. Stepping and twirling in formation. Tossing the canes and catching them and rolling their hips so the females whistled catcalls and threw dollar bills, which were scooped up quickly and unapologetically by the people who threw them, everyone calling that trife and laughing and holding their sides.

Titus and Vonny sat on the top step of the landing drinking their Steels observing, knowing the other was noticing the same things. Deep in their chests was a peace and appreciation. A wholeness. All this drinking in broad day, the police nonexistent. Somebody broke out a super soaker backpack. Pumping the handle and giving chase to some females bouncing and jangling and screaming but with smiles and it was allgood. It was hard imagining times better than these. Everybody was going some place better after this, name brand graduate schools, up-all-night cities along seaboards. If not better, at least not worse.

36

Down the road from the Blackout BBQ, Alvis Rogers—
people called him Muffin—knelt to the turf and dug his
fingers into the chalked white line that the equipment
manager laid down this morning. As he had feared despite
his father and teammates gassing him up, all 32 NFL teams
passed on him. And passed repeatedly. The draft lasted a
whole 3 days and by the end, his father was convinced that
someone had sabotaged them. They were certain the Giants
would call and were so angry at the scout that they considered not returning his message. Muffin consoled his father
and looked up on the internet some names of a few NFL
players that had gone undrafted and gone on to successful
careers. His father did not relinquish his belief in a sabotage
yet they called back the scout. The private workout was
scheduled for Tuesday the 27th.

Tuesday the 27th, the last day of classes, the day of the
year end BBQ, Muffin woke up alone, having told his girlfriend that he would treat this workout like any other game
day, and he needed the space to get in the right mental state.

Digging his fingers into the turf that morning, Muffin raised his rear and visualized 6.625 on the scout's digital timer, the numbers God-sized in his vision, then he blinked and saw nothing but cones. 3 cones. Arranged in an L. One cone beside his fingers in the turf, the next 5 yards up and 5 yards to the right of that one, the last cone stood. He'd run this drill a hundred times awake, a couple hundred more times asleep. He was at the point where completing this drill required the brainpower of scratching an itch on his calf. He didn't have to think about his path up and back and around those cones, the number of steps, the number of breaths required for 6.625. Stay light. Stay quick. He didn't have to think about the many opportunities for doom along the way, a scout's slow trigger finger being one that kept him up at night. While it had occurred to him at some point that his body could fail at any moment, it didn't occur to him now as he stilled his breath and let his body expand in the dull air rising from the grass. He had a taut right hammy as of this morning, a twinge in his neck that warned him not to turn his head too far to the left. It didn't occur to him that running a time over 6.625 was possible. His mind's eye couldn't see it, which meant it didn't exist.

The scout from the Giants stood with a timer and clipboard. I'll start on you.

Muffin slowly drew his free hand to his hip, let it rest there for a half count. He burst outward and swiped the middle cone with his middle finger. He pivoted back to the original cone keeping his hips low, chopping his feet, light, light, light, like the trainer said to do. He halted in near splits and knocked the cone over with his other hand then reverse pivoted, his foot slipping in the bed of his cleat, his big toenail ramming itself against the seam and he felt a bright pain shoot over the front part of his foot. His whole leg twitched. He bound towards the far side of the middle cone on the horizon. Light, light, light. Feeling his elbows fly away he pulled his limbs into his core and regained his balance as he threaded a figure 8 around the last cone and back through the middle one. He threw his chest forward crossing the finish past the scout who squatted and wrote the time on the clipboard.

6.876.

Muffin untying his cleat with the throbbing big toe, Lemme run that back.

The scout let him run it again.

Muffin tumbled across the finish and popped up off the turf again, scowling over his knees when the scout told him his time had worsened by a tenth of a second. Look sir I can beat that—Muffin untying his cleat—I run 6.6's all the time in practice. It's that these shoes aren't broken in.

The scout let him run it 2 more times. Not even timing the last one.

C'mon Alvis 6.8 is the best we can do. We still got to do the shuttle. What they don't deal with fatigue in the League? The scout laughed. Go get some water and some shade and I'll give you plenty of time before we start the shuttle. You're lucky I'm not averaging these times.

The scout watched Muffin go over to the side of the building where there was shade, and lay on his back with a towel over his face.

The scout glanced at his wrist where a watch had been a few days ago, forgetting he had left it in a Tampa hotel. Today he had to be at Dulles by 5. He remembered that he had hit traffic the last time he was coming up this way through Virginia. The scout looked at his bare untanned wrist again, and crossed his arms, not able to suppress the anxiousness of missing his flight. His oldest daughter had driven in from Cincinnati with the baby. He very much missed his daughter and felt guilty about missing her last visit in February.

He clicked through the modes of his stopwatch, knowing the time and date were off since he'd changed the battery. All the chances he had to set it. He knew it would come back to bite him. He considered going over and asking Muffin the time. He probably had the time right? They all had cell phones these days? But the scout knew it wouldn't look right. The kid would know right away.

The scout tried to do some calculations in his mind based off the time he left that little diner and he remembered asking the waiter the time and the waiter had to look at the clock on the wall ... and the scout was getting fidgety about not knowing the precise time and resenting this kid for missing his flight. Probably wouldn't make the 53 anyway who are we kidding? But the scout kept telling himself the right thing to do was to let this young man finish. Words such as duty and obligation ran through the scout's mind, then he began to question what those words meant, and if he had a greater duty to tell this young man the truth. What could a man call this obligation? Where did it come from?

The scout tore a little strip off one of the clipboard pages and wrote GET A WATCH and walked over and thanked Muffin for his time but that it wasn't going to work out. Muffin hadn't even removed the towel from his face when the scout started in, Look son I'm not the one to tell you that the road ends here. That's only for you and your family to decide...

Muffin had removed the towel and was looking at the scout standing over him, the brightness behind the shoulders, the face shadowed. The mouth was moving, the brow knitted. Muffin sensed the man was being truthful, so Muffin said okay. They did not shake hands. The man walked away and there was just the brightness, which stretched and stretched around him in all directions. By the time Muffin left the facility his joints were so stiff from sitting on the ground he had trouble getting up.

37

Vonny leaned into Titus and said aye look. Over there. Titus gazed across the dancing bodies in the courtyard towards the gazebo. He squinted at the familiar oblong head, then saw the high, well-defined cheekbones of their roommate Kev, who they hadn't seen in weeks, and he was talking to some people, the slips of his white teeth clear from a distance. They rolled up to him warm and happy, punching Kev in the arm—Sup boy!—and clapping the back of his neck and rubbing shoulders and cursing at him warmly fuck you doon here you big block head nigga? You booed up with that new girl and you never wanna kick it no more? Titus and Vonny were so happy to see their sporadically long lost roommate they forgot Kev was in the middle of talking to some other people. Two bigass silverback niggas. Football players. Hahaha aye yall know Artie and Shai? We did the Fashion Show together. And the two big niggas turned toward them, taken aback but their hands were already up for dap, and Titus and Vonny, surprised too, saw the hands up for dap, and just went with it. Sup. Sup. Sup.

Kev was in the middle of explaining what he was doing after graduation. It was that program that stuck him in the hood to teach for a few years. He'd gotten in. He was trying to use a metaphor to illustrate the difference between two things but the metaphor had too many parts to it and nobody knew what his point was in the first place. The football players nodded in agreement but had nothing to say.

Vonny asked where the school was. Miami. Oh word? Kev nodding. The football players and Titus and Vonny all chuckling softly because they knew what that meant, Miami. Man. You lucky ass faggot man. Titus clapped him on the shoulder. Vonny hung his arm around Kevin. Yo you gon let me slide thru stick man what's good? The football players said forreal. I might need to lay up at your crib down there. Aye Kev you got a spot there yet? And excitedly asking Kevin questions about Miami they slowly formed a circle around him, closing in, taking turns clapping him on the shoulders and back and dapping him up and laughing, laughing at the same time at stuff, and what the other group said, and looking up and noticing they was laughing at the same time, then Vonny tapping one of the football players sayin he heard the clubs down there don't close till 5 in the morning and the big ol silverback nigga going 5 in the A-M???? and Vonny confirming, his hand over that big nigga shoulder bruh, you could get bent, go to sleep, wake up and the club still open, and they were all laughing at the same time at the same stuff feeling real good and no longer self conscious about the fact they belonged to different squads.

And at a certain point, one of them big niggas leaned in and asked what he felt needed to be acknowledged ... and he said to Titus what's good? Titus looked at him whatchu mean by that. Come walk with me dog lemme holla at you. And they walked off to the side and talked some, saying to each other that this whole beef that might of existed was dumb. Nobody could say how or why it started. How'd we let this go on so long? Aint nothin really happened if you think about it. True, true. You can't let the beef go on like this. Yeah we shoulda deaded it in the first place. True, true indeed. They gave each other dap, shoulder tapped and said to each other, making sure to look the other in the eye, Squashed? and nodding solemnly.

They came back to the party feeling relieved but they kept their faces hard and told their people what had transpired. Everybody nodded. Made sense. Was the right thing to do. Yeah you right. How'd we let it go on that long? Yeah over what? The answers evading them, the feeling of doing right spread. Then there was a feeling that the end of the beef should be made official. That oaths be made, palms be slapped together. Proper witnesses present. Heads nodded. Yeah that was the right thing to do. Clumps of bodies, mostly football players, forming in the courtyard. Nodding, dapping. Titus all yo niggas here? Yeah Vonny here. Whaddabout that one dude you run with? Who? The nigga from New York? Vonny where Joe at? Callum. He still in the crib. Go gettum then.

Joe was in his room playing poker on the computer when Vonny came through, You *still* playin that shit? Joe not turning to look, Aye could you put a sign out there that say BATHROOM OUT OF ORDER or something? Joe rifled amongst the spent tissues on the desk and found one that wasn't soggy. He blew his nose and wiped at it, smearing the mucus around more than removing it. That's disgustin dog haha, just go getta new one. I'm serious about that sign son. If one more nigga bang on the door asking for the bathroom —Don't let them in then hahaha—It was a 200 dollar pot

not too long ago. You lucky these niggas is garbage son.
Come outside we got niggas out here tryna squash this beef.
What? Football niggas. What they wanna say to me? Sall-
good cuh, they just tryna squash shit properly. Make that
shit official. Squashed? I aint got nuttin to do with them
niggas. Just come outside then. Why? I aint got nuttin to do
with that, that's you and Titus beef. Vonny softening his
voice, rubbing his palms together, Look Joe you know how
niggas is. It won't take but 2 seconds...

Joe and Vonny came out after Joe finished the hand, Joe
wrinkling up and wiping his face and snorting. Too fuckin
bright out here gotdamn. Hope disshit don't take too long.
Vonny brought Joe in front of the football players in the
courtyard who had their heads cocked laughing it up with
Titus by the picnic tables, shoulder tapping and dapping
each other up. And their eyes turned to Joe, their smiles
dissolving somewhat seeing the nigga wiping and
scrunching his face looking irritated and inconvenienced
and there were wet spots of snot along the collarbone areas
of Joe's shirt but they tried to keep optimistic in spite of that,
and they pursed their lips coolly and even found Joe
amusing in his triflingness. Joe's cornrows old as hell lookin
like shredded wheat.

Titus put his arm around Joe. You good baby? Yeah. My
allergies.

A football player approached, punched his palm. So we
all good now Joe? Scratching his chest Joe looked at the
ground, snorted and reached in his pocket for a tissue. So
we all good now Joe? Joe man you good there baby? Joe
coughed and mumbled and scratched his chest and his eyes
went out of focus with all those people out there lookin at
him and he knew how triflin and snotty he looked gotdamn
why all these muhfuckers lookin at me this cornyassshit.

What he say? The circle of observers and oathtakers closed in a little more. What he say? DAMN MAN! I SAID WE STRAIGHT. Fuck wrong with that nigga?

Another football player, a youngbuck on the team, punt returner, punched his palm with eyes big and not so drunk but jumpy—My nigga we still got prollems? Aint no prollems. Joe wiped his face. Aint gon be no prollems man. We straight I told ya. The youngbuck leaned in eyes bigashell, his voice high and tight. So we good? We good man I said we good. If you don't touch me or my niggas they won't be no prollems. Joe patted his waist at the end of saying that. What? Ya heard me. WHAT???!!?? Young-buck shoved Joe in the chest and Joe fell back into Titus. Fuck he say? Fuck what he said you aint see him pat his waist like that? HE SAY HE GON SHOOT FOOTBALL PLAYERS!!!! Another youngbuck climbed up on the picnic table holding his beltbuckle, WE GOT GUNS TOO FAGGOT! Titus tried to wrestle Joe back, shut the fuckup and don't say nothin nigga. Fuck off me yo! You football niggas is pussy! Aye he don't mean that. Joe you don't mean that you dumb muhfucker. Titus turned and shoved Joe towards the apartment but the football players were pushing up on him and Titus kept pushing Joe towards the door as hands reached over and past him. They were on the landing outside their unit and Titus shoved Joe through the door and stood guarding it with Vonny lookin at some 20 30 football niggas surrounding them. Titus with his hands up, Aye man don't listen to that nigga Joe. He aint been right in the head lately. HE SAY HE GON SHOOT FOOTBALL PLAYERS! We seent him pat his waist like he gon do somethin. Titus still with his hands up, Chill niggas we gon talk to him and sort this nigga out. Best believe aint nobody wanna beat his ass worse than me and Vonny. BRINGUM OUT HERE! Titus and Vonny ignoring the demand. BRINGUM OUT HERE THEN! He a grown man Titus. If he got sumpin to say to us, then let that man speak his mind. Titus said alright, went inside and deadbolted the door behind him. The football players pounded on the door cursing HE AINT COMIN OUT, I TOLE YOU!!!!

Titus shouted Joe where you at? JOE! Joe came out of his room with his llama hanging at his side. Titus stepped in front to block him. Move nigga. You aint gon shoot allem niggas out there man. I said MOVE. Joe raised his hand to mush Titus. Titus reacted quick, shoving sharp and hard enough for Joe to come off his feet and Joe ran up on him again and they rammed chests and their arms got tangled and Vonny saying hey yawl be careful with that, then wedging himself inbetween, It's gon be cool yawl, and meanwhile the door continued to bang and the football players continued to shout.

On a dime the sounds turned. The police. Titus and Joe stopped clenching and they all listened. Slowly they leaked to the den, Vonny first to look through the peephole, then Titus to shut the blinds, then Joe sat on the loveseat still gripping his pistol.

They sat quietly, their shirts dirty, collars stretched out, listening for the trajectories of bodies outside. People being chased. Collisions, escapes, and people herded off one way or another. Cars in the lot leaving, honking and cursing and people shouting for their friend to come over here hurry. Glass shattered in the lot and Vonny got up to look through the blinds. He said it wasn't his whip. Joe your car good too. Joe said thank goodness.

Popping the top of some Steels they listened to the last of the scragglers in the courtyard getting surly with the police. They listened and laughed wanting it to be funnier than it was but they were tired. It was about 5pm now.

Titus went to his room and peeked through the blinds. DJ Tone Capone had packed up his gear. Dixies and crinkled foil, a bottle or two glinting in the grass. It was ghost out there.

Titus caught a nap. When he woke it was barely 6 and there was plenty of light still. He went out to the den and saw Joe slumped over in the loveseat, snoring, the llama nested in the trash on the coffee table. Vonny had his shoes off laying across the couch. He was still up playing on his phone. You get some sleep stick man? Yeah. Vonny said he was going to hit up Q's man for a dub right quick. Titus said he'd go too and changed. Vonny looked him up and down. Yo you dressin to go OUT out? Yeah I can't stay cooped up in here. I wanna get something to eat too. What you aint hongry too? He gave Vonny a new tee since all he had besides his wifebeater was his UPS work polo. They figured they might as well bring some of this brew and started grabbing what they could, leaving one, never mind that 2 bottles for Joe in the fridge.

Joe woke up and was looking at them blinking, unsure. Vonny had a bottle under his armpit and a case in the other hand, which he set down on the edge of the coffee table and held out his hand for Joe. Aight boy we get up with you later. Where yah bout to go? We gon holla at Q and them real quick. Where Q live? U Heights. Yah coming back? We might. Yah goin to the after party joint? Vonny shrugged and asked Titus what he wanted to do. Titus was already leaving out the front door. Vonny said we might slide through. I gotta work tomorrow though. Aight hit me up if yah leave. I aint tryna go up there dolo or nuffin.

* * *

Vonny and Titus rolled up to that new Subway down the way and it was jumpin. The line was long but moved quickly. Since the cashier was black, Vonny got up on his toes and leaned in scratching the back of his ear saying under his breath in his tidewater drawl wassgood? The cashier understood and rung them up for only one combo.

They sat and ate. Titus could still feel that vibration. It was quiet but there. A layer within all the other layers. Watching Vonny eat he could tell Vonny sensed it too but it didn't seem to bother him. They threw their arms over the backs of the booth and chewing they looked around at the people, most of which were students, no one noticeably bent but everybody was happy and talking. Felt like there was plenty more day left.

Titus balled his napkin. You mighta been right it being more than a physical thing with Joe. Huh? What you said earlier, him being depressed about shorty, I agree with you. Vonny couldn't remember what he was talking about so Titus asked what happened when you went inside to get him? He was playin poker, I own know, seemed aight to me stick man. Titus sucked his teeth, Knew it. Was a mistake getting him. Fuck was I thinkin? All I had to say was I don't know where he is. Or that the nigga left.

They tried talking at it some more but the itis was setting in, the spaces between their replies growing longer, their backs sliding down the plastic booths. It won't nobody's fault stick, it's all good ... But I'm sayin tho, he aint been right lately, we shoulda seent it comin ...

Afraid they'd fall asleep, they got up, thanked the black cashier and left.

* * *

They went over to Q's spot. It was crowded cos he had his boys from outta town staying there. As Titus and Vonny stepped through the door with bottles in their armpits and cases of brew in their hands, heads tilted from the couch. Look it's them troublemakers again. Haha. Dap exchanged all around. Questions about what went down earlier. Titus and Vonny shook their heads, said yall might ask that nigga Joe cos I don't even know.

It was hot in there and Q had one tall oscillating fan. Doods laid around in their wifebeaters with their faces long and sweaty. Titus sat drinking looking at the TV. Vonny paid Q's man and started splitting the dutch in the kitchen where the fan didn't blow. When the smoke got too strong, Titus went outside to the front balcony overlooking the parking lot. He leaned on the rails and looked at the cars. He thought about Brooke. Where she was today. He pictured her surrounded by a bunch of people, everyone trying to get her attention. Her head tossed back laughing when another person came up to her, and she would cover her mouth, bout to die she was so surprised to see this new person, it'd been so long. He was happy for her and sensed he would see her again, maybe even tonight, and there wouldn't be any coldness or awkwardness between them.

Vonny came out there after a little while and leaned on the rails with him. Vonny said that he remembered what Titus was referring to earlier about Joe. I was just joking about him being depressed. I didn't know he had these mental issues going on. Titus kept bobbing his head to the bassline coming from a car parked below, already over the topic, going it aint nothin. Q came out there and was talking real slow. It wasn't clear what he was saying but he kept holding his hand up for dap, saying yall feel me doe? And Q had the idea in his head that Vonny and Titus were laughing at him and he was a little irritated and Titus said shuttup Qazi and your Taliban lookin ass. Don't make me bust your lip again. Q leaned way out over the railing and said yoooo to someone down there. Vonny grabbed him, laughing, Nigga you don't want to fall and die haha. What they gon say on the news about you? Vonny helped Q inside. A few minutes later Titus followed.

There were doods sprawled across the couches and the floor napping, one guy snoring under the music, and periodically someone coughed and had a big swallow. The room was growing darker. One by one doods woke, each staggering with their doo rags to and from the bathroom. The music got louder and the volume on the TV rose up in competition. There was a debate going on by the couch about the NBA playoffs, about whether the game was changing and players were putting themselves above the team more and more, and someone accused the other of looking too much into it. If I woulda hit that shot I'd do a lot more than point at my chest. He aint point at his chest. He pulled his jersey back to show his heart. Same difference. Someone else pointed out that none of it mattered because his team ended up losing in the end. So? They going up against the 1 seed. Of course they gon lose...

By this point the brew flowed and shots were taken to the dome and there was ironing and showering and babypowdering of ballsacks and mists of Coolwater being sprayed and walked into and someone broke out the clippers for a quick touch up and the bluntsmoke was thick enough to violate so Titus went out to the balcony again. The sun had fully set, the drama from the BBQ earlier in the day was a whole nother lifetime ago. He looked at the cars in the lot below hoping, expecting to see something, someone, a sign of some sort, if only a glimmer. He found himself getting a little excited at the rustle of keys in the pocket of someone walking to their car. He didn't even know why people were celebrating today. Yeah it's the last day of classes but we still got exams starting this Friday. We aint do nothin yet. Why we patting ourselves on the back already? Vonny came outside and Titus relayed to him this convo he'd been having with himself. Vonny said yup that's true stick. But that aint never stop no one from drinking haha.

Eventually everybody from Q's spot cobbled themselves together and descended the stairs in a cloud of wobbly vapor. They packed tight into several vehicles all ass and elbows. They drove past Sigma Nu and saw that it wasn't jumping yet. They lingered on the road analyzing the security out front but a cop flashed his high beams and they pressed the gas and kept it moving. They parked in the cut and headed towards their old spot. Vonny led the way through the mulch and they reached a part behind the house where the ground rose high enough to almost reach the window. Titus boosted him up to look and no one was in there and Vonny started pushing on the jamb, his whole body shaking with effort, Titus shaking too and gripping Vonny by the knees tighter. It was locked from the inside he said. They checked some of the other windows and Vonny decided him and Titus were going to go through the front and let niggas in that way. Vonny pulled a bottle out of his pants and handed it to Q. We see yawl in a lil while. Vonny and Titus got inside but all the other doors in there were locked. Vonny consulted his instincts, then his imagination, then grew tired suddenly and called Q and told him we get up with yawl later. We gotta wait here for Joe. Over the phone Q said that they'll hit up the Corner for now and come back when it's a little more deep.

Vonny and Titus posted up in the foyer where they could see everyone coming through. The security didn't let in no townies, not even no out of town people who said they went to college too. It was strictly UVA. The party was ass for a while cos of that. On top of the usual. People was dancing but friend dancing. Not no freeks. It felt like junior high. Titus told Vonny to call Joe again. He on the way stick I just called him. Eventually Joe rolled up alone. He was looking a lil better, like he took another shower, and by this point the party was thickening up a lil, and non UVA people were sliding through the cracks. Then there weren't cracks. People coming through. Q and his people came, Q slipping the bottle of brown to Vonny. It was getting crowded and they got pushed back from the foyer to a long narrow hallway next to the downstairs stairs, which were blocked off by a couch. People slid by with their bodies rubbing against one another and the walls sucking in their guts. Polite for the time being. Nobody stepping on nobody toes. Titus and Vonny were standing on both sides of Joe dapping up the people they knew and hollering at them a quick word or 2 before the current of traffic carried them away to wherever. The stream was slowgoing but steady, Vonny and Titus chanting just below the surface of their respective consciousnesses I just want to get the fuckonnup outta here already before something happen. Then Vonny sensed someone shoving through the crowd. Tremors. Nothing visual at first. Then it was visual. A big arm swimming over, bodies being dislodged in the path. The path coming straight. Muffin's eyes red and swollen and not peripheral but just aimed straight ahead and slightly down and through. Vonny swerved in front smooth and tried to box Muffin out nonchalant but he almost fell over. Muffin was about to swim through Vonny but he stopped, recognizing him. Muffin and Vonny lived in adjoining dorms first year and had gotten fucked up together once or twice, nothing too crazy, and were still on dapping terms whenever they saw each other around, the memories of first year still warm but evaporating quickly. Their acquaintance never developed, and they never thought about the other, but they both liked each other and smiled a lot whenever they happened to cross paths.

Recognizing Vonny again, oh shit, Muffin dapped him up and whispered in his ear, Lemme holla at your mans right quick. Naw dog, Vonny tryna play it cool, it aint a good time right now. How come? Not a good time. Then the line of questioning rebooting, Lemme holla at your mans right quick. Naw dog ... Muffin leaning in breathy with a hand paternally across Vonny's shoulders, his tone reasoning as Vonny shrugged feeling small bracing the weight of this football player's ropy arm. I just wanna holla at him. It'll be quick. Vonny could play it cool but for so long before Muffin picked him up off the ground (Vonny's eyes bulging, oh shit this nigga a big boy) and flung him to the side.

Joe hadn't even noticed Muffin had been right there the whole time. Joe had been hollin at shorty he had a class with. Muffin was standing right behind him, Excuse me, I heard you been going around saying you was gonna shoot football players. Joe turned halfway then continued talking to shorty. Aye I'm talking to you. Joe turned his head, his expression annoyed and rolling his eyes and Muffin reached out and started choking him. Titus said oh shit and jumped in and tried to pry Muffin off him. Vonny grabbed at Muffin's other arm. Muffin grinding his jaw tight and shaking Joe's neck with each word, That's—what—yagit, as Joe slowly slid down the wall with his legs kicking everywhere. In a moment they were able to separate Muffin's hands from Joe's neck. Females was cryin and screaming and hardly no one was laughing. Someone shouted that the cops was at the door. IT'S THEM BOYS!!!! Bodies jerked in all directions. Vonny was shouting to Titus. I can't find him stick. What? I CAN'T FIND HIM. Find who?

* * *

Joe staggered across gravel. Then the crunch of gravel stopped and he was on grass. He tripped and tumbled partway down a hill and he tried to stand up and slid the rest of the way. He pushed off the ground and limped towards the dim orange lights of the parking lot across the field. He could hear people running past him. They were flying past him, the sirens pushing them just a little more than they were capable.

Eventually Joe reached the parking lot. His head was spinning and he ducked between two vehicles, wheezing and weak. He tried to suck in the air but he couldn't and he choked on himself. He heard himself gagging so he bent over and hacked and his eyes filled with water and the world was shards of light and his throat shards and the pain shooting through him as he heard people laughing and howling, HERRY UP FAGGOT! and getting into their cars. He could finally breathe.

Joe sat in his car. He tried to call Vonny but his hands were shaking too much to press the distinct numbers. He sat looking at his hands shake in his lap. When that passed, it was replaced by a singular, and suddenly all consuming urge to find that nigga who had tried to hurt him. He just wanted to find him. Look at him with his eyes. The man who wanted to end his existence. He wasn't sure what he was going to do. He needed to see him. Then it would be clear.

As Joe pulled out of the parking spot, he made out, through the shards twinkling in his vision, a few broad shouldered figures on the other end of the lot. They were laughing going on about something. Walking nice and easy.

Joe pulled the car up slow. Those big niggas were still walking nice and easy, then they spotted Joe lurking with the headlights off. They started to run but Joe was already out of the car with his palm heavy, Sup now. The doods put their hands up, said they didn't want no trouble. They was just walking to their cars. Where Muffin at? Who? Joe asked if they were football players. Two out of the three said yeah. The other one said he played basketball. Joe continued looking at them. The car was still running. He asked if they knew where Muffin was and as the words came out of his mouth, Joe felt that his voice sounded a lil off. Like he was begging. Immediately he got embarrassed and angry. He got back in his car and left.

The three athletes, instead of feeling relief, had a hard time breathing so they put their hands over their head and paced or bent over panting and eventually one sat down on the pavement just staring off, still unbelieving that a pistol had been pointed at him. Once they got over that, they whipped out their phones with the quickness and called everyone they knew.

Word spread. Quicker than quick. A noxious gas. Niggas was beyond heated. Saying they was tired of this nigga man. First he said he was gon shoot football players and yall said it was talk. What now? We got people said he pulled the tool out talkin where Muffin at? They shoved eachother in the chest right in front of Muffin.

Muffin did not react outwardly. Sitting in his truck he watched his teammates pacing restlessly across the beams of his headlights. What had happened today with the scout from the Giants, that had seemed so long ago. He began to doubt whether that was real. Then he remembered the scout standing over him telling him he wasn't good enough, using other words, but what did it matter. If he'd only let me finish.

Muffin's teammates worried that they'd never see this Joe Reed again. Just who was this nigga anyway? I never heard of him before today. How the fuck is this nigga even qualified to come at us?

More cars pulled into the U Hall lot. Teammates getting out and walking into the chain of headlights with more fuel, more fanning, and doods were getting in Muffin's ear now. Whispering. Whispering more hate, pleased seeing the scowl form on Muffin's face. Getting all up in his ear going on about you gon let this nigga do that? You gon let this man call out your name? And asking accusatorily when Muffin wouldn't answer explicitly, asking how you gon let him say your name like that? How you gon give another man permission to use your name like that?

Muffin rocking in his seat not saying much but staring blankly with his lips wide and distasteful. You gon let him do that captain? C'mon captain you gon let him do that? Other people walking around yapping into cellphones. Spreading it, fanning it. Letting it grow.

Pretty soon they felt a part of something larger. It had to do with the universe now. If they didn't make this right, they couldn't live with themselves for the rest of their lives.

They all rolled up to what they believed to be Joe's crib, where the party was at earlier that day. The caravan stretched deep. Bumper to bumper up the hill of Faulkner apartments. Cars pulled up onto grass. They walked with purpose across the courtyard and up the steps, Muffin out in front pounding on the door. They couldn't let this stand no more. *He* couldn't let this stand no more. Muffin screaming at the door that you said you was looking for me nigga. Pounding the door. It's me nigga. I'm here.

Joe had been in the apartment. Anxious, sick. Something inside him sliding down. Inevitable. He was about to go when someone else walked softly into the den, pale, shaking all over. It was Kev. Kev had been passed out in his room the entire time. Now shivering oh shit over and over shit and stopping suddenly putting his hand out, Don't, when he saw the llama dangling from Joe's arm, No don't go out there. Joe shoved him to the side and walked out onto the landing and it was deep, not that he could see anybody distinctly but the bodies in haggard rows stacked one behind the other and the whole landing swelling and Joe barked to the first and closest face he sensed WHAT NIGGA and the dood reached out to grab Joe by the throat and Joe raised his arm not even halfway, not even aiming, and popped. One side of dood buckled and his big body staggered back sliding through the arms and legs of the doods behind him and he landed on his haunches. Looking at his leg he sounded amazed, almost asking. He got me. This nigga got me? The other players were standing back looking down at Muffins leg hanging limp. When the dark spot started spreading things got loud again out there, first one nigga yelling GRAB HIM then everyone shouting and the shouts multiplying against the hard surfaces. Joe didn't wait around for this yelling. He went back into the apartment and locked the door and sat on the couch and looked at Kev, his face all twisted up and red and babbling, but not recognizing that it was Kev, but a person in a lot of pain. Feeling weak Joe slid down the couch and onto the floor. His ears rang. He felt weird all over. Like he was far away from the things he was looking at right now. The table, the TV, hands, shoes. He didn't know where he was. This room. This other face in here a million miles a minute. The people yelling outside. What time was it. The YEAR? Yelling. BANGING on the door. Screams out there of godawful agony. Someone, the sum of someones out there wanted to hurt him. Why? What they want? BANGING. Inside here it was dark. The surfaces were moving. And the dark smell of powder on his hands. His hands, he was looking down at them. He couldn't recognize them. The phone on the table buzzing. Glass breaking all around. He wanted to stand and run. His hands, these hands, for some reason they just wasn't movin.

PART IV

ROOST

38

Two days passed since the shooting.

Kevin Arancillo, who had been staying at his girlfriend's place off Madison, returned to the apartment to let in the cleaning crew. They took down the tangled metal blinds in the den and his bedroom, and picked out what remained of the broken panes. Cardboard was cut to size then spools of duct tape were stretched over the bare openings. Temporary, they said. Sweeping, vacuuming. His rug, rolled up and leaned against a corner, sagged in a sickly looking way. Bedsheets were piled on top that. The police had already recovered the hammer that had been thrown through the den window, but the other perpetrator, a chair, obviously not of this unit, remained in his bedroom. He asked that it be taken away.

Student Housing could do nothing about his computer. His computer, caught in a net of blinds and cords wrapped around the spinning legs of that demon chair, had been yanked from his desk. The monitor had a crack clear across it but still turned on. But when he pressed the power button, a faint whirring came on, followed by a kind of crunching that sounded productive, then there was not-so-good crunching, and the whirring died and the power light extinguished. Slapping seemed to help. When he was on the brink of a breakthrough, he gave one good slap and the whole unit stopped powering up. He called around for copies of files and presentations. His thoughts lingered but couldn't quite comprehend all the other stuff on the computer that was perhaps now irrecoverable.

Checking his chair for bits of glass, he put his feet up and tried to study out of a notebook for a few hours until the detectives came. Occasionally he went to the bathroom, overcome with the sick feeling he was about to say something wrong to the detectives, whether inadvertently or the result of his own desire to submit. He had never in his life spoken to law enforcement. He didn't trust himself to lie successfully, at least not to professionals.

Generally he avoided lying, not for any other reason but convenience. Everything was easier when he stuck to the truth. People asked, he told it as he saw it and so moved on with his life. He avoided situations in which he had to lie, and as a consequence, had very few close friends and many, many acquaintances.

He was trying to figure out which of these two groups his roommates fit into. Had these years living in this apartment with Titus and Vonny amounted to anything? Beyond the booze and laughs, what was their relationship? He hadn't partaken in any of their beefs, their drama, never approached them with his problems, nor they to his. If he had any problems to speak of, real ones, the kind that involved the potential for scars, he was sure they'd do the decent thing. How could they not? After all these years?

Kev lived his life such that he wouldn't be a burden to anyone. He kept his head down, worked hard, didn't complain. Didn't ask nothing from no one. He was raised that way. His parents were poor people from a poor country whose example taught him it was selfish, and ultimately degrading, to ask anything of people outside the family. And that included asking for concern or pity. Only Americans did that. To demand was simply unthinkable. Favors were regarded suspiciously and if it weren't for the church's teachings, panhandling would be met with outright hostility. Everyone had their own problems. The world was at least tolerable when people kept their suffering to themselves. Titus and Vonny seemed to respect that. Before today, they asked nothing of him.

Joe was a different matter. Kev never particularly liked him, but that was neither here nor there. That Joe went outside despite his plea to stop—Kev could barely comprehend it. How a person could destroy his own life like that, how simply it could be achieved, how quick, he had seen it himself how quick, it didn't seem real. Kev hadn't slept since that night. Being shoved out the way by Joe, the helplessness he felt watching the door open, then the body passing through with its round shoulders, and specifically the sound of the door closing, the perfect and cruel finality of it he could still hear.

Kev tinkered with his computer, thinking on things, now and then scanning the rest of the room for bits of glass Housing had missed.

* * *

There was a knock on the door.

There were two detectives, one white and somewhat young, the other black and noticeably older. They convened at the dining room table. As the younger one sat, the older walked straight to the cardboard duct taped over the den window, inspecting the hasty work, then turned to face everyone. There sure is a lot of cigar tobacco in here.

The young detective set his leather planner on the table and asked Kev if he was aware of any marijuana being smoked in the apartment. Kev shook his head and said he wasn't around much. The young detective cracking a smile and scooting his chair closer, Never noticed a funny smell? Kev consciously remained as still as possible, keeping eye contact and consciously avoiding touching his face, but didn't want to look too stiff and unnatural even though he was now seeing all the blunt guts and the ash in the room and kicking himself for at least not cleaning a little out here, but the young detective was smiling and leaning forward and trying to invite Kev to do the same—Kev shook his head, his expression plain. I'm really not here that often. The young smiling detective turned to look at the old one leaning against the wall back there and his smiling face returned to Kev. You're not under investigation here. We just want to ask a few questions about your roommate Joe then we'll be out of your way. We know you've got some studying to get back to. What's your major by the way? I'm in the Comm School. Communications? No, Commerce, it's what they call the Business major here. Business, oh I heard that's tough.

The detective opened his leather planner. Some of this stuff will be very basic but I've got to ask it. Then we're going to get to what we need to get to. When we're there I'll let you know okay? I'm sure you heard what happened here

Tuesday night. Right outside that front door right there. A student was shot. Pretty serious stuff. Not a graze mind you. The detective patted his thigh. There's a big artery here. A lot of people bleed out. Luckily that's not the case here. Then again I'm not a doctor. He turned to his partner and asked if he'd heard any updates from the hospital. The older detective shrugged, From what I hear the best case is he loses his leg. His whole leg? Oh that's a shame. Losing his leg I said that's the best case. He's not out the woods yet.

The young detective made the cross and said he'd pray for him then he clicked his pen and got to the questions. He asked the basic stuff. Then he asked some stuff about how well Kev knew Joe. Kev said not very well. He explained that Joe moved in partway through the year. In that time they had not spoken much beyond pleasantries. The detective asked if Joe was a secretive person. Secretive? Yeah did he behave like he had something to hide? I can't say really. I'm not here very often ... The young detective put down his pen and scooted his chair closer. His knee touched Kev's. Look I get it. No one likes talking to the police but now we're going to talk okay? That talk I mentioned earlier, we're here now. I want you to be real with me Kevin. There's a young man in the hospital right now fighting for his life. Somebody's baby. People forget that. We're all somebody's baby. I don't need to tell you how serious this is. You go to UVA, you study Business. Your brain comprehends stuff like this. Can I ask your nationality? I'm Filipino. That's what I thought. My wife's friend is Filipino. Nagtatagalog ka ba? Not really. But I can understand a little. Born there? No, I was born in Woodbridge. That's where I'm from. The detective had a puzzled look and turned to his partner by the window who chimed in that it was Northern Virginia. Prince William County. Yes that's what I thought. The young detective leaned back and wiped his palms on his slacks and asked Kev what it was like in Woodbridge and the conversation fell into the basics again and somehow or another they got to talking about the big ol mall up there, Potomac Mills then the detective began talking about his son and pulled out a picture from his wallet and showed Kev. He asked if Kev had any kids. Kev shook his head. You want any one day? Maybe but not any time soon. You're a smart man. The detective asked if Kev considered himself religious. His wife's friend, the Filipina, was a devout Catholic. Kev said yes somewhat. How about spiritual? Kevin said yes more so. That's good. I was talking to my sister the other day about the difference between being religious and being spiritual. To me they're the same. Then again I'm no scholar. My sister did much better in school. In any case she says to me, the difference comes down to a relationship with God. With religion a relationship with God is not necessary but with spirituality that's kinda the whole shebang. This is her breakdown of the situation. The detective asked if that made sense. Kev said yes. Then he asked his partner who crossed his arms, You really think you said something deep there didn't you? This man is a student at U-V-A. Kev let out a chuckle and the young detective turned to face Kev, grinning. Well I thought it was something.

The grin still there and with the pitch and intonation of his voice not wavering from how it was before, and with no break in the flow of the conversation, the young detective asked so where were you Tuesday night? Tuesday? Yes Tuesday. Walk me through the night. The detective by the cardboard pane was very still. Kev could tell he was listening very closely, very very very closely. Kev began speaking and he described being picked up by his girlfriend around 7 to check out the party at Sigma Nu. They drove by, didn't go inside because it looked weak. Then she drove them to a different party on Rugby, walked around some, down to the Corner for a bite to eat, and he ended up staying at her place off Madison. They asked her name and he told them Tabitha. They asked for times and he gave some. The detective wrote all of this down. The detective asked when was the last time he saw Joe. Maybe three, four weeks ago. I had to run inside to grab something. He was around. The older detective was pacing. He picked Joe's NBA patch coat off the couch. Whose coat is this? Kev said he didn't know. Not mine. The young detective asked his partner if there was anything else that needed to be asked, and right as he asked that the young detective said he remembered something. Standing up and picking up his leather planner. Can you show us which room is Joe's?

Kev walked with them down the hall and pointed at the door. Is it locked? Kev said he didn't know. Can you check for us? Me? Please. Some math occurred in his head. He hadn't been coached on this contingency. Everything else—the friendliness, the nonchalance, the small confiding smirks—he had been warned about. If in doubt, Titus told him, say you didn't know because you wasn't there. But now an officer of the law was making a request that was physical in nature. Kevin simply could not compute. He felt his body twitching all over.

He reached for the handle and depressed the lever. It was locked. That seemed to satisfy the detectives. The old one said see I told you. Tell me what? They were walking back to the living room when the young one asked about Kev's girlfriend, if it was serious. With the summer coming up and all. Kev said not just summer. He was about to graduate. Good for you. They shook his hand and seemed genuinely happy for him. You two gonna stick together? I don't know. We still got a few things to figure out. She's got one more year left here. The detective wanted to talk all about her some more. What she was studying. What she was going to do after college. Where she was from. What she was like. How they met. Kev stuck close to the truth, omitting that he and Tabitha had broken up back in October. The detective kept saying he was happy for him and Tabitha. Real happy. It was an exciting time for him. Long distance is hard but if you both want to make it work ... He asked what Kev was going to do the rest of the day. Kev said study. Yes that's right, and the detective got up and got his things ready. He took out his card, crossed out the number on the front and wrote a number on the back. You leaving town soon? Next Wednesday I'll be done with exams. Before you leave I want you to call me. He pointed at the number on the back of the card. This number, not the other one. I don't want you leaving without getting in touch. There's a chance Joe will come back for his things. If that happens, the detective pointed at the number on the back again, this number okay? We had a good talk. You're a sharp guy. I wish you nothing but success. More friendly Tagalog was spoken that Kev could barely understand. Yeah you too. One last time at the front door the detective turned back, They don't have a maid service here? Kev said nope. Aren't you the lucky guy. Maybe Tabitha can help you clean up before you leave. You don't want to lose your security deposit.

Kev peeled back the cardboard from the den window and waited for the sound of their car to sink down the road. A vague but strong guilt came over him. He wasn't sure exactly, but it felt like he had snitched somehow. He hadn't used his current girlfriend's name, Camille, or mentioned that they'd gotten into an argument, which was why he took the cab back up to Faulkner alone, pounded those last two brews in the fridge, and passed out in his room. He didn't mention how he and Joe escaped the apartment, where they were picked up and by whom, and how they had disposed the pistol in what body of water, according to the exact instructions of a self-announced expert on this matter who shall not be named. None of this he disclosed yet every sense in his body told him he'd done something to hurt his friends.

He called Vonny's cell and waited in the den for the sound of his car to pull up, and peeled back the cardboard and saw the faded, partly peeling green Corolla in the handicap spot with the arms chickenwinged out the sides. The passenger door opened, and Titus walked quickly up the ramp.

Studied closely again, Kev recounted the interview with the detectives. They didn't ask about me right? No. Only about Joe. And about all these blunt guts out here. Titus apologized, said he'd help clean up as soon as stuff cooled down. They asked one more thing. They wanted to know which room was Joe's. So? So I told them it was back-left. They go in? I don't think so. Think? Chu mean think???? They wanted me to open it for them. So did you??? I'm sorry Titus.

Kev needed to sit down.

Sorry for what Kev? Huh? What you do? I told you Kev, all you had to do was say you wasn't around. No need to be cute. I know how you are, all friendly and shit. Just stay in the box, keep it simple. Now tell me. They go in there or not? HEY, Titus clapping his hands, we don't got time to fuck around Kev, tell me.

Unable to look at the man standing over him, Kev dropped his head. He confessed to pushing the lever. It had been locked but the fact that he complied—Kev continued apologizing. He'd never done nothing like this before, he didn't know. He didn't want to do it. Everything else he did perfectly, exactly how he was told, but how was he to know they'd test him like that?

When Titus realized no betrayal had been committed, that Kev was shook, that's all, he held back from interrupting, his eye glancing now and then at the door, then at the patch of dirty carpet where his face would be if they had to surrender, then gave it a few more moments and formed an apology, pursing his lips at the end to make sure it landed, and got to work.

Snapping open a fresh garbage bag Titus picked the NBA patch coat off the couch and a pair of jeans slung over the chair, a pair of basketball shorts with a bleach stain going down the front. He found a plastic convenience store bag under an empty case of brew, approached Joe's door with the bag over his hand. He took out a key and unlocked the door and smelled the smell of Joe. In the bottom dresser drawer balled up in a black sock was a knot. He took it out and eyeballed it. Maybe 200. He put the knot back in the sock and dropped it in a garbage bag with the clothes from the den. He stood in the very middle of the room muttering to himself trying to remember what was next. The screwdriver. He took it from the desk drawer. He had a little trouble unscrewing the stop on the drawer so he gave up on that for the moment and pushed a chair up to the wardrobe and reached around blind up there with one arm for the shoebox. He felt it and brought it down. Another knot. He had dust all over his shirt now and didn't feel like counting. He gave the desk drawer another try with the screwdriver and he got the track loose this time. Pulling out the drawer he felt around and felt that ziplock taped to the interior of the desk. He screwed everything into place. Now the cell phone charger. He ducked to look under the bed. Looked in corners. Went out to the den, pulled apart the tangle of cords under the TV and couldn't find a charger anywhere. He went back into Joe's room and grabbed a clean pair of drawers, socks. Then thought about the kind of stuff he noticed Joe wearing most often and found a few shirts in the closet that Joe could choose from, and some weird looking jeans with a painted on pattern on the cuff and this weird stitching that Joe never wore.

He locked the door with the plastic bag over his hand, regretting a little that he didn't wear something over his hands while he was in there. He was standing there beginning to obsess over it then he stopped himself. He was gonna be out this place for good in a lil while.

He apologized again to Kevin. We didn't want to drag you in this. Yo listen me, you didn't do nothin wrong okay? You been tryna help the whole time. Joe, he appreciates all this. It'll be over soon I promise.

Kev asked if he would get in trouble for helping them. Titus repeated that it would be over soon.

Titus threw the bag with Joe's stuff in the trunk and got in. Vonny asked sup with the bag. Titus said it was mostly clothes. Ha you think you got enough? I don't know. Give the nigga options I guess.

They drove past the soccer field and took a left at the light, then all the way down past the basketball arena and took a left, then went down and took a left at Blockbuster above which was the phonathon office, then they went down and took a left at Copeley and they were back at the bottom of the hill at Faulkner and it didn't seem anybody was following them. They pushed toward the loop again and they took the first two lefts again and kept going straight down 29 easy and the traffic was light. It was hot out, but not as hot as earlier in the week, which made the day feel like a lazy Sunday even though it was only Thursday. Titus said turn into here for a min and they dipped into the Seminole Square Shopping Center parking lot and waited there with the car idle, both of them sunk in their seats with an eye on the side mirrors. Without AC, it was beginning to get uncomfortable sitting there. There was a Hardees in that shopping center. That seemed like a good idea. They ordered a 16 piece mixed, a jug of tea, hush puppies, cole slaw, mac. They asked for plates and utensils. Will that be all? Yes.

They more or less went straight there after that, to Vonny's crib. They leaned in their seats untalking and the shadow of the forest canopy passed over them, the road winding and they made it out of that forested part and there was the big parking lot of Sterling in the middle of a field of nothing. They cruised past Vonny's building, all the while their eyes flicking from the front to the sides and the rear view. They made a lap and came to the construction and went around to the other side and Vonny backed into a spot. Before they got out of the car Titus asked if Joe had made that call yet. Vonny shrugged. They both sat there a moment, absorbing the implications, then got out.

The TV could be heard from out in the hallway. Vonny put his ear to the door and knocked gently with one knuckle a few times before unlocking the door. Joe was laying on the couch looking at the TV. He sat up slowly, a towel sausaged around his neck. Thank god yahniggas brought something to eat. Titus set down the bag with Joe's stuff and said he couldn't find the charger. I looked all over for that bitch. Everything else I got but that charger man. Joe said it was cool. I can always buy a new one. Let's eat, I'm starving.

They joined hands standing at the dinner table. Vonny said the prayer. Father God we come before you today to give thanks and we ask in your name to bless this food so it can provide us nourishment and strength in this time of need. They squeezed hands tighter, almost so that it hurt. Lord we thank you for all the blessings you've given us, all that you've sacrificed, have done and will do for us in the future and in your name Christ Jesus, Amen. They opened their eyes, allowing themselves to return to the present, the room, the food on the table. Taking a deep breath in, they felt the spirit humming in them and they grabbed at the food a little slower than they would have.

They ate and watched whatever was on BET. Music videos. Chrome wheels spinning and the redbones and mamacitas with bright shiny half-open lips crawling towards them slowly and in slomo, it was hard to tell. Keeping their eyes on the screen, they talked out the sides of their mouths at one another chewingly, catching the other up on the news. Nothing had changed really. Kev didn't tell the detectives nothing. They had nothing to go on ... And Crime Stoppers was upping the reward. And UVA's President had issued a statement in response to public calls to suspend finals because the shooter was still at large. How could you call grounds safe President Casteen with that gunman out there? How can anyone study when the basic human need to feel safe has not been met? Blahzay blah. I can assure you that the University makes no compromises with student safety. I remain in constant contact with the University and Charlottesville-Albemarle Police ... The interviews with people on the news. That was the worst. So bad it was almost funny. Seeing the people they knew up there on the TV. Tryna get they shine. People talking about Muffin like he was some kinda nigga brightening everyone's day. Some heel clicking kinda nigga. Even people who were there at the party watching him choke Joe the fuck out testified to that. The chick sobbing. Every time I see him he always had a smile on his face ... He's not the type of guy that looked for trouble ... and on and on. She was there that chickenhead, everyone saw her screaming and squealing and scuffling trying to get a better view. All of that didn't matter. It was the same as before. None of this was news. Joe said he heard some police coming down the hallway. He blew his nose into a napkin, looked at it. The more I think about it, it was probably maintenance out there.

Titus gathered everyone's plates. The trash in the kitchen was full. He pushed it down. It didn't give as much as he thought. He closed the cabinet right before he could see the pile rising again.

Titus managed to squeeze in some studying. Vonny was sleeping sitting up. Beside him Joe was coughing into his fist. Joe cricked his neck to one side, winced. Started tasting his own mouth. Coughed again. He took one of the chairs from the dining room table and set it next to the window. He cracked the window open and lit up a Newport, blowing smoke out the crack and resting his wrist on his knee, which was bouncing up and down. The sun was getting low. It was orange outside. Titus asked him if he had made that call yet. Joe shook his head. I thought about it though. Been thinking about it. Titus told him to take his time. Do what's best for you. You can always back out if it don't feel right. The lawyer works for you. So what's best for me? I can't tell you that my nigga. That's what that number's for. I'm asking you Titus. What's best for me? Titus closed the book in his lap, went to the fridge and cracked 2 brews. They clicked glasses. Titus took a pull and set the bottle on the table. The rest of this for you. Titus studied until it was time for his review session. He woke Vonny up and told Joe he wasn't coming back tonight because of his final tomorrow morning. Prolly spend the night in Clemons. They hugged hard and Titus clapped his back asking you good? My neck still fucked up but I'm straight.

In the car Vonny was moaning. So tired, so tired, so tired. Yawningly he twisted on the lights and pushed the car out of the spot and they resumed the process of looping around in the same place and taking wrong turns and meandering.

You know when I saw Kev—Titus broke off the thought. The picture was too too unpleasant. All I can say is I feel bad. I aint too worried bout him though. But Joe man. Vonny he's making it harder on himself the longer he waits. You know what he told me just now? Who told you? Joe. He told me he aint even call that lawyer yet. I already told him if it's taking you this long to turn yourself in, aint no way a judge will grant bail. And look Vonny tomorrow Friday. Titus was chopping his open palm to emphasize. Now if he don't go by tomorrow he gotta wait till Monday for a hearing. If that. They all backed up on Mondays so ...

Vonny listened along and sorta grunted as he drove. He was so tired his brain wasn't doing the driving. It was all the memory in his muscles, which he allowed to happen. Vonny stifled a yawn, kinda chewing at it. Do alla that really matter stick man? Titus asked what he meant by that. Maybe I'm saying, well I don't know how to say it stick man but I don't know how much heat I want on me. I just started at UPS. I can't be missing no days cos my ass in jail too. My pop aint paying for this crib, it's all me. Titus agreed then asked what that had to do with what they were talking about just now. Vonny shook his head, I don't know I'm tired. I still aint used to this schedule. I know my boss knew I was still drunk the other day. I know he did. Only reason I aint fall asleep that night is I was still hype from coming to get Joe.

Vonny allowed his hands and feet to guide the nose of the car around the corner and into a narrow side street lined with parked cars. They were here finally behind the Chem building. Titus got out and walked around to the driver's side and leaned on the sill. He could see how bad a shape Vonny was in. Titus said maybe we can put him up in a telly this weekend. He got enough bread for it. Vonny nodded, not even looking at him.

The review session was ass but for some reason Titus lingered till the end. The professor musta caught wind of what was going on because the TA wasn't giving answers like he was before. The room was packed at the beginning but as soon as people figured out the answers weren't coming like before, the room began to dwindle. And it wasn't like people weren't trying. Asking follow up after follow up. At first slick, then more direct. Could you work out an example for us in a manner that would appear on the final? The TA shrugged and apologized and clung to his canned response, That you must find on your own. Titus wasn't too mad about it. The final wasn't until next week. The one tomorrow for PSYC, now that one was giving him problems.

He was taking the back way to Clemons. Cutting through the Old Dorms. UVA had laid some new mulch down and the smell of it was sharp as he walked along. It was dark out but he could smell the grass as it was newly cut, and he crossed a bridge and crossing it he connected 2 and 2, that graduation was almost here and this all was primping. Kinda fake but what could you expect. Walking along he came upon the backside of Clemons. He always liked the way it looked at night. The fact that it was built into a hill and you could see each floor distinctly, the tall windows wrapping around and they were bright. He climbed the stairs. Remembering again that he was graduating soon. It was easy to forget. He could barely vision it.

39

Titus ended up sleeping at Alderman Library, having found himself a nice hidden spot way deep in the stacks. On one of them half floors. He got up early and checked his email again on the main floor. The professor still hadn't gotten back to him about the extension. All the others was cool but this faggot for some reason. He re-read the email he sent yesterday. I DON'T KNOW IF YOU HEARD ABOUT THE RECENT ... MY WORLD IS IN A BIT OF TURMOIL WITH THE POLICE COMING BY. I CURRENTLY DON'T HAVE A PLACE TO STAY AS MY APARTMENT HAS BEEN DECIMATED. IT IS A CHAOTIC TIME FOR ME AND I WOULD APPRECIATE IT IF I HAD A LITTLE MORE TIME TO ...

He rolled up to the Psychology building early. There were folks lining the hall sitting on the floor studying. Flipping through single pages quickly and he could hear them from around the corner. He pushed past the double doors and there were a few people inside dotting the seats around the auditorium. Down at the bottom the TA's stood chatting, the thick stack of exams on the table beside them. They broke off their conversations as he approached. In a low voice Titus said I got a serious emergency. The TA's looked at each other, eyes wide but there was a smirk deep inside having heard so many excuses like this before, and the male TA with the brown curly hair said to the other one, a woman, that he would handle it.

The TA pushed open a door behind the lectern and they were in a basement hallway where it was empty and quiet and there were hardly any doors. This was the floor they conducted experiments on. The TA held his face lightly clenched with concern but as soon as Titus asked him if he heard about the shooting on campus earlier in the week, his eyes grew wide, the rest of his face unclenched. Yes of course. It's all over the news. How could I not? I didn't even want you guys taking this exam with the guy still out there. The shooter, he's still out there right? That wasn't your friend that was hurt, was it? The TA was very still as Titus explained that the shooting had taken place at his apartment. He went over the condition of his room, the fact that his computer had been smashed in the aftermath. Someone had thrown, what was it? a chair through my window? The TA covering his mouth and Titus continued claiming the destruction to Kev's room as his own, his tone even. He went over the fact that the police kept coming in and out, and he threw in the word DECIMATED and CHAOTIC from the email, and the TA put a hand on Titus's shoulder. I do *not* think you've had a fair opportunity to prepare for this exam. That much is clear. But I emailed Professor Haidt about this and he hasn't gotten back to me. The TA shaking his head vigorously, Professor Haidt is overseas right now. He's been very hard to reach. Tell me your name. Titus Stevenson. Titus looking at you right now I can say you're dealing with much bigger things. Tell me are you safe? Yeah I think so. The TA cursed under his breath and paced. This makes me sick to my stomach. No one should be here right now with some crazy asshole on the loose. Is there anything more I can do for you? Titus shook his head.

The TA showed him back through the door to the main auditorium, and took down his information and said he would be in touch.

The auditorium was more than halfway full now and the lights were coming down bright and Titus thought, is it always this bright standing down here? Walking up the steps and against the stream of cloppity, slouchy bookbagging traffic, he was fighting back a grin. He felt a little more space inside him. A little more air.

He was outside and feeling good. He leaned against a wall with his arm. Closing his eyes. There was a gentle burning beneath his lids but his breath was coming and going nice and easy. He didn't know how long he was there leaning against the wall before he heard the dean's voice behind him, You and me both.

Daniels standing there with his hands on his hips, sleeves rolled up, his face and shirt damp like he'd been in the sun a while. Despite that he seemed full of energy, happy even, and was turning away, beckoning, Come walk with me.

They went along the main road, the grass and mulch not smelling as strong as last night. They were headed toward the OAAA not saying much, squinting, and Daniels put his hand over his eyes to shield the sun, You eat yet? and they got in his car, a maroon Caddy. Clean inside. The kinda clean that made Titus sit up straight and not move too much.

The gravel crunched beneath the tires. There were no other cars parked out front the Aberdeen Barn. It was supposed to be fancy in there even though it looked like a barn on the outside. Titus had never been. The sign said CLOSED but Daniels knocked and a tall man with a pony tail came out grinning. A little early isn't it Mr. Daniels? Laughing, the dean shook hands with him and made quick introductions, and they were led to a table.

Tablecloth was laid down and they were finally able to sit. The tall man came back with a menu for Titus. Daniels ordered the crab cakes and a whisky sour. Titus went down the menu and found the next to cheapest thing. Young man are you sure you want only a sandwich? It's on me. The entire menu is available, right Gus? Well obviously not the prime rib but we can slice off a ribeye and throw that on the grill for you. Nah that's okay. Just the sandwich.

They ate, talked, pawing at a few subjects. It had been a while since they'd talked. Really talked. They were trying to get used to each other again, their rhythms. Daniels finished his drink and declined another one. He was rubbing at the wet circular spot on the tablecloth when he explained that he needed some fresh air today. His phone had been going nonstop. I'm just repeating myself after a while. I don't know what gives some people the impression that we're dealing with another DC sniper. I'm guessing this is an isolated incident. From what the police say it's just one guy. Drunk, nothing premeditated. Some cheap pistol, who knows. I don't know what kind people carry these days. I suppose you would know wouldn't you Titus? The dean smirking, then lowering his eyes. It amazes me to hear such words come out of my mouth but we really have arrived at that point Titus. You know, we like to spend all our time pretending. Now here's some truth if you're ready for it. Two decades I've been here and there's never been anything like this in the black community at UVA. Well I'm lying. At a party once but that was a long long time ago. It wasn't a student so I guess it wasn't on me. Daniels began chuckling, apologizing, then stronger laughter came as he tried to suppress it.

Titus looked over his shoulders and the dean chided him, no one's here Titus. Besides we're not even saying anything. The dean took a drink of blunt wet ice and gestured across the table, towards Titus. Now that I'm paying for that sandwich the least you could do is be honest with me. How did things come to this? I would love to hear your perspective. Because you know what my colleagues are saying to me? They're saying how could you let this happen on your watch? Like all I am to these people is some mammy when I am *in fact* the architect of this fine house we're standing in. These white folks they sleep at night based on the work I've done, I'm sure you know that. I'm the one who built this. If I were to leave tomorrow, black student enrollment would drop off a cliff. The dean sniffed, and they have the nerve.

The tall man with the ponytail filled their waters and dispersed quickly. So what was it over Titus huh? I would at least like to know. Was it over a girl? Money? Please tell me something. I don't know Dr. Daniels. It happened pretty quick. Didn't nobody want this to happen—You know my generation we fought for things. Ideas. Even if we were misguided, there was some cause behind it. Something larger than ourselves guiding us. But young people these days—Daniels was pointing his big finger across the table— you have no cause above yourselves. You have no under- standing of what other people have sacrificed. And I am sick of dealing with people who only think of themselves. You, all of you, my God you're adults. I am no one's mammy. Is it possible for me to be any clearer than that?

Titus began to apologize but that made Daniels even more upset, and the dean was repeating nothing, sometimes as a statement, then as a question ... over NOTHING??? really? ... Titus could see the old dean was shaking and Titus said no more.

The check was brought and they left. Driving Daniels seemed alright. Pulling up to Faulkner Titus said just stop here. You don't have to drive up. Titus got out at the bottom of the hill and Daniels looking at him with his sunglasses on and said don't forget your doggie bag. The trunk was popped and Titus got the container and saw the dean's hand summoning him to the driver's side window. When you see Joe, tell him I said this: You have to be a man. You got that? When you see him, you tell him for me. Exactly how I put it. You tell him you have to be a man now. Let the process take its place. If there's anything to be done, it's that. You tell him it'll be okay. I'll come see him in there.

40

Joe called one of the lawyers in the phonebook. The lawyer knew right away who he was. Joe walked him through what happened. The lawyer made him go back and explain why he left the apartment and went out onto the landing. They was banging on the door I told ya. Did they manage to break it down? What, the door? You can't break em down it's metal. So what did you hope to accomplish by going outside? I told ya they busted one of the windows. Were they coming in through the window? This guy right, the guy had put his hands on me earlier and when I went out there he did it again. Wait why couldn't you have stayed inside? Joe was getting irritated. The guy put hands on me. It's self defense.

Joe called the next number in the phone book. This lawyer interrupted him right away. You from Jersey? New York. Oh okay. My first guess. I went to law school at Fordham. Joe continued and the lawyer seemed kind enough. He let Joe talk a bit longer on his upbringing. His brother being shot. Then him having to take some more time off after that townie popped him. He still had a sister up there some-where. Another brother. Inevitably they were led back to the same part of the story as with the previous lawyer, and this one told Joe point blank there wasn't a good case for self-defense without fault. How much time I'm lookin at then? It depends. Do you have any prior convictions? Joe told him no. The lawyer thought on it and said again that it depends, but that Joe's priority right now was to turn himself in. But I wanna find some representation first. I don't wanna go in there and then have to deal with that there. Let me be frank Joe you're going to have a hard time finding someone to take your case if you don't look like you're cooperating with the process. I know you think you're getting all your ducks in a row but from the perspective of the legal system, it only looks worse the longer you delay. Joe finally asked the lawyer if he would take his case. The lawyer told him no, I will not elect to represent you at this time. I'm sorry. You sound like a good person Joe. I hope you'll find justice.

Joe hung up the phone, strangely relieved. He looked at the phone book and the rest of the names printed in there. He had just called the two with the nicest looking ads. He smoked through the rest of his pack of Newports and knocked on Vonny's door, asking if he could go run to the store for another pack. Joe was holding out the cash, extending his arm into the darkness of the room. Vonny mumbled from the sleeping bag on the floor just gimme a minute, just one more minute. Joe went back to the couch waiting. He tried lighting some of the butts left in the tray, burning his fingers like he knew would happen, and he sat back thinking on things.

* * *

Titus's room had been spared any damage, yet he kept his shoes on, afraid that any slight twinkle was a shard of glass. He did some studying. After an honest hour he set up shop in the den and took his shoes off and did some more studying laying on his side, stopping when the anxiousness in his chest had subsided. He finished the rest of the sandwich from the Aberdeen Barn and went into the kitchen and found a can of sweet corn high up in one of the cabinets. Sitting on the couch, the spoon rattling in the can, he heard the phone ring. An on grounds ring—Brooke.

Energized he stepped into his boots. Looking down at the loud ringing phone he paused a moment. It was within the realm of possibility that the police were borrowing an on grounds phone. A trap.

He pressed speakerphone button grunting coolly from the back of his throat ulloh. May I speak with Titus Stevenson? Yeah speakin. Hello Titus this is Carey Waters from the University Judiciary Committee. I've been assigned as one of the investigators of your case. We've been trying to reach you. Is now a good time to talk?

Titus stood looking at the bright red dot indicating that his phone was in use. The voice from the phone continued. Now if you have a few minutes to set up an appointment— Titus took the receiver off the hook, Chu tom bout case? Who is this? This is Judish. Did you get a chance to review the official notice? A chuckle coming from a remote part of Titus's body, Notice? Yes a notice was sent in the mail earlier this week. It was sent Wednesday. I see you live on grounds. You should have received it Thursday. Thursday? Titus squinted at the things in his room. The blinds, bed, rug. Calendar.

A smile began to spread across his face. Tell me your name again? My name is Carey Waters. Aye Carey man c'mon you gotta quit the bullshit man. Tell me what's going on. Titus walked with the phone into the hallway. The flat cord only got him to the edge of the den. Titus set the base down and the cord from the receiver unkinked enough to reach the couch, where he fished around his can of corn as the dood from Judish continued apologizing for how awkward this was. He explained that they try to time things so that the accused learns about the charges in writing first. But with graduation coming we think it makes sense to press the issue. Normally this doesn't happen over the phone. Should I call back once you've had the opportunity to review the charges in writing? Yo you know I'm bout to be up outta here right? Carey apologized again.

Titus convinced Carey to read the relevant charges. Getting to the end, Titus was scratching his ribs going dayum. All those? Yall is comical man. Whose pressing them? Dean Barbara Staunton from the Office of Student Life filed the complaint. Yeah I thought so. She been tryna get me for a while now. You know my background right? Carey hazarded a response, African-American? Is that what you were asking? Titus said forget it. Carey said they should sit down to meet about the case. Why we're talking now aint we? I'm sorry Titus but I really need you to come in. But we talkin now. Go ahead and ask whatever you gotta ask ... It went back and forth like that for a little bit and eventually Titus relented. I can't keep clowning around with these niggas. He agreed to meet at the UJC office at Newcomb Hall tonight at 7pm.

He was still laying on the couch, an hour or two later, laughing about the charges and how petty Dean Staunton was being when Vonny pulled up. Vonny said he doin it dog. Who doin? Joe. This nigga gave me some loot and said go

get a bottle of Remy, go get some Guadalajara's, and we gon
drive to the joint tonight.

They made their run to the store and took the straight
way back to Sterling what the hell, showing up with liquor
clinking in one bag and the Mexican food in two others. Joe
was on the phone with someone. Titus clapped him on the
shoulder and Joe said yah can start eatin ahready. Just bring
me a brew for now. Joe stood pacing on the phone by the
window. Listening and talking quietly and smoking his
cigarette, rubbing his head and nodding. From time to time
he turned away and cried into the wall. Titus and Vonny
nursed the brews. Slowed the rate at which they ate. They
didn't crack the Remy till Joe was finally off the phone. Joe
was in a decent mood and a few shots had him feeling right
and they were cracking on each other and the laughs came
real easy.

They waited around a lil to sober up then got on the
road. It was a little ways. Joe was in the front passenger seat
leaning. Looking out the window. Looking up at the university banners hanging up from the streetlights along the
highway. The big UVA decal on the road, the one right past
Barracks shopping center, had been repainted recently. The
colors were bright and defined even in the night. The car
curled up the onramp and there was nothing interesting on
the side of the road for a bit, and Joe began mumbling to
himself, Just what am I gonna do now huh? Vonny looked
over briefly and kept driving. He turned on the radio a
moment later. The music made them feel dumb and small
and helpless. Vonny turned it off and they went along
feeling the warm wind coming in the windows, smelling the
faint smell of rain from earlier that evening.

Glancing at the time on the dash, Titus recalled his 7pm
meeting with that Carey dood from UJC. He was at peace

that he was here now attending to something more important. He asked if Joe remembered what they had talked about before about dealing with the police. Cos they might seem real nice, like they your friend or something. You don't gotta call em out. Just look at em and smile. Say you don't gotta answer they question. It sound easy now but when you up in it, it's always a different story. Joe was nodding. Me and Vonny will come through tomorrow first thing just to check. Just make sure you put us on that list. You know who else you should put on that list? Maybe Dean Daniels. Make sure you put him down. He a good dood to have in the back pocket.

When they got there there were a few people ahead of them. Joe gave his name and showed ID. They looked him up, said yes we see you in here, Can you please step around this way? Titus and Vonny said aight Joe hold ya head and Joe went through a door where he was read his rights and they had him take off his belt and shoelaces and was then promptly told to sit and wait. He filled out some forms. His personal items all went in one clear bag and his prescription went into its own bag by itself. He filled out some more forms for his medicine and waited in a bright ass holding cell, the wisps of liquor still turning and turning inside him. Being with Vonny and Titus, drinking and laughing in that apartment, that all seemed so long ago now. A completely different part of his life. Maybe some other one. At least his belly was full and for that he was glad. He didn't want to get too low right now. Not yet. He waited for his name to be called. The other doods in holding seemed to know what was up. They closed their eyes and stole some sleep leaning against the wall.

His mind did not cast back only. It went wide. Upwards. Outwards. He'd never been locked up before. He thought on everyone he could, particularly the people who believed in him. What they would think if they'd seen him right now. How surprised or unsurprised they'd be. If that would disturb or disfigure their day. Or if they'd shrug and keep on doing whatever they was doing.

The shooter now in custody, the university released their statements. The statements were full of congratulations. Everybody and they momma was congratulated, even Muffin, who was looking like he was going to pull through. His NFL Dream was another matter.

No one else was taken into custody. Not the football players who busted up the windows at Faulkner apartments, and several other windows in the parking lot, and committed property damage such as to one Dell Pentium III personal computer, and who had ignored repeated requests by the police on scene to clear the area, who had to be physically restrained for breaking past the yellow tape.

Ultimately vandalism charges were pressed. Not obstruction of justice or public intoxication. The official police report took special care to note that the players did not direct any profanity at the officers on scene. Despite ripping police tape, needing to be physically restrained to avoid doing so again, and presenting themselves as visibly and by all other senses intoxicated, not happening to direct profanity at police, but only to the faggot muthafucka that shot their friend, spoke to their character.

Since two out of the three players facing charges were projected as starters next year, Coach Groh preached patience out in the press. These men deserve their due process. The athletic director promised to continue to monitor the situation.

Exams continued unabated. And the warm late afternoon rains, starting and stopping throughout the weekend, smelled marvelous.

41

There was a rare silence in the apartment now, interrupted only by the occasional scuff of flip flops in the stairwell. It lent a new degree of focus to Titus's studying. Concepts that mystified were now child's play, and there was a sense of different interlocking parts gliding into place. From time to time he looked at the letter from Judish, chuckling at it. These niggas is comical man. And when he was done with his stretch break he set the letter down and got back to work.

After lunch, it was harder. He covered up the answers with his hands, guessed, uncovered. Kept missing the medium hard ones. Should be getting them by now. He paced around the unit, and convinced himself he could get it going better at another one of his spots. It was too dirty in here to think.

He walked over to Darden library and found a good spot on the second floor. He got up to use the bathroom and didn't have to worry about nobody stealing his stuff. The library closed right at 5 and about a half hour before the lady went up and down the stacks telling people that. He could hear her a couple rooms away and when she saw him with his bag of funyons and his bigass headphones and his black ass staring back at her black ass she said it to him like he was extra dumb anyway and he chuckled at her. He went back to the crib and looked at the Judish letter again. It amazed him the pettiness. He felt like he needed someone to laugh with.

Cracking a brew he called one of his boys from back home. Asked how his family was. He hadn't thought of him in a while but told him he was thinking of him today outta the blue and his boy said oh yeah I seen your mother the other day at the Shoppers Food. Oh yeah? Yeah she said you graduating in a few weeks ... As soon as he got off the phone he sat with the Judish letter again intently studying it this time, the language, whether certain phrases meant more than they let on. He called back that Carey dood from the other day and Carey told him come down to Newcomb tonight. I'll be there all night studying in the offices. We definitely need to get this interview done.

Carey got straight to it. They went through the charges one by one and since there were so many they got bogged down and they decided it was easier to just go more or less chronologically through things. Carey asked about the disclosure thing from the summer and Titus had to do a bunch of explaining there. Then came a bunch of questions about the meetings with Daniels, if there was a sign-in sheet or some sort of procedure to track his attendance. Nah not at all. It wasn't like that. Carey asked if he was sure there was nothing in writing and Titus could tell that funny stuff was going on in the background of all this. A lot more was going on. So Titus asked him straightup if Dean Daniels said something different about the meetings. Carey said not to worry about that, to answer what he knew to the best of his abilities. They got onto Winter Ball which was pretty straightforward. Titus knew the name of the judge who dismissed the charges, the dates, all that. Then they got onto the topic of Joe. What he got to do with it? Carey talked and Titus said he didn't get the connection at all, and no disrespect but maybe I need to talk to a lawyer about this. We talking about a case that's still pending. Carey assured him that despite UJC's involvement with university police, UJC was an entirely independent student-run organization. I can guarantee you that we are free from any outside interference. That didn't seem to be an answer to a question Titus had asked. Titus asked if they could take a break. Carey went out into the hall for some water. Titus went downstairs to one of the free phones on the 2nd floor.

He told Vonny he had a real bad feeling about this. They tryna get real funny on a nigga here. Aint you say Q caught some UJC charges for something? Yeah for drinking in his dorm first year. Vonny started chuckling. They fined him and made em write a apology essay. My dumb ass helped him too. Titus was laughing. Yall niggas was quoting Nas lyrics right? They laughed and Titus was surprised his laughed travelled. He looked around and the floor was empty in both directions. Vonny told him to stop being paranoid man. They just tryna get you shook. Everybody know Judish don't do nothin to you. Honor System maybe. But not no Judish. Vonny asked if he remembered Mike? Who Mooselim Mike? Nah the Mike live downstairs from us at Copeley. They say Mike was stalking some whitegurl and UJC made him go to counseling. That's prolly the worse I ever heard happen to somebody. So whatever happened to Mike? Shoot man. I think that nigga went back to Baltimore. Doon what? Working. I talked to Fatima and she say he work for Sprint.

Titus went back upstairs to finish the interview. He answered all of Carey's questions about what all went down last week. By the way dood was asking it sounded like someone out there was talking. It was like they knew more than the police. Kev ass talkin? Titus stuck to the facts. That he had been there at Sigma Nu and tried to break up the fight. Then the police came ... At the end Carey asked if he had any questions himself. Yeah if I'm such a threat to safety and such a disruption to the learning process, then why don't yall just let me graduate so I'll be outta your way. Carey said that was a good question. It wasn't his job to speculate however. In a week they'll mail a packet with their preliminary findings. Things may be clearer then.

Vonny came through the crib later that night and helped him move Joe's stuff out of his room. They piled the clothes and posters and the computer in the corner of the den. They accomplished this more quickly than anticipated and left for the ABC store where they spent a long time looking at the bottles higher up on the shelves, recognizing the names of brown and clear liquors from the popular songs they'd heard, and debating whether or not they were being reckless spending that much money. Oh well.

Sweaty and bent, they kept having the same conversations. Hey they not Honor. Why my trippin? They can't kick niggas out like Honor. You said it stick man. Shit even Honor don't kick niggas out no more. They don't want that hanging on their head you feel me? These Judish niggas is just too comical man. Just too comical. That bitch Staunton so fuckin petty. Desperate. That nigga Daniels warned me too. He said they *been* wantin to get in a nigga ass, I'm tellin you Vonny ...

Titus went to his room and came back with the official Judish notice that had come in the mail last week. For the first time he had showed it to another person. Not even reading the page, the amount of writing made Vonny immediately ask, they just list out all the standards of conduct or is this all the charges they pressin? Titus said they were pressing all of them. Vonny went gotdamn inside, they really threw the book at a nigga, and he read the charges to himself quietly.

I. PHYSICAL ASSAULT OF ANY PERSON ON UNIVERSITY-OWNED OR LEASED PROPERTY, AT ANY UNIVERSITY SANCTIONED FUNCTION, AT THE PERMANENT OR TEMPORARY LOCAL RESIDENCE OF A UNIVERSITY STUDENT, FACULTY MEMBER, EMPLOYEE, VISITOR, OR IN THE CITY OF CHAR-LOTTESVILLE OR ALBEMARLE COUNTY, OR PROHIB-ITED CONDUCT, AS DEFINED IN THE UNIVERSITY OF VIRGINIA POLICY ON SEXUAL AND GENDER-BASED HARASSMENT AND OTHER FORMS OF INTERPER-SONAL VIOLENCE.

2. CONDUCT WHICH INTENTIONALLY OR RECK-LESSLY THREATENS THE HEALTH OR SAFETY OF ANY PERSON ON UNIVERSITY-OWNED OR LEASED PROPERTY, AT A UNIVERSITY SANCTIONED FUNC-TION, AT THE PERMANENT OR TEMPORARY LOCAL RESIDENCE OF A UNIVERSITY STUDENT, FACULTY MEMBER, EMPLOYEE OR VISITOR, OR IN THE CITY OF CHARLOTTESVILLE OR ALBEMARLE COUNTY.

3. UNAUTHORIZED ENTRY INTO OR OCCUPATION OF UNIVERSITY FACILITIES WHICH ARE LOCKED, CLOSED TO STUDENT ACTIVITIES OR OTHERWISE RESTRICTED AS TO USE.

4. INTENTIONAL DISRUPTION OR OBSTRUCTION OF TEACHING, RESEARCH, ADMINISTRATION, DISCI-PLINARY PROCEDURES, OTHER UNIVERSITY ACTIVI-

TIES, OR ACTIVITIES AUTHORIZED TO TAKE PLACE ON UNIVERSITY PROPERTY.

6. VIOLATION OF UNIVERSITY POLICIES OR REGULATIONS REFERENCED IN THE RECORD, INCLUDING POLICIES CONCERNING RESIDENCE AND THE USE OF UNIVERSITY FACILITIES.

8. DISORDERLY CONDUCT ON UNIVERSITY-OWNED OR LEASED PROPERTY OR AT A UNIVERSITY-SANCTIONED FUNCTION. DISORDERLY CONDUCT IS DEFINED TO INCLUDE BUT IS NOT LIMITED TO ACTS THAT BREACH THE PEACE, ARE LEWD, INDECENT, OR OBSCENE, AND THAT ARE NOT CONSTITUTIONALLY PROTECTED SPEECH.

9. SUBSTANTIAL DAMAGE TO UNIVERSITY-OWNED OR LEASED PROPERTY OR TO ANY PROPERTY IN THE CITY OF CHARLOTTESVILLE OR ALBEMARLE COUNTY OR TO PROPERTY OF A UNIVERSITY STUDENT, EMPLOYEE, FACULTY MEMBER, OR VISITOR, OCCURRING ON UNIVERSITY-OWNED OR LEASED PROPERTY OR AT THE PERMANENT OR TEMPORARY LOCAL RESIDENCE OF ANY STUDENT, FACULTY MEMBER, EMPLOYEE OR VISITOR.

10. ANY VIOLATION OF FEDERAL, STATE, OR LOCAL LAW, IF SUCH DIRECTLY AFFECTS THE UNIVERSITY'S PURSUIT OF ITS PROPER EDUCATIONAL PURPOSES AND ONLY TO THE EXTENT SUCH VIOLATIONS ARE NOT COVERED BY OTHER STANDARDS OF CONDUCT AND ONLY WHERE A SPECIFIC PROVISION OF A STATUTE OR ORDINANCE IS CHARGED IN THE COMPLAINT.

11. INTENTIONAL, RECKLESS, OR NEGLIGENT CONDUCT WHICH OBSTRUCTS THE OPERATIONS OF THE HONOR OR JUDICIARY COMMITTEE, OR

CONDUCT THAT VIOLATES THEIR RULES OF CONFI-
DENTIALITY.

12. FAILURE TO COMPLY WITH DIRECTIONS OF
UNIVERSITY OFFICIALS ACTING UNDER PROVISIONS
1-11 SET ABOVE. THIS SHALL INCLUDE FAILURE TO
GIVE IDENTITY IN SITUATIONS CONCERNING
ALLEGED VIOLATIONS OF SECTIONS 1-11.

Vonny gave back the notice. He didn't know what to say
right away so he asked when Titus received it. Saturday.
They said they mailed it out Wednesday. Titus was grinning
and swigging the VSOP. So what you gonna do then stick
man, about these charges? Titus shrugged. Vonny said they
can't put a block on your degree can they? Titus frowned,
offended, Oh fuck no, then thinking, thinking, they better
not be able to. Vonny said maybe it was like how if you had
unpaid overdue libary fees, you could still graduate but they
wouldn't give you a copy of the degree until you paid up.
Yeah that's what I think too. Titus took another swig of the
VSOP. I'll call this nigga tomorrow to check. Yeah stick man.
It's prolly just a fine or sumpin.

After the last exam in a long career of them, Kevin experi-
enced what he always did at the end of each semester, a
conspicuous lack of joy. His survival had hinged on an
ability to obsess about certain very small imaginary things.
Suddenly removing those things did not immediately cure
him of the symptoms. He knew he would feel better days
later, and even begin to appreciate this milestone, that in a
few short weeks a ceremony would occur and he would officially be in the company of different people in society:
adults.

There was still cleaning to do before moving out. When they spoke over the phone, Titus said to leave Joe's stuff there in the corner. Him and Vonny would both come by later to help.

Kev detected a certain something in the voice that became obvious the more he thought it about later. It said I like you but you're not that important to me. Kev did not take it personally and resumed working on the parts of the den unoccupied by Joe's stuff. The quiet he appreciated, the thinking, and Camille came by to help after her exam, then finally he heard the squeaky fan belt of his parents' old minivan.

They were amused by the dirty pile of Joe's belongings but looked with concern at the cardboard windows, now covered by a translucent layer of tarp due to the periodic rains. He said it was a random drunk and they had no reason to dispute the story. They continued loading the van.

His mother, a housekeeper, could not be persuaded from picking up a broom. She angled it in the AC intake and dislodged previously unseen handfuls of fuzz, scolding under her breath the roommates who were not there. Kebbin is your roommate the one smoking hah? He said he didn't know. Wasn't around often.

Kev took out the business card from the young detective, the one where the number on the front had been crossed out and the new number had been written on the back. He looked at it for a long time before releasing it into a trashbag.

He cinched the bag and walked it to the back of the parking lot where beneath the mound of bags and abandoned furniture he remembered there being a dumpster. Kev gave it a good aim and flung the bag toward the summit only to watch it bounce and tumble down the near slope, and become snagged on a torchiere lamp, dragging that down too, and now the hours of diligent cleaning were scattered on the ground. The detective's business card was somewhere in the wads of paper and tobacco, calling out, through the flies and filth, one last time.

Kev looked around and was happy to pretend that he had fulfilled his duty to this place and so walked off, free of the guilt that would've once hounded him, and boarded his parent's minivan. Riding through the campus, he saw it through their naive eyes, the pretty buildings and unspoiled history. The knowing hand beside him squeezed. Camille asked how it felt to be done, which drew an amused sniff from him and many more minutes of silently looking out the window.

42

May came. The robes gathered behind the Rotunda where the green, acid burnt statue of TJ was. Then the robes, school by school, each school led by a banner, pushed up the wide white steps, forking off 2 ways around the building. In deadlock, listening to the roars tunneling down the Lawn and the pre-recorded trumpets sailing, they leaned on the cool marble rail, some suppressing grins, and many arms were draped around shoulders, pettiness melting under Kodak barrages. Flip flops scraped, the hem of robes tickling those toes. Quite a few cigarettes were smoked in the waiting. It wasn't too hot, just a dull downward moving gray overhead. More roars, trumpets. Heads tilted, measuring and comparing relative volumes, which figured somehow into calculations of how much longer they had to wait. Eventually the standing broke and the 2 streams waddled and waddled and eventually conjoined on the other side under the broad columns. The Lawn opened before them, black robes rolling forward between flanks of flashbulbs, the colonnades on both sides reflecting the cheers, and they giddily chopped down the steps, the sound starting at their ankles then was at their shoulders and giggling they were inside the sound now, completely dipped inside and deep in it and it was pulsing, can you believe it? They shucked off footwear at the bottom of the steps. Women leaning on friends and strangers as heels were removed. The grass between their toes, the absolute best, like you wouldn't believe. Nothing was corny anymore.

At the end of the procession they settled into folding chairs brimming their hands to their heads. They squinted at the speakers sitting on the dais, trying to figure who was who, who was famouser than the other. Beachballs bounced across the crowd from punch to punch and as the speakers took the lectern, the realization struck: This was it. They were running out of time. Their peripherals were preoccupied with finding that one someone they'd been meaning to talk to before forever set in. That someone. The drama of loose ends lingering was the thing that kept them awake during the speeches. The US Senator—supposedly he was famous—focused his remarks on terrorism. A beach ball was apprehended by security. A new one spawned somewhere else. The Senator bore a steely gaze into the crowd because terrorism has no boundaries. It has no boundaries, but this nation will succeed. I am privileged to be in a position today to try and make those decisions, which I'll address momentarily, to keep America strong and to follow the rule of law, whether it's the Geneva Convention or in the trials that are about to take place to redress great wrongs. We are a nation of a rule of law and will always be that way.

Out of the sea of robes her figure, that neck, that long beautiful neck from ballet stretching out the regalia of sashes and leis, the sight of it leapt out to him. There. Unmistakable. Titus stood halfway, getting a better view. Rows and rows ahead, her head tilted to talk to the girl next to her, some whitegurl he did not recognize. But Brooke always knew allkinds of people. He studied the tossing of her head from side to side as she engaged in polite conversation and concluded it was her. Definitely her. He told Q he'd be back and stepped across and on toes, and made his way.

She saw him coming down the aisle and snapped her head away covering the side of her face with her hand, smiling and mortified. People scooted their chairs. Side conversations parted as he knelt to the grass, rubbing his palms. Look girl I aint tryna argue. I just wanna know if you got my message from last week. She crossed her arms, the corner of her mouth cocked disdainfully. What do you think you're doing? You want to do this right now in front of all these people Ty? Alright lemme be point blank with you then. Rubbing his palms. They not lettin me graduate. A laugh squirted out of her. Well it doesn't look like it's working. I aint booshittin you Brooke. They pressin Judish charges. They put a block on my degree. What? She had been all hardass to this point but her voice changed and they both recognized it. It's booshit Brooke. All for old shit but I don't wanna get into it right now. I'mma beat these charges you best believe. Judish? Like what happened at Winter Ball? The stuff with your roommate? Titus was increasingly noticing all the people listening by, not even hiding it at this point. Well Brooke it's all of the above. They even bringing stuff up from before here. She shook her head, the disbelief rushing in all at once. She asked about law school. Aren't you set to go to George Washington? He dropped his head and he heard her groan above him. Shaking his head he agreed, yeah I know. They can't do this Ty you know that. They not. I just need you to write a letter for me. He went ahead and explained to her that she needed to testify in writing to his character. He didn't

expect her to be there in person. It didn't have to be long.
Just the fact that it came from her, someone with as many
leadership positions as her, someone who'd known him a
long time, means a lot. If she wanted to speak on Winter
Ball she could but he had a few people lined up already to
write on that. Standing from the grass, he said he didn't
want to take more of her time. Who are you sitting with? Oh
just Q and them. I don't know where Kev is for some reason.
Sensing there was nothing more to say, he said alright and
as he turned to leave, she held onto his hand. Come find me
after this. Alright. Walking back to his seat he looked back
at her. From time to time his mind lingered on how cold she
had been to him just now. How ready she was to ignore
him. He couldn't get it out of his head this disposable
feeling.

After the hats were thrown he gave dap to Q and them
and told them all that he'd get up with them later. You
going to the aftaparty joint tonight? Man I don't know. I
might come through. I'll hitchu up. He walked back up the
Lawn against the stream. He bunched his robe under his
arm and did not bother to pluck his hat off the ground. His
family was under the colonnade. Pop stood sober and
expressionless behind dark glasses, his half sister Rebecca
swaying with the baby on her hip. There were others from
the Stevenson clan, the branches from Philly and Georgia,
about dozen in total. Four pre-pubescent cousins, Roger,
Deion, Samira, and Kenny who had been promised a trip
to King's Dominion this weekend. One set from his mother's side, the Sampsons, Aunt Wilma and Uncle Ricky; their
kids, now grown up, had graduated from here a decade ago.
Far in the back, safe in the shade under the colonnade was
his mother and Grandma Boothe, blind and wheelchair-
bound and perfectly happy. He slid his index finger into

one of her shaky hands, watched her bones squeeze together and quiver rheumatically around his finger and he looked up at her, awed by the effort as a nearby camera caught him in profile. Grammama, you doin good? Her face was shaking and he kissed her on the cheek. Uncle Tim, his mother's younger brother, clapped Titus in the back and jammed his hand into his palm. Somebody take a picture of us! Titus was punched in the arm and told to smile. Now everybody wanted a picture. He put his robe back on and a hat was placed on his head. It was hard but he did it. His father sidled up, his hands in his pockets and the last of the pictures were taken. Jeremiah how come you don't look too happy? Your boy got to that finish line aint he? Pop walked quietly off to the side and one of the uncles joked that he still got the loans to pay off that's why he aint smiling.

As they got ready to leave Uncle Tim asked how come he aint walk across the stage and shake somebody hand? Titus said they just mail you the degree. An eavesdropper nearby kneeling next to a cooler said that degrees were conferred according to school. The program has all different venues listed. You just have to find your school and go to that site. Uncle Tim booming triumphantly, You hear what this man said? We gotta go find his school. It's on the program. Titus's mother said it was okay, it's just a piece of paper. Uncle Tim was bout to throw a fit. Loretta I aint come all this way to not see my nephew on some stage shaking somebody hand and getting that slip of paper he worked 4 years to get. They stood around for a little bit plucking air into their shirts. Grammama couldn't stay out in the humidity much longer, someone said. Plus the kids were hungry. Rebecca said the baby was due to eat too. What time is it? Wilma how bout you? Ricky?

So it was decided. They went to the Red Lobster on Route 29. Uncle Tim ate with conviction and was now itis-stricken. His eyelids dim. He was quiet and it looked like he was praying. He tapped his temple mumbling grinningly it was smart that they came straight here. Beat the traffic. The kids chased one another throughout the restaurant and nobody was tripping.

43

They held the trial on the top floor of Newcomb. A small conference room full of long wooden tables and big leather chairs tacked in brass. Titus and his parents arrived before everyone else. The A/C was out of service. The Stevensons jiggled open the old wood-framed windows. They made fans out some blank paper laying around. The trial chair came and told them there were refreshments outside. When they returned to the room, case packets were on their table. They perused vacantly. Vonny came. Then Dean Daniels poked his head around the door, then vanished behind it before anyone could say something. Titus's counsel, Sam, a third year from the general pool, came next and his hair was wet with sweat from the walk over. The panel members arrived one by one with their bookbags, asking if they were in the right room. The stack of blank papers was passed around and more fans were made. A police officer, a bigass bailiff looking dood appeared at the door in uniform, and stood there silently looking ahead. Titus asked his counsel if that was normal. Sam said he's heard of police being present. I can't lie, it doesn't happen often.

It was 1 or 2 minutes till the start time and the opposing counsel's table was still empty. Titus was hoping Brooke would make an appearance. She had mentioned maybe doing that. But that was some time ago and they hadn't talked in a while. He was holding onto that, the sight of her coming through the door, fresh off a plane from New York, that beautiful long neck, when he heard heavy hard soles clacking up the hall, accompanied by some throat clearing.

Two men, two grown ass men Titus had never in his whole life seen before, heads full of white hair, carrying briefcases and coffee, walked briskly into the room and sat at the opposing counsel's table. Clearing their throat again, their jawlines fluttered and they snapped open their briefcases and sorted their papers.

Titus was blinking big eyed at their fucking white hair. You gotta be kiddin me dog. Sam said he'd never seen anything like this before. So you just gon sit here my man?

Samuel went to the front to confer with the trial chair. There was explaining and nodding and pointing at paperwork. Sam came back looking dejected. I mean this is ridiculous. The chair told me they updated the packets yesterday. You can look for yourself. Titus flipped through the packet and found the addendum in the very back: DUE TO THE SPECIAL CIRCUMSTANCES AND GRAVITY OF THE CHARGES ...

Titus didn't know what to say. He just asked Sam can they do this? Sam said look at the bottom of the addendum. Look who signed it. The VP of Student Affairs. Titus said they can't make up the rules as they go along can they? This sposed to be student run. Samuel didn't have much to say. Titus said fuck disshit I'm gettin my folks and we gettin the fuck outta here. Sam put his hand on Titus's shoulder as he began to rise out of his seat. I already told the chair we were leaving but he strongly advised against it. They'll try you in absentia. I'm confident in our case.

Standing outside the door with his folks and Vonny, Titus explained what was going on. Ma covered her mouth, horrified. Pops didn't trip. I don't know son. Everybody's here ready to go. If you in the right, you in the right. Ma looked at him. You don't think that do you Jerry? You seen them. They're grown men. The guy we have looks like the boy who delivers our paper. When Vonny was asked he put his hands up quick, Aye this between you and your family. C'mon Vonny. You here, you family. Stick man I can't really say but sumpin don't feel right.

Titus crossed his arms and went down the long hallway alone. At the end of the hallway he paced punching his palm muttering to himself. Then he came back, his arms swinging loose and free. Let's get back in there.

His mother wanted to know where Brooke was. You said she was going to be here. I don't see her. When Titus told her Brooke wasn't coming, his mother tore herself from the group and was halfway down the hall before Titus caught up with her. Her voice ached. Son I don't like this at all. All these last minute changes. Outside lawyers. You have to be crazy to think I'll let you go back in that room.

He explained to her, guiding her by the arm as he talked, saying yeah he thought about all that. But if we don't like the decision we can always get it thrown out on appeal. Just think about it Ma. Someone told you you could be done with the drama today? All this drama from UVA? Done before dinnertime? You know how long we been dealing with this? All this? We don't have anything to lose. Me and Sam, we've been preparing this case for weeks.

Out in the hallway they all thought on it a bit more, frowning and mumbling and shifting their weight side to side. They said it made sense yeah? a win-win? and they returned to the room.

* * *

The trial got going. There were no real surprises. The private attorneys went about their business. Stuck to the talking points. Repeated things. But there were these little gestures and turns of phrase that Titus noticed. The subtleties of what they did. Glances, pauses. They didn't seem in a rush but if you stepped back, you realized they had spoken in entire paragraphs that gathered and ebbed, and up close you could tell that it wasn't like they had things strictly memorized. The facts, the story, it was all inside them. A part of him recognized, even admired their craft, and it was easy to fall into that because the picture they had rendered wasn't even him, though it sounded plausible as hell.

At the beginning the professional attorneys posed the main questions. Aren't the members of this community entitled to know if a student convicted of a serious violent crime walks among us? Studies among us? Resides in our dormitories? Withholding information of that nature does the community a grave harm. Most of all, it deals a grave harm to Titus. If the university could have learned of his violent history earlier, then proper steps could have been taken to re-integrate this young man into the community.

Their big thing was the repeated pattern of recklessness. (RECKLESSNESS—that was one of the terms they kept coming back to. There were a few others.) This wasn't a one time thing but a cumulative PATTERN. They made the Winter Ball stuff sound pretty bad but Titus was prepared for that. Then they said he skipped out on all his mandatory meetings with Dean Daniels in the spring. Then they got onto the Joe stuff. They had lined up several police statements and pieced things together so that Titus came out as some sort of ringleader in the whole saga. When Alvis Rogers got shot, that was the culmination. Mr. Stevenson had many opportunities to avoid escalating things but look at his decision-making. After the melee at the cookout, he goes to the after party later that night, well aware that members of the football team would be there. We have witness statements claiming he snuck into that party as well. Regrettably but not in an unforeseeable turn of events, another altercation ensues. If by now the panel does not recognize a pattern ... The lawyer did not bother completing the thought.

Later on his partner paced the middle of the floor, wandering freely from the lectern. You may be wondering why now? Why not let this young man move on from the university where he could no longer be a threat to our community? I wondered that initially before I agreed to participate in this case. And I realized that allowing Titus Stevenson to receive a degree would be sending one of the worst messages possible. It would say, look you're free to be a danger to people for 4 years and at the end you'll receive your degree like everyone else who had followed the rules and abided by the Standards of Conduct. As I say that aloud, I'm sure you know that doesn't sound right at all. It's unfair. I say, there's no better time than now to take a stand. Our institutional values are at stake.

Then his own counsel got up there with his notecards. All the big words Sam used at the beginning somehow didn't sound right or natural, but at least he stuck to the script about this case being excessive and egregious. To be brutally frank, we should not be convened here today. Titus

Stevenson has already paid his debts for the actions in question. By trying him under the UJC Standards of Conduct, we are in essence committing double jeopardy. They want to talk about messages? What message are we sending when a student fights the odds to make it to college, fights once again to put his life back together after getting out of jail, and takes on an accelerated course load just so he can graduate on time and honor an oath he made to his parents? What do you call that? I call that a model of perseverance.

Throughout the speeches, the panel sat there behind that long wooden conference table burying their heads into their packets. When the floor opened for their questions, the panel members glanced at one another awkwardly and said nothing. The trial chair leaned into the microphone, There are no questions from the panel at this time. Titus remembered getting emails this summer about 2 of the panel members being alternates. One was an alternate of an alternate. Dean Staunton didn't even bother to show up. They granted a continuance and she piped in her testimony through a blinking red light on an intercom. She was just reading off something. But Brooke. How come she didn't bother neither? He looked over her character letter in the packet, again underwhelmed at what it had to say. Is it too much to ask? You show up on my doorstep in the middle of the night, shit. Me and Joe was ready to kill. Ready to put in that work. Didn't even think twice about throwin away our freedom. I really got to beg you?

Daniels refused water and sat dabbing the sweat from his forehead in a chair placed in the middle of the room between the two lecterns. Daniels said he believed in second chances. I've had my share of them. But I'm not chained to the belief that all of one's second chances lie in one place. A change in setting might be best for this young man and in the best interest of the community. I don't take this lightly. My personal charge is to graduate each and every single African-American student that comes to the university. Yet at the same time I am cognizant that you've got to be a participant in your own education, your own rescue. There's not more I can do to help Titus if he's not showing up to the meetings. Simple as that. There are obvious safety issues under consideration that I'm sure Dean Staunton has detailed. There was no way my colleagues and I would have permitted him to remain in our community without safe-guards in place and an intensive plan for remediation.

When it was time for cross-examination, Sam pointed out that Daniels had no paperwork asserting the mandatory nature of the meetings. Daniels denied the need for paper-work. No one has invested more time into Titus Stevenson than me. I will not have *you* question my commitment to the African-American student community. Daniels started going on about the vital nature of the meetings, how Dean Staunton went through all the trouble to arrange them. He kept going on about something else, going without resis-tance, repeating some of the same points as before, lapsing into his own credentials and his biography. Titus felt himself getting so worked up listening to Daniels go on about how he cared, cared more than any man who ever existed. Dr. Daniels, if I could follow up there—Frankly, I'd rather you not. I'm offended by what's implied by this line of questioning.

Daniels was allowed to leave at the end of his testimony. Titus was preparing some slick remark when the dean would pass close by, and had narrowed down his choices. He gazed straight into the dean's face and felt his own lips move around, the sound inaudible over the shuffle of papers in the room. Daniels gazed back, smiling faintly, unbothered that he'd been called a fuckin pussy to his face, and nodded at the bailiff holding open the door.

Next Vonny was called up. He said his piece about Titus minding his own business when the cops tackled and sprayed him at Winter Ball. Mr. Childress are you aware that your version of the narrative differs from that found on the official police report? Vonny shrugged and reached behind his head for a handful of hair that was no longer there. I can only tell you whattaw saw myself.

Then came the moment when Titus had to go up there. He had a suit on. He answered questions from his counsel. From the professional attorneys. Just when they were about to relieve him from the stand, he pulled the damp piece of paper from his interior coat pocket. The trial chair told him they don't allow prepared statements from the stand. Can I add just one thing to what I said earlier? The trial chair said go ahead. As long as it isn't too lengthy.

ESTEEMED PANEL MEMBERS. YOUR HONOR. I FIRST WANT TO EXPRESS MY RESPECT FOR EVERYONE WHO HAS BEEN INVOLVED IN THIS PROCESS. I UNDERSTAND THAT TAKING ON THIS CASE, IN THE MIDDLE OF SUMMER VACATION NO LESS, REQUIRES GREAT SACRIFICES OF TIME, TIME RATHER SPENT AROUND LOVED ONES. I WANT TO THANK YOU. LET ME JUST SAY I HOLD NO GRUDGES AGAINST THE UNIVERSITY FOR PURSUING ITS INTEREST IN SAFETY. IT HAS EVERY RIGHT TO DO SO. BUT IN THIS PARTICULAR CASE, MY PARTICULAR CASE, I FEEL THE UNIVERSITY HAS EXCEEDED THE SCOPE OF ITS POWERS AND HAS GONE OUT OF ITS WAY TO MAKE AN EXAMPLE OUT OF ME. IT'S UNDER-STANDABLE WITH ALL THAT'S HAPPENED BUT THAT STILL DOESN'T MAKE IT RIGHT. THAT'S ALL I

WANTED TO SAY. THANK YOU ALL FOR YOUR TIME. NO MATTER WHAT YOU ALL DECIDE I WILL BE AT PEACE WITH IT BECAUSE I KNOW THAT I AM IN THE RIGHT AND THAT GOD RECOGNIZES THAT.

The trial chair thanked Titus for his testimony and told the panel to disregard the prepared statement.

44

The panel deliberated for an hour. An hour? That normal? Sam shrugged and said he'd give him a moment with his family.

They joined hands in the hallway and prayed then they all walked into that tiny room with the big chairs past the bailiff and up front were the panel of five judges who didn't want to be there over the summer. His own chest was pumping, his head down, his chest about to burst. And now came a stretch of yawning uncontrollably, and as the yawn passed from his chest to his face, the yawn came out of his ears, his eardrums popped and he couldn't hear a thing. He yawned again, seeing the university's professional attorneys with their full heads of white hair, and he yawned again, his whole body shuddering and with his shuddering body, his shaking hands and his face stretched wide and contorted with the yawning, he forgot for a moment where he was.

He was only aware of his heart about to burst as he searched for some vacant chair to plop himself into. As he sat down and regained a sense of where he was again, this room, these people, he remembered again that there were people in this room who knew more about his fate than he did. This bothered him. He fought a yawn by scowling through it and burying his head into his chest again. The maddening realization continued to build. These people sitting there, straight faced, almost sullen, knowing everything there was to know. How they had the nerve to watch him walk in here with his family, to sit and look at him right now. The whole thing felt perverted. Like how are you gonna just sit there. You prolly tryna analyze me right now. You want me to be gassed, is that it? Yall about to tell me I'm guilty and you want to watch me be shocked as hell as if there was ever a question. He could feel his toes gripping the insoles, a feeling shooting up the inner part of his leg. Huh is that it?

The door was closed. A gavel banged. His counsel stood and placed his hand in the small of Titus's back, helping him rise into the hot room, into the congestion of his head. He had barely stood up all the way when the voice from the front of the room said guilty.

After that he only heard vaguely the sound of the man continuing to read off a sheet at the front of the room. No other precise words coming together. Just the vacant murmuring and movements of a jaw he could barely see over there, the head bowed, the faces beside him plain and placid, and the guy was done reading the sheet and things kept moving. The gavel banged again. Everyone sat down. There was more to do. Stapled packets slid down the line. The chairman took out another sheet and began reading off it. Someone from the panel finally looked up, looked at Titus in the eye, blinked, looked again and looked away. The corners of the room vibrated with what Titus thought was an air conditioner. Then he saw the windows behind the panel thrown open and no, couldn't have been an air conditioner and he realized he was still standing. Covered in sweat. His collar was soaked and the back of his shirt under his shoulder blades clung to his body. He tried to blink, tried to breathe, but it was like there was a tight band across his sternum, some chicken wire wrapping tighter and tighter. Despite that, he could feel everything most precisely right now in the sweat of himself, every bead running down his face, his temples, his back, down and through the hairs of his calves beneath his slacks, his toes wet in his shoes squeaking against his insoles curling, digging.

Another panel member looked at him, darted the glance away, and he could feel his counsel putting an arm around his shoulders, It's okay. We have to sit now. What's going on? It's okay Titus. This is normal.

The trial chair at the front of the room looked up from his sheet and his voice continued to come out of his face steady and dry. His hand came up and signaled for Titus to sit, the fingers pushing down the air. Sir we need everyone seated. Titus was shaking his head. Yall can't do this. Sir we need everyone seated. C'mon Titus let's sit. Your chair's over here, his counsel's arm still around his shoulder. I earned them credits. I know Titus. Not everything's settled yet. Counsel, should we break for another recess? No chairman. Please check with the accused.

His counsel's face was big in his vision, the big pink face enunciating slowly, You think you need a minute? Titus wagged his head, mumbling through the congestion, Yall don't understand. I'm already going to law school in the fall. George Washington. I already put my deposit down. I gotta talk with someone next week to pick out classes. The counsel nodded his big head deliberately, I know, I know. Just sit Titus. It's all part of the process. Now we're getting to the critical part. He put his arm around Titus's shoulder

again. Titus stiffened. You in on this too dood? Please Titus
sit. The counsel letting the weight of his arm sink into the
shoulder pads of Titus's suit, pressing down more firmly. It
was at this point Titus felt something inside begin to rip. He
stood up quickly. Aye nigga don't you fuckin touch me like
that. His counsel backed away, hands up, Please, I'm trying
to help. Huh you think I'm gon hit you? Titus approaching.
You think I'm that dumb huh? A scream—a woman's, his
mother's?—lit up the edge of his awareness. Then things
started happening real fast. The gavel banging and his folks,
Vonny were rushing to him. The rented bailiff reaching out.
He felt his own chest about to burst again, his lip quivering.
His whole body tight and vibrating, each molecule buzzing
and he was far gone. He knew it. He absolutely knew it and
who gave a fuck right now, nigga, you think I fucking care if
you keep banging that thing. And his knowledge of knowing
how fucking stupid and ignorant and wild he was being at
this very moment in this room of people made him stupider
and ignorant and so fucking retarded because he was so far
gone and now a collection of breathing and muscles and
sweat and despite pop grabbing him, despite the bailiff
hugging him down, I'm gon walk up there and shove it up
your ass you keep bangin that shit. His mother wailed and
Pop directly in his face, SON YOU DON'T WANT TO DO
THIS. The congestion was so thick in his head right now
swelling it all and YALL HAD TO CHEAT AND BRING IN
THE OUTSIDE LAWYERS!!!!! and he lunged at his own
counsel again, knowing exactly that the nigga was in on
it too.

The bailiff got a hold of him. But Titus's suit coat was 4
sizes too big and he ducked out of it easily and he was a step
away from his counsel, the faggot in on it too. Quickly the
bailiff had a handful of his white soaked shirt, the part that

wasn't stuck with sweat to his body and momma back there still wailing through a shaky hand covering her mouth, PLEASE JESUS WILL YOU MAKE HIM STOP and that shit man, hearing that shit made his skin crawl and made him angrier like see what yall made me do in fronna her and he struggled to take one more step with the cop holding onto his shirt, and one more step was accomplished, his sole gaining traction on the carpet and his knee shaking with the force of his thigh driving down and the buttons of his shirt popped and papped and he had that counsel by the pant leg yanking at that terrified leg before the bailiff got a complete hold of Titus, twisting his wrist backwards on itself so he could crumple in the pain that shot straight through his nervous system and popped his eardrums back into full hearing and just in case he was too far gone to feel that, the cop swept his legs from under him and Titus fell forward, one of the cop's knees dug down through his bicep to the bone and the cop bending the wrist back further and another hand at the base of Titus's skull pushing his face to the carpet. Titus shouted at the sound of feet and papers filing out the room, How else am I sposed to act huh???? HOW ELSE??? WHAT DID YALL EXPECT!!!

With the people gone, Mr. Stevenson approached the officer. Sir I myself am retired police and I'm not trying to tell you how to do your job but I believe my son is dehydrated. A cup of water may be in order. The bailiff hooked his arms through the chickenwings formed by Titus's bound wrists and pulled Titus to his feet which hung limp and useless. Mr. Stevenson pulled an armless chair and they placed Titus down in it. The bailiff grumbled that this could've been much easier for him and that he should know that as the son of a cop. Mr. Stevenson held the cup of water to his son's face.

* * *

The trial continued in Titus's absence. Without much delay, they settled one floor below in a room almost identical to the original one. The professional lawyers went about their business albeit it with less flair as the day wore on. Sam spoke as if in a daze, sure that everyone wasn't listening to him but pitying him and by the end Sam began to resent everyone in the room. This entire trial was a sham.

The panel deliberated once again, quickly, urgently, some suggesting that what had happened upstairs should be taken into account. I don't see why not. You all saw that. I was surprised that the complainants didn't touch it. Well they can't. What do you mean they can't? They looked at the trial chair to resolve the dispute, and he put his pen to his lips in thought.

The panel continued without the chair's input. I don't mean to state the obvious but the guy clearly has anger issues. Another panel member raised her hand to speak and was told she didn't need to do that. Shouldn't we consider if there is a mental and psychological issue here? Another panel member scoffed. Why should we consider that? His counsel made no mention of any condition. He had the opportunity to file for a psych eval but he didn't. End of story. So we have to conclude that his meltdown was a result of character. Result of character? Let's see how any of us would hold up if you had already gotten into law school, paid the deposit, and were blindsided days before graduation. The first panel member waved his arms pantomiming Titus's thrashing earlier. I wouldn't react like THAT, that's for sure. Oh you say that but you have little understanding of where he's from. What do you mean by that? She did not respond and he asked her if she was accusing him of being a racist. She shruggingly asked if she had used those words, a smile almost forming.

The trial chair finally tried to quell the bickering. He reminded everyone once again that UJC did not operate like a typical courtroom. There was no contempt-of-court equivalent in the UJC bylaws. If we want to punish the accused for the display upstairs, a new complaint would have to be initiated and the process would have to run its course once again. Some panel members asked him to cite the specific bylaw and when the trial chair could not, he said he would make a phone call.

The trial chair went out into the hallway and checked to see if anyone was around any corners or hidden in the cubby by the water fountain. He opened his cell phone and without turning it on, he held it to his face, nodding his head a few times and going uh huh until he had decided that a real phone call would have concluded by now. Returning to the room he simulated the heavy pained expression of a person who was relaying bad news. I just got off the phone with another E Board member and here's what I have been told. For the sake of simplicity I'm going to ask you all to do something. As impossible as this sounds, I want you all to treat whatever happened upstairs, those few minutes of your life, as if they never happened.

* * *

Titus's counsel came downstairs and standing beside the bailiff, told Titus's father and Vonny the sanction. Mrs. Stevenson was sitting and did not join the men and their questions. Vonny clapped the counsel on the shoulder. Good look man. Thank you. I'll tellum.

Vonny walked up punching his palm and pulled up a chair. Aye stick they aint kick you out. They say you on suspension for a semester. When you come back in the spring—a laughter started in Titus's throat—you just have to take enough credits to be considered full time. It don't even matter what you take ...

When Vonny was finished explaining Titus shook his head grinningly and told him go head with that. I aint comin back to disshit. Not after this. It's a wrap can't you tell? Stick just listen to me. Listen to you? You know I shoulda never listened to you and my pop in the first place. We shoulda walked out as soon as we saw them outside lawyers. Whatchu tryna say stick man? You putting this on me? Titus sniffed and pressed his lips tight. What is you gettin at there huh? Titus refused to speak. You know what Titus you got a lotta people here who love you and we all tryna—Vonny made an involuntary sound. It stopped him from saying what he was about to say. It sounded like a hiccup but Titus kept looking at him, a scowl developing as he watched the thing occurring. Titus squinted for a long while. Vonny turned his head away. Vonny dog you aint doin what I think you doin? Aye Vonny man. Vonny you need to quit with that. Vonny went into the hallway where Titus's mother was holding herself in a chair, absolutely still. He sat beside her and she kissed him on the forehead. Rubbed his back as Vonny covered his face and sobbed.

Now his mother stood and wandered into the room. Titus saw her moving toward him slow, her face swollen, shoulders pinched. I'm sorry Ma. I know I promised but this place, shaking his head and sniffing, this place Ma, I don't know what it is. I spend another second here I swear I'm gon hurt somebody. I know God gotta plan but it aint here. I'm sorry ma. You my heart. You always be my heart.

She helped him to his feet. She called for the officer to undo the cuffs. His arms loose now in their sockets, Titus finally felt relaxed, became overwhelmed with that peace he remembered feeling after so many verdicts. And as he moved in to allow her embrace, smelling that perfume that had been muddled by sweat, she slapped him across the face. She jerked her hand up again and he flinched covering his head. Holding her hand up there for a moment, her face was wadded up with disgust. She let her arm drop to her side, spent. She went back out into the hallway where his father was rubbing Vonny's back, Vonny sitting down and holding his head. They told him it would be okay son.

45

Vonny was used to having a summer break. But working people don't get those he now understood. Except maybe teachers. He worked early as hell. Had to be at UPS by 3 in the morning. The trucks needed to go out by 6. And for the trucks to leave the depot, there couldn't be no mistakes with the packages. As a belt supervisor, his job was to minimize those mistakes. To keep those conveyor belts moving.

There were always mistakes though. What withall those packages. And new guys coming in all the time and trying to do too much not knowing what to do in the first place. When one loader made a mistake, the other loaders on the belt yelled fuckin new guy just do your job! Then management came in and piled on with more yelling hell you guys yelling for? Then the drivers came out from the break room with their coffee and yelled for everyone to hurry up. They had their own numbers to meet. Everybody had numbers to meet.

Vonny was good at the numbers, which was one of the reasons they liked him so much at UPS. He could do that math easy. Never fucked up. So after a few months they gave him his own conveyor belt to supervise, a decent wage and the promise of full-benefits around the corner.

Everybody there was grownups. Doods with families. But every time they came to him, they weren't like people older than him. They were all the same age now. If that make any sense. But the funny thing was whenever they had problems, the problems seemed like childish ones to him. This dood didn't wanna share. This dood said somethin slick. Vonny would pull them to the side, some of them with mortgages and wives and children. Fellas fellas we all grown men here. Rocking a wide stance and rubbing his hands together and nodding as sides of stories were told. He was a good listener. Didn't interrupt or nothin. And at the end of the testimonies, he had his questions. Honest questions. The kind anybody would ask. So if you was confused man how come you didn't say nothin? The onus on you to tell somebody. This other man can't read yo mind. Any objections and Vonny barely raised his voice. Fellas fellas we just gotta communicate a lil better, feel me?

He soon gained the reputation of being the fairest supervisor there. People working other belts came to him seeking advice and he hit them up with the power of common sense. They listened to his slow tidewater drawl awakening the long dormant part of their brains, a part that could see beyond their small petty egos, and they left the conversation renewed, as if they knew the answer already. You right Vonny. I just gotta do a better job communicating.

Hitting his numbers by what would be breakfast time for normal people, Vonny watched the last of the packages roll down the conveyor belt, the boxes jiggling down the winding lap as ready hands awaited. The package was tossed into the darkness of a truck ... and that was the bulk of the work. It would be dawn and he'd be thinking to himself how he was getting a leg up on niggas out there. Rising early and getting so much done. Niggas aint even had they Frosted Flakes yet. Haha.

Each day rising early and completing his work with no mistakes, the weeks and months passed and he realized hey, I might be doon alright. Won't nuffin to being a workin man really. Not too much to it. He said his thank yous to the Lord and while the Lord did not respond audibly, just that one time in the Chinese buffet, Vonny still felt His presence on most days, a kind approval that kept him quiet and grateful.

He had a few more scheduling things to do on the computer and doods always wanted to hang around him. Get him to tell him a story about some female. Get his opinion on something. Hey Vonny look at this. Hey Vonny when was the last time ... He was the young guy. The UVA kid. Funny, because you don't seem like the other UVA kids we've had here. Remember whats his name? Matt? Yeah I remember Matt. Vonny is definitely no Matt. That Matt, I tell you. He really kept to himself. Not a real people person. Sharp guy though. Vonny shrugging and punching his palm, You gotta have people skills if you wanna make it. It aint all about book smarts.

* * *

Titus took the bus to his job. He spent the days indoors on the phone asking people if they were willing to answer a few questions about the most pressing issues of their lives. As long as those issues were national security and global terrorism. And could be ranked on a scale of 1 to 7 according to their level of concern. 7 being the highest. He always forgot that. Easy to get the numbers mixed. Most hung up on him. Not once in his first month did he hit his numbers. It made no difference to his boss. Or anybody for that matter. There wasn't any yelling over there when doods fucked up. Matter fact there wasn't no way to fuck up really. You had a script, which he stuck to. Hardest part was remembering the knock some of that bass out of his voice. But after a while, he didn't bother. As long as the script was delivered and the checkboxes were marked. He drank alot of Diet Coke in there. Wore a tie. And they paid. Biweekly. That was the best thing, the frequency of the paycheck. Not the amount. When he thought about it, it was aight. All things considered. They left you alone. It could be whatever man sometimes, of course, but as long as they left you alone. Better than nothin. Which was what he had been working with. Beat being at the crib all day.

Back in Manassas he had few options. He tried to explain to his father that aint nobody messin with nobody who gotta record, yet his pops insisted on driving him around, Titus in his buttoned shirt and resume in hand, to wherever the phonebook guided them.

Towards the end of July a break seemed to come. One of his favorite middle school teachers was running a summer rec league for girls basketball. She needed a few referees. What can I say, Ms. Lane. I like working with children.

He knew it was a wrap as soon as he saw the words BACKGROUND CHECK on the application. The clerk at the district office guided his hand to the box, rolled his thumb back and forth. Rub your fingers like this and it will all go away.

Eventually, inevitably, he hit up Vonny who was still in Charlottesville. Vonny said there were no openings at UPS but he knew somebody who knew somebody who worked at this polling place by the Taco Bell in Seminole Square Shopping Plaza. Sounded like Titus's line of work. Government and politics surveys. It was easy. Just calling people on the phone.

He got the job. Moved in with Vonny back at Charlottesville. That same off campus crib deep in the woods. His Prince William probation officer signed off on it since Vonny had no priors. Still Titus had to go through the whole paperwork transfer again. At least his Charlottesville PO spared him from the intake office visit. I still got you on file. I hadn't even moved the folder to the other drawer.

* * *

On weekdays Vonny came by to scoop him. Sometimes they took the long way back to the crib. Past Daniels's house. Titus wanted to see that old nigga crib. Jus cos. Joe had peeped them on where Daniels lived. His 2 story stood at the end of a cul-de-sac with a basketball hoop over the garage. There was that maroon Cadillac. Titus said he was going to pour sugar down the tank of that bitch. Late one night. Stick you know if that actually work? Hell yeah it do. Hold up stick. You done it before? I personally haven't but niggas back home do it all the time.

They got so far as to visit Wal-Mart to pick up ski-masks. They had already bought the sugar the other day. Standing there in the store and holding the mask in his hands and looking at the holes for the face and mouth, Titus felt the air go out of him all at once. He told Vonny forget it.

They stopped by Best Buy on the way home. Vonny kept saying they needed to replace the TV. We gotta upgrade stick. Fuck outta here with that man. We aint got no bread for that.

The sugar. All the sugar in the house went straight to Kool-Aid instead.

And that was their summer. They worked, came home. Worked, came home. To that unit that had the bare minimum furniture. Not even beds yet. Samo shit. On different sleep schedules. Joe's things, in a few lumpy trash-bags with a poster or two sticking out them, were pushed into a corner.

Every so often Joe called. Every so often they visited him at Regional. Less and less as the summer progressed. There wasn't much to talk about. They had nothing else to prove by being there. One time Joe called and said his brother Zeke had been shot dead walking down the street. The judge was going to release him to go back home to attend the funeral. They drove to Regional to pick Joe up and they had a lil welcome home party and drove him to the Grey-hound station the next morning. He was supposed to come back 3 days later. He didn't. Then out the blue they got a phone call from him. A Pennsylvania area code. Time passed. A call, New York City area code this time. Joe said he was in Florida. It's complicated man. I'm good tho. He asked if his stuff was still there. Yeah still here.

Titus and Vonny sat around on that couch sipping brews and not talking much. Samo shit.

* * *

Titus's supervisor called him into his office. There was a fridge in there full of Diet Cokes. Titus asked if there was a reason he was called in. No I just wanted to convey to you how well you're doing. Titus said okay and was getting up to go back to his desk when the supervisor revealed he was a UVA grad too, did you know that? Titus did not know yet he nodded. I like you Titus. I've been listening in on your calls. You read well. What I mean by that is you don't sound like you're reading. It's natural. The rest of the people here, it sounds so artificial. I wanted to let you know, you can go off script if you like. The boss was smiling. He was not well liked. Everybody who worked there chain smoked outside to get away from him. It had required a lot of effort for the boss to say all these kind things to Titus. Titus said okay and went back to his desk.

Later on that night, Titus's leg was bouncing as they hit the brews on the couch for the small sliver of time their waking schedules overlapped. You ever see yourself like this Vonny? Still here? Still chillin? How Vonny responded—a long sip, a long pull, maybe a shrug of the shoulders or of the lips—Titus would not remember. It was too deep a question. The answers would slide off somewhere and Titus fell asleep in his workclothes that night like many others, the ends of his tie splayed across his chest.

Sometimes, when drinking primarily, Titus thought of Brooke. Not much. He tried to imagine this new life she was making for herself. It was hard to vision clearly. What he knew of New York from TV and the movies, from music, it wasn't prolly like that, at least not the kinda places she was going to. Whatever, whoever filled her days. She prolly don't spent not a single second thinking about me. Why should I to her? Even thoughts of other men, when he allowed them in, did not so much as anger but annoy him, and he sniffed, adjusting himself on the couch and Vonny would look over expectantly before his eyes returned to the screen.

* * *

Vonny kept campaigning for a new TV. Driving home from work, they passed Best Buy. The same line. Yo we gotta get with a flat screen, that kind that's flat all the way straight across. Like my brother's. Doan gotta be big. Jus flat. For the glare.

Vonny said he couldn't see the screen from the dinner table. The glare, stick, I'm tellin you. A flat screen solve all that. C'mon Vonny you can jus eat over here on the couch like you normally do. Vonny said he knew someone who worked at the returns department at Best Buy. We can get that TV for nuffin. There might be some dents or scratches but the joint will still work guaranteed, I'm sayin.

Samo shit. Samo.

* * *

They bought the flat screen in August. Went in on it 50-50. It was perfect except for a piece of plastic coming loose off the side. You can't really see it unless you force yourself to stare at it. Titus shaking his head, Shit is painfully obvious to me, my nigga.

Soon the math became apparent that they would be short on next month's rent. Their parents had long cut the cord so they made due on bad credit. They relied on ingenuity. Instincts. They ate nothing but sandwiches. Mayonnaise. Syrup. They ate these sandwiches and watched people cook steaks on that big flat TV.

They got by alright. They lost weight. They were alright.

Vonny was resourceful though. Every so often at UPS, someone picked up a package from FedEx. They just left those in the corner, too lazy to take it to FedEx themselves, which wasn't nobody's job anyway.

Vonny kept his eye on this one box that showed up. All day. A nice sound system. He could see the brand printed on the outside of the box. All the features listed on the side. Would go perfect with the TV. That's all day right there. Every time he stood up to do something, he took a detour to look at the box, its labels. He nudged it with his foot. Felt its heft. When no one was looking at the end of his shift, boom. Copped it. Driving home he couldn't stop smiling at that box chilling in the passenger's seat. Thoughts of God did not intrude.

When Vonny got home from work and everyone was just leaving for work, he napped, woke up, sat around and listened for the delivery trucks.

Vonny popped up off the couch. He looked down the empty hall in both directions. If he saw a package by someone's door he slid over to it nice and smoove, old mail under his arm and he was jiggling his keys. He looked around again, looked at the box, and nudged the box with his foot nonchalant. Measured its heft, its sounds. Heavier the better. Looked at the address. Its origins. Looked at the old mail in his hands as he scooted that thing with his foot. In his head he was whistling. Heavier the box the better. Scooting. He got the new Xbox that way. They didn't know any of their neighbors. Home from work, Titus stared at the Xbox. What's this? You spend money on that? Naw. No more was said.

* * *

It was Vonny's idea to start eating at the dining halls again. They could save more taking their lunch there. Newcomb was still open in the summer. Titus didn't like it but fuckit if it could save us a lil loot. Tired of cold cheese sandwiches all the damn time. Vonny had nothing to do so he came back and picked Titus up and taxied him down 29 to the

Newcomb Dining Hall. After they ate, they waited around hoping for some cheeks. Stranded here in Charlottesville for the summer cheeks. They got to know the workers there. They were surprised alotta them were still in high school. Tattoos on their necks, the girl saying how old you think I am? Vonny laughing, Only kinda people ask that is either too old or too young. She squirmed, fiddling with her hands behind her back. I'm 16. 16? I guess I'm done talkin to you. Nigga, I wasn't gonna giyou nunna this anyway.

She was the cardswiper. She let them in free. They got their groceries from the dining hall. They filled one bag full of styrofoam to-go boxes. In another bookbag went the jugs with juice and milk. Around the corner was the bathroom. They looked in the stalls. OK, stick, lock the door. They cracked open the dispensers and took the paper towels and toilet paper. There was a big mirror there over the sink and they avoided gazing at their own reflections.

They were eating pretty good until the fall semester started up again. There was traffic on the road again, construction, joggers overflowing from the sidewalks. The line curled out the door and past the bike racks.

At the front of the line was the regular term cardswiper. An old lady with a young weave. Squatting on her stool. When they tried to pass on through nonchalant she hollered at them. Yawl two got to slow yo roll now!!! A strand of fuchsia bang covered one of her eyes. They knew her. She beamed sitting there on top her stool. They came up and gave her a hug. Yawl two tried to slide by on me? Yawl come back and now you tried to big time somebody like ... Look at yawl two. You especially. All dressed up. All big time. Where yawl work at now? We still here up in Charlottesville. Yawl fell in love with the place yawl stuck around after graduation haha. Yeah.

It was deep in there. Everyone hitting up the ice milk machines, the waffle machines. Trays piled high. They claimed a long table in the back where the black people were and had been for as long as they knew. But it was deep in there, the beginning of the year, and all kinds of people were sitting back there unaware of the time-honored divisions. Strangers, strange people. Lookin younger all the time these people. These people didn't even have the common courtesy of leaving a chair of space between them. But that's how they are at the beginning of the year. Glistening. They wanted to shake hands, ask names and all that. Majors. Years. Hometowns. The whole run down. Did you guys know that the food they serve here is the same as what they serve in prison? I'm not kidding you. The same company. Titus and Vonny chewed and said nothing.

These people. When the strangers left, more strangers replaced them, more courteous ones who just reciprocated the ignoring.

They saw niggas they knew. Niggas who came up rubbing their palms. Came up in their new schoolyear clothes, a new hitch in their step, a diddy bop even. Fake niggas. They dapped up Titus and Vonny, Titus and Vonny sitting full and with napkins crumpled on their plate, eyes listing as these niggas they knew threw out all the slang they had heard on the radio and in the music videos over the summer, rubbed their palms and punched them, chanced a sneer, tossed invisible cud in their molars, laughed loud and demonstratively. Whass rully rully rully good mah niggas? Maintainin man. Ussgood whichoo? I thought chow niggas lef. Naw. We here. Gotdamn, Titus lookin all GQ'd up. You

got that clean look goin with the pink tie and you know they
say real niggas wear pink tho. Aye, mahnigga, don't fuck we
deese two. Vonny, whoo, I remember you. Yeah, he snatched
that nigga off his feet. Oh man straight suplexed that fat
nigga man, on some Royal Rumble shit, forreal hahaha. I
aint even tell you tho that it was a football nigga. Real talk.
Football nigga? Tellum Vonny. Yeaaah, it was wunnadem big
boys, can't lie. So why Titus you all dressed up for? Titus
wiped his mouth with a dirty napkin again. Tossed it on his
plate. Workin man now.

On the way out they stopped by the drink machines.
Vonny was filling up a thermos with chocolate milk. Titus
watched the slow stream. Look I aint tryna come back here
again Vonny. Vonny screwed the cap on. Looked around.
Yeah, it is kinda deep in here, stick. We aint needa come
back. It's all so fake Vonny. What happened? Happened to
all the real niggas?

* * *

It was one in the morning now. One of those indiscriminate
nights. Whatever season. The blunt had burned its course.
On the flat screen were sparkling, glare-free images of giant
clapping asses and mirror-finished chrome wheels that
went on spinning after the car stopped, kept on spinning
forever. Sometimes Vonny slept all day and he'd be good
through the night just staying up and watching the videos
on that flat screen and occasionally chatting with the Lord.
He'd stay up all night, put on his clothes and be ready for
work the next day no problem.

Vonny nudged the slump body on the couch beside him.
Wake up stick. Titus was sleeping in his workclothes again,
his tie loosened across his chest. Vonny was going to nudge

harder but stopped—man he look so peaceful asleep. Face look different. Calm. Never do he look like that when he wake.

Vonny continued looking at the TV, eventually the sleep coming up to snatch him too, so he got up off the couch and slumped toward his bedroom. He left the door ajar. Just in case. Sometimes Titus would get crazy out there. Shouting in his sleep. It had happened. Scruggling and kicking and saying some craziness. Something about, YOU DISGUST— either it was YOU DISGUST-ING or YOU DISGUST ME. Last syllable was hard to catch. Shoot. The man just might fall out of the couch and crack his skull on the corner of the table if he don't be careful. This one time in the middle of the night, Vonny went out there and saw him facedown in the middle of the floor. His legs tangled in the blanket. Hands reached up like he'd been laid out. You wake cuh? Yeah. Vonny knelt to him. Nah leave me here. Dog the couch right there c'mon. It's not too far. Vonny helped him to the couch. Stick we need to buy you a bed. Nah I'm straight. Vonny laid a blanket on him. Pulled the coffee table away. He emptied the ashtray and threw away the cups and fast food wrappers before heading back to his room to reclaim the few hours left before getting up again. Before work.

Vonny was wondering, sometime in the last moments before the sleep finally caught him, something about oh man, how come he can't just sleep like a dead man. Just go to sleep and be still. Like dormant. When you dream it shouldn't be a place that, I'm sayin. God you might wanna consider that. As if it aint bad enough when a nigga wake. Pardon the expression. Sleep should be rest. Peaceful yunnow. That's why they call it sleep. And dreams. Dreams dreams dreams. I'm saying tho. I'm saying. There must be sumpin you can take that can make it so you don't even have to dream no more. You can jus go to sleep and wake up ready to go again. Feelin fresh. Don't even gotta bother with no dreamin. Don't wanna take no chances. Cos really what use is dreams if they be hurting you all the time to havem?

Printed in Great Britain
by Amazon